Through
the
Green Doorway

A novel by

T. P. Majka

INFINITY
PUBLISHING.COM

Copyright © 2009 by T. P. Majka

ISBN 0-7414-5557-9

Published by:

INFIꞨITY
PUBLISHING.COM

1094 New DeHaven Street, Suite 100
West Conshohocken, PA 19428-2713
Info@buybooksontheweb.com
www.buybooksontheweb.com
Toll-free (877) BUY BOOK
Local Phone (610) 941-9999
Fax (610) 941-9959

Printed in the United States of America
Published September 2009

Acknowledgments

I want to thank all my family members and friends who allowed me to beat your ear with bits and pieces of this tale. You know who you are.

Thanks also to my lovely and helpful wife, Beatrice, my motivator.

Thanks to my niece, Amy, for finding the flaws I missed.

Thank you to my nephew's wife, Meredith, for designing the cover of this book...

Last, but not least, thank you God / J.C. / The Ghost with the most, for all you continually do for me.

This work of fiction is dedicated to my dad,

Marjan Majka

I might have only known you for six years,
but I know you've been with me in spirit since you passed.

To the Reader

Welcome to the theater in my head.

You are about to embark on a journey that has spilled out of my brain and onto the page. First off, thank you for taking this book home with you. I know there are plenty of folks who would rather see a movie. By reading this, it tells me that there are still people who believe in allowing the power of the written word to take you places only the mind can go. So, again, thank you.

Within these pages, you'll find all the ideas, images, thoughts and words that were brought together like a giant jigsaw puzzle. A process that was both slow and painful. And, I do mean really, really slow and really, really painful.

All the characters in this tale are just people in my mind and are not to be confused with the real world. Any similarities are purely coincidental. My hope is that as you begin this adventure, you'll soon find yourself at its end and wanting more.

So, if you are ready, grab a blanket and sit back and join me. I have a spooky story to tell. Listen closely, once upon a time...

Part One

Wishes

1

At four years old, his first wish was granted. Ishmael Alastor would get plenty of wishes, but his first wish happened to be a good one. Because a child's younger years should be happy ones, they shouldn't be frightful ones.

While many a night sitting in his crib, Ish watched his father physically and verbally abuse his mother. Only four, but he knew something wasn't right.

His tears always went unnoticed.

Ish liked parties, especially birthday parties; more to the point, his birthday parties. Having everyone gathered around (except his father) singing to him as he stared at the candle flames.

He loved staring at the flames.

"Happy Birthday, Dear Ishhhh… Happy Birthday to you!"

When the clapping started, his cousin Frankie sat beside him with his napkin tucked nice and neat under his chin. He clapped and clapped; his hands moving so fast, it made Ish laugh. "Go ahead, little Ish, make that wish!" he said with a smile.

Ish thought and thought, and thought real hard, thinking of the best wish he could make. *I know,* he thought to himself, *I wish, I wish, seal it with a kiss, I wish Daddy would stop hitting Mommy!*

And he did, the very next day.

The day after Ish made his first really thought-out wish, his father would never hit his mother again. On the night after Ish's fourth birthday, his father got behind the wheel of his car; drunk as a skunk, like almost every night,

3

and proceeded to go home for a workout on his punching bag of a mate.

Only he never made it, a tree got in his way.

No one else was killed, just a scumbag named Samuel Alastor. On his tombstone were the words: <u>Loving Father; Devoted Husband.</u> Put there by his wife, Sondra, she knew it to be a lie. A big one at that, but she didn't want anyone to know the truth. The truth was too painful. Sondra just wanted to get on with her life. The Bible says: God will have compassion on whom he'll have compassion. The Good Lord showed his kindness by having the pain of being abused taken out of the picture. Only the memories remained. Those too would fade, but only if she let them.

Her older brother, Jonah, was a Godsend. He had always been there for her when she was growing up, and even more so after Samuel's death. Jonah took care of all the funeral arrangements. He never actually liked Samuel, and he had had bad vibes about the guy, but he wasn't about to tell his sister how to live her life.

His wife Trish put forth the idea that Sondra and Ish move in with them.

Sondra wasn't looking to be a burden on anyone. She was, in fact, just happy to be in their company, away from her home where the memories would close in and surround her. Trish made the suggestion and Sondra thought she was just being polite, but when she kept insisting, saying it wouldn't be a problem. The house was big enough for everyone, plus Ish would have his cousins, Frankie and Judy, for company. So, after giving it some serious consideration, Sondra decided to take her up on the offer.

It actually didn't take her long. She secretly hoped someone would throw her a lifeline, someone who could pull her out of the hell she called home. A home that held hate within its walls.

Even after Samuel died, she still heard him in her mind. At times she even thought she heard him with her ears. She believed getting away would be the best thing for her. She believed that with her whole heart; ignoring her secret suspicion that he would never let her go, even from the grave.

Jonah's house was a large ranch home, sitting on a hilltop in the peacefulness of the woods about an hour's drive from downtown Seattle. An ideal location, Sondra knew it would be a big change from living in the city, but it was a change she was willing to make. A change she needed to make.

She loved the hum of the woods. The trees softly blowing in the breeze, the noise of woodpeckers busy at work. It was a peaceful place, a quiet place. Sometimes a little too quiet, but Ish made up for that whenever he played with his cousins. They could be so loud at times, but Sondra loved that sound as well. Hearing their laughter always made her smile.

Everyone accepted them as part of the family. The children were a big help with Ish; they were a number of years older than he, but they loved having him around; if only for the fact that he would now be the baby of the family.

Since the death of her husband, Sondra's life began to change for the better. She found a part-time job in the city with an ad agency, working "The Pit" as they called it: the secretary pool. Going back to work, even for a few hours a day, helped her forget about the past.

A past that still had a strong hold on her.

She never spoke to anyone about just how bad things had been with him. The beatings, his foul and loud mouth, and the mind games he liked to play. Samuel had been such a charming guy when they first met. But, that turned out to be sweet icing, on a sour cake. She met him at a Christmas party. She was so young, naïve, and he was so much older and handsome. Some people said the relationship wouldn't last. Most wished her well, but she herself actually believed they were meant to be together.

When they first met, she felt—Love at first sight, if such a thing is possible. Samuel, on the other hand... he felt what every male on the planet feels—Lust at first sight. After all, she was a knockout. At five foot, four inches tall, with a body built for the centerfold of *Playboy*, no red-blooded American male could resist a second look. And, second look is exactly what he did, which turned out to be something Sondra would later regret.

Samuel had an eye for the ladies. He never even tried to hide the fact, but Sondra still thought she was the only woman in his life. Sometimes, he would look at a woman and suggest that the two of them have sex with her. She always took it as a joke, playing it off as if he didn't mean it, when the whole time, he's insisting she go over and talk to a complete stranger. And yet, she still believed that he only had eyes for her. She went out with him with blinders on. His charm had a lot to do with her inability to see the truth. That, plus the fact she couldn't see past his good looks, didn't want to believe that any other woman could take her place. After they got married, that's when she started to take notice to his roaming eyes.

But that was in the past.

Except, sometimes the past liked to creep up on her. At times, crawling fast like a centipede running down her spine, sometimes sluggish like a snail, she would usually bolt out of her sleep in a cold sweat, seeing his face with that twisted drunken grin still hovering in front of her eyes, even after opening them. Then, it would fade away, and her shakes, sometimes-violent trembling would cease as well.

2

Problems, problems, everyone has problems.

Sondra kept hers to herself. She thought she could handle them alone. She thought wrong.

Yes, things were going well on the outside. Her looks, her manner, all worked well at hiding what was growing like a cancer on the inside. She couldn't forgive him. How the hell could she? After all that man put her through? Forgive? She was having a hard time trying to forget about him, let alone forgive him. Yet, that's what she needed to do. Deep down she knew that's what needed to happen. Instead, she chose to try to forget but couldn't put it behind her. Oh, she played along, acting as if she had a normal life, and she did a great job of it. That is until some guy should smile at her.

It's what Samuel had done when their eyes first met.

Any and every guy who smiled at her, either on the job or on the streets, quickly became him. First their face, then the smile, and suddenly and always without warning, no matter how many times it happened, Samuel's face with that sweet smile and then just as fast, his drunken grin. She pictured him wiping away the drool on his chin after he slapped her around, standing there swaying back and forth laughing at her, telling her she wasn't worth shit.

"Mommy, I want these. Can I have them, Mommy, huh? Can I?" Ish asked, as he pulled on her skirt.

His voice, along with the tugging of the dress, snapped Sondra out of the trance she'd gone into. She stood in the fresh fruit aisle of the supermarket holding a melon with one hand and pressing her chest with the other, as if that alone was enough to slow her heartbeat.

Sondra held her breath and exhaled slowly, watching the back of the head of the man who had just smiled and walked past her down the aisle.

Tugging... tugging... that constant tugging, "What do you want!" she snapped.

Ish's smile quickly faded and a frown took its place. He held a bundle of grapes in his tiny arms. She felt guilty for the outburst and quickly dropped to her knees and took the fruit. "I'm sorry I yelled at you, Ish. Do you forgive me...?" His smile said it all. That smile was the only smile that didn't cause her to flip a switch. "... of course you can have these."

She put the grapes in the cart and then picked him up and sat him in the cart's seat. "Let's get some milk and then we'll get out of here. What do you say?" Ish laughed and began swinging his legs back and forth.

Sondra rolled the cart down the aisle, picked up the milk and then headed to the checkout counter.

It took twenty minutes to get through the line. If it weren't for the old man in front of her with his cat treats and cat food, canned and bagged, cat litter and cat toys and oh who knows what else, she would have been out in two minutes flat. But that was all right, she wasn't in a hurry.

Trish told her not to worry about getting anything, they had everything covered, but she couldn't do that, she had to get something. So, she bought the milk and the grapes, and of course, her favorite read: *Star* magazine.

After getting Ish strapped into the car seat, she rubbed her finger against the indentation on the tip of his nose, then kissed his forehead before taking her seat behind the wheel. She took a deep breath and pulled her seatbelt on. Running late already, it looked as if rain was about to fall any second.

Oh I hope it doesn't rain, she thought to herself. She started the engine. It kicked over, but it made a screech until she let go of the key. *"And watch when you start her up,"* she remembered Jonah telling her. *"Sometimes she likes to squeal."*

Everything was still new to her. She'd been living with Jonah and Trish for two years and still couldn't believe it. She didn't even realize that fact until the day of Ish's sixth birthday. Now, here she was keeping Ish out of the house while Jonah and Trish and the kids fixed up the place all nice with decorations. They were likely waiting right now for Ish to come walking through the door, so they could all yell "Surprise!"

Just as she pulled out of the parking lot, the rain began to fall.

"Oh sure, you couldn't wait!" She shouted at the sky. As if in response to her yelling, the rain came down even harder with big splashing drops. She had to switch on the windshield wipers at the highest speed, but it still couldn't swipe the water away fast enough. *No sense in even trying to go anywhere,* she thought to herself. She pulled over to the side of the road and waited the storm out.

Only, the storm had all the time in the world.

As she sat there, listening to the raindrops on the roof and Ish's singing along with each little splat, she began to think about things she'd been trying so hard not to. Like when Ish was two and had come down with a high fever. She remembered crying, wondering where Samuel was and with whom while she wrapped Ish in cold towels trying to get his fever down. She could still hear his cries when the icy wet towels were pressed against his hot, tiny body.

He was never around when you needed him, she thought. Married a little over a year and pregnant with Ish, he had gone out with his drinking buddies until all hours of the night. She remembered the first time she had the nerve to ask him where he was all night. That was the first time he slapped her across the face. Just once, but it should have been enough to send her packing, but it didn't. "I was bowling!" he screamed. "You got a problem with that!" She'd been stunned by the slap. It wasn't until Ish jumped in her belly when she finally came out of her daze and found that Samuel had left her standing there while he went to take a shower.

"Mommy, can I have a grape?"

Ish's voice brought her back to the present.

"Sure, baby, you can have one." She pulled a handful out of the bag and dropped three in his waiting hand. He smiled and shouted, "Rain stopped!" as he pointed at the front windshield. The clouds had finally broken and in the sky the sun began to set. Bright colors of orange, red and yellow splashed across the horizon as the last of the thunderclouds rolled away.

It would be at least another fifteen minutes before dark, but Sondra had a feeling she wouldn't make it home before then and of course she got stuck in traffic. It seemed the storm that rolled through dumped enough rain on the highways to cause a major problem; she hated the thought of being stuck in a traffic jam.

She clicked on the radio and the speakers blared, "... in the news this hour..." Sondra quickly turned the volume down. She guessed Jonah had a hearing problem. "That was loud, Mommy!" She could see Ish in the rearview mirror holding his hands to his ears. His face was all smiles. "Yes it was, wasn't it!" she said with a grin. "Remind me to yell at Uncle Jonah."

By the time they finally got back to the house it was nearly eight o'clock. The sun had gone down and now the sky was covered with a blanket of stars. The starlight was bright enough to light up the pathway leading to the front door. When Sondra opened it and flipped the light switch, everyone jumped out from their hiding places and screamed, "Surprise!!!!"

Later that night, after everyone had finally gone to sleep, Sondra settled Ish into his bed, pulling the covers up and tucking him in real tight. "Good-night," she said as she kissed him on the top of his head. "Sweet dreams."

For the longest time she sat next to him on the bed, not saying a word. It was times like this that would make Ish feel strange; her sitting there staring off into some other place. Whatever her thoughts, he couldn't be sure, but the expressions on her face were enough to make a young boy wish for some strange things.

He wanted to be famous.

3

Now, lying in her bed, she closed her eyes and tried to sleep. Maybe she would get some rest tonight, then again, maybe not. Sure, Samuel was dead, and he could never again hurt her, but the scars that were left behind never really left at all. The cuts and bruises she always hid were faded, but the emotional pain still lingered. A pain no amount of drugs could take away. The sleeping pills she took before going to bed began to kick in, and Sondra found herself slipping into a dark tunnel. Sleep would come tonight, thanks to *Sominex,* but how peaceful the rest would be was anyone's guess.

They say your dreams occur just moments before waking up, but for Sondra her nightmares began to follow her into her waking hours. She couldn't tell the difference from the real or the unreal, the dream or a night scare and it was beginning to show in her daily living.

She dreamt of the events of the day. It started out dark and dreary with rain slapping against her bedroom window. It wasn't the kind of day that makes a person feel like jumping up and going, but go she must, if only to get out and about.

From the bedroom to the boardroom in a flash! Only she knew she shouldn't be there, she was just a secretary; this had to be a dream. Yet, there she was sitting amongst the bigwigs of the agency. Suddenly, every male in the room became her dead husband. All of them, staring at her with *his* dark blue eyes. Every pair of eyes, gazing: on and on; each face with *his* eyes and all of them ripping at her clothes with *his* hands, pulling them off and then feasting on her flesh with forked tongues.

She bolted upright in bed with a soundless scream in her throat.

† † †

Ish, being a bright boy, never had a problem with any of his teachers in school, and his grades were above average. He did, however, have difficulty making friends, but as he grew older, he found that with exactly the right birthday wish, that problem could be solved.

Only birthday wishes came true. Birthday wishes were all that mattered. Every year after realizing that his birthday wishes became reality, he wished for whatever met his need at the time. If that meant wishing for something devious, then so be it.

He also came to realize what he could get away with when it came to his mother. He knew which buttons to push and when to push them. He also knew his mother was hiding something inside. He didn't remember much of his father, but by the way his mom talked about him, it was just as well that he didn't. He liked hearing the stories though, especially if it kept her from getting on him about something he didn't want to hear about. She never directly talked to him about his father, but whenever she got mad about something he'd done, she'd rant and rave about how his dad had done one thing or another and how much she hated it.

But there were a few times when he heard her talking to herself while she sat alone in her room, unaware of him just outside her door. It scared him at first, but he learned to use it to his advantage, telling himself it was just a normal routine with her, nothing to be ashamed of, or afraid of. Besides, he found he could fix just about anything with a wish. Not just any wish mind you; it had to be a birthday wish.

Wish after wish and year after year. Whatever Ish wanted, Ish got.

Once, when he was eleven, he wished for the power of invisibility. He wanted to take care of a bully that constantly bothered him. He never actually saw himself disappear, but he gave it a try. Just once, but it was enough to convince him that he did, in fact, have the power—a power that could come in handy in sticky situations.

The years ticked by, tick-tick-tick, like the calendar ticks away the days; before they knew it, Ish was a senior in high school. His senior year turned out to be his best year in high school. He had everything he wanted, except that wasn't enough. What he needed could only come from a willing woman, but he never had much luck with the ladies. Tall like his father and having the features of his mother, he looked so handsome in his cap and gown.

"Ishmael Alastor."

Sondra was so excited to watch him up there on the stage receiving his diploma. *He's a good-looking boy, or should I say man now,* she thought to herself. Sitting next to her brother and his wife, the three of them felt so proud. Jonah was sitting there looking businesslike in his black pinstriped suit. He thought about how nice it would be to finally get the last child in his house, out. And Trish, in her low-cut red dress, imagined the possibility of seducing her husband's nephew before he went off to college.

The names were called one by one.

To Jonah the whole ceremony was long. The only other thing that could be so numbing to the brain would have to be church. Like everything else in life, this too passed and the four of them were once again in the car heading home. Knowing it was a silly question but asking it anyway, Trish said, "So, are you going to miss high school, Ish?" Jonah looked at his wife with an expression on his face that said **Dah!**

"The only thing I'm gonna miss about that place," said Ish with a smile, "... is being able to get some good smoke."

"Hey!" said his mother looking annoyed. "What did you say?"

"Relax Mom; you know I'm only joking. Besides, I'm past that stage."

Sondra never even knew he got to that stage, let alone pass it. Maybe it was best if she took it as a joke. *That's it, he's only joking around,* she thought. "You'd better be kidding me!" she cowed. Ish sat forward in his seat playing with his aunt's hair, but he quickly slumped back with a sorry look on his face. "Jeez, doesn't anybody know how to take a joke?"

Only it wasn't a joke, and he knew it.

He'd been smoking grass since his freshman year. Being always slick about it, no one ever caught on. But pot faded when he started doing blow. He never actually bought the stuff but always managed to be around at the right time when someone else had it. His official nickname with his buddies became *Sleaze.*

Everyone was quiet the rest of the way home. Only the hum of the tires on the highway was heard. By the time they pulled into the driveway, the sun had set and the sky was a dark pink and growing darker with each passing moment. The crickets chirped, but suddenly went silent when they heard the crunch of tires on the gravel. They waited for everyone to go inside the house; sure enough, as soon as the last one went inside and the door was closed, they began chirping again, singing the night sky a lullaby.

Ish had said all his good-byes to his friends in his class. They thought college would be in his future, but Ish never let on that he had other roads to travel. Only he didn't know where those roads would lead. He'd soon find out that some roads were best left alone because they come to dead ends.

One night before slipping into the land of Nod, Ish thought of Todd, the lead guitarist of his friend Billy's rock band. He thought of how he told the guys he wanted to go to college and become a famous writer. Todd had said, "Man, you don't have to go to college to be a writer. You can write songs for the band and become a famous songwriter!"

He didn't think much about it then, but later on he would, and that's only because there's so many roads for those that are young. Ish stretched out in his bed staring at a poster of Albert Einstein. Under that, a bumper sticker read: Why be Normal?

Above him, on the ceiling, were glow-in-the-dark stars and moons and planets. They glowed for what seemed like hours and Ish would stare at them. Even though they didn't twinkle or anything, he still liked to look at them and imagine all the possibilities.

Fading, fading—out.

Sleep came so peacefully. He slept with a smile on his face, as if he were getting laid. Whatever it was, it didn't last for long. Soon, his eyelids began to flicker, and he fell into an even deeper sleep. Deep, deep, suddenly he's surrounded by darkness.

He could barely see himself, and it became even harder to see, as the cold darkness seeped around him, hugging him. It seemed as if he was thrown into a freezer, and the darkness was eating him alive. Chunk by chunk, icy fingers finding their way to him, ripping each hunk of flesh until it dissolved into black. Coldness took its place.

Soon, all that's left of him are his eyes.

He's alive, yes, and his body has been used like a meal by the hungry darkness, yes; and yet here he was—only a pair of eyes in the darkness. Only eyes but still he trembled from the coldness that surrounded him. Darkness so frigid his eyes begin to tear. In fact, it felt as if sewing needles were being pricked into them. They were being used as pincushions and the pain was ripping his mind—if it was still there—apart. The worst thing about it was the fact that he couldn't close them. He had no eyelids. If he could just close his eyes, maybe the pain would stop.

He heard a sound.

What was that, he thought to himself, momentarily taking his mind off the pain. Listening... listening, straining to hear and then it came again, like the wind blowing across a cornfield. The corn stalks rustling, as it roared past like a wave. A voice, and it came in a whisper, *"Ishhhhhhhhh..."*

In the distance he can see two red flickers of light. They float in the blackness, coming closer and closer and all the while the voice called, *"Ishhhhhhhh..."*

To Ish, the red flickers of light looked like a car's brake lights. As it got closer, he could see two spots of white lights along with the red, making it look even more like a car in reverse. It was coming fast.

"Ishhhhh..."

Now, the lights were upon him. Except, they weren't lights at all; they were a pair of eyes: blazing blood-red eyes with a flicker of white in the center of each. They were only inches from his own now; he could feel waves of icy air crashing into his pinpricked eyes.

"ISH!" The voice called.

The voice bellowed his name over and over, sounding as if it came from the very depths of hell. It scraped at his nerves like fingernails scraping against a chalkboard. He wanted to run, to hightail it out of there, but there was no place to go; there was only the cold and dark.

"Listen to me, Ish," said the voice. And listen he did, for what else could he do? But, how could he listen if he had no ears?

Dreaming... dreaming...

"You'll pay!" said the eyes. He had no idea what the eyes wanted, and would, in fact, not know until the time was right. This dream, this nightmare, was just something to awaken his inner self; the self that *wants* only and nothing more, which is what the eyes had hoped to achieve.

"Whatever you want, Ish, it's all yours. Just remember, you'll pay!" Laughter filled his head as he awakes in his bed, soaked with perspiration from head to toe.

The dream faded, but he was still filled with the sense of lying in a tub of ice water. Slowly, ever so slowly, that coldness which kept him lying there, trembling like a newborn child, finally slipped away, and he pulled himself up and out of bed with no memories of the dream.

So began another day, only today was the day he would tell his mom about his plans for the future. Sure, she wanted him to go to college to get that all-important "degree," but in what? That was his whole reason for not wanting to go. She told him, in fact, that he could go for whatever he wanted, but when he decided he wanted to be a writer, she gave him a look that said: You have to be joking! He spent all this time deciding on what he wanted to do, and she threw cold water in his face with that one remark.

Ish knew that Uncle Jonah might not like the idea of him joining his friend's rock and roll band, but he thought, *To hell with him.* They told him he could do whatever he wanted, and when he told them about becoming a writer they all asked, "You joking?"

"Well this won't be a joke," he mumbled to himself as he looked at his reflection in the mirror. He knew his mom would flip out when he told her his plans. *She's just going to have to understand,* he thought to himself. *I'm going to do what I'm going to do and if she doesn't like it then she can kiss my ass.*

Ish knew that only one person would be on his side. Aunt Trish would agree with just about any vocation he decided to choose because he knew that Aunt Trish wanted more than what she was letting on. How many times can you walk in on somebody naked if they don't want you to see them naked? It seemed every chance where it could happen with nobody else home, it happened.

He'd walk into the living room, sit down and flip on the TV and in she'd stroll wearing nothing but a towel. As if she's coming out of the shower, the shower was upstairs so what the hell was she doing down in the living room? Then the towel would happen to slip off her body, exposing her nakedness.

Oh, he wanted to grab her and take her, but he also knew right from wrong, and that would most definitely be wrong. But, how nice it would be, and he seemed to be thinking about it more and more.

Maybe it was the fact that his friends would point out to him just how lucky he was to have an aunt that looked *so fine!* "Getting any from Auntie?" His friend Joey always asked. Ish would get all red in the face and not say a word. That, plus the fact he didn't actually do anything with her. But oh man, how he wanted to; yes indeed, he wanted to, and so did she. But did she? He was afraid to go for it. What if he made a move and she screamed, Rape! What then? Maybe he might actually fuck her before he went off with the band. If not, there most likely would be groupies to be had.

4

At eighteen, not many people know what they want to do with their life. Ish knew what he wanted to do; he'd been hanging out with his friends from school. Most of the time just to listen to them *jam*, and *jam* is what they did best. They called themselves *Psycho Punk and the Drones.*

The thrashing of the music always brought Ish's blood to a boil, and he loved it. One day he started singing along with the band, and before he knew it, he was jamming with the fellows. He even wrote some of his own original songs. He was a writer after all, and if he wasn't going to college for that, then he could just as well write songs with his friends in the band. He knew nothing of writing music but he figured somebody else in the band could do that; the only thing that concerned him was getting the words out. The music could come later.

Sondra took the news of her son's decision to tour with the band as expected. She was making eggs and bacon at the time, and it was the smell of said bacon, which brought Ish out of his bedroom. She stood by the stove wearing her long brown robe. The bunny slippers she wore were comical to Ish, but he kept his comments to himself.

With her back to him, she seemed to be staring off into space, lost in her own little universe, yet she knew without ever turning around that he had entered the room. "Go ahead and sit down, Ish. I've got your breakfast, it's almost done."

When he pulled the chair out to have a seat, it made a screech so loud and piercing that Sondra dropped the spatula. It fell to the floor, finishing off that screech with a loud *CLACK!*

She swung around with fire in her eyes. "Will you please lift that chair, don't pull it out!" Ish gave her a puppy look to cool her down, but for some reason it didn't work. "Did you hear what I said!" she hissed. Ish plopped into the chair feeling rejected. Maybe now wouldn't be the best time to share his news. "Yes I heard; jeez, I'm sorry!"

She picked up the utensil and placed it into the sink. She pulled another one out of the cupboard and proceeded to finish what she started; all the while with her back to him she complained, "How many times have I asked you not to do that... You never listen to me."

On and on she babbled. Sometimes it actually sounded as if she were talking in a foreign language or maybe it was the fact that he'd lost interest in what she had to say and tuned her out.

"You seem to be picking up more and more of your father's habits."

That's when she went silent.

Ish didn't remember a whole lot about his dad, but there were some memories deep down inside, and when she had said what she said, Ish heard nothing else. At that moment, a trapdoor opened up under his chair and he fell.

Falling, falling, everything turning black; going from a young adult to an infant in a *flash;* sitting in his crib crying because Mommy had to go out. She left him with his dad. "Don't worry, Ish. Mommy won't be long; I'm just going to the store for Daddy. You be a good boy."

Except, he wasn't being a good boy; he was crying for his mommy just like any other three-year-old, crying because he didn't understand why she had to leave. The only thing he cared about was being with his mother.

"Shut up, you little brat!!"

His father's voice, always thunderous when he was mad, made little Ish wet himself. Of course the yelling did no good. It did, of course, make things much worse. He was only a child who didn't know any better, but his father's anger erupted. He picked the baby up and began to shake him.

"Shut up... shut up... shut up!"

Now, the memory of the pain from his dad squeezing his tiny arms, shaking him like a rag doll, his head jiggling around like Jell-O, all of it came to him. And suddenly, sitting at the kitchen table fifteen years later, waiting for his mother to give him his breakfast, a pain shot through his left eye. It felt as if a knife had been thrust into his head. He cupped his eye with both hands and winced in agony.

Sondra took no notice, she still babbled on and on, only she wasn't mad anymore. Now she was talking about how she'd have to get used to not having him around after he went off to college. "Which reminds me," she said as she turned to hand him his breakfast. She stopped when she realized Ish was in pain. "What's the matter? What is it?"

He waved her off with his hand, "Nothing, I'm all right," he wheezed as he wiped a tear from his eye. "Must of got something in my eye, that's all, I'll live!"

She rubbed the top of his head and said, "You sure?"

Ish hated when she treated him like a child and he pulled his head away from her hand. "I'm fine, really."

Sondra smiled, "O.k., fine; good; anyway, like I was saying... What was I saying?" She stood there scratching her head. To Ish, she looked like a ghost. She looked in fact as if she'd gone over the edge. *She looks like she's lost it,* he thought to himself.

"Oh... now I remember. Have you decided what you're really going to school for?"

Ouch! That hurt, Ish thought. For a moment he said nothing. He let the question hang in the air like a smoke ring from a smoker's mouth. It floated, twirling and twisting up and up until it finally broke apart and disappeared. "I told you I want to be a writer…" His voice was cold, "Apparently since that's not to your liking, I've decided not to go to college at all."

That's when she snapped.

"What did you say? You're not going to college!" The pitch of her voice rose with each word. "Just what do you think you're gonna do? If you think you're gonna loaf around here, you got another thing coming!"

Her screaming woke everyone in the house. Hell, she could have awakened the dead. Jonah and Trish watched as Sondra turned beet red. Ish stood up and pushed his food off the table. The plate hit the floor and shattered into a thousand fragments.

"Don't worry!" he screamed. "I'm not gonna be loafing around here. I'm gonna join my friend's band and we're gonna be famous someday!" He stormed out the backdoor, leaving it open in his wake. A cool breeze slipped into the room, and its caress on everyone's bare ankles brought shivers to their spines.

Ish was gone.

He didn't care what his mother thought about his joining the band. Had he stayed, he would have seen firsthand what that news had done to her. As the cold air drifted into the kitchen, sucking out all the warmth, Sondra stood in the middle of the room, still holding the spatula in her hand. In her mind, he was becoming more like his father the older he got, and although that may or may not have been true, she believed it, and that's all that mattered.

Suddenly she saw Samuel's face hovering in the doorway Ish had just gone through only seconds before. It swished and swooped as the chilly breeze rushed inside.

"You stupid Bitch!" the apparition screamed. ***"You worthless piece of shit!"***

That's when she fainted.

†   †   †

Ish flew out the door so fast he didn't bother to grab a coat. Now, as he walked the mile or so to Billy's house, wearing a flannel shirt wasn't exactly the warmest thing, especially if that's all you had to fend off the gusting and chilly March winds. *At least the sun is out,* he thought to himself.

He walked as if on a mission.

With both hands jammed into his jeans pockets, arms pressing, his head down, he walked, and when the wind really let loose he broke off into a run, wishing he at least would have gotten around to fixing the flat tire on his Schwinn.

The warm sun on his back felt great so he slowed his pace. Ish listened as the wind whistled through the white pines on either side, and in the rustling he could hear a beat. At first it was only faint, but as he got closer to Billy's house it grew increasingly louder.

Billy had been a friend since freshman year. When they first met, they almost got into a brawl when Ish cracked a joke about Billy's last name. Ish had called him, "Billy *gay* blade."

Billy didn't hold it against him. After all, how could he with a last name like "Blade." No matter how many times Billy may have heard a joke about it, he always managed to laugh it off. He was into music, loud music. In fact, the louder, the better. It was Billy's idea to start up the band, and Billy who pushed them into gigs, because Billy was the brains of the whole deal. Not to mention the fact that he had the speakers and the rest of the equipment. It seemed Billy's dad had a habit of always trying to buy his son's love.

24

The other guys were all members of his class. Joey Boil played the drums as if possessed. Tony Sharpton strummed the base guitar so fine, you would think he was born with it in his hands, but the band wasn't complete until Todd Striker decided to go on the tour. Without Todd's angelic voice, the band could never take off.

Nearly ten-thirty by the time Ish showed up, the guys were in the garage doing what came naturally. The rolling of the drums, the wailing of the guitar, the organ's howl—they were only tuning up but even that was music to his ears.

Ever since they graduated they did nothing but practice, and here and there, Billy would find a place where they could play, usually without getting paid.

When it came down to it, Ish would make the tour as well, even though it wasn't actually a tour. They were just taking the show on the road, pulling up stakes, hoping they could make something of themselves. In the process, Ish would end up leaving behind an uncle he didn't really care for, an aunt he wanted to screw, and a mother who was never really right in the head. At least not that he could remember. Even as a small child, he felt something was not right with her, and he was glad to leave that whole scene behind.

Things couldn't have been better; they were moving from town to town, playing in more places than they could count. At first the money wasn't so great, but that changed with time and they had all the time in the world.

Along with time and money came women and drugs. Todd had told them they were going to make it all the way to the top. They just needed the one break they were all looking for: a record deal.

Then one day it finally happened. They landed a deal with a major producer, and things started looking great. The night they heard the news, they partied until they couldn't party anymore, slopping down drinks until four in the morning.

Then, the accident that wiped away their dreams came. For Joey, Todd, and Tony's life would end on that rainy night. Ish and Billy would survive, but the band had died, and so too the dream of fame.

5

For the longest time, Ish couldn't bring himself to open his eyes. He was afraid he might see what he didn't want to see because if he looked at it again, he'd surely go mad. But he had to open them; he was alive after all. Hurt for sure, but he was alive. He remembered last seeing Billy lying strapped in his seat, *thank goodness for seatbelts!* He didn't know how he survived, but he did.

Stupid! Stupid! Ish thought to himself. *It was the booze, damn it! It wasn't my fault!* Oh, but it was; he was the one driving the damn van. Everything was going so well and looking better with each passing day, but now there was nothing! All gone—all because of what?

Hell, they were all pumped up when they heard the news about the record deal. Billy, who seemed to know all the right people, found Louie, their manager. Louis Marks was a man who kept his word because he told them that if they took him on as their manager, he'd make damn sure the band would get a deal.

Damned if he didn't do just that. They'd just finished a gig when they found out, so they decided to stay at the club awhile and do some celebrating.

That turned out to be a mistake.

But, he knew the biggest mistake turned out to be deciding to race that damn train. Who the hell egged him on?

He couldn't remember.

Stupid! Stupid! He remembered crossing the first set of tracks, then slamming his foot on the gas, because damn it we can make it! Who was that screaming in his ear, "You can make it! You can make it!" He couldn't remember crossing the second set of tracks because that's when everything went black. In that blackness he found his father. Yes, the man had been dead since he was a child, but he remembered what his dad looked like; it's hard to forget such a mean face.

It was you! Ish thought to himself. He now realized who was yelling, "You can make it!" It had been his dad wailing at the top of his lungs from the other side, "You can make it!" And he believed him. Why?

The van had been split in half. Ish and Billy were alive but the guys in the back! Oh man! The guys in the back! They had been erased like a teacher swiping the blackboard clean of all the answers before a test.

Gone…

"… all because of you!!!" Ish screamed at his father's dead and angry face.

He remembered seeing all that blood.

That's what kept his eyes closed. He didn't want to see the blood, so much blood. But it seemed the longer he kept his eyes closed, his mind would begin to piece the picture together like a giant jigsaw puzzle, until all of a sudden, Ish was staring at the bloody remains of his friends.

All gone now, damn it! All because of you! Ish looked away from the mess and into his father's eyes. Each pupil in those eyes flickered with a yellow and orange flame.

"Forget about them!" His father screamed. "You are your father's son!"

Those eyes seemed so familiar, and he wasn't afraid any longer. He was in fact caught up in a pleasure web of some kind and he couldn't move. Those eyes flickered and Ish became mesmerized. "Yes," Ish mumbled in his sleep. "I am my father's son. Yes, yes." Then the darkness began to fade and sunlight took its place.

Slowly, ever so slowly, the sunlight, which poured in through the window blinds, flashed his eyes until it finally brought him back from the other side.

Ish opened his eyes.

He found himself lying in a hospital bed with a stranger staring down at him. He wanted to grab the man's arm and ask, "Who are you?" But he couldn't move or speak. He was awake, yet it felt as if he were in a dream.

"Don't move." The stranger said, as if reading his mind. "You're banged up pretty bad but you're going to make it."

Ish stared at the stranger for the longest time, as if studying the man. *Who the hell is this guy*, he thought to himself. And again, as if reading his thoughts, the man said, "My name's Mitchell Blade, Billy's older brother."

Ish's eyes widened when he realized who the man was. He'd heard a lot of things about him.

Being stared at was something that not only made Mitch mad; it also freaked him out. Ish could almost read him like a book, the big, bad, older brother who went off to become G.I. Joe. MISSION: Save the world!

Mitch's facial features looked as if they were chiseled out of stone. His cleft chin gave him that Kirk Douglas look, and that thought seemed to tickle Mitch's fancy because he was smiling now, a fake smile but a smile just the same.

"You and Billy are in Mercy Hospital, west of Pittsburgh. You're both gonna be o.k. But... "

Now Ish was reading Mitch's mind. *Your friends didn't*, he thought.

Then Mitch said, "Your friends weren't as lucky as you and my brother."

Ish gave a slight nod of his head without saying a word. He wouldn't know what to say even if he could; his jaw was wired shut.

Mitch felt bad for the kid, but he was also pissed off. He'd heard that Ish was the one driving the van, and he was planning on finding out what the hell happened. Now Mitch was staring, his eyes commanding attention. Ish tried to look away but he couldn't.

Oh well, he thought, *if I can't beat him, I'll join him.* With that, he shot back a cold and careless stare of his own, which caused Mitch to blink.

"Don't worry about a thing," Mitch said. "When you and Billy get out, which shouldn't be too long, you both can come and live with me till you're feeling better." He knew he was rambling, but he couldn't help himself. That cold stare made him mad and it freaked him out. It seemed this kid knew it was working on his last nerve.

What did Billy say to this guy, Mitch thought to himself. Whatever it was it must not have been very nice. Why else would he be so jumpy around this punk. When the staring game had ended with a blink, Mitch made sure he'd never give those eyes a second chance to steal his soul, because that's what it felt like, a cold hand wrapping around his soul, trying to pull it out of his heart.

"You go ahead and get your rest," Mitch said and smiled, again a fake one. "Be talking to you." He opened the door and left the room feeling more than a little relieved.

Seeing that kid didn't do me much good, he thought to himself. He thought he got all the information he needed from the head nurse before he went in; she said Ish was noted as being the driver of the van, but that was all the information she had had at the moment. She could have mentioned the fact the damn kid had his jaw wired shut. She would have saved him from wasting his time, thinking he was going to get the kid to talk. From the looks of things, the kid wouldn't be saying much for a while.

He knew he had other things to worry about; the doctors had said Billy was lucky to be alive, but he had some serious head injuries that called for some serious praying.

That's just what Mitch did.

Billy was indeed a lucky boy. After being in a coma for more than six months, he awoke from his sleep with the dead, a new man. The day Billy came out of his coma, Mitch had a strong feeling in his gut. At first he thought maybe it was just indigestion, but as it tightened, he had a hunch Billy was in the process of waking up.

He didn't know how he knew, but he figured he'd better check it out just the same, and while he was at it, he'd go and see, *what was his name?* Mitch thought, *Ishmael Alastor; the weird dude.*

Mitch had been so preoccupied with getting settled into a place while he waited for Billy to come around to the living that he completely forgot to check on this punk Ish more often. The kid had checked out of the hospital weeks ago. The hospital didn't have any records of the kid having family in the area. He could be anywhere by now.

Mitch decided maybe it was best that it turned out this way. He didn't much trust himself around the kid. If he had his way, he'd beat him within an inch of his life, forgetting the fact that the kid didn't have more than an inch to give up at the time.

Mitch talked to God often. He never thought of himself as a religious man, never really thought about God or his Son or his Holy Ghost, but since Nam, that all changed. He thought at the time that it was just a way to get through that living hell. He thought that once the threat of having his head blown off from a sniper, or his balls blown to shreds from a land mine was gone, so too would be the thought of God.

Lucky for Mitch that wasn't the case. He found the more he talked to his Maker, the better he felt about everything life had to offer. That's where the feeling in his gut about Billy came from. He knew that was God's way of saying: Go see your brother.

He was in the room for maybe a half-hour, sitting next to the head of the bed, listening to the machines that monitored his brother's life signs. In walked a nurse that Mitch knew he had to get to know. He noticed her name, Darla Mates, on the nametag of her uniform.

"Can I help you?" He asked with a smirk.

Man oh man, he thought to himself, *you sure could help me!*

She proceeded to write down the information from the monitors. "Just checking his progress," she said and smiled.

She looked great in her nurse's uniform, and Mitch let his imagination run wild as he thought about what it might be like to be with her. He hadn't been with a woman since God knows when, and her body was sending his head into a dizzy binge.

Suddenly Mitch noticed movement from the bed.

Billy was raising his hand.

He stood up and watched as his brother's hand rose higher and higher. The nurse now stood beside him, watching Billy reach for the sky. The doctors said Billy might have trouble remembering things. *Would he remember? Only God knows,* Mitch thought.

He reached for Billy's hand as Billy opened his eyes.

Mitch smiled. A tear swelled in his eye as he said, "How's it going, tough guy?"

With a twinkle of recognition in his own eyes, Billy said, "Better now… big bro."

Part Two

Obsessions

6

It was like any morning, except there was something in the works that made it unlike any other morning that would follow. The phone rang. The shrill scream pierced his hung-over brain like a dentist's drill to a tooth. It took awhile before it finally nudged him out of his sleep. His hand scrambled through the sheets as he reached for the phone.

In seconds, his fingers are fumbling for the receiver. It fell to the hardwood floor where it made a loud *Bonk!* A voice is barely audible, "Mitch! Yo! Mitch, wake up!"

Mitch found the cord and pulled the receiver to his ear. In a hoarse voice he said, "Yo! What the... What time is it?"

The voice on the other end of the line sounded excited. "Mitch! Man, am I glad you're awake!" It was also recognizable. "Billy? What the... "

"Calm down, Mitch, and listen up. You're not going to believe what just happened... "

Jack Daniel's began whispering in his ear and Mitch screamed into the phone, "What already!?"

He sounded peeved, but what else was new; Billy had heard him go off on more than one occasion. Hell, Mitch didn't need a reason. Mitch was Mitch, and there was no changing him. "Mitch, listen!"

If there was anything about his older brother that rubbed him the wrong way, it would have to be Mitch's inability to listen. He pulled the phone away from his ear as Mitch continued to scream, "Come on, Billy! What's so damn important, it can't wait!" When he put it back to his ear again, he yelled, "Mitch, shut the fuck up! Get dressed and meet me at the Motel-4 pronto! I have to make another call. See ya!"

… CLICK…

Mitch listened to the dial tone as it irked his ear. When Jack Daniel's launched into another taunting session, he hung up the phone. His head was in a fog. He seemed to be in the fog a lot these days. Get dressed, he says! Meet me at the Motel-4, he says! His anger wasn't directed at Billy. He was angry with himself, angry that he let himself fall prey to his archenemy, Jack Daniel's.

He dragged himself out of bed and made his way down the hallway to the bathroom. He didn't bother to turn on the light because that would only send knives into his bloodshot eyes. He was still dressed in the clothes he passed out in. That was another thing he was doing a lot of lately.

He planned on taking a quick piss, but it turned out to be longer than expected with the constant stop and go, stop and go. The smell of booze came with it, and it caused him to choke back a gag. He hated falling off the wagon. That meant another long run behind it before finally climbing back onboard, if he had the strength to make the climb.

When he finished, he washed his hands in the sink and splashed the cold water on his face. It helped, but not much. Five minutes later he was in his car heading to the Motel-4.

The ride wasn't long but it felt like it. He managed to catch every red light before getting off the main highway. By the time he rolled into the parking lot, the clock on the dashboard showed 3:40 a.m. Jack Daniel's sang sweet nothings into his ear again, so he pulled his car across from Billy's and flashed the headlights.

He sat and waited for Billy to get out of his car and flashed his lights again. He wanted a shot. He thought he needed one right about now. Again he flashed the lights. "What the… You're going to make me come to you?" he mumbled. Reluctantly, Mitch finally opened the car door and pulled himself out of the driver's seat.

He slammed the door. He wanted to make sure Billy knew he was pissed off. *It's almost four in the morning and this guy's playing detective dick,* he thought to himself. The morning sky glowed with the silvery rays of the moon. Only the sound of the gravel, crunching under his foot with each step, could be heard.

A slight wind caressed his face. It felt as if a hand from another time had touched him. As he came closer to Billy's car, he could see his brother slumped over behind the wheel. "What the… !"

Mitch ran to his brother's aid.

■   ■   ■

Waiting in a hospital was something Mitch hated the most. His mind raced with a million thoughts. They all led to the most difficult one of all. Who? He would have to wait for the answer. Billy was out. He'd been shot once in the gut. It was the waiting that was ripping him apart.

He was mad at himself, mad about getting so ticked off when Billy called. He did that a lot these days too, always getting himself worked up over nothing. He had a problem but he knew he could deal with it. He hoped he could deal with it. His divorce from Darla only made it worse, or was that the reason for it? He jumped, his mind coming back to the present when a hand touched his shoulder.

Looking up, expecting to see a doctor, his jaw nearly dropped off from his head. "Darla? What are you doing here?" Seeing her again made his heart flutter. *It's been a long time*, he thought to himself. *She still looks great.*

"I heard about Billy," she said as she took a seat next to him. "I thought you might need someone to talk to." She cupped her hands over his and smiled. That smile always could make him smile, but at the moment he just couldn't do it. Not because he didn't want to, God knows he did, but because he couldn't, his mind was still reeling with other thoughts.

As she spoke, he drifted off into his own world. Watching her lips move but not hearing a word. *Who the hell pumped my brother with lead,* he thought. *What was it he said on the phone, 'You're not going to believe what just happened?' What happened, besides the fact that Billy was laid up with a hole in his gut. What happened?*

Her voice snapped him out of it again. "Are you listening to me?" With a grin being the best he could muster, he said, "I'm sorry, what did you say?"

She reached up and pulled her long auburn hair away from her face. "I said... you look lost. Are you gonna be o.k.?"

Mitch reached into his breast pocket and pulled out a cigarette. "I'm fine. It's Billy I'm worried about."

Darla reached out and snatched the smoke from his lips. "There's no smoking in hospitals." Mitch managed to smile at her as he said, "Sorry. I forgot."

The smell of her perfume made him remember a time when that alone was enough to drive him wild with desire. But that was then. Now all he desired was a jolt from the bottle, yet oddly enough the desire was just that, a desire and nothing more. Was it because she was here with him now? Did she still hold that kind of an effect on him? She had helped him in the past.

As he gazed into her deep blue eyes he thought, *I could get lost in those.* He'd forgotten about a lot of things. He forgot how her laughter had always picked up his spirits and there were a few times when his spirit really needed a pick-me-up.

He forgot just how great it had been waking up with her lying beside him, how warm and comfortable it had been on cold winter mornings. The passion that flared between them was never to be repeated with anyone else. At least not as far as Mitch was concerned; he hadn't thought of any other woman let alone actually meet one.

"So how've you been?" he asked, trying not to sound interested and failing miserably. He hadn't seen, nor heard from her since the divorce was finalized, but he still had a soft spot for her in his heart.

"I'm fine," she said and managed another smile. She too still held feelings for him but was too proud to show it.

They'd been married for seven years and divorced for nearly five. Mitch always thought that trying to get to know her was like trying to read a book without an ending. Someone ripped out the last five pages, leaving the reader hanging. She would never open up, never allow her inner thoughts to be known. That's how it had been and he remembered that it was her idea to call it quits. *What's she doing here*, he wondered. She had grown distant the last year of their marriage. His job as a private investigator kept him busy for sure, but he thought they could work through it.

He never thought that maybe his job was the straw that broke the marriage's back. If only he stopped to think about it. How wrong he had been to think that two people could continue on, day after day, living the same routine without ever communicating. It was only a matter of time before the foundation crumbled. Had he been that stupid not to see it coming?

Maybe he missed it because of the way he was brought up, or maybe it was the environment in which he was raised, but no matter what, all Mitch knew was that the man was the king of the castle, the head of the house, the breadwinner. He thought he was meeting all her needs, except he was to busy hunting down deadbeat dads or sneaking around taking snapshots of cheating spouses.

He never really asked her what she needed, let alone spend time with her, and by the time he got around to it, she wasn't interested in sharing. He met her after he got out of the military. He literally swept her off her feet. They went out for a few months before he popped the question.

I never really knew her, he thought to himself.

So his marriage had ended and so too his life, but that of course was not the case. At fifty-five and still looking like forty-five, a guy quickly finds out that the single life isn't as hard to pick up again, not really. You just had to get used to the idea of doing things for yourself. It was a slow start but that's what happens when you're married for a few years. You get rusty. He only needed to do some polishing up.

He would come to realize, after the divorce, how wrong he had been in his thinking. No one ever told him that marriage was a job in and of itself. Had he known then what he knew now, he might have done things differently, but he knew in his heart that that was a lie. He was too much the bloodhound, always looking for a trail to follow.

He loved the idea of being a P.I. He loved the whole idea of law enforcement. He had a taste of it as an MP in the Army. He did his twenty and got a nice pension for his efforts. When he left the military, a lot of changes had taken place in his life. He tried working on the police force, but it wasn't long before he tired of that and opened his own P.I. office. He went to work on building his new business for his new life and his new wife. When his business shot through the roof, he needed help. That's where Billy came into play.

For the longest time they said nothing. The two of them sat there, her looking out the wide-paned window and him staring down at the floor. Each lost in their own little world. As Darla gazed outside, watching an airplane slowly descending from the early morning sky, she thought, *Please God if you're listening, please let Billy be o.k.*

Mitch interrupted her thought when he asked, "How'd you know I was here?" His voice sounded confident and sure, but Darla had a sense that Mitch wasn't as confident as he seemed; she knew Mitch was scared. Billy meant the world to him.

"Your mom called me and said Billy was in the hospital." Mitch looked at her with question marks in his gaze.

"Who called—Ma?"

She smiled a wider smile and said, "It seems Billy has her name and number in his wallet for whom to call in case of an emergency."

Still the mama's boy, Mitch thought as he fought back a chuckle. Darla put her hand on his shoulder and gave it a gentle squeeze. "Billy's gonna be o.k."

She hoped.

7

Finally, after what seemed like days on end but in reality had only been an hour and a half, a man in doctor's greens approached Darla and Mitch. They looked at each other and then back at the doctor. The man standing before them brought back memories of the Jolly Green Giant. Mitch half expected him to laugh out loud like the big guy in the commercial, "Ho, Ho, Ho."

The man removed his mask and with a hint of excitement he said, "Detective Blade?" He stuck his hand out, expecting to shake Mitch's, but he just sat there staring at it, more like through it.

After an awkward second longer, he dropped it back to his side. With a smile he said, "I've heard a lot about you, Mr. Blade. It's not every day I get to meet a celebrity."

Mitch mustered up a lame smile and said, "How's my brother?" *And who the hell shot him,* he thought to himself. He was still upset with himself. Jackie Boy was trying his nerves again, but a quick glance at Darla and his nerves seemed to settle to a more manageable quake.

"Your brother's a lucky man, Mr. Blade. If you hadn't brought him in when you did, we would have lost him."

The doctor, who had been a fan, now only viewed Mitch as a jerk-off, and an ignorant one at that. "We're gonna keep him here for a week, maybe longer. He's lost a lot of blood."

Mitch was relieved to hear that Billy would be all right. So relieved, in fact, that he forgot Darla was with him.

"When can I see him?" he asked.

The doctor pulled the latex gloves off of his unusually large hands and said, "You and your wife can see him when he wakes up, but that might be awhile. You'd be better off going home. We'll... "

Mitch cut him off as he finally stood up from his chair, his own height exceeding the doctor's by at least a half foot. "If it's all the same with you, Doc, I'd rather wait." Darla, for reasons unknown to her, reached out and grabbed Mitch's hand and said, "We'll wait, Doctor. Thank you."

"O.k.," he said. "Like I said, it may be a long wait. Now if you'll excuse me." With that said, the doctor walked down the long hallway and turned the corner. Mitch took his seat as Darla still held his hand. "Are you gonna be o.k.?" She asked. Mitch gave her a big grin and said, "Yeah, I'm gonna be just fine. Why don't you go home and I'll call you if I need you."

For a second there, Mitch thought he was still married to her. It actually felt like it deep-down inside, way down inside where she refused to go. God how he wanted to know her beauty from within; he thought it'd been great, but now it was only a memory and a painful one at that, because he knew even deeper within himself that he'd never find any better than her. She was once in his life, and he blew it and just now knew it.

He was deep in thought. So deep, he didn't even feel the kiss she laid on his cheek as she stood up from her seat.

"Call me," she said and then she too walked down the corridor and rounded the same corner as the doctor before her had done. When Mitch looked down at his hands and found a folded piece of paper, he opened it and stared for the longest time.

She's got such sexy handwriting, he thought to himself. On the notepaper was an address and phone number, along with a smiley face. Under that was her name, always in that neat "I'm a Star" signature.

.   ■   ■

The doc wasn't joking around when he said it might be a long wait. Mitch was thinking maybe it would be an hour or two tops before Billy woke up. When his stomach screamed for some fuel, he found his way to the hospital's cafeteria and curbed its bellowing. The food sucked but that was only because his stomach still had some booze twirling around in it.

He had a huge pile of scrambled eggs, some toast and topped it off with lots of coffee. He thought about seconds but decided against it, which was a good thing too because later he wound up sitting on the can, losing his bowels, cursing the eggs and himself for eating so much of them in the first place.

Hours never lasted so long. He had at one time wished he could find a way to slow time, did in fact wish he could go back to the carefree days of his youth, but never in his life imagined that time could crawl as slow as it had.

Mitch looked at his watch. *If this day went any slower, it'll start going backwards,* he thought to himself. He read every magazine they had available to read. *Sports Illustrated, People* and *Time*. He even allowed himself to thumb through the pages of *Ladies' Home Journal, Better Homes and Gardens* and *Glamour*. He reread *Glamour*; it had a lot of interesting photos.

When he got bored with that, he sat and watched the soap operas on the 19" color TV which was mounted high on the wall in the far corner of the room. He soon tired of watching that as well, the screen flickered and jumped so much it was useless to watch. Besides, he could only keep his head up for so long before getting a kink in his neck.

Every thirty minutes or so, he found himself outside smoking his cigarettes.

He sat and waited for nearly twelve hours. He watched the waiting room go from near empty to over-crowded, then back to a more comfortable four or five people, all waiting like him. Mitch had to laugh as he watched the old man sitting to his right trying to watch the TV. Its jumpy screen began to get on the old geezer's nerves and it was comical to observe.

Ten minutes later, the old goat was fast asleep.

8

Mitch couldn't hold out any longer; the waiting was causing him to think about things he didn't want to think about. The old man had the right idea, so Mitch allowed himself to rest. *I'll just close my eyes for forty winks,* he thought. By the time he got to thirty, he was out like a light.

In his dream he was arguing with his dad. It was the day he told him about his plans on going into the Army. His father hit the roof. Mitch never saw his father so angry. His face red as a beet, his eyes practically popping out of his head, his dad did everything he could to talk Mitch out of his decision, but it was too late, Mitch already signed all the paperwork. It was just a matter of time.

He woke from his dream with the sound of his father's voice still shouting in his head, "If you join the Military, you're no longer my son!"

It felt so real. It was as if he had gone back in time.

Mitch thought about it awhile, and decided he didn't give a rat's ass if his dad didn't approve. He knew his pop was just pissed because his eldest son wasn't going to follow in his footsteps. There are some things a guy has to learn, but as far as Mitch was concerned, plumbing wasn't one of them. No matter how hard his dad tried to push him in that direction, Mitch knew it would never happen.

When he first entered the military, he ignored most of the letters from his mom, wanting to forget home, but with time, he eventually started reading them. His mother would tell him about his father and how he was treating her. She said he didn't like the idea of his wife writing to a stranger.

He remembered that most of the letters upset him. His dad was making life miserable for everyone. Mitch

46

remembered that at one point he even wished his father would just kick the bucket, and then he remembered how horrible that thought had made him feel when one of her letters told of his suicide, which led to Billy taking off and starting a rock band.

He'd joined the Army to get away from his dad. The man could sometimes be so overbearing. And possessive! He was worse than a woman, always asking where he was going, or what he was doing, top all that off with his constant nagging about learning "The trade!" It just got to be too much.

He never gave his mother or Billy a second thought. He knew he had to get away, so he just went. He spent most of his time as an MP, and while he was gone a lot of changes took place on the home front. Since his dad died and he wasn't around, there was no one to see to it that Billy stayed on the straight and narrow. Not that his father made a great role model. Hell, Mitch thought it better that the man was dead.

Sure, his mother tried but there's only so much a woman can do; a kid needs a mother and a father, and of course with kids being kids. He remembered a lot of those letters talking about Billy and how his mom was afraid for him. Apparently, he did manage to occasionally call, but he never told her where he was at the time. Mitch knew he couldn't do anything to change things, but he made a promise to himself that he'd do right by Billy when he got home. When he enlisted, he never thought about home. If his mother never bothered to write, chances are, he would have moved on with his life without them.

Mitch spent his second year of the service in Vietnam. The fighting was winding down by then, but he volunteered for sniper school and passed without difficulty. The training was tough but he fed off the stuff; the tougher it got, the more he loved it. But he wasn't totally prepared for some of the shit he had seen. He remembered everything about his time over there.

It was the only thing that was on his mind for the longest time. Then he met Darla and she helped keep his mind off that whole ugly scene. He thought he could forget about it, but he dreamt about it almost every night. Even after he got married, the dreams still held him captive. It was always the same dream of him crawling around in his camouflage, mixing in so well with the jungle; then, an explosion, and the screams of his partner. In a flash he's up and running. Everything moving in slow motion, he slips, falls and finds that he just stepped into what still remained of his partner's guts. His spot man is lying there screaming for God to have mercy. What's left of his body is nothing but a mesh of flesh from the stomach on down. With flailing arms, and eyes in a state of shock, Mitch holds on to what's left of the man and tries to comfort him. Then the poor slob finally gives up the ghost.

Many a nights Mitch woke up hugging his pillow, thinking he was still holding on to that guy. So many thoughts… so many memories… It seemed the more he tried not to think about it, the more his thoughts would turn to it.

How long have I been waiting, he wondered. Sitting here waiting for the chance to see Billy, this was déjà vu. He remembered sitting in another hospital years before, wondering if he'd ever see his brother alive again. He had just processed out of the service and wasn't home for more than an hour when word came to him and his mother that Billy had been in an accident. She'd been filling him in on everything that was happening, telling him how the last she had heard, Billy was playing in a nightclub somewhere in Pittsburgh.

He remembered the call as if it were yesterday. His mother's face turned white as a sheet as she sat there in her chair with her mouth hanging open in shock, holding on to the receiver with all her strength. It took Mitch a good thirty seconds to wrestle the damn thing out of her hand. He asked the person on the other end of the line if they could repeat the message. The man on the other end was from Mercy Hospital in Pennsylvania, a long way from Washington State. He remembered how pissed he had been at Billy back then.

Damn, seems like he's always been pissing me off, he thought.

Good thing Mitch had the money to fly out to get him; he could have left him for dead or, even worse, left him to fend for himself, but Mitch couldn't do that. Mitch had a conscience after all. He was worried back then, worried that Billy wasn't going to pull through.

He prayed that Billy would fight his way out of it.

That's what Blades do: fight their way out of every tough situation. He promised himself that if Billy made it, he'd see to it that his younger brother stayed out of trouble no matter what that may entail. And that's just what he had been doing ever since, or at least he thought he had. He knew Billy was in the mess he was in this time because of Mitch's own stupid obsession.

All this thinking was beginning to take its toll. He closed his eyes again and was just about to nod off into never-never land when a hand touched his shoulder. A nurse with emerald green eyes was smiling at him. "You can see your brother now, Mr. Blade. He's awake."

■　　■　　■

If the memory train was coming to a stop, it was an awfully quick one. Seeing Billy lying in the hospital bed brought back even more memories. How long had it been? Twelve, maybe thirteen years since Billy had been laid up in that hospital's bed in Pittsburgh? Back then the doctors had said Billy was a lucky boy and that was true, but now, seeing him lying in this bed with a tube in his nose, Mitch realized that his brother had to be one lucky son of a bitch. One of the luckiest that ever walked the face of the earth.

The nurse told him Billy was awake, but Mitch found him lying there with his eyes closed, looking more like he was ready for the morgue than having visitors. He was surprised a tag wasn't hanging on his big toe; he looked that bad.

Mitch approached the side of the bed feeling like a kid who's afraid to see his sick grand pop. He watched Billy's chest rise and fall under the sheets. Billy's eyes began to roll around in his head, and then they were open, looking up at Mitch. They were smiling, and then so too was his face as his lips pulled upwards into a grin.

Mitch took his brother's hand, gave it a reassuring squeeze and said, "How's it going, tough guy?"

Billy's smile grew even wider as he said, "Better now, Big Bro."

Oh, POW Wow! Mitch thought. This is getting weird. Back so long ago when the world was merely sitting on the edge of insanity, back in that hospital Billy had said the same thing then, and the memory came to Mitch's mind through a tunnel of time. … Better now, Big Bro…

… Big Bro… Big Bro… Big Bro…

That fast, Mitch was zapped to another time, another place. The doctors had said his brother was lucky but they also said they hoped he would be fortunate enough to remember anything before or after the accident. They said he might not remember anything, ever again. They believed he should be thankful Billy was still alive. They said he could help him build new memories and try to help him remember the old, but Billy didn't forget everything. Mitch had been away for so long, but Billy still remembered him.

Mitch had asked the same question then, and Billy had smiled and said, "Better now, Big Bro."

… Big Bro… Big Bro… Big Bro…

"Hey Mitch… Earth, calling Mitch!"

The sound of Billy's voice yanked Mitch back into the present. He tried to hold back a chuckle but was unsuccessful.

"What's so funny?" Billy asked.

Mitch wanted to say how he liked his choice of words, but instead he said, "Just remembering something… How're you feeling?"

Billy, in an attempt at looking tough, sat up and snatched the tube out of his nose and with his best Rambo impersonation he said, "Good enough to get the hell out of here."

Mitch reached out and put his hand on Billy's shoulder and said, "Cool out, Jack!" and regretted saying those words, because in an instant, Jack Daniel's was beginning to fill his head with nasty thoughts again.

"You're not going anywhere until the Doc says otherwise," he grumbled.

Billy knew it was useless to argue with Mitch. His body knew it too, because he was just now feeling the results of his show of toughness. Lying back in his bed, feeling a bit dizzy, he put the tube back into his nose. His big brother always did know what he was talking about. That was one of the reasons Billy envied him so.

Mitch pulled a chair close to the bed and took a seat. His sigh was that of an old man. For the longest time he said nothing, lost in his own world. Billy didn't care; he was just glad to have him here; for some reason it made him feel safer.

Mitch closed his eyes and rubbed his temples with his thumbs trying his best to ignore the bitching of Jack in his head. *Time-out! TIME-OUT! Take a freaking time-out! Just cool out, Jack!!*

Finally he opened his eyes, looked at Billy and asked, "So what happened?"

Now it was Billy's turn to dummy up. He was inside himself, searching for the right words, trying to remember and knowing it would be easier. Easier because this was something big! This was something that was going to make life easier to handle. Sure, Mitch had made a name for himself in the business, but this was something that would make both their lives more comfortable.

"You told me to keep my eyes open, remember?" His voice was low and his words came out slow. Mitch knew it was for effect; Billy always did like to make everything more dramatic than it had to be. "You told me to call you anytime, remember?"

Mitch scratched at an imaginary itch on his scalp. As much as he hated to admit it, he said, "Yes. I remember."

"I was keeping an eye on the place just like you asked me." In his excitement, he began to pick up the pace. "I thought I was wasting my time. I thought for sure it wouldn't happen but damn! You proved me wrong, again!"

Mitch was smiling and it was the kind of smile that always made Billy laugh when he was a kid. That smile that said, "Oh my gosh… stop it, you're making me blush!" Billy found himself laughing as he realized he actually remembered something else from his past.

Mitch asked, "What's so funny?" and covered up a chuckle of his own.

Billy's smile faded and his face became serious. "How did you know the killer was going to strike there?"

Being tired and busy fighting with Jack in his head, he wasn't in the mood to hear how great he was at his job, especially from his kid brother. "Just a hunch," he said. *That, plus the fact it's happened in a freaking Motel-4 a number of times,* he thought. In between bouts with Jack, he struggled to remind himself that he wanted Billy to know as little as possible, thinking that that would somehow keep Billy in the safe zone.

Only it didn't work.

If it had, Billy wouldn't be lying there with a hole in his gut. The silence between them grew thick as they thought about their own situation or station in life. Mitch was busy piecing the puzzle together. This case was turning out to have a lot of tiny pieces, a case that seemed to draw him in, and a case with more questions than answers. He didn't understand why or what drew him to it, but he was determined to find out. In his determination (or should it be called obsession?) he had nearly gotten his brother killed.

Billy was still reeling from remembering pieces from his past, the time before his accident. It wasn't the first retrieved memory and he felt for certain that it wasn't going to be the last. He was feeling great (other than his wound); he knew what he was going to say would make Mitch a very happy camper. Finally, when he felt he couldn't hold it in any longer, he said, "I saw the guy."

9

A moment ago Mitch was feeling worn down, ready to call it a day, but when he heard what Billy said, he sat up in his seat with a jump. "You saw the guy... the killer?"

In his excitement from hearing the news, Mitch started drumming his hands on the edge of the bed. His little brother had seen the guy he'd been trying to sniff out. He thought he was getting close, and now he could almost smell the bastard. "Could you pick him out of the books?"

Billy watched, as Mitch continued to tap his hands on the edge of the bed, drumming "Wipe Out" on the mattress, looking like a kid that just got his second wind and wasn't about to go to bed now. He reached over and grabbed Mitch's left hand, stopping the beat in its track. "If he's in there, but I'd be very surprised."

"What makes you say that?" Mitch asked.

Billy gave him a big grin and said, "Just a hunch."

Mitch sat back in his chair, allowing himself to relax, telling himself to chill out; you're getting a little too giddy kiddy. He had told Billy some things about the case, but left a lot of holes, so as far as Billy was concerned, he was just doing his older brother a favor. Sure, Billy would have thought that the stakeout was odd but that was beside the point.

"I'm guessing he's the one that shot you?" he asked.

Billy started to tell him the whole story, but declined to talk about the part where he fell asleep. He said he was sitting in his car, trying to be nonchalant, when he saw someone who looked weird, someone who looked out of place. It was too dark to get a good look at the guy so he decided to follow the creep to wherever he was headed.

Sure enough, he followed him back to one of the rooms, which wasn't hard to do since all the rooms were on the ground floor. When he got to where the guy had gone, he peeked in the window and saw what he thought for sure he wouldn't. It was a quick glance, and he only saw it because the guy must have accidentally brushed up against the curtains making them swish back and forth, offering a slight view until the curtains settled back into place. But he saw it just the same: a woman, lying in the bed with a sword sticking in her chest and through the bed. He said he'd be willing to bet that if you lifted up the bed's covers, you'd find that the tip of that sword was sticking into the floor.

"I was freaked!"

His excitement was evident by the way he babbled on and on, "I wanted to call you. Call the cops. Get this freak locked up." He caught his breath, trying to make himself relax. All this reminiscing was beginning to tire him out. Mitch didn't say a word. He just waited to hear more. He'd been waiting all this time, what the hell were a few minutes more.

Billy closed his eyes, remembering the whole thing as if it were happening now. "I got back to the car and called you…" He opened his eyes again and glanced out the window. The only thing he could see was the sky, and it was an awesome blue with puffy white clouds floating by. For some reason, it reminded him of the Macy's Parade.

"I was just about to call the cops when I look up and see this guy standing outside my window with a gun in his hand. Next thing I know I'm waking up in this bed." He didn't dare tell Mitch about the creepy feelings he had about the dude. He didn't want Mitch to worry about dumb shit. So what if the guy spooked him; anyone would have felt the same way. Wouldn't they?

Mitch sat back into his chair, feeling the never-ending pull of sleep. He yawned, putting his hand in front of his face in order to stifle it. He held up his index finger as if to say, "Wait a minute," and finished his yawn with another sigh. "Can you give a description of the guy to a police sketch artist?"

Billy knew where Mitch was going with his thinking, and he wished that it could be as easy as that. He said, "It wouldn't do any good. The dude was wearing a mask. The wacko was dressed like freaking Zorro."

Mitch knew it was too good to be true. His high hopes were falling fast, ready to smash into a million pieces. It seemed this particular case was filled with one question after the next, and all of them leading to nowhere. All of a sudden he needed a drink, a good stiff one. As nice as that thought sounded, he knew it was the last thing he wanted. What he desired more than anything was to sleep.

"That explains the swords," he mumbled to himself as he fought off another yawn.

Billy was feeling a bit sluggish himself and told Mitch so. He told him to go home and get some rest. He said he needed his own rest; his stomach was beginning to hurt again.

Mitch knew he needed a time-out of his own, some time off to relax and unwind. He had been busting his hump nonstop with this case. It pulled at him the way a magnet pulls at a refrigerator door. It had been so many years of chasing shadows; he lost track of how long he'd been working on it.

Seeing Billy again, talking to him, made Mitch both relieved and exhausted. He thought for sure he'd pass out right here in the chair. He reluctantly pushed himself up and out of his seat. He found out what he needed to find out. Billy was o.k. And that's all that mattered. He smiled and said, "Since you're going to be o.k., I'm going home and crash."

When Mitch stood up to go, Billy's heartbeat began to do double-time. Was it getting hot in here? As Mitch reached for the door's handle, a bead of sweat stung Billy's left eye.

"Mitch."

"What?"

Billy wanted to tell him not to go. He wanted to tell him how afraid he was but he couldn't do that. Mitch would have looked down upon doing something like that, or at least that's what Mitch always liked to say.

He squeezed out a grin and said, "The killer... I felt like I knew the crazy son of a bitch, something about his eyes."

Mitch managed a grin of his own and said, "Get some sleep." Then he pulled the door open, and he was gone.

10

Since his accident, Ish's dreams had become strange. He dreamt of the dead. He dreamt of the living too, but mostly his dreams ended up with the dead. People he neither knew nor cared to know called to him and he did his best to ignore them. When someone he didn't know popped into the picture, a siren went off in his head. The day he woke up and found Billy's brother standing over him, looking like a guy searching for answers, that's when he got the first warning blast. He was laid up in that bed, and all of a sudden his head's throbbing because the blood is pumping like he just ran the mile in three seconds flat. That warning pang shot straight to the center of his head and exploded like fireworks in the sky.

Ish remembered Billy telling them he didn't know his older brother all that well because he'd joined the Army when he was just a kid. Billy may not have known him that well, but Mitch was definitely Billy's hero. He never actually came out and said it using those words, but it was obvious to all of them by his expressions and body language. Billy did everything but build a monument. That's how proud he was of his brother. He was quick to defend him when his father spoke ill of him too; he was always the first to put in a good word on his brother's behalf.

Billy's old man made it a habit of coming out to the garage while the guys were practicing for a jam session. He would get Billy pissed off because he'd say something rotten about Mitch. Mitch who couldn't do anything wrong, the great Mitch, who had all the brains and Mitch who had all the muscle. All that changed when they found Billy's dad hanging from the rafters.

It may not have been so bad if he did it in the attic or someplace else, but the son of a bitch hung himself in their practice space, the place where inspiration was king. The shock of finding him swinging back and forth would forever be imprinted in their minds.

Billy blamed his father's suicide on Mitch. He didn't realize that his dad had problems he couldn't handle. Some people are quick to take the easy way out. Weak-minded souls are often swift to do a dance on the end of a rope.

Billy's father, along with all the others, walked in Ish's dreams. He said the same thing as all the rest, but Ish ignored it. They were dead after all; what did they know?

Warning pangs continued to go off every time Mitch paid him a visit. Every visit, Ish pretended to be sleeping. Sometimes Mitch would stay for a few minutes, sometimes a little more than an hour. It always gave Ish plenty of time to think. He knew his life had taken a major turn, but he wasn't sure where this new direction was leading him. He would soon find out that no matter where it led, he had no choice but to follow it. He alone chose this path; he'd have to see it through.

Everything he'd ever known was in the past, finished, no more. Ish didn't need any hassle with Mitch. He already screwed up; he didn't need to be reminded of that fact. He knew the only thing he could do was to run at the first opportunity. Until then, he'd allow himself to relax and heal.

Ish prayed to his God.

A God his mother would not take kindly to. He prayed late at night, with his hands held out in front of him as if he were casting a magical spell, muttering under his breath and mentally projecting his will, repeating over and over again, "Stay away! Stay away!"

He had a strong will. His God only made it stronger because Mitch's visits became fewer and fewer, until he stopped coming around altogether. What turned out to be bad luck for Billy (his being laid up for six months in a coma) turned into good luck for Ish. When his chance to run finally arrived, he took off like a bat out of hell and never looked back. Not knowing where he was going, only knowing that he needed to run, he slipped into a city that was both new and unknown.

They'd only been in town for a short time before the accident, so he'd never gotten around to seeing the sights. Being out on his own was something new. Sure, he'd left home and toured with the band, and you could say he was on his own, but he wasn't. The band had taken the place of his family, had become his family. So, he was never really on his own, until now.

With no money and only the clothes on his back, Ish set out to rebuild his life. He didn't know what to expect. He thought it would be easy too, because up until now everything he ever had had come so easily.

Ish found out just how harsh life could become. Reality stepped up and slapped him in the face. Being in a band was all he ever knew. He thought of starting up a band of his own, hoping that that would somehow get the magic back, but that faded out fast. Billy had been the brains of the old band. He was just lucky enough to get pulled along for the ride. Ish even tried joining other bands, but that never panned out either. Not many bands needed somebody to shake a tambourine. He couldn't sing to save his life, and he didn't play an instrument, so his band days had become a thing of the past.

The pressure of being on his own with nobody to turn to in a new town began to mount and depression set in. Ish felt as if everyone was out to get him. No matter what he did, nothing went his way. He wondered what he was doing wrong but could never find an answer. It wasn't long before he found himself begging for spare change in the city.

Ish hated himself for doing it.

He had always looked upon the homeless with contempt, and now he was doing what he hated. It wasn't something he was proud of but he also knew that pride wouldn't put food in his stomach. Before he ever lived the life, he thought people who lived on the streets deserved to be there. He thought they wanted to be there, as if they had a choice in the matter. He saw them as scum of the earth and now here he was living like a bum.

"Hey buddy, can you spare some change?"

Ish held out his filthy hand, hoping to get some change for a cup of coffee. A man in a black business suit pushed his hand aside and said, "Get the hell out of my way!" He brushed by so fast; Ish thought the guy was heading for a fire.

People are cold, he thought. *Can't they see I need help?* He could only see the cold and careless stares of strangers staring at him as if he were a piece of trash that needed to be disposed of.

"Fuck you very much!" Ish shouted.

The man continued to walk, but he then stopped long enough to turn around and flip the middle finger.

The world had abandoned him, and his God had forgotten about him. Now, hatred for both simmered under his skin. There was a time when he had a dream of becoming a writer. That dream was dashed on the rocks when his family failed to support it. In rebellion, he ran away from home, thinking he'd show them how wrong they had been. He didn't realize that maybe he would be running for the rest of his life.

When Ish had been laid up in that hospital bed, he told himself to hope for the best, but expect the worse. He certainly wasn't prepared to live on the streets. How do you prepare for something like that? He thought he had prepared himself mentally, thought about all the what-ifs, the how-tos and the wheres. He now realized being mentally prepared for something you knew nothing about was a lot harder than he thought possible.

His depression only made matters worse. Maybe, just maybe, being mentally prepared wasn't all that it was cracked up to be. Being sane in an insane world wasn't always easy. Feeling bogged down from all the pressure tends to make people snap, and his situation was clearly a case of feeling bogged down.

He thought he would be on the streets for no more than a month, but when one month turned into four, he began to feel as if he stepped into quicksand and he was sinking deeper and deeper into the mire with each passing day.

Six months.

Twelve months.

Eighteen months.

Ish managed to keep himself fed by finding every shelter the city had available. Sometimes, if he was lucky, there would be a bed on hand, but most nights he found himself huddled under an office building's fire escape, using newspapers as blankets. He never went to the same shelter twice in one week. He alternated between places to eat, not wanting to be noticed by anyone who could cause him trouble. But trouble had a way of finding him.

He found out that just because people are homeless doesn't necessarily mean they're stupid. As hard as he tried to go unnoticed, they still noticed him. Ish became a trouble magnet. Since living on the streets, he'd been mugged twice. You would think being homeless, you wouldn't have to worry about being mugged. The first time it happened, he was caught off guard, asleep at the helm. He was dreaming at the time, dreaming about the band days, when all of a sudden the wind gets punched out of his lungs as someone gave him a body flop, then wrestled his shoes off his feet. If that wasn't bad enough, the same guy came back and kicked his ass again, chasing Ish away from his cardboard home and then claiming it as his own.

Living on the streets during the day was bad enough, but when nighttime rolled around, it became a living hell—Mama always said, "Watch what you wish for, son. You just might get it." At times he thought he'd rather be in the real place, at least there he'd have all his friends with him.

There was no one for him here.

He thought about taking his own life, about ending it all and getting it over with, but he never really had the nerve to do something like that. Whenever he thought about it, memories of Billy's father swinging back and forth would remind him that that was the coward's way out.

Living on the streets was nothing like touring with the band, although it did have its similarities. They did after all just pick up and hit the road, going from town to town, finding places where they could play and making their money as they went, but he had his friends with him then; now he was all alone and money was hard to come by.

He walked in a daze, feeling rejected by a world that once had embraced him. A world that at one time gave him the belief in all the possibilities of greatness. Now it shunned him. He realized that the world had two faces, one of love and kindness, the other of hatred and cruelty. His thoughts went deep, and Ish lost himself in them.

He bumped into a heavyset man and the man shouted, "Hey, watch where you're going!" then pushed him aside.

He felt nothing, heard nothing. He just kept walking in his own world, lost in some other time, another place. The jeans he wore were soiled with grease, grime and his own waste. He smelled like a dead rat and looked even worse. His once wild to the eyes tie-dye shirt was now so soiled with dirt it made its vibrant colors nonexistent. His head of hair, once short and groomed, was now long and matted.

If anyone who knew him should see him now, they'd never believe it was the same guy. Ish was a proud man. That was one of the reasons he was in the mess he found himself in. He thought of his mother. The last time he'd seen her, she was standing in the kitchen making him breakfast. There was a time when he would have done anything for her, and then she had to piss on his dream.

He hated her for it, but he still wanted her approval. He didn't know why; it was just something that came naturally, like the way a baby will quickly find its mother's breast when it's hungry. He just needed her to say everything was fine, to reassure him that the things he thought and did were o.k. Even as he got older, he continued to seek her favor. He got ribbed about it from his friends, but he didn't care; it was as if she had some kind of hold on him, a hold that had finally been broken when he left home.

He thought about going back but he knew he could never go home again, not after the way he just walked out the door and never returned. He never called, never wrote. For all he knew, she could be dead.

That thought scared him.

What if she was dead? It would be his fault. When he left, she was standing there looking as if she was out in left field without a glove.

Another thought came to him. What if she wasn't nuts like he thought she was; what if walking out is what sent her over the edge? He didn't want to think about that— couldn't think about it because it made him feel things he didn't like. Besides, he had enough to worry about living on the streets. He didn't have the time to worry about things he couldn't change.

As much as he wanted to hate her, as much as he wanted to forget her, he suddenly wanted, more than anything else, a chance to talk to his mother.

When Ish finally allowed himself to return to the present, he found himself in front of a McDonald's with a cup in his hand. The loud clinking of the half-dollar hitting the tin is what snapped him back to reality.

Somebody was feeling generous.

11

Being mid-morning, the streets were alive with people that were either going to work or those already there. As a city bus pulled away from the curb, exhaust erupts out of its tailpipe, and a black cloud momentarily covers his vision. The sunshine cast a shadow of the building out in front of him, so whenever anyone walked by, they stepped out of the sunshine and into the shade, or vice versa.

Watching the people go by gave Ish a peculiar feeling. An elderly woman in a motorized wheelchair, a little boy and his mother holding hands, stepping out of the sunshine and into the shade. To Ish, it was like watching people who were living one minute, and then dead the next. In the sunshine, they were alive; in the shade, they were dead.

As he watched, he began to laugh. Not an out loud laugh, but a chuckle under his breath.

Someone shouted, "Hey Sleaze!"

Ish continued to watch and laugh. Another bus pulled up and stopped. An elderly man with a cane was stepping out. He moved so slowly the younger woman behind him was beginning to get annoyed. When the last person got off, it pulled away leaving another cloud of black muck.

"YO! SSSSSleaze!"

Finally, Ish said, "Huh?" He turned and looked to his left, and as he did, he saw him standing there in the same clothes he died in. It was Todd Striker. Only it couldn't have been Todd because Todd was dead, and Ish knew it, yet there he was standing in the shade.

Dead!

No, Ish thought to himself, but he was looking at him, plain as day. Todd was wearing the same blue jeans with silver studs running down the sides of each leg. His denim jacket also had silver studs, and he used a bicycle chain as a belt. *No, it couldn't be.*

"Hey, Ish… You Fucking Sleaze!"

But it was.

"Todd?"

A couple of guys wearing military greens stepped out of the sunshine and into the shade, going through and then past Todd's ghost. Ish pushed himself up off his ass, using the building to steady himself.

"Todd?"

A younger man stepped by Ish, dropping a couple of quarters into his cup. The clinking of the coins was music to his ears. He didn't bother to say thank you. He was too busy thinking about Todd.

Before he could take a step towards him, Todd was suddenly standing next to him.

"Yo Sleaze, I got a message for you from your dad."

Todd's ghost was standing so close. Ish could have sworn he smelled his breath and the aroma of Death, decay. He never stopped to think that maybe the stench he smelled was reeking off his own body.

Ish leaned against the wall and slid back down into his yoga position. More people stepped out of the sunshine and into the shade, out of the shade and into the sunshine; back and forth, alive and then dead. Dead, and then alive. Ish was in a trance. He forgot all about Todd.

Someone tossed another quarter into the cup. Ish just stared at it with surprise. *A lot of people feeling generous this morning,* he thought.

"SSSSSSLEAZE!!!!!!"

Todd's voice sounded like a wild boar; it screeched so loud it scared the piss out of him. The dry concrete underneath him quickly became wet. *I need a drink,* he thought. All of a sudden Todd was in his face. So close, that if Todd blinked, Ish would feel his eyelashes tickling his own.

"Your dad says you've got to earn your degree."

Ish was confused. In his dreams, all the dead folks had said the same thing. He just ignored them. He knew he'd never earn any kind of degree. "What kind of degree?"

Todd's face crinkled up as he grinned, giving him a demented look, a look of madness. When he smiled, blood began to trickle out the side of his mouth. He puckered his lips as if looking for a kiss, and then said, "A degree in sin."

Ish closed his eyes, hoping that would end the lunacy. *This can't be happening,* he thought. *Todd's dead. Worm shit by now; there's no way in hell he's sitting here talking to me.* The sounds of life were all around him, a cabdriver shouting profanity at an ignorant SOB in a BMW. Police sirens howling in the distance, shuffling feet as more people walk by, and of course, another clink of a coin in his cup.

He opened his eyes. Todd was gone.

Relief swept over him like a wave. He placed his cup at his side keeping his hand over it, tapping his fingers on the tin. At one time it contained Bumble Bee Tuna, now it served as his begging dish. He thought using anything bigger would be pushing his luck.

"Hey Sleaze, did you hear what I said?"

Yes, he had heard. But he didn't want to believe it, didn't want to hear it. He closed his eyes again, trying desperately to ignore the voice that spoke in his left ear. *No! No! No!* He put his fingers in his ears, hoping that would stifle the voice.

"What's the matter, aren't we friends anymore?"

Ish started humming to himself, rocking back and forth and side to side. That sinking feeling was coming on strong. He continued to rock back and forth, humming to himself, hoping that things in his head (because that's where it had to be) would settle down.

An old witch of a woman stepped out of the sunshine and into the shade and was about to continue on, when Todd screamed, "Hey lady! Give this poor excuse of a man some money; can't you see he's down on his luck!"

The woman stopped as if she had been slapped. She began to fish around in her purse, her beak so close to it; she looked as if she were sniffing for the correct amount of change. She pulled out a dollar and stepped in the direction of Ish. He didn't notice. He was still rocking back and forth, humming a little louder, trying to fuzz out the voice.

She stuffed the dollar into the cup beside him and quickly covered her mouth. His disgusting odor was like a punch in the nose. "You poor man...," she mumbled as she held her breath. She walked off feeling as if she'd done her good deed for the day.

When Ish was absolutely sure everything was back to normal, he opened his eyes. He looked to his left, no Todd. Then from his right, Todd said, "You really look like shit, Sleaze."

Ish jumped in surprise and screamed, "Man, what is it you want from me!"

A woman, who was jogging by, steered clear, giving him a look that could kill. He didn't notice anything other than Todd. Anyone who walked by saw a man talking to himself. But to Ish, he was talking to the pale ghost of Todd, his friend from the great beyond.

The seen and the unseen became a blur. Was Todd really here with him now? Ish was staring at him and seeing him as sure as he could see his own hand. He reached out and touched Todd's face. The touch was both hot and cold, as if he'd just put his hand on a block of dry ice. His fingers felt like they might be stuck to his face forever.

"Is it really you?"

"It's really me." Todd grinned.

That grin was something that Ish never saw Todd do when he was alive. In fact, he couldn't remember ever seeing Todd smile, let alone grin. Even when the band found out about the record deal, Todd had kept himself businesslike, not allowing himself the joy of celebrating, for fear of having it all fall apart, which was ironic because it fell apart anyway. Sometimes fate can deal a lousy hand.

"We're here to help you."

Ish gave him a light slap on the face. Todd just kept grinning. "What do you mean 'We're' here to help me?" he asked. Todd pointed down the street, and as he did his jacket opened up, showing a black T-shirt with Black Sabbath on the front.

Ish followed the direction of Todd's hand, and saw Joey Boil and Tony Sharpton running back and forth to people that were heading in Ish's direction.

"Us man, who do you think?"

Todd's voice had gone hollow, as if he were talking inside a tunnel. His words echoed one after the other, "Do you know what they're doing, Sleaze? They're giving everybody a suggestion. They're telling them to help out a man who looks like shit, and that's you, Sleaze."

That grin began to stretch to a horrifying length, and the hair on the back of Ish's neck stood at attention. The echoing stopped as Todd said, "It always helps if we remind them they'd be doing a good deed."

He laughed and the sound of it made Ish's skin crawl.

There was another clink in the tin and Ish quickly snatched it up, forgetting he had put it down in the first place. He poured its contents into his lap, looking around as he did, making sure nobody was going to steal it. He counted five dollars and some odd change. Someone had been a dick and put a piece of chewed gum into it as well. He picked it out of the can and put it in his mouth. He was in luck; it still had its Juicy Fruit taste.

The smile on Ish's face made him look like a nine-year-old kid who just opened his Christmas presents. He stuffed the money into his pockets and began slapping them listening to the change jingle. His first thought was to get himself a cheap bottle of some Boone's Berry Farm: strawberry flavor. Then he decided he wanted a smooth jolt of Southern Comfort.

A cold hand touched his shoulder.

Ish turned to look, and when he did, he saw that Todd's face wasn't pale anymore. It wasn't even there. It looked like it had been put through a meat grinder. Where the eyes should have been were two black sockets and, inside each, maggots swarmed. The flesh and muscles of his face dangled on the bone dripping tiny little droplets of blood. Blotches of green slime pooled in what used to be his cheeks, bubbling like some kind of hot lava.

Todd was grinning again, and the dangling shreds of flesh bounced around like puppets on strings. "We're here to help you... Get you back on your feet."

Ish wanted to close his eyes, to shut out the horror that was before him, but he was in a trance. He couldn't take his eyes off Todd. That grin was so wide and getting wider; it looked as if Todd's face was about to split in half. In the blink of an eye, Todd's face became its pale, dead self again.

His eyes were staring at Ish, and Ish thought for sure he would get sucked into them if he didn't look away, but he couldn't, even if he tried.

A feeling of guilt washed over him and he began to cry. Since living on the streets, he had had rerun after rerun of the accident in his head. He tried to convince himself that it never happened; that he wasn't responsible for putting three of his friends in an early grave, but his own memory betrayed him.

"How can you help me after what I've done?" he asked. A long line of slime hung from his nose, and Ish wiped at it with his grease-stained hand.

Todd said, "It's all right, Sleaze. We know it's 'snot' your fault!" and began to laugh.

The laughter was catchy because Ish started laughing too. They say laughter is good for the soul, and it must be true. Ish hadn't felt this good since the first time he got laid. When they were still alive, the guys had chipped in, pooling their money together for a streetwalker. She had been a fine piece of ass back then, and Ish had been grateful. Now, even in death, his friends were still willing to help him out.

Ish couldn't control his laughter. He felt like a new man. Memories of his days on the road flowed through his mind. He remembered a night when they actually had enough money where they could sleep in a cheap motel instead of the van. He remembered how they sat up all night bullshitting about everything from religion to politics. They made a promise to each other that if any one of them should die before the others, they'd come back from the grave and let everyone know if there truly was life after death.

He laughed some more, because at the time he thought it was all talk, never believing or thinking that any of them would die. Now, here they were: The Three Musketeers, sitting around him outside a McDonald's on a sunshiny day. The four of them laughed as they talked about old times.

A whale of a man wearing a McDonald's uniform came barreling out the front doors. His face red as if he were either angry or choking on something he ate.

Ish didn't notice. He was still laughing with the guys. Tony Sharpton said, "Oops! Looks like we got company." Ish lifted his head and saw a blob towering over him.

"You can't sit here!" The man bellowed.

Ish wanted to laugh, almost did laugh, but Todd nudged him on his shoulder. The man was so large and his uniform so small, Ish hurt himself holding it in. A nameplate was pinned to the man's shirt pocket. It read: Simon Shoetree – Manager.

"Did you hear me? You can't sit here. Get moving before I call the cops!"

No problem, Ish thought, *no problem at all.*

He pulled himself up without saying a word. He didn't have to; the guys did all the talking for him. Joey Boil shouted, "Hey Lord of the Lards, get a real job!"

Tony Sharpton chimed in with, "Yeah! Stop eating all the profits!"

And finally, Todd Striker added his own two cents, "Yo! Fat ass, go home and fuck your dog!"

Ish walked off, laughing to himself and with his long-lost friends.

12

First things first: Ish was a mess and he knew it. He also knew that during the three years being homeless, he had come to see it as part of that whole scene. Had, in fact, come to the realization that he liked his down to earth smell.

The guys led him to Zen's Laundromat where he stole himself some newly washed clothes. He stuffed them into a plastic bag that he pulled out of the trash and walked out without being noticed. From there, they found a YMCA where he washed the stench off his body. The manager wanted to give him a hard time about it, but the guys talked him into the idea. The man never even knew it.

Ish's luck began to change, and it looked to be changing for the better. He had been given a second chance at life again, and he wanted to make darn sure that he wasn't going to be ungrateful for it. The guys had come through for him, and if showing his gratitude meant doing whatever the guys wanted or needed done, well then, he was sure as shit not going to let them down. They helped him in every way and he promised he'd pay them back.

He no longer begged for his money, but with odd jobs and the guys' never-ending help, he made enough to take a bus out of, and away from, Pittsburgh.

The first stop on the road to his recovery would be Atlantic City: the place where Miss America swings her ass and gamblers go to lose.

The ride was a long one and traffic made it seem even longer, but he enjoyed himself all the same. He hadn't been on the road in years and had almost forgotten what it was like to be rolling down the highway. It may have only been a tour bus, but it still brought back all the memories of his days and nights on the road with the band.

He gazed out the window, watching the scenery change with each passing mile. He looked so sharp dressed in his tan khaki pants and a brown button-down dress shirt. The sneakers he wore didn't go well with the rest of his wears, but he had gotten them from the last shelter he'd stayed at before hitting the road, and he couldn't seem to part with them. Other than that, he looked as if he just stepped out of a JC Penney's catalog.

By the time the bus rolled into the terminal, darkness ruled. The lure of the lights pulled Ish into Bally's Casino. The whole atmosphere caused an instant high as if the air inside the place had been spiked with laughing gas. The clicking of the money wheel, the sounds of dice clapping on the tables, the rustle of cards, and the ringing of slot machines, all were enough to give Ish a head rush.

He was standing next to a twenty-five cent slot machine staring out at the floor, watching all the people with their high hopes of hitting a big jackpot, and seeing the faces of those that revealed their losses.

"Go ahead, Sleaze. Try your luck."

Todd stood next to him with his ghostly hand on the knob of a one-arm bandit. Ish fished through his pockets, pulling out his last two dollars in quarters. His hand shook as he fed the first three into the machine. The arm slowly began to come down on its own, and Ish quickly grabbed it, looking around, making sure no one saw.

The three symbols spun into a blur.

Click—Seven, Click—Seven, Click—Cherry.

"Damn!" Ish mumbled as he slapped the machine.

He fed three more quarters into the machine, pulled the arm and came up a loser again.

Todd said, "This is it, Sleaze." He was grinning that grin again; that grin that constantly gave Ish a sudden urge to pee. He put the last two quarters into the machine and was about to pull the handle when Todd said, "No! No! Let me do that." The arm came down and the symbols began to spin.

Faster and faster they spun.

Ish was nervous, afraid someone might have seen, but it was all right, only one man saw, and he was so smashed he passed it off as it being the workings of his own drunken imagination.

The symbols spun and spun. It seemed as if time had stopped all together, but those damn cherries, bars and sevens just kept spinning and spinning.

Click—Seven, Click—Seven, Click—Seven.

The bandit began spitting out quarters. The flashing red and white lights on top of the machine nearly blinded him, and the clanging of the bells rattled his head. The coins poured out, singing as they filled the machine's bed. Ish laughed and began scooping his winnings into one of the complimentary buckets. When the slot machine finally stopped, he'd filled three buckets nearly to the brim with silver.

A man, who could have been Curly Howard's twin with a mean streak, approached Ish and asked if he needed any assistance. He read the nameplate on the man's jacket: Ralph Bender – Security. "You most certainly can, Ralph. You can help me take my winnings over to the window, so I can exchange it for some green."

When tallied, he had close to seven hundred dollars. He tipped the man who looked like Curly with a twenty-dollar bill and thanked him for his help.

Things are finally looking up, Ish thought. He was standing near the payout window gazing around with a smile on his face, watching everybody and everything, feeling like he was on top of the world. He wanted to pull a Jimmy Cagney by shouting the words out loud: *I'm on top of the world, Mom!*

"It's not over yet, Sleaze."

Now it was Joey Boil's turn to call the shots. He led Ish to the roulette table, telling him when to play red, when to play black; back and forth, black and red, red and black. Then Joey started giving him numbers: 13, Winner. —26, Winner. —34. On and on, number after number.

From there he went to the blackjack table where luck had absolutely nothing to do with it. 21 —21, —Blackjack... Blackjack... Blackjack! Next: the crap tables. Everywhere he went he won more money than he could ever need. By the time midnight rolled around, Ish had nearly a hundred grand.

He was on a high. No booze high like normal, not a joint or any other drug high, it was a natural high, one of the best highs he ever had. If not the best, it was certainly close enough. He felt so high; he almost forgot how getting this high was made possible. He nearly forgot who was behind it all. Ish thought since he won so much money, he could afford to splurge, enjoy it while he had it.

He was lying in the hotel room's bed, watching the television, enjoying the comfort of the bed and the quiet of the room. He figured since everyone in the hotel was treating him like a king, why not live a little and be a king, if only for one night.

He could have gone all out, could have gotten the penthouse suite but chose instead to settle for something less expensive, not realizing that the guys were calling all the shots—all the time. When he agreed to pay them back for their help, they'd been serious; more than he happened to be, that was for sure. After all, how and why, would you pay back a dead man, let alone three?

There was a commercial on the TV. It was an ad for Motel-4. The advertisers must have paid a pretty penny because the spot had come on three times within the last five minutes. Ish loved it. The slogan alone was enough to bust your stitches. It always made him laugh. The announcer's voice rose in volume as the slogan came on, "Don't forget. You get more, at Motel-4."

Ish laughed without fail.

You get more, at Motel-4. Sounds like a motel owned by pimps, he thought. He flipped the channel and stopped to watch the weather, hoping for some hot sun, thinking he was on vacation. As he feared, a storm was coming.

He got off the bed and went to the window and pulled the curtains aside in order to get a look at the sky. As he gazed out the window, he could see dark clouds building in the east. The coastline looked beautiful at the moment, with every hotel lit up, the boats out on the ocean lit up, and a few stars managed to twinkle above it all. The whole scene made him feel majestic.

He watched the waves as they crested six to eight feet before crashing onto the beach below. He wanted to open the window to let in some of the ocean breeze, but when he looked around for a way to open it, he found nothing. His ocean breeze would have to come from the air-conditioning vent.

Guess the hotel doesn't want to take any chances with jumpers, he thought.

Ish hopped on the bed, rolled over on his back and changed the station. The movie *Planet of the Apes* was on; Charlton Heston was on his hands and knees in the sand; the ruins of the Statue of Liberty was in front of him and he's yelling, ***"You maniacs... You blew it all up!... God... damn... you... all... to... Hell!"***

Without warning, the television fuzzed out.

Ish changed the channel: snow, every channel, nothing but snow. Outside, lightning began to light up the night sky. Thunder rumbled in the distance.

Again he took to the window, looking out at the sky, watching as the black clouds that looked so far away only a moment ago now raced toward the shore. The last of the stars were gone. Only gray clouds with thick black centers swept the horizon. That majestic feeling had been replaced, with dread.

13

This storm is going to be a mean one, Ish thought. He could almost feel it in his bones. As a kid, he had a thing for watching storms roll in, and he still got a kick out of it now. He pushed the curtains back as far as they could go, pulled up a chair and sat in front of the window, waiting for the show to begin.

He didn't have long to wait.

A flash of bright light just outside the window caused the hair on his body to stand on end. A tingling sensation, like an electric shock, shot from his head to his toes; then, a split second later, his hair went limp again. The light was so bright; it left a block of green in his retinas. He closed his eyes, thinking he'd at least check things out. Maybe the guys wouldn't give him a problem if he checked it out. He began staring at the green block, watching as that green glob slowly shimmered and morphed into a door. He saw himself hesitantly reaching for the skull doorknob, turning it, then walking through the doorway.

He opened his eyes.

He wasn't in his suite anymore. He was in a motel room, that was obvious, but it wasn't Bally's. This place was nowhere near as nice as the suite he'd just been in. In the corner of the room was a high-back wooden chair and a table, both reeking of cheap. An orange and blue piece of cardboard sat on top of the table, advertising Motel-4 with an 800 number in bold print, **1-800-Motel-04.**

A full-size bed with its brown and white checkered bedspread looked as if an inch of dust had settled onto it. Next to the bed, another cheap wooden nightstand. The lamp sitting on it was a small one, no more than seven inches high. Its yellow lampshade, way too big, also had a layer of dust.

A black rotary phone sat next to the lamp. It looked to be the only thing in the room that was clean. Across from the bed, a thirteen-inch black and white television set sat on top of another piece of wicker shit.

Ish thought of the slogan in the ad, 'You get more at Motel-4.' What a laugh, this place was definitely owned by pimps.

"It's payback time," Todd whispered. Hearing his voice, even in a whisper, was enough to cause Ish to jump.

"I wish you wouldn't sneak up on me," he complained. "You're gonna give me a heart attack."

Todd began to grin again, and Ish quickly wished he hadn't said what he said. He closed his eyes again and saw the green doorway still there. He stepped through it and opened his eyes.

Another bolt of lightning lit up the suite. Ish was back in his chair, looking out at the storm. The television behind him was still fuzzy, all snow. He watched unafraid as the lightning flashed here and there, spiking white-hot light through thick black clouds. Todd slowly appeared in front of him on the floor to his right. He was sitting in a yoga position and his grin seemed even wider. "You have to go back, Sleaze."

Then Joey appeared, sitting in the same position on the floor to his left. "Yo! Sleaze, you got to please… "

"Where's Tony?" Ish asked, not knowing why he even bothered. He knew Tony was there all along.

"I'm right here, Sleaze," he said as he finally appeared sitting directly in front of him.

When the lightning struck closer to the building, the guys faded in and out. Another flash, and then all three of them were standing over him. Todd growled, "Come on, Sleaze!"

"You got to go back, dude," said Joey.

"What do you say?" asked Tony.

"What's it gonna be!" they all screamed.

They'd been through this before. They told Ish he would have to pay back the help they gave him. When he asked how he was supposed to do that, they laughed at him, looking at him as if he were crazy. They told him, so yes he knew what they expected him to do, but why did he have to kill anyone? Wasn't it bad enough he had accidentally killed his friends?

Another burst of light and more rumbling from the skies, this one was much closer than the last. As the thunder rocked the building, the snowy TV set went black.

Now, the only light in the room was that of the lightning, each strike flashing faster and faster. Ish could see the three of them, standing around him, fading in and out with each strike. He tried to ignore them by staring out at the storm, but he could see them out of the corner of his eye, hovering there like pieces of laundry hanging on the line, blowing in the wind.

It gave him the creeps. He was trying his damnedest not to show it, but his own body gave him away. He had goose bumps everywhere.

They wanted him to kill somebody in Pittsburgh but he couldn't do it. He promised that as soon as he had enough money, he'd do it. Ish thought that would buy him some time, but it turned out to be not nearly enough. He didn't think there ever would be enough time; he just didn't think he could do it. Sure, he talked trash, but if it came down to it, he just didn't know.

Ish didn't want to let the guys down, yet at the same time, he didn't want to hurt anybody either. He could hear the voice of Anthony Perkins in his head saying, "I wouldn't hurt a fly—I wouldn't hurt a fly." He thought if he asked for more money that would stall their plans. He wanted to get some sleep tonight, play and win more money tomorrow. He was thinking tomorrow. He'd do it tomorrow.

He tried fazing them out by watching the storm as the rain finally began to fall from the sky.

It started out slow but quickly gained momentum. Each drop slapped at the window, sounding like snapping bones. The hair on the back of his neck stood straight up. He always hated hearing his cousins crack their knuckles; it drove him up a wall. This was pulling him apart.

The sound grew louder as the rain fell harder. Snap, snap, snapping, thousands of bones were cracking. He put his hands to his ears, hoping that that would somehow silence the noise. It wasn't working. The sound just grew louder.

Snap—Crack—Snap!

Ish told them back in Pittsburgh that he couldn't do it; had promised them that he would. They told him if he couldn't do it, then he should pretend to be somebody else. They asked him who his favorite hero or villain was; his first thought was Zorro. They laughed when he told them.

They told him to imagine himself as Zorro.

Be Zorro!

Snap— Crack—Snap!

The rain was relentless as it struck the glass at blinding speeds. It rolled down the windowpane, giving Ish an acid-trip view of the outside world. Lightning lit up the cancerous red and black skies, and he could see a face in the clouds. It looked, in fact, like the devil himself. The face shifted as the winds blew and lightning lit it up in an ugly fashion.

It looked like Satan was laughing.

The guys had told Ish about the green doorway. They said, "Look for the green doorway and pass through it." At first he didn't understand, and he was scared, afraid of what he might find. They said the doorway wouldn't last forever; they said to do the job and come back as soon as possible. That made him even more nervous. What if he got stuck? What would happen then?

Todd had told him he'd have to find his own way back, and at the time, Ish didn't want to argue about it, not when Todd had that grin on his face.

Ish closed his eyes again. The doorway waited.

This is it, he thought. He began to imagine himself as Zorro. He imagined that he had everything: the hat, the mask, the gloves and the sword. He could hear the guys in the background cheering him on, "Be Zorro! Be Zorro!"

The rain continued its attack as it snapped and cracked against the glass. Ish no longer heard it. In his mind's eye he was becoming Zorro. He saw himself stepping through the green doorway again. When he opened his eyes, he found himself back inside the Motel-4.

Still raining, the thunder continued to rumble along but inside this room everything was so peaceful, so quiet.

Ish was standing near the window, dressed in black from head to toe. He didn't know how, or even care why; the only thing he knew for sure was that he had a job to do and he was going to do it, even if it killed him.

14

After Mitch left his brother alone in his hospital bed, Billy had all the time in the world to think about his run-in with the killer. It all felt like a dream, and if he hadn't been lying in the hospital, he would have believed it to be just that, a dream, but it wasn't, and knowing that fact made him uncomfortable.

There was something about the man that kept gnawing at his brain. He hadn't felt like this since the time he came out of his coma. Back then, memories had picked at his head as he tried desperately to remember. With time, he recalled some memories of the past, but he still struggled, and he still fought, trying to piece his life back together.

That's how he felt now, struggling to remember where he might have seen the guy before. He didn't know why his mind raced with questions; he'd only seen the man's eyes, yet that was enough to drive him up a wall.

There was something about his eyes.

Dark green eyes: cat's eyes. Billy had looked into them, then at the .22 aimed at him, then back into those eyes again. The killer had given him a smirk, a smirk he had seen hundreds, if not thousands of times before, but he couldn't place it. He kept seeing that smirk over and over again in his mind, and then flash went the gun, and out went his lights.

Billy didn't want to go sleep. As tired as he might have been, he still didn't want to sleep. Maybe it had something to do with his dream. While he had been knocked out, he had a dream about Zorro. Billy didn't want to tell Mitch about it; Mitch would just blow it off as being a dream.

In the dream, Billy was at a distance, watching the killer. The guy was standing in front of an open grave, wearing his Zorro outfit, running his sword through a woman as she screamed for her life. She fell into the grave and another woman took her place. She also let out a horrid scream as the sword plunged into her gut.

Over and over, the bodies kept falling and the grave got bigger. On and on he thrust his sword, a sword that's already stained with blood; then he kicked them into the pit because that's what it became—a Pit, with flames darting out along the edges, licking at the legs of the next victim.

Then the dream changed. Billy found himself sitting inside a huge van. He looked to his left and saw Zorro behind the wheel. Behind Zorro was a hideous creature on all fours, its body was that of a giant lizard with the head of a cobra. Its head inches from Zorro's ear, hissing with deadly intent. Then came a flash and Billy had awakened with a dry scream in his throat.

He couldn't tell Mitch. He didn't want Mitch worrying about him. Billy knew who he was. He knew who Mitch and his mother were, but for some reason he couldn't remember anything about his dad. He thought he remembered bits and pieces of being in a band but that too seemed more like a dream. He couldn't remember anything about the accident.

He knew he'd never remember a lot of things, but he never let on. He never wanted to give Mitch the impression that he was someone who had lost half himself. He fooled them all too, even himself.

Mitch had been there for him; that was true, but Mitch could never give him back the missing pieces of his life. The pieces that were shattered in a flash, shattered by something he couldn't even remember. It was a total blank.

Waking up in that hospital bed so long ago, and finding out that he'd been in a coma made him wonder where the time had gone and who stole his soul. Mitch had taken him under his wing like a big protective bird, and his mother had taken care of him around the clock, nursing him back to health.

Billy felt badly having to lie to Mitch or his mom whenever they asked if he remembered something about his past. They would ask, "Remember that?" and Billy would smile and shake his head yes. Most of the stuff he remembered or at least he thought he might, someday.

When Mitch asked him to be his partner in the P.I. business, it had been one of the best days of his life and one of the worst. His big brother was doing everything he could to be a good brother, and Billy was being a rotten brother by telling lies about remembering things he might not ever remember again.

He wasn't lying when he told Mitch about the man's eyes. He remembered those eyes. Thinking about them chilled Billy's blood. Dreaming about the killer was another matter all together; none of it making any sense, but it was equally disturbing.

With half his memory washed away like the sands with the tide, life had become so much harder. He was thankful for the things he could remember and hopeful that other memories would follow, but life just wasn't the same. He felt cheated. He hated having to lie, but he had to; Mitch was being so nice. It seemed the deeper the lie went, the harder it became to tell the difference between truth and fiction, and he began to believe his own lies.

He thought he was pulling himself together, thought he was making some serious strides in the right direction, then Mitch started working on this one particular case and suddenly his life was turned upside down. Now he realized that he had been going in the wrong direction after all.

It wasn't the case itself; Billy liked keeping busy and being on this case kept him busy. It was the way Mitch had become obsessed by it. Mitch had stumbled upon the damn thing when the two of them were out in Kansas City chasing down a bail-jumper.

He'd been thumbing through the newspaper and came across an article about a murder in a Motel-4. The article was a small piece but the story still made for interesting reading. A call girl (who turned out to be a missing senator's daughter) had been found slain inside one of the rooms. There was no one registered in the books; no one saw anything, and the only fingerprints found at the crime scene were those of the victim. The sword that was used as the murder weapon was the only other evidence left behind.

Billy had been trying to catch some Z's when Mitch read the article out loud.

The whole tale gave him the case of the willies, but he didn't think much about it other than it being strange, but Mitch couldn't seem to let it go. It started with Mitch talking about it all the time. Then he got deeper still, by using his own personal time on the case. It got to the point where he was asking Billy to stake out the only Motel-4 in the area almost every other week.

At the time, Mitch was having some tough days, going through the motions and emotions of getting a divorce. Billy thought that that was the reason for Mitch's interest in the case; it was just something to keep his mind off his marital problems.

Billy put up with it but only because he felt he owed Mitch that much. Put up with the dumb shit. But when Mitch started asking him to cancel dates to do stakeouts; that was going too far. As far as Billy was concerned Mitch had stepped over the line. Billy finally told him he wasn't going to waste his time chasing ghosts. That had been just over five years ago and he thought that was the last he'd ever hear about it. But it wasn't, because he ended up staking the place out again.

Billy thought maybe Mitch's experience in Nam had something to do with it. He thought if that was the case, then he would do whatever was asked of him, just to keep the peace.

Hell, Mitch was paying him for his services. It was easy money considering the only thing he did was sleep most of the time. He'd been asleep on the night he saw the killer. Mitch had been in one of his moods, and instead of arguing with him, Billy decided to merely sit in the car and get some long overdue Z's.

He dozed off sometime after midnight. He'd been asleep for over three hours and would have slept longer if he hadn't knocked his head against the window, waking himself up in the process. His head, still fogged over with sleep, quickly cleared when he spotted somebody who looked like they were dressed for Halloween. He knew something wasn't right and decided to follow the guy. When he saw the victim, his blood iced over. That's when he ran back to the car and called Mitch.

Now, lying in his hospital bed, thinking about the killer's eyes, a memory tugged at the back of his mind. Billy had the feeling that Mitch wasn't going to be the only one obsessed with this case.

15

For Ish, the hard part was over. He had passed his first test of loyalty with flying colors. Todd, Tony and Joey seemed utterly pleased that he didn't let them down. They were so grateful; they helped him win even more money. Ish didn't mind; he was learning to live like a king and didn't want it to end, ever. After all the shit he went through, he felt he was getting his just reward.

He knew the rules: *Payback* could be called for, at any time. He found that the job wasn't as tough as he thought it would be, not when he was dressed as Zorro, but he didn't think he could do it without his outfit. The whore he killed didn't seem to mind it either. In fact, she thought it kind of sexy. Odd yes, but sexy. He knew that each new job would become easier. The guys, of course, would continue to show their gratitude.

With cash from his casino winnings, Ish bought himself a forest green Firebird, no questions asked, and cruised out of Atlantic City in style. He decided to take the back roads, wanting to see the scenic route to his next stop, never knowing where that next stop might be.

He eventually headed west on Route 30.

Hitting the window switches, both the passenger's and the driver's windows went down. The air rumbled inside the car and the breeze felt great blowing through his hair. He never felt more alive, more alert. This was the best taste of freedom he ever had, and he was ready for anything and everything.

Ish had left A.C. at ten in the morning, and by noon he was driving through the town of Paradise, Pennsylvania. He wanted to stop, not only because he liked the name, but also because he needed a bite to eat; his stomach was grumbling.

On his left he spotted The Paradise Diner. A small place with only six parking spaces, but he was in luck, there was one space open. He jerked the wheel and quickly pulled the Firebird into the parking lot, his tires screaming from the quick motion. The black minivan that was behind him blew its horn as it continued on its way. Ish could see the man driving. He made eye-to-eye contact, then flipped him the bird.

He heard the man yelling as he drove by, "You ass-hole!"

"Fuck you," Ish mumbled under his breath. He flipped the switch and the windows went up. After turning off the engine, he sat there stewing in his anger. *Got the nerve to blow your horn at me!* Then, as quickly as his anger came, he became calm again, in control.

Inside the diner, locals shared the latest town gossip while having lunch. The minute Ish walked in, everyone clammed up. He paid them no mind. He took a seat at the front counter and waited to be served. The waitress was an older woman but she couldn't have been older than thirty-one, thirty-two tops.

The first thing Ish noticed was how much she looked like the girl he'd killed in Atlantic City. Her blond hair was the same red; her green eyes were the same hazel. She looked so much like the woman that Ish couldn't stand to look at her.

He ordered a BLT without making eye contact and noticed her nametag. He quickly looked away, not wanting to read it because if he did, he'd know her name and he didn't want to know her name. If she looked like anyone else, he might have read it. Hell, he might even have tried to hit on her, but it was too damn weird the way she looked like his first job. He ate his sandwich and swallowed it down with a Coke.

He ate fast, extremely fast. Ish ate as if he were a trainee in the Army, wolfing down his food before the Drill Sergeant had a chance to yell in his ear, "Move it! Move it!"

Ten minutes later he was on the road, glad to get away from a ghost of his recent past. He'd been successful at putting the thought of the woman behind him, and now he was singing, without the use of the radio, that Willie Nelson song "On the Road Again."

He had no idea where he was going and didn't really care. As long as the guys were willing to help him out, he was planning on *trucking on.* Driving on the bypass of Route 30, cruising at a speed that was just beyond legal, he spotted a hawk flying high above the tree line. For a split second he became that hawk (another special birthday wish granted) soaring high in the sky; then, just as quick, he was back behind the wheel, cruising down the highway with the wind in his hair.

By nightfall he was in Pittsburgh, not realizing that his next job was just around the corner. Ish thought driving in the city at night was a breeze; there was no one else on the road. When the sun went down, a chill stirred the air, but Ish kept the windows open in spite of the cold.

As he drove, he began to hum a tune from years gone by.

He couldn't remember where he'd ever heard it, but it was stuck in his head, like a fly stuck to a strip of flypaper. It was a tune his mother used to sing to him as a child. When he couldn't sleep and he was crying, his mother would rock him back and forth. Sitting in a rocking chair with Ish in her arms, she would sing, "Hush little baby don't you cry..." Todd appeared sitting shotgun in the front seat. "Hey... Sleaze." His voice snapped Ish to attention.

He could see Tony and Joey in the rearview mirror, sitting there in the back seat looking at him with grins on their faces.

"Hey!" Joey chuckled, "What's ya humming, big guy?" Ish smiled and said, "… I don't know. It's something that's stuck in my head."

With the wind rushing through the car, his hair flipping into his face, he swiped at it, constantly trying to keep it out of his eyes. He noticed the guys' hair wasn't blowing around at all, as if the windows were up the whole time.

"Hey, Sleaze." It was Todd again. "Make a right up at the next light." Ish did as he was told, and when he did, he saw the Motel-4 ahead on the left. He couldn't help but look at the place as he drove by. Two blocks further up the street, there was a Holiday Inn. Todd told him to pull into the parking lot and again he did as he was told.

A storm was brewing to the south. By midnight, it would fall upon the city with a vengeance.

Once inside his room, Ish threw himself onto the bed.

Lying on his back with his legs spread wide and his arms outstretched, he stared at the ceiling and waited for the storm. He knew it was coming; he could feel it like a hot breath on the back of his neck. It seemed to follow him like the plague.

In a way, that's what he was becoming, Death charging into town on a black horse, taking with him the lives of his victims.

†   †   †

After his next job was completed, Ish slept like a newborn baby, without a worry in the world. As he slept, he began to dream. He dreamed about the job he had just done.

He was sitting on the edge of the bed inside the Motel-4 with the phone to his ear.

"Hello, is this Heavenly Escort Service?"

He was nervous and hoped the tone in his voice didn't give it away. The voice on the other end of the line was that of a woman's; her tone was soft and sexy, which didn't help Ish with his nerves.

"Yes, this is Heavenly Escort Service. May I help you please?"

At first, Ish didn't know what to say; then, as an afterthought he said, "Yes, could you please send an escort to the Motel-4 on the corner of Brinton and Blvd. Allies?"

Ish could hear the smile in the woman's voice as she said, "We sure can, sir. If you tell me your name and room number, we'll have her there in no time. You did want... a woman, correct?"

Ish felt hurt. Her questioning his manhood was the last thing he needed.

"Yes, most definitely, a woman." He said, his voice sounding flustered. "My name is Mr. Green and I'm in... Could you hold please?" Ish hopped off the bed, its springs squeaking as he did, and went to the door. He opened it, looked at the number, and then closed it again. Returning to the bed, he picked up the phone.

"Yes. Hello? I'm sorry, I'm in room 106."

For a split second he thought the phone had gone dead. "Hello? Are you still there?" Finally the woman said, "Yes sir, Mr. Green. We'll send her to room 106. You can expect her in about twenty minutes."

He thanked the woman and hung up the phone.

Still sleeping and still dreaming, Ish tossed and turned in his king-size bed. He tossed and turned until he finally rolled into the fetal position, sucking his thumb. In his dream, he's with the woman from the escort service. The two of them are rolling around, using every inch of available space on the bed in a hot embrace. Rolling and rumbling, lapping and licking, until they find themselves on the edge of the bed, with Ish on the bottom and the woman on top, rocking and reeling. Except, Ish is dressed from head to toe in black, his mask showing only his eyes, which seemed to have a slight greenish glow.

The woman becomes inflamed with lustful desire, riding up and down, slow and fast, rubbing her naked body against the silky black cape he wore, howling at a moonless sky. Finally after all the rockets had been launched, she collapsed in a heap and fell asleep in his arms.

Then, in his sleep, he felt a jolt of electric shock rushing through his system and began to jerk and twitch.

He's staring at his victim's sleeping eyes—**Twitch—Jerk—Twitch—Jerk**—his hand slips over her sleeping mouth—*Twitch—Jerk—Twitch—Jerk*—her eyelids pop open in a flash. Those eyes staring in terror as they realize the danger. Those eyes showing the pain as the cold steel sinks into her flesh—**Twitch—Jerk—Twitch—Jerk.**

In an instant, everything turns red.

There's a river of blood, with corpses bobbing up and down, like logs. Some of them are face down; still others are face up, bloated and decayed with millions of flies buzzing around, giving the appearance of a black fog rolling across the water. Ish is in a rowboat sloshing his way through the carnage. The wind blows the smell of death into his mouth and nostrils, and he sucks it in as if it were fresh air, huffing in a mouthful of the filthy pests as well.

In the wind he can hear a voice. It's calling his name.

He woke to find himself dressed in black, lying in the hotel room bed. The faint sound of a siren cried in the distance, and for a moment Ish thought it was screaming his name. He felt disoriented, as if he'd been drugged. Then, as sleep finally released its hold, he realized where he was and quickly jumped out of bed.

After showering, Ish was able to hastily change into his regular clothes, because... just like his last job, they were waiting for him in a nice neat pile, sitting on the corner of the bed.

He grabbed the whole Zorro outfit and rolled it all together in a ball, then grabbed a pack of matches off the dresser, went to the bathroom and threw the bundle into the tub and set it ablaze. *No sense in keeping the damn things,* he thought, *not when he could just imagine up another set of work clothes.*

The evidence burned.

He'd see to it that any mess he made was cleaned up before he left. If that meant scrubbing the black crud off the tub, then so be it, no problem. He couldn't leave anything incriminating behind, because... *that* would be a problem.

16

It's been said that time flies when you're having fun, and if that's true, then Ish should have sprouted wings because he was having the time of his life roaming around from town to town. He never stayed in one place for too long, choosing instead to hit the road because that's where he felt like he belonged: the trail.

He believed everything was his for the taking; if there was a scam to be had, Ish pulled it off. Lady Luck seemed to cling to his arm wherever he found himself. And, as always, whenever he thought he could do it all himself, he was reminded that he still had the help of his friends.

Friends, from the dead side.

They were his only friends.

In fact, they would put him in his place if even a hint of any other kind of friendship developed. So, instead of putting up a fight, he would take heed to their protest and move on to the next town, next unsuspecting place. It was always easier that way, just go somewhere where he could fade into the background and start the whole process over again. It's always best to keep a low profile.

Ish couldn't remember how many times he heard his Uncle Jonah say those exact words, but it got to the point where he thought the man was a criminal in hiding. Over time, Ish came to realize that that was a good piece of advice. Stay low, under the radar. Become as small as possible. Make yourself invisible. Funny how things work out.

Ish could relate to hiding because hiding was something he was always good at as a kid. He always did like to play hide and seek with his cousins. In a way, playing it back then was his training for playing it now. Kind of.

It may be a totally different game, but the basic rules apply: Mix and mingle with the masses but at a safe distance.

Time was never an issue with Ish. He went wherever the guys told him to go, without any questions. Even though there were times when all he wanted—more than anything in the world—was to be left alone. He had mentioned it to them once, then quickly regretted it.

The guys got nasty and it wasn't pretty.

They hounded him constantly, day and night, with their nagging questions and horrible laughter. They finally drove him to his knees, begging them to shut up. He was in tears, pulling the hair out of his head in handfuls, looking like a man being pulled in three different directions, a man who was about to burst like a bubble.

They laughed and laughed, and laughed some more.

When silence fell upon his ears, he thought he had died and gone to heaven, even though that was a fat chance. Silence never felt so good. He never again asked to be left alone.

Things continued smoothly enough, crisscrossing around the country had its good points as well as the bad, but all in all, Ish couldn't have asked for better luck. He got to see more of the countryside than he ever did touring with the band. Most of that time was spent riding in the back end of the van. He never really got to see the beauty of the landscape.

Everything seemed to be going great. That is, until the job he pulled near Kansas City, Missouri, that's when his luck slowly began to run dry. The job itself went clean as a whistle, just like the previous jobs, but there was something that made it stink to high heaven.

Maybe it was the fact that it was in a town called Liberty. The place where Jesse James and his brother Frank committed the first daylight bank robbery, or maybe it was the fact that he tried to phone home, tried to make things right on the home front, only to have the phone hung up in his ear.

Ish knew it was a mistake the moment his Uncle Jonah picked up the phone. When he told him who he was, his uncle went ballistic, yelling and screaming, calling him every name in the book. He said as far as he was concerned, his sister's son was dead. Then, bang! The call was cut off.

Ish couldn't blame him; he never even thought about getting in touch with them. He never let them know how or where he was; it was only natural that his uncle would consider him dead. Wasn't it? He didn't know why he made the call. It was a spur-of-the-moment kind of thing, something done without much thought behind it, but he did seem to be thinking a lot about home lately.

It became an obsession. As much as he tried not to think about it, as much as he tried not to dream about it, that thought would always bubble its way to the surface without fail.

Something else irked him too.

Ish suspected that there was someone poking around where they shouldn't be poking around, and somebody was looking into matters that didn't concern them. He could feel it. It felt like someone had tied a rope around his neck. At the end of that rope was a huge block of cement and it weighed him down.

It worried him some, not knowing who was sending him the bad vibes, but he knew he would find out sooner or later, and when he did, he would know how to handle it.

He always did know what to do with troublemakers. Growing up as the smallest kid in school always did appear to attract them. Ish never let his size get in the way when it came to getting even. When he was in the sixth grade, he got even with a bully. He waited for the perfect moment to seek his revenge.

After making a birthday wish, a wish to be unseen, under the cover of invisibility, he walked up behind his adversary like a shadow, and pushed him down a flight of steps.

It was a long flight, at least thirty steps in all. They led down to the basketball court and the pool area. The poor sap was heading to the court to practice his three-point shot. He missed practice. In fact, he was out of school for three months. So, yes, he knew exactly what to do with anybody who would dare get in his way.

But then, that nagging feeling would rear its ugly head, making him second-guess himself. He became cautious. Cautious to the point of paranoia, always double tracking, extra checking. He had a constant need to cover his ass. When he finally realized that that one phone call might come back to haunt him (he'd been dumb enough to call from the same room which held his victim), it became a mission to head towards the place where he grew up, the place where he felt he belonged.

It was time to go home.

Ish planned to do just that, but of course making the suggestion was out of the question. He didn't want to start another howling session from the guys. He would have to make it seem as if it was their idea, but how to do that was the hard part. He knew it wouldn't be easy getting the guys to see things his way, but, he figured, they were heading west anyway; he'd find a way to convince them when the time came.

Until then, he'd keep his trap shut about the whole scheme.

17

The closer Ish got to his home state, the more dreams he had. It was always the same dream over and over, night after night. He dreamt about the day he woke up in the hospital and found Mitch Blade standing over him like a warden.

After killing his latest victim in San Francisco, he began to piece it all together. The person who was responsible for his many sleepless nights; the bastard that was snooping around, sending him bad vibes, had to be Mitch Blade. Didn't the dream make it obvious? Not certain, but feeling good about his train of thought, the guys confirmed his suspicion when they finally filled him in. They said they had known all along, but decided they wanted to let him sweat it out. They got a kick out of watching him squirm.

The whole time he spent plotting in his head ways to get the guys to suggest he head home had been a waste. All those nights of lost sleep, thinking about going home, wasted. Those bastards let him ride the roller coaster of hell. He wanted to explode on them, but he checked his feelings at the door, keeping his cool.

In spite of his anger, he was glad to be going home. With that put to rest, he found his own rest and slept like a baby. Total peace. So peaceful, he didn't want to wake up. The warmth of the covers and the fluff of the pillows, all were enough to keep him where he lay. At 8:30 in the morning, he rolled out of bed.

The curtains covering the window certainly did their job well. If he didn't have to pee, he might have slept longer. Looking in the mirror, he saw a stranger. The years had not been kind; his receding hairline went so far back, he was starting to look like Bozo the Clown. Wiping the sleep out of his eyes, he stretched the wrinkled skin around them, staring at himself. He could see the real him, the worn-out him.

With a long ride still ahead, he hoped traffic wasn't a total mess. If he didn't stop more than twice, he'd make it into Seattle in about fifteen hours. He hoped.

By 9:15, Ish checked out of Westin St. Francis—one of the grandest hotels in the city of San Francisco—and hit the road one more time. To Ish, the ride was a familiar one. He remembered when he was younger, how the whole family would make the excursion every year for vacation. Back then it seemed to take forever, first the day to come and then the trip itself, but the one thing that never failed was the fact that the whole event would fly by and everyone would endure the ride home without saying a word. Going on the outing was always the noisiest, everybody yapping and laughing, singing and howling like a bunch of baboons, excited about the coming two weeks. Uncle Jonah had a friend who had a friend, who had a place near Stinson Beach.

Ish was lost in thought as he drove east on Interstate 80. He was six years old when they first made the journey. He knew where to go because he had studied the route every year. While everyone else kept busy reading a book or playing games, Ish would be sitting in the front seat watching the road and his Uncle Jonah. It was funny watching his uncle with his constant gesturing at the other drivers, which turned out to become a bad habit of his own.

A red corvette blew its horn as it whipped past on his left, and Ish gave the man driving the middle-finger salute.

By the time he was heading north on Interstate 505, traffic became so thick it came to a crawl. Ish kept himself upbeat by playing eye-spy with the guys. He always did enjoy playing it as a kid. A lot of people on the road got to see a kook in action. When Ish realized people were watching him, he quickly acted as if he were singing.

Traffic opened up again on Interstate 5, and he was doing seventy-five, making up for lost time. It was nearly 1:30 in the morning by the time he was close to home. He had made good time, considering he only stopped twice, once to eat and fill up the gas tank, and a second occasion to go to the bathroom and fill up again. He was tired from the long ride, hence when he spotted a Best Western, he pulled into the parking lot, eager to get a room and thus he could finally get some much needed sleep.

He fell asleep the minute his head hit the pillow. In his sleep he began to dream. Everything is blue, until a fluff of white swirls by. He's sleeping on a cloud, floating high above the skies of the city. The cloud is so fluffy and white and he's so comfy and light, floating like a balloon in the wind. He can feel the breeze as it caresses his skin.

Floating higher and higher, and then the wind began to blow harder, the cloud started to thin out. Suddenly he's falling, falling like a rock. The earth below him gets closer and closer as he's falling and falling. He can hear them calling, so far away but they're calling, "Be Zorro! Be Zorro! Be Zorro!" He's still falling but he begins to make the change, and just before he hits the ground, he wakes to find he's made the change all the way.

He's lying in a bed, but it's not the one he fell asleep on. He knows this because he's wearing black, his work clothes. *This is a first,* he thought to himself. All the other jobs had been made available to him via the green doorway. This was the first time he ever fell into a job by way of a dream.

So, he found himself in a Motel-4, just a few miles down the road from where he was staying at the Best Western. He noticed it on the ride in, but he always tried not to think about work until the job was called for.

How far back had it been? He wondered. He knew it was at least a mile, maybe two or three. Either way, he knew he'd have a long walk back. But it wasn't the walk that bothered him; it was the fact that he would have to wear his work clothes. That was a thought he didn't like, not one bit. The guys never said anything about pulling a job like this. They never said anything about falling into one from a dream. What about the green doorway!

There was one thing he did know.

He knew he'd better keep his cool or risk blowing the whole job. He'd have to keep off the main road, stay within the trees so nobody could see him. He would be all right; right?

He made the call and didn't have to wait long at all. His victim had arrived twelve minutes after picking up the phone. Apparently the escort service had someone close by. The job was just that, a job; he couldn't enjoy it, considering he kept thinking about the damn walk back to his room at the Best Western.

He finished her off in grand fashion and rushed out the door so he could get the walk out of the way. Only he was in such a hurry, he had forgotten his stupid hat and had to go back and get it. He never left anything other than his sword—hell, that was his trademark—and he wasn't about to change things now.

It's a good thing I left the fucking door unlocked, he thought. He was upset with himself, but happy he hadn't gotten too far before realizing his mistake.

Ish had sensed that someone was following him, so when he got back inside the room, he purposely brushed against the window blinds, and as they swished back and forth, sure enough, he saw somebody out there looking in.

He grabbed the hat and jammed it on his head. The rubber band holding the mask to his face yanked at his hair. Snatching the dead woman's purse off the floor, he flipped the contents out onto the bed: a pack of gum, a roll of bills, some rubbers, a hairbrush and a gun. He reached for the .22 caliber Beretta Bobcat and checked its chamber.

It was loaded and ready.

Apparently, 'Little Miss Cum Fuck Me' was thinking that it would somehow protect her. Lucky for him she was packing. It made things a lot easier. He put everything but the money back into the purse, and then threw it at the corpse. It struck her in the face and landed next to her head. He stuffed the cash into his pocket and stepped out the door in search of 'Mr. Nosey Body.'

It didn't take him long to find the asshole. The guy was sitting in his car out in the parking lot.

Ish crept up on him like a cat stalking its prey. He could see the son of a bitch dialing a number into the phone. He pulled the car door open and stood there for a split second, looking at this guy who couldn't mind his own business, and he was thinking how familiar the guy looked.

Then, he aimed the weapon at the man's gut, and with a smile on his face, he pulled the trigger. The weapon's report echoed in the woods. It sounded like a miniature dog barking. He aimed at the man's head and pulled the trigger again.

The gun jammed.

He tried again and still nothing.

Ish cursed himself for not aiming at the guy's head in the first place, and then cursed the gun for jamming up at the most inopportune time. He slammed the car door shut and quickly slipped into the woods. He didn't think anyone heard the gunshot, but he was more concerned with whom the bastard was talking to on the phone. He knew he would have to get back to his room quickly.

Ish made sure he kept himself well within the trees. It was dark but he managed to see his way through because hundreds of stars helped light his way. He shivered from the cold as puffs of steam swirled around his head with each breath. Every step echoed softly: Each snap of a twig, every brush of dry leaves, mimicked deeper in the woods.

Every now and then a car would pass in either direction on the main road. When Ish saw any headlights approaching, he'd stop and take a seat on the cold and damp forest floor, waiting until the car was well out of sight. *No sense in taking any chances,* he thought.

All in all, it took Ish forty-five minutes to get back to the Best Western. But getting across the street and past the gas station on the corner without being seen would take some thinking.

Before making the last trek to his room, Ish walked deeper into the woods. He broke off into a jog, pushing tree limbs out of his way as he ran, searching for the perfect spot to dispose of some evidence. One hundred, two hundred, three hundred yards, until finally, he fell to his knees at the base of a giant redwood and began to dig like a dog burying his bone. Clawing and digging, the frozen soil reluctantly came loose as he worked with the power of ten men. He felt like Superman. He worked until he had a cavity one-foot by two-feet deep.

Ish slapped his hands together, cleaning the muck off his gloves, then reached into his pocket and pulled out the gun. He placed it next to the opening, pulled off his gloves and put them aside as well. After yanking off the hat and mask and dropping them to the side, he ran his hands through his hair, feeling a little more than worn out. He picked the gun up and looked at it.

Piece of shit, he thought to himself, as he dropped it into the hole. He yanked at the frilly collar of his white shirt, the ripping sound whispering off with the wind. Ripping and ripping until it was completely off, he stuffed the shreds into his pockets. He wanted to make sure he looked like your average run-of-the-mill Joe. He didn't want to stick out like a sore thumb. *This should help,* he thought.

He was deep in thought as he grabbed the hat and stuffed the gloves and mask into it and dropped them into the hole with the gun. He wasn't fond of the idea of burying this stuff, considering how he usually burned the shit, but he wasn't about to take any unnecessary chances. Lighting a fire would definitely be taking an unnecessary risk.

Nobody is going to find this shit, he thought, *because nobody is going to be looking for it, let alone know that it's here.* He covered the entire hole with the dirt, packing it with both hands; then he smoothed out the soil as evenly as he could and brushed twigs with leaves over the tiny mound. Having done that, he pushed himself up off the ground.

His legs felt like someone had stuck him with pins and needles. He slapped at them until the sensation melted away, and then headed back toward the road.

He would have to walk across a two-lane blacktop, pass the well-lit Texaco station, and then over to the Best Western. There were no cars on the road or in the gas station. Only the attendant could be seen sitting inside the glass booth. He was reading a newspaper with his back toward Ish.

He couldn't have asked for better luck. He slipped past like a ghost on the prowl, entered the hotel and headed straight to the elevator without looking in the direction of the clerk on duty. The clerk hadn't even noticed Ish; he was lost in a good read.

Just before the elevator doors opened, Ish realized he didn't have his room key with him. *Damn*! he thought, *that means I will have to talk to 'Mr. Can I Help You Sir.'*

Ish looked in the clerk's direction. He was a young man, maybe in his late twenties. "Let's get this over with," he grumbled to himself. He gently slipped his way over to the counter. The man behind it was wearing thick Coke-bottle glasses, and Ish could see the reflection of the smut magazine in them.

"Excuse me," Ish said with a cough.

The man jumped in surprise, then tried to cover the filth he was reading with his elbow, knocking over a Pepsi can in the process. Ish could hear the soda fizz as it rolled off the counter and began to puddle on the floor. The man's glasses started to fog up, and Ish could tell he was embarrassed.

"Can I help you, sir?" He asked with a forced smile.

Ish grinned and said, "Yes you can. I mistakenly left my key in my room. Room 305." The clerk looked puzzled but he gave Ish the key without asking any questions. He thanked him and went back to the elevator.

As the doors opened and he stepped inside, he could hear the clerk mumbling and cursing at himself as he cleaned up the mess he made. Ish laughed and pushed the floor button; the number three lit up.

The doors slid softly closed and the lift began. Music filtered out from the overhead speaker. It was a Barry Manilow tune, "Copacabana." He hated Barry Manilow. But by the time the doors opened on the third floor, he found himself humming along with the damn song.

He walked down the hallway to his room. Passing room 301 on his left, he could hear the TV. It was way too loud for this time of the morning. Passing room 302 on his right, he swore he could smell pot seeping out from under the door. All was still in the next two rooms, but as he slipped his card key into the lock, he heard a loud cackle; *must be somebody in 302,* he thought, *stoned out of their head laughing at a* Flintstones *cartoon.*

Ish opened the door and stepped into the room quickly locking the door behind him. The light on the nightstand was on, and he wasn't surprised to see his clothes sitting in a nice neat stack on the end of the bed. He stripped out of what remained of his work clothes, knowing they'd have to be burned, but first things first: He needed to take a shower. He let the hot water pour down over his head, enjoying the feel of it. The water began to get hotter still, but he just stood under it, loving the feel of it rolling off his face, his hair and down his back. With so much steam blowing around, the bathroom literally became a cloud.

After washing up, he stepped out of the shower and toweled off. He wiped at the steam-filled mirror, expecting to see a tired face because he was drained, but when he saw a bone-white skull staring back at him, he screamed. His eyes blinked, and when he saw his own face screaming back at him, he stopped. He continued to wipe the mirror with the towel; his hand shaking like an old man.

Ish knew he couldn't stay at the Best Western for long. He knew it was too close for comfort. He also knew he'd have to put some distance between himself and the Motel-4, and Mitch Blade, because he knew Mitch was close by—he could feel him. He decided he would check out of his room first thing in the morning.

18

By the time Ish crawled back into bed it was nearly 5:00 a.m. He didn't even know why he was going to bed; the hot shower had energized him instead of making him sleepy. His mind was alive with thoughts of times gone by, along with his more recent troubles.

Something didn't feel right.

Ish pulled the sheet up and folded his hands across his chest. He looked like he was ready to be laid out for a funeral. He kept thinking about 'Mr. Nosey Body,' kept thinking of the dumb look he had on his face when he was staring at the gun. It was a look that screamed: Stupid!

He was angry with himself because he knew he totally blew it. He couldn't believe he was dumb enough to slip up like that. How could he have been so stupid? The only thing he could hope for now was that the *asshole* bled to death before anyone came to his rescue. That was hopeful, but just a tad.

One thing he knew for sure, the situation needed closure, and for the first time in a long time, he was scared. Really scared. Ish knew he would have to hear about his mistake all because he paused for a second, staring into the man's eyes thinking, *This guy looks like somebody I know.* Was that why he aimed at his stomach first? And who the hell was that anyway?

If fear had a face, it would have been his very own at that moment. The longer it took for the guys to show up, the deeper he sank into his quicksand of terror. Time seemed to slow down, and then go backwards altogether. The last time he looked at the radio alarm clock it was 5:15, but when he looked at the clock after what he thought was five minutes later, it read 5:05.

A smell began to permeate within the room. It was faint at first, but it grew stronger with each passing second. Only, the seconds were ticking, but the little flip number clicked back to 5:04.

The scent was foul, a cross between human waste and moldy books. A nasty taste stuck to the back of his throat. He put the pillow over his face in a lame attempt to cover the stench, but the pillow was reeking with the odor and he threw it across the room.

They were coming.

Ish was lying with his eyes closed and didn't notice when Todd appeared. "Yo Sleaze."

Todd's voice made his flesh crawl and his heartbeat began to race as beads of sweat trickled down his forehead. He opened his eyes. They were all there: Todd on his right, the others standing at the foot of the bed. Ish hoped he didn't look as frightened as he felt.

"What's up, guys?" he asked. As if he didn't know, he knew just as sure as a cat shits in its pan.

The question went unanswered.

He glanced at the clock, afraid to look at them, and watched as it clicked back to 5:03. He was expecting another 'Let's drive Ish up a wall' kind of deal. He waited for their taunts, their sarcasm and their horrible laughter. That was the worst part of all, the laughter. He knew if he heard their laughter that would surely send him running in front of an oncoming truck. But he heard none of that, and slowly his heartbeat returned to its normal pace.

The shit didn't hit the fan after all. The guys were being so damn understanding about the whole thing, it hurt. Hell, he was madder at himself than they were with him. They told him why 'Mr. Nosey Body' looked so familiar. It had been Billy Blade, his running buddy back in the days of the band. Ish hadn't seen him since the accident, but it was as if time hadn't changed Billy one bit.

He wondered if Billy had remembered him. When he looked into his eyes, they seemed to be saying that maybe he had been recognized, and that thought made him nervous, but the guys put his mind at ease by telling him that Billy didn't remember.

Time became normal again, and the clock began its constant tick forward.

By five minutes after six in the morning, Ish was checking out of his room. The clumsy pervert clerk was off duty, which made the whole process go that much smoother. The guys told him about a room he could rent so he decided to take them up on it. Only, when he found out where the one room would be, he nearly broke down in tears. It was his old house, the place where he grew up.

At first the thought made him nervous, but the more he thought about it, the more it made sense. He could show his Uncle Jonah that no matter what he said, he was still alive, still kicking. Maybe his mother would understand, and maybe she would insist that he come into the house. He couldn't wait to see the shock on their faces. The guys led him to believe that he was going to see his family, and he went with it hook, line and sinker, right up until the moment he rang the doorbell and the door opened.

Behind it was an old woman. *Must be the cleaning lady,* he thought. He was expecting his aunt or uncle or maybe even his mom, but he wasn't expecting to meet the little old lady who lived in a shoe. She was no more than five foot, three inches tall, and her back had a hump on it the size of Texas.

Ish wanted to ask her about the room for rent, but her left eye distracted him. He couldn't help staring at it. He wondered if maybe it was a glass eye. He finally asked about the room and was led inside. Seeing the house again brought back so many memories; even though it was furnished differently, it still felt like the same place, only smaller somehow.

He was sitting on the living room couch, waiting to speak with the old woman's husband, and remembering some of the good times he had in this very room: the make-out session with Mary Lou Larson, his high school crush. The all-night parties when the grownups were gone; all these memories made him smile, something he couldn't remember doing in a very long time.

The old couple turned out to be a Mr. and Mrs. Milton Brown. Their son Roger landed a fat-cat job and wanted his mama and papa close by his side. He had bought the house not more than six months ago. They said they were happy in their home in North Carolina, and would have stayed there if it wasn't for the constant hounding their son had made. "So hell, what can we do?" They asked.

Ish nodded his head, trying to make it seem as if he actually was paying attention, but his mind wandered off in other directions. He remembered the first time he saw his Aunt Trish drop her towel, showing him her all, and she had a lot to show.

"Would you like some iced tea?" The old woman asked.

Her question snapped him back to the present, and he nodded yes to be polite but continued to listen to the old man as he went on and on about how much they missed North Carolina, how the weather was so much nicer down there. When the old woman returned with the tea, Ish took it and thanked her with a huge smile and a wink.

The old man babbled on and on about how he and the missis got into a big argument with their son because they wanted to rent out a room. He said they told him the house was way too big, and besides, they could always use the company, the place felt so empty. He said his son finally caved in and said, "If it'll make you happy, then go ahead and rent out a room."

When they finally asked him about himself, Ish gave them an assumed name. He turned on the old charm and lied through his teeth. He told them he was new in town, hoping to find a job in his field. When they asked, he told them he was a radio talk-show host.

† † †

At about the time Mitch Blade was busy packing his bag for a well-deserved vacation, Ish was settling into his new home with the Browns. They gave him the house key and laid down the ground rules. They were simple enough: no loud music and no women in the house after midnight.

He knew he could live with that; he wasn't planning on being around much anyway. He had a lot of work to do. The guys told him that Billy was alive and well; that meant he would have to pay him a visit sometime soon.

Take care of business.

He was sitting in what used to be his cousin Frank's bedroom—his old room was currently being used as a storeroom with tons of boxes of all shapes and sizes—seems the Browns were genuine pack-rats—anything and everything they could pack, they brought with them from their former home.

This room wasn't much to look at, but at least it was a place to stay. It felt so much bigger back in the day, but then again, that was a long time ago. Where does the time go? It's true what they say, 'Life is short'; sometimes a little too short. Ish knew a lot about that; he had been cutting lives short for some time now, but what he didn't know was the fact that he was making a name for himself. The woman he had knocked off near Kansas City turned out to be a runaway daughter of a state senator.

He had no way of knowing who she was; she had run away from home years before and was thought to be dead. He just made it official, and made himself an overnight, unofficial celebrity in the process.

Ish never bothered to read a newspaper or watch the news, never kept up with the rest of the world, so when he picked one up as he was having coffee with the Browns one morning and saw the headlines, he nearly laughed out loud. In bold black print it read: Mystery Madman Still At Large.

Now, as he sat on the edge of his bed flipping through the channels on the television, he thought of that headline and the story it entailed.

Things were falling apart at the seams. Of all the places his troubles had to start, it had to be in Liberty, Missouri, so much for Liberty. The story explained a lot about the bad vibes he'd been getting since that job. It said that Mitch Blade, the world famous private dick, was on the trail and hopeful that the man they called the Motel-4 Madman would soon be caught.

It was bad luck. Something he hadn't experienced in awhile. The fact that the woman he killed was a senator's daughter was bad enough, but even worse, knowing that the phone call he made from the crime scene was truly going to bug him now. When he first read the article and realized that it was talking about him, he felt giddy with his newfound fame. But now, thinking about it made him mad. What really made him hot under the collar was the fact that the guys let it happen. Were they turning on him after all this time? Why?

If they were turning on him, they certainly didn't show it. He couldn't understand why they would do something like that anyway; he was doing the jobs that they asked him to do—what more did they want?

Still, the question—why they didn't tell him who the girl was—drilled at his brain.

The paper said that the police along with the help of Detective Blade were confident that the murderer was closer to being caught. It told of the latest murder and how Detective Blade's brother, William Blade, had been shot while on a stakeout. The police believe the murderer shot him. They said that the bullet taken from Mr. Blade's stomach had pinpointed the gun to be that of the victim herself. A carrier's permit for a .22 had been found in her purse. As of yet, the gun hadn't been found.

And it won't be found, Ish thought to himself. On the TV, three kittens swayed back and forth, singing the Meow Mix song. "Meow... meow... meow... meow... "

Ish turned off the set.

It had been over two weeks since reading that article but it continued to bother him even now. He sat in his bed with the lights out. The pale glow of the moon, filtering in through the blinds of the window, was his only source of light.

Living with the old couple for the past few weeks began to shed some illumination about what had happened to his family. He got enough information to deduct that they moved out after they eventually had to put the man's sister into the hands of the State. They, in turn, checked her into the psycho ward at Overlake Hospital in Bellevue.

Apparently the old couple's son told them how he got such a great deal on the house. Seems the owner wanted to get out and start over someplace else. The man's sister had become mentally unstable. They said it got to the point where they were afraid she might either hurt herself or someone else. So, they put her away and wanted to get away themselves.

The thought of his mother being locked away in a padded cell, a room most likely the size of an outhouse with a single light bulb hanging from the center of the ceiling, swaying back and forth, rocking shadows up and down, it made him think of his own state of mind. Wasn't mental illness something that corrupted every branch of a family's tree?

The contemplation of family madness called to him.

Was that why the guys showed up? Not to help, but to somehow push him over the edge of reality like his mother? Isn't that what they had done? They called him the Motel-4 Madman, didn't they? He couldn't sleep, and he wouldn't, not until this whole state of affairs was cleared up.

Ish closed his eyes.

Thinking back to when the guys first appeared, saying they wanted to help him out of the mess he was in, he couldn't understand how he didn't know he was becoming the most wanted man in the country. But as he reflected on the situation, he remembered there would always be some sort of interruption; either the guys would show up or something else altogether would prevent him from finding out about his notoriety.

Sure, he never got to watch the news, never read a newspaper, but deep down, didn't he already know? His mind fought with the question. It was a question that went two ways. First: Didn't he know he was making a name for himself, and second: Didn't he know he was as crazy as they said he was?

He longed to weep, but grown men don't shed tears. *Oh well,* he thought. *No sense blubbering over spilt milk.*

19

The doctor told Billy he would have to stay a week, maybe ten days, but when ten turned into fourteen, he became livid. At first, being hospitalized didn't bother him much; in fact, he liked getting all the attention from the good-looking nurses, but he quickly grew tired of the whole hospital scene. It was too damn depressing and he wanted out.

They were hesitant to let him go, but Billy caused such a stink about leaving, they let him go just so they didn't have to hear his complaining. They told him he might still feel some pain now and then; that he should take his pain medication every four hours. Billy took their advice with a grain of salt; he wasn't thinking about pain at the moment.

By the time he knocked on Mitch's apartment door, the pain was back and it was starting to really kick in. He wished he'd gone to the pharmacy and picked up his Demerol. He wasn't expecting to need it so soon, but he was glad he took the sample painkillers the doctor offered him. Otherwise, he'd be up shit's creek without a paddle.

Billy stood in the hallway holding his hand to his stomach, grimacing with each sharp stab. Maybe it was a good thing he stayed in the hospital for as long as he did and he was thinking, maybe, just maybe, he should have stayed as long as they wanted him to. When no one answered his knock, he had to reach up and run his hand along the top of the doorframe, find the key and open the door. It didn't help his stomach any.

Once inside, he flipped the wall switch to his right and the overhead fluorescent lamp flickered, flickered, until it finally lit up the hallway. To his left was the door to

Mitch's bedroom. On it was a sign that read: ENTER AT YOUR OWN RISK!

Billy could imagine the mess behind that door, and wasn't planning on going in there. He had made that mistake once before, and once was enough. The room to his right was the living room and kitchen combined. Since Mitch worked out of his apartment, the room was set up as his office.

Billy went to the sink and turned on the faucet. When the water was cold enough, he poured himself a glass. He reached into his pocket and pulled out the package of painkillers. With shaking hands, he ripped open the pack and popped the pills into his mouth. They went down easy enough, but it would be awhile before they began to work.

He flopped into the leather rocking chair behind the oak desk and waited for the pills to take affect. Glancing around the office, seeing how neat everything was, it made him think that Mitch had two sides: the nice, neat, business side, and the private, "live like a pig" side.

On top of the desk was an Apple computer to his right, an answering machine to the left of that, and in the middle was a silver picture frame with a picture of Mitch and Darla in happier times. The two of them were dressed in fishing gear; both holding a trout for display. Mitch's face looked as if someone had stomped on his toes as he held the smallest of the catch, while Darla's smile was as big as the fish in her hand.

A notepad was sitting in front of him with a note from his brother.

Bro,

I need to regroup. Don't know how long I'll be gone, but in the meantime, help yourself around the place. Stay out of my room!

Mitch

Billy noticed one saved message on the answering machine and hit the playback button. It began to rewind and then stopped. *Beep...* "Hi Mitch," it was Darla's voice, "I was hoping to catch you but obviously I missed you. Call me when you can, o.k.? You got my number. Bye."... *Click... Beep!*

Her voice was so fine like sweet chilled wine; Billy couldn't forget it if he tried. He reminisced the first time he met her, waking out of his coma, and finding her and Mitch standing over him with smiles on their faces. When she asked him if he remembered his name, her voice had turned him on, causing a rise under the sheets, and it still held the same effect.

Billy fought back his arousal and noticed the pain in his gut beginning to subside. He laid back into the comfort of the chair, closing his eyes and began rocking himself ever so slowly.

He thought of the past. If he tried to think further back into his history, his head would begin to throb. It was like banging his head against the wall whenever he tried to recall something that happened before the accident.

As he rocked, he rubbed his temples with the palms of his hands, desperately trying to remember something, anything. His mind was a blank, black as a slate chalkboard. The pain in his gut had been replaced with the pain of trying to remember, and no amount of dope could help relieve that.

Suddenly, a flash of a memory from years gone by, he was sitting by the banks of the river with Mitch. He was six again, and Mitch was teaching him how to fish. The two of them were watching the water, waiting for the bobber to bob, and hoping for the first catch of the day. The sun twinkled off the water, into their eyes, making it difficult to see.

Mitch put his hand to his forehead, trying to shade his eyes, but it was just too bright. "Are you going to miss me when I'm gone?" He asked.

Billy stopped pulling on the gum in his mouth and said, "I guess so."

"You guess so? What kind of answer is that?"

Switching his baseball cap around on his head, with a smile Billy said, "Why you got to go in the Army?" He turned to face the water again, and Mitch must have seen the tear building up in his eye because he put his arm around his shoulder and squeezed tightly.

"I don't *have* to go. I want to serve my country. I'll be back, bro." As the tear trickled down Billy's cheek, he turned to look at his older brother with a sparkle of hope in his eyes, he said, "When? When you gonna come back?"

Mitch squeezed even tighter, trying to reassure his best buddy. "I don't know how long I'll be gone, kid. I guess I'll come back when I'm ready to come back. I need to get away."

FLASH—FLASH—FLASH—FLICKER—FLICKER—FLICKER.

The memory changed.

FLASH—FLASH—FLASH—FLICKER—FLICKER—FLICKER.

There's a mob in front of him and the lights are on strobe. Billy's singing and jamming on the keyboard and the crowd roars its approval. The lights strobe at various speeds, slow one minute and faster the next; every head in the audience bounced, bobbed and weaved as the music thumped, thumped, thumped. His fingers are flying across the keys; each note is so sweet to the ear. He glances to his left, and standing there shaking a tambourine is a figure in black. There's no face under its hooded head, just a bony hand clamped around the tambourine, shaking and shaking;

its clanging sounds like two knives, each blade sharpening the other. Yelping like a puppy getting its tail stepped on, Billy opened his eyes.

A shiver rippled down his spine, and suddenly there's a song jamming in his head. It's a song he hasn't heard in awhile. He can hear the singing, "Laaaaa, Laaaa, Laaa, La, La..." He tries to remember the name of the song, but it's lost somewhere in the Outer Limits.

He pushed himself up and out of the comfort of the chair, steadying himself with his hands on the desk. His legs felt like rubber; they were shaking so badly he nearly fell to the floor.

The temperature in the room began to fall. Soon, it was so cold; it felt as if he were in a meat locker. He could even see his own breath. Now his legs were not the only thing shaking, his whole body was trembling. The air seemed to be circling around him, around and around like a tornado. The notepad on the desk, he could see the pages flapping and rippling in the frigid breeze.

The phone began to ring. Ringgggggg... Ringgggggg... The sound made him shudder even more. Ringgggggg... Ringgggggg... He picked it up.

"Hello?"

Nothing, Nada, Zip! Except the line was open, someone was listening. For a moment, Billy thought he heard something. "Hello, is anybody there?"

There was nothing but dead air. He wanted to hang up, wanted more than anything to get the hell out of there, but he couldn't move. The receiver was glued to his ear as he listened.

Listening... listening... straining to hear. He could've sworn somebody was saying something. "Who is this?" He screamed... *Click*... Billy stood there with the phone to his ear, listening as the dial tone buzzed his brain.

He noticed that the room had become warmer; the cold breeze that had circled him gone. He stopped shaking and hung up the phone.

What the hell was that, he thought. As he stood there, wondering who had been on the other end of the line, he was suddenly overcome with feeling dirty. Deep down, black-as-sin dirty, as if something foul had seeped into his skin. He went to the sink, turned the faucet and splashed his face with the cold water, hoping that would somehow cleanse him of this awful feeling.

It worked. He was beginning to feel like his old self again. Then the phone began to ring once more. He froze in mid splash, his hands still touching the water, and with the ringing of the phone, he began to tremble all over again.

The phone rang and rang.

Get a hold of yourself, he thought; *it's only the freaking phone!*

Billy picked it up after the fifth ring. "Hello?"

"Billy?"

It was his mother, and she sounded scared. "Billy, is that you?"

"Mom?" Of all the people to call, it had to be her? Billy's first thought was that something happened to Mitch. "What's wrong?" He asked.

"Billy… you all right?"

That's just like Mom, asking a question like that, he thought. She always hounded him when he was a kid. Anything and everything that she could hound about, she had, and he didn't like it one bit. *There's an easy memory to remember,* he thought. "I'm fine, Mom!" The tone in his voice had been sharp so he quickly softened it. "What's the matter? You sound upset."

Being in her late seventies, she had a tendency to repeat herself, "Billy… you all right?" He said nothing. He was trying his best not to get angry. His mother had a way of getting on his nerves. Finally he said, "I'm fine, Mom!" Again his tone was harsh, but it fell on a deaf ear. His mother was always the worrier. She said, "I was just checking. I had a dream you were over at Mitch's place and three guys were beating you up."

She's just checking, he thought. She never could let go, always checking, always trying to control. "It's all right, Mom; it was only a bad dream." *Was it really a bad dream?* He wondered. One thing for sure, her dreams were tame compared to the ones he had.

She kept him on the telephone another fifteen minutes. To Billy it felt like days. As he listened to her go on and on, he fought to keep his cool, hoping she would finally give it a rest.

At long last he couldn't take it anymore and eventually said, "I'm gonna be staying here while Mitch is gone." Before she could say another word, he said, "I got to go, Mom. See ya, love ya, bye," and finally hung up the phone.

20

Ish thought going home would somehow make his life easier, he thought wrong. Home was something he wanted; hell, it was something he needed, but now, now he wished he was still homeless and living on the streets of Pittsburgh. At least back then he didn't have to keep looking over his shoulder, not like now. Sure, life on the streets was no picnic, but he dealt with it, didn't he? Living on the streets had hardened him to the harshness that life had to offer. Then the guys showed up and softened him into Jell-O, a big lump of soft yellow goo, wiggling and jiggling, doing anything and everything they asked him to do.

Since coming home, his nights were agitated ones; he tossed and turned, struggling, trying to bury himself into the arms of bliss, that place between those that are asleep and those that are dead.

In the morning, he awoke feeling as if he just ran a marathon. He pulled himself reluctantly out of bed, and prepared for another day of stalking his prey. He paid Billy a few visits at the hospital, and both times Billy had been asleep.

Ish was lucky today.

Today his prey was wide-awake, looking well enough to be set free. That's what he was planning on doing, setting him free. Free from all the worries of the world, freeing him, in fact, of life—period.

He overheard the conversation between Billy and the doctor. He couldn't have missed it; Billy had been so loud and obnoxious. He hoped what he heard was true, and now as he waited outside, the moment of truth had arrived. Ish sat in a red pickup truck, parked in front of the hospital, waiting for Billy to show his face, and after twenty minutes of waiting, his prey was on the move.

He watched him hail a cab, then followed at a safe distance. The truck he drove was a used one, and it showed its age by coughing as Ish stomped on the gas. It was a far cry from the car he started out with, but his days of living like a king were long gone. He had used a number of cars since then; this truck was the worst of the bunch.

Twenty minutes later, Ish was pulling the truck over, parking a block away from where the cab had stopped. It pulled in front of a five-story apartment building; Billy got out and limped up the steps in obvious pain.

When Ish was confident it was safe to follow, he got out of the truck. Walking at a normal pace, not wanting to be noticed, he stopped at the building where Billy had entered. Staring up at the double stained-glass windowed doors, he wondered if maybe he should just go home.

When he got up enough courage, he climbed the steps. There were twenty-four total. He had a habit of counting steps. He remembered counting the number of stairs that led down to the school's basketball court, counted them so many times before he shoved his nemesis, Tommy Hathaway, down them. The habit stuck ever since.

Once at the top, he found he could only get inside if he had a key or if someone buzzed him in. He had no key.

Ish was about to turn and run down the steps when Todd suddenly was standing beside him. "Go ahead and buzz 2B," he said with a grin. "They're waiting for the cable guy."

Ish had no way of knowing how Todd had known that fact, and didn't really care; the only thing he cared about was getting inside.

He pushed the button for 2B. A few seconds went by and he pushed it again. Finally, the speaker began to crackle, and a female voice said, "Yes, can I help you?"

With his mind firmly set on getting inside the building, Ish calmly replied in a southern drawl, "I'm here to fix your cable."

Cable was the magic word.

"Okay… one second while I buzz you in."

Ish put his hand on the doorknob, and within seconds, the loud buzzing could be felt as well as heard. He pushed the door open and stepped inside. The hallway walls were painted a really ugly mustard yellow; the sight alone was enough to make him sick. To the left was an elevator. On it, a sign was posted. He didn't know what the sign said; there was handwriting plastered all over it with words like: What else is new!—Piece of shit!—Fix this fucking thing!

To his right was a flight of stairs. Todd slowly appeared at the top of the steps, leaning on the railing, looking as if he were waiting for a bus. That smile was on his face again, a smile that said, "Follow me."

"Don't bother with the elevator, Sleaze. It's out of order." He pointed up the stairs. "Your man's hiding in apartment 5A."

Ish climbed the narrow staircase, counting all the way. One… Two… Three… Past the second floor, third floor, fourth floor, huffing and puffing until he stops at the top. "Fifty-three… fifty-four… fifty-five!" he mumbled as he caught his breath. He was hunched over with his hands on his knees, wheezing like an old geezer.

He glanced down the hallway, still huffing and puffing, trying to catch his breath, when suddenly he felt boxed in. Darkness seeped from the walls. The only window at the end of the hallway had been boarded up. He could still see some sunlight trying to creep in between the boards, but it wasn't enough to make a difference; it was still pitch-black compared to the rest of the building.

When his eyes adjusted to the dark, he stood up and began his search. It didn't take him long; 5A was the first door on his left.

Ish pressed his hands to the door. He could feel his heartbeat throbbing through his fingers. Slowly, like a safecracker putting his ear to a safe, he pressed his ear against the wood.

At first, the only thing he heard was his ear sucking itself to the door like a plunger to a clogged sink. Then, ever so faintly, he thought he heard a beep. Yes, yes, that's what it was, an answering machine kind of beep. He couldn't make out everything being said, but he could hear enough to know that it was a woman's voice. He strained to listen, but that sucking sound made it difficult.

"You got my number. Bye."

The voice was replaced with another beep.

He's in there, Ish thought. *He's in there listening to his messages. Who was she?* His eyes were closed the whole time he was listening, so when he opened them and found the guys standing there, he nearly jumped out of his skin. All three of them had their finger to their mouths in a 'Shhhhh' pose.

His heart felt as if it would burst from his ribcage. How many times had they crept up on him? He couldn't remember. It was a wonder he wasn't dead from a heart attack years ago.

"We're gonna have some fun," Todd whispered. Ish wasn't sure why he would do that; he was a figment of his own imagination, wasn't he? It's not likely that anyone else would hear him.

One after the other, they passed through the door. First Todd, then Tony, and finally Joey, but before he went all the way through, he stopped and gave Ish a big 'This is going to be fun' wink. Then he was gone, leaving Ish alone in the hallway once more. He swiftly put his ear to the door.

†   †   †

They found Billy situated behind the desk in the living room sitting there with his eyes closed, rubbing his temples, looking like a guy trying to hold it all together, but not doing a very good job of it.

Standing around him, they each began to taunt him in their own special way. Todd leaned in close to his ear and whispered, "What's the matter, Billy boy, not feeling well?"

Then Tony knelt in front of him in a mocking gesture of worship, and said, "All hail King Psycho Punk!"

Billy continued to rub his temples, not aware of anything around him, lost in his own private hell.

Joey started to sing.

It was a familiar tune, one of Billy's favorites: Blue Öyster Cult's "Don't Fear The Reaper." The song had the desired effect. Within seconds Billy's eyes shot open as he gasped a deep breath. He jumped out of his seat and stood on wobbling legs.

They were all singing now, running around Billy, as he fought to keep himself from falling over. Around and around, faster and faster, they laughed as they sang, "Laaaaa, Laaaa... Laaa... La... La... "

†   †   †

Out in the hallway, Ish struggled to hear what was happening inside. His right ear had gone numb, so he switched over to the left, and that's when he heard the phone ring. He wondered what could possibly be happening, and

129

wanted to be a fly on the wall, if only for a second; the guys sounded like they were having a hell of a time.

Ish slid his head against the wood, trying to find the best spot to hear, and as he did, he suddenly winced in pain as his ear snagged on a splinter. Cupping his ear, rocking back and forth, biting his lower lip, he cursed his own stupidity. Inside the apartment, he could hear Billy shouting, "Who is this!"

A few minutes went by before the guys passed through the door and stepped into the hallway. The pain in his ear had been replaced with excitement when he saw them. They all put their finger to their mouths again.

"Shhhhhhh… "

Ish couldn't control himself; he was like a kid, rocking up and down on his toes, smiling all the while. *Killing all those women wasn't nearly as exciting as this,* he thought. Hell, that was work—this was play. Within the apartment the phone rang again. Ish wanted to put his ear against the door but had second thoughts about it. He wondered if maybe Billy was talking to the woman that was on the answering machine, but Todd cleared that thought from his head when he said, "Billy boy is talking to his mommy."

Todd's humorous tone of voice sent Tony and Joey into hysterics. Ish wanted to laugh, man how he wanted to laugh, but he knew better than to do something stupid like that, so he let them do the laughing for him. It felt just as good.

Oddly enough, this was another first. There was a time when he dreaded the sound of their laughter, but now it was a tranquil sound, a calming sound, like the music brought on by a running stream with its soft trickling melody.

The music stopped when Todd said, "You'll find everything you'll need to do the job down there." He pointed toward the boarded-up window down the hall.

Ish made his way down the hallway, his eyes totally adjusted to the darkness now, and as he got closer to the window, the sunlight beaming between the boards was shining directly on the sign on the door to his left. It read: Storage Room.

Ish tried the knob and the door swung open. He stepped inside and closed it behind him. It might have been dark, but his eyes seemed to have the power of night vision. He stepped in closer, and as he did, a cobweb brushed his cheek. He brought his hand up, ready to clear the web and found that it wasn't a cobweb after all; it was a piece of string. He pulled on it, and the light went on. A forty-watt bulb hung over his head, swinging back and forth.

On the wall to his left, rows of shelves were stacked with all the necessary janitorial needs: paper towels, toilet tissue and liquid soap. To his right were more shelves holding other odds and ends: Spic and Span, Windex, Glad trash bags. Finally, on the bottom shelf was a box of condoms, some blankets and a stack of girlie magazines.

Looks like Mr. Janitor likes to use this room to take in some smack time, Ish thought. In front of him was a bucket on wheels. A mop stood in it, and perched on top of the mop handle, a pair of workman's gloves.

He instantly knew what to do. He pulled the gloves onto his hands, yanked the mop out of the bucket and began twisting the bundle of damp yarn off the handle. The wooden handle, at least three inches thick, was splintered here and there. He knew it would be perfect for the job at hand.

Soon, darkness would fall.

Ish turned off the light and waited patiently inside the storage room. He knew no one would be coming, it being a Sunday, the janitor being off duty. The only thing he hoped for was that Billy stayed put. As long as he didn't go anywhere, everything would be fine.

Ish could feel the outside world becoming darker and darker. He planned on waiting until his victim was fast asleep. Hell, he'd wait as long as it took. He wasn't in a hurry.

He spent the time reminiscing about his younger years, wondering where they had gone, and why they had to go so damn fast. Everything about life went fast; those long-awaited vacations, all those special occasions always flew by, leaving everybody wondering where the time went.

He didn't mind the wait, knowing full well that the wait would be worth it, in the long run. Waiting was like foreplay; he loved every minute of it because he knew the pleasure he'd feel would make up for any lost time.

As he waited, he remembered not only the good old days but also the bad. There were a lot of bad things to think about. He thought he'd buried them into the far reaches of his mind, never to hear from them again, but waiting in such cramped quarters began to take its toll on him.

The room felt like it was shrinking.

He remembered when his father put him in the closet because he wouldn't stop whining—that's what his dad called crying—and he could still hear his old man on the other side of that closet door, so long ago, "You'll stay in there until you stop whining like a bitch!" Ish couldn't have been more than three at the time.

Memories of his mother, once thought of as being pleasant, began to show their true ugly side. A memory, buried deep: How many nights did she make him kneel on a broom handle for something he'd done wrong? She made him kneel for hours while she stood behind him, demanding that he pray to God for forgiveness from his evil ways. In his mind, he kept telling himself she did it for his own good, but at times like that he could phase out the pain and become numb to the truth.

The truth being that she was only doing it because of things she may have done wrong as a mother. Wasn't it her fault he always got into trouble? Maybe if she hadn't treated him like a helpless child, maybe then he wouldn't blame her for the shit he got himself into.

Deep inside, rage began to boil.

Hatred rankled inside him like a lion prancing back and forth within its cage. The memories were falling like dominoes, one after the other, each stirring the cauldron as it boiled. His flesh became hot. His dimple-tipped nose flared like a bull before its charge.

Ish held the mop handle like it was his victim's throat, twisting and squeezing, his teeth grinding. In the darkness his eyes pulsed with a green glow.

The time had come.

He stepped out of the storage room and headed back to 5A. The guys were waiting for him. Ish stopped in front of the door as Todd put his ghostly hand through it, unlocking it from the other side. Still holding that maniac grin on his face, Todd said, "He's all yours."

Ish opened the door and stepped inside the apartment. He had waited nearly twelve hours, hours spent seething with hatred, and now at long last the time had come.

He moved down the hall, passing the door with the funny *Enter at your own risk* sign, down to the spare room, the room where he knew Billy was now fast asleep.

Part Three

Warnings

21

The sound of the wind, rushing through the leaves in the trees, pulled him out of his sleep.

Mitch wanted to sleep, to dream, but the howling of the wind wouldn't allow him the pleasure. When his eyes finally opened, they focused on the top of the tent, watching the canvas as it rippled with the breeze. The sun was beginning to rise and the birds sung their praises. It was going to be a beautiful November morn.

He closed his eyes again and pictured the leaves in his mind. He could see them clearly as they struggled to keep themselves adhered to their branches. Twisting and turning, as the wind rushed through them, he could see some of them breaking free...floating away with the gust. It wouldn't be much longer before all of them were gone. Winter was coming. Out of all the seasons, Mitch loved "winter" the most. If he could, he would skip *summer* and *fall*. Fishing and Camping, and Camping and Skiing: three things he could never get enough of. With his eyes still closed, he watched as the leaves, in his mind, kept floating and floating.

That's when things went black.

The sound that woke him was also the sound that sent him into a dream. *Was it a dream?* He wondered.

Mitch was staring at the top of the tent again, listening to the wind. His eyes were only closed for a minute, maybe two. He wasn't sure if what he saw was a dream or not. But it had to be. He could still see it. The image was burned into his mind; it was a mop handle dripping with blood.

He pulled the zipper of his sleeping bag down, pushed its warmth away from his body and sat up. Wearing his white tank top (the kind Darla liked to call his 'wife beater' shirt) and gray jogging pants, the cold air sent his bare flesh rippling, like a stone being tossed into a calm lake, as goose bumps popped out like massive zits.

He stretched out his arms and yawned like a cow, sucking in huge amounts of the fresh morning air. It filled him with enough energy to start him off with a go at sit-ups.

With his arms behind the back of his head, he pushed himself to the limit. Up, down. Up, down. It was his morning ritual whenever he went camping: three reps of twenty sit-ups; and three reps of twenty pushups. It helped get the blood flowing, made it easier to ignore the cold.

The wind, still howling outside the tent, sounded as if it was cheering him on. Mitch rolled onto his stomach and began his pushups. It was funny how he could always find time to work out whenever he went camping, but he couldn't seem to be as disciplined about it at home. At home he would just roll out of bed and go on about the day without even thinking about exercising.

As he pushed himself up and down, he thought of the phone call that waited for him when he got home from the hospital. He wanted to call her back, wanted to more than anything, but he wasn't sure what to say to her. He knew they needed to talk; he needed to tell her how miserable his life was, without her. But that could never happen. That would be giving her control of the relationship. Opening up to her would only make him vulnerable to more misery.

Mitch shoved his thoughts of Darla aside and finished his last set of pushups.

He couldn't think about her right now, not when he was so close to finding the Motel-4 Madman; that son-of-a-bitch was in *his* territory now, and he was planning on taking him down.

Camping had a way of calming him down, slowing the fast pace of life to a more manageable speed. That's just what he needed and planned to do. He was half tempted to invite Darla along, knowing it was something she liked to do, but he knew he needed 'time-out' time to get away and think things through, and having her along, no matter how nice it might have been, wouldn't help matters one bit.

Mitch dressed and stepped out of the three-man tent.

The winds seemed to become calmer as the warmth of the sun spread across the horizon. He could hear the sound of the Wenatchee River hidden within the ever-calming wind and immediately had to relieve himself.

He leaned against the nearest tree, holding his manhood in his palm and closed his eyes. He could hear the trickling of the river and within seconds his own stream began to flow. As he finished up, shaking the last drops, the image of the bloody mop handle flashed into his mind.

It had to be a dream, he thought. He had no idea what it could mean (because every dream has a meaning, doesn't it?) but he couldn't imagine what, if anything, this dream could mean. He pushed it out of his head.

Mitch had enough supplies to last a couple of weeks, because that's how long he planned on taking some downtime.

Now, his basic necessities were dwindling. He fired up the mini-burner and made the last of the coffee. As he waited, he lit up a cigarette. He knew he shouldn't, but it helped to take his mind off other things, particularly the thought of drinking something stronger than java.

That was another reason he was here camping.

He'd fallen off the wagon and had to get back on. What better way to avoid getting drunk? Being out in the woods, far away from any bar or State store. It kind of made the odds of getting smashed slim to none. When the coffee was ready, he filled his cup more than halfway, making sure to leave room for the cream and sugar. Using a plastic spoon, he stirred till the count of ten, then carefully sipped at the steaming brew.

Ahhhhh, he thought, as he leaned back in his folding chair, *there's nothing better in the morning than a cup of coffee and a smoke.*

Mitch pulled a black book out of his army jacket that hung on the back of the chair, and thumbed through the pages. Most men who have a little black book would be looking up a hot date's number. Not Mitch, his book didn't have anything like that; his book held every piece of the puzzle to the case at hand.

He stopped at the pages marked in red ink and began to read his own handwriting, which wasn't an easy task, considering his handwriting was thought of as chicken scratch. He took one last drag on his smoke and then crushed it into the ground with his finger.

Every detail that he'd been able to come across in the case was marked down in this book: the names of the victims, the cities and states where the murders took place, and notes from interviews with the unfortunate ones who found the bodies.

He read from an interview he'd had with the owner of the Motel-4 chain. The guy's name was Karl Smyth. Mitch had paid him a visit not long after he first involved himself with the case. Mr. Smyth had been a burly man, one who looked as if he ate nails for breakfast, and Mitch had made note of it.

Question: How many motels do you have across the country?

Answer: Eight... so far. Plans to open more...

Question: Have there been other bodies found, other than the one found in Liberty, Missouri?

Answer: Yes. Note: If said answer gets out to public... expect lawsuit.

Mitch remembered the look on the fat man's face when he said it; it wasn't a pleasant one. The bottom line for Mr. Smyth was making money, and if word got out that his motels were havens where some sick fuck got his kicks, he'd be out of business.

He sipped his coffee, imagining he would be getting a call, now that the story of Billy, getting shot while staking out one of Mr. Smyth's establishments, was in the news. He lit another smoke without even realizing it, as he continued to read.

Question: Where are the other motels located?

Answer: Atlantic City, NJ; Pittsburgh, PA; Liberty, MO; Reno, NV; Las Vegas, NV; San Francisco, CA; Portland, OR and Seattle, WA.

What the hell drew me to this case, he wondered.

Mitch thumbed through the pages once more, stopping at the pages marked in green ink. Red ink for interviews, green for locations, black for miscellaneous items. It was his way of being organized.

Every location had a check mark beside it except Portland and Seattle.

Check marks were where murders had taken place. He pulled a pen from his jacket and made a check mark beside Seattle. *Every place but Portland,* he thought, as he circled that city's name over and over again. He flipped to the back and began to make notes to himself. There had to be something he overlooked, something that was right there in front of his face; he just couldn't see it yet. Double check all records, he wrote. Talk to Billy about possible stakeout in Portland.

Today was his last day of vacation, his downtime. Tonight he would get his rest and in the morning he would head on home. For the moment, it was time to relax, and he knew just how to do that. It was time to go fishing.

Mitch closed his book and got ready to catch some lunch and dinner.

The day, like all good days, flew by without Mitch once looking at his watch. He wanted to, but he knew it would be his luck the fish would make a hit on his line as soon as he did. He had what he thought were plenty of hits, only they turned out to be snags or twigs, nothing more. If there is anything one learns from fishing, it has to be patience. Something he had a tendency to lose now and then, but when it came to pulling in that first catch, it made the waiting well worth the effort.

As Mitch kept his eyes firmly on the bobber, watching it bob up and down, he thought of the times when he and Billy sat and watched the water for hours in this very same spot. Their Uncle Norton had always been a big fishing nut, and he took Mitch along almost all the time. When Billy was old enough, Mitch took up the tradition of bringing him along. Right up until Mitch went into the service.

All of a sudden, the red and white bobber took a nosedive and all past memories were shattered as Mitch pulled on the fishing pole, reeling in what he hoped to be his first catch. It was a big one; that's for sure. Mitch pulled and reeled, pulled and reeled; then the fish was jumping out of the water, quickly taking another nosedive back into the rippling waves as it fought for its life.

His first catch, a beauty: a thirteen-inch, eight-pound rainbow trout.

Mitch finally glanced at his watch and saw that it was nearly half past two. He couldn't believe how fast the time had gone; he'd already missed lunch; this bad-boy would have to be his dinner.

Putting his prize into a cooler that was only big enough to hold a six-pack, he walked back to his tent with a smile on his face. He spent the rest of the day walking the many trails, taking in the surrounding beauty of the fall season, trying not to think about having a drink.

He felt as if he were riding a wild horse, being without at least one shot in a full two weeks. It was hard not thinking about it, but he felt it getting easier with each passing day. He had forgiven himself for falling off the wagon, which was something he needed to do in order to get on with his life.

By the time the sun started to set, Mitch was back sitting in front of the tent preparing his catch for dinner.

He worked like a natural-born chef on speed, gutting and chopping the fish, trying to get the job done before the sun went down, sending the woods under the cover of darkness. Not long from now, the campfire would be the only source of light.

A cigarette dangled from his lips, sending smoke into his eyes as he worked like a pro. He took one last drag and tossed the butt into the fire.

Scraping the chopped fish into the hot and waiting frying pan, he listened as it sizzled. When the smell hit his nose, his mouth began to water.

Cooking had always been something he enjoyed, especially eating the food he cooked. He learned how while in the Army and liked doing it ever since. It gave him the sense of being on his own, not needing anybody else. It was yet another part of freedom, real freedom. Freedom to come and go as you please, freedom to do whatever came to mind, anytime, anywhere.

Afterward, when the sun finally set and his meal was in his stomach, Mitch sat and watched the heavens. One by one, the stars made themselves known, popping into the black velvet sky, here, there, until the entire horizon was speckled with lights. Mitch wondered if there was life out there, somewhere far, far away. If there was, did they have the answer mankind so desperately needed? Could they provide any help to the many problems we face?

Answers to his particular questions were slowly coming together, but he didn't feel any closer to catching the killer now then when he first started working the case.

He reached for a log out of the pile of wood next to his folding chair and tossed it into the flames. The campfire popped and hissed as the fire began to eat the new wood; flames reached higher and higher, pushing back the darkness a fraction of an inch more. As he watched the flames do their dance, he thought of Billy and wondered if he was out of the hospital by now.

Pulling himself out of his chair, Mitch went to the tent and unzipped it just wide enough so he could reach inside. He had to reach further than he thought, his hand hopping up and down like a Halloween spider on a bungee string, until he found what he was reaching for. He pulled the tote bag out of the tent, fumbled around inside and found his cell phone. He tossed the bag back into the tent and zipped it shut.

Mitch punched in the phone number of the hospital as he walked back to his chair; then he hit the send button and sat down. As the phone rang, the fire popped and hissed. After the third ring, a woman's voice came on the line.

"Northwest Hospital, please hold."

Music filled his ear before he could say a word. He listened as Men at Work sang about the land down under. The flames in the campfire seemed to dance in time with the music in his ear. He just started to get into the song when the woman came back on the line.

"I'm sorry to keep you on hold, this is Northwest Hospital... how may I help you?"

Mitch began to wonder if it was becoming a habit; all day long, thoughts of Darla kept popping into his head; now he was beginning to hear her voice as well. His mind momentarily wandered off. He could hear her voice on the answering machine. "You got my number... Call me... Bye."

The voice on the other end of the phone said, "Northwest Hospital. Can I help you?" Mitch's thoughts snapped back like a rubber band and he said, "Darla? Is that you?" The words came out of his mouth too fast. What if it wasn't her? What if it was just in his head?

"Mitch?"

His heartbeat picked up a few beats when he realized it was really her.

"Darla, since when do you work at Northwest?"

"Since a few months ago."

"Why didn't you tell me when I saw you there?"

He could hear her laughter through the sudden static, "You never asked. Are you calling to check up on Billy?"

"Yeah," he said as he shoved another log on the fire. "Can I talk to him?" He leaned back in his chair and closed his eyes. The campfire crackled and hissed as sparks went flying into the air like a mini-fireworks display.

"I would, if I could, but I can't," Darla said. "He checked out early this morning."

The image of the bloody mop handle suddenly filled his head. He could see droplets of blood dripping off the end of the handle, slowly, like a leaking faucet. "Mitch, did you hear me? I said Billy checked out this morning." The image popped out of his head like a bubble; he said, "Yeah, I heard you. I just got distracted there for a second. Do you know where he went?"

Mitch could hear someone talking in the background when Darla said, "I'm sorry, Mitch. Hold on a sec, o.k.?" Before he could say anything, music filled his ear again. This time it was The Beatles singing "Let It Be." A moment or two passed and Darla was back on the line. "Mitch?"

"Yeah, I'm still here."

"I wasn't on duty when he left, but I heard he made a big stink about leaving, so they let him go."

"That sounds like Billy."

"Takes after his older brother," said Darla.

Mitch knew she was right. She had seen him go off the deep end plenty of times, so he didn't acknowledge her jab. Instead, he said, "I got your call. I was planning on calling you as soon as I get back."

"Get back? Where are you?"

"I'm out here at Tumwater Campgrounds… gonna head on home first thing in the morning." Mitch could hear someone else in the background asking her a question and knew his conversation was going to be cut short, so, before she could put him on hold again, he said, "Listen, Darla. I have to go. I'll call you."

"I'll be waiting," she said and then hung up the phone.

Loneliness covered him like a blanket the moment he hit the end button. He wanted her now more than ever. Why did it have to be her? Why couldn't it have been someone else answering the phone? He tried not to think about it, but he couldn't help himself. He was actually considering hooking up with her again. Deep down, he wondered if she would be willing to give it another try.

Mitch looked at his watch. Damn! It was almost ten-thirty. Time goes too fast.

If his thinking was correct, and it almost always was, Billy would be at Mitch's apartment either pigging out and watching the tube, or kicking back with the headphones on his ears, jamming to one tune or another. He punched in the phone number, hit the send button and hoped Billy wasn't doing the latter of the two.

The phone began to ring.

22

He knew what he needed to do.

He had to crush the enemy, to squash any and all who would stand in the way of the will of his God. A God he made a vow to, a commitment to—a commitment he would fulfill no matter what the consequence. Billy had been a member of the family. But by the looks of things, it seemed he either forgot or chose to walk away, as if walking away could change anything. Only a fool would believe that lie.

Ish knew the truth.

The outside, the body may change, but on the inside, the soul remains the same. Once down, there's no turning around. That's why the band had died. Billy's failure to take it to the next level brought on changes, but in the end, fate found a way to even the score, because here he was, about to make Billy's brains a bag of mush.

Ish stood in the blackness of the hallway in front of the spare room door, rocking up and down on his toes, slowly twisting the mop handle in his hands.

The thought of bashing Billy's brains out of his head while he slept seemed to be a cowardly thing to do, but he didn't care. As far as he was concerned, Billy had brought it on himself by sticking his nose into things he didn't need to be concerned with.

He deserves it, Ish thought.

Oh how he wanted to make Billy pay. For so long he thought he was the cause of the band's demise (and he was) but now he realized it was Billy's fault all along.

If Billy had gone along with the idea of sacrificing a human infant, hadn't turned his back on the family—the rock band—then maybe things would be different now. The band could have gone on to be immortalized, could have gone down in history with the rest of the great bands like The Rolling Stones, Led Zeppelin or The Who. Too bad Billy had gone soft, blowing it for everybody else.

Payback's gonna be a Motherfucker, he thought to himself as he stood in the hallway, at one with the darkness that covered him and at peace with the job at hand. It wouldn't be a problem; the friendship they used to share was only a memory, nothing more.

This was it. It was now or never. *Where the hell are the guys?* He wondered. Why were they off somewhere else when he wanted them here? He wanted an audience—hell, he needed spectators—this was going to be one for the books, a job like no other.

He decided he wasn't waiting around for them to pop in and enjoy the show.

He slowly managed to uncurl his fingers from the mop handle and reached for the doorknob, gripping it with such force that if it were a soda can, it would have crumbled in his fist. With frantic delight, he began to turn the knob; then suddenly the telephone started to ring.

Ish froze in place, like a deer caught in the headlights of an oncoming car.

He gazed down the hallway in the direction the ring came from. *Was there a ring inside the spare bedroom as well?* He put his ear to the door as the phone rang again. *No, there's no phone in there;* he was certain of it. Now his only concern was if Billy had heard the ring. *Was he pulling himself out of bed right now?* His only hope was if Billy was still a sound sleeper.

Like a rat looking for cheese in a maze, Ish ran to the living room and pulled the phone cord out of the wall before the fifth ring. His catlike ability to move about in the dark without any problems was no surprise. It started the first time he went through the green doorway, way back when he was new to the game of killing. His night vision had grown stronger with each crossover.

He stood by the desk, looking around, listening for any sounds of movement. *Was Billy awake?* His ears zoomed in as he listened to the sounds in the darkness. To his left he heard a steady drip and ping: *Drip, Ping!* coming from the kitchen sink. From behind, an occasional thump from the radiator; there was no shuffling of feet, no creaks from an opening door, all else, relaxed and still.

In his excitement of running to cut off the phone, he forgot he was still holding the mop handle in his left hand. He grabbed it with both hands now and began to twist. It wasn't long before the friction made it warm enough to be felt through the work gloves. Still, he twisted, as if trying to rip a chicken's head off.

"Hey... Sleaze!" Todd sat at the desk with his feet up, waving his right hand. The sight of him made Ish a bit edgy. *Why was he sitting there dressed as if for a family meeting?*

His black robe clung to his body like a second skin. The hood was over his head, but Ish could still see that wild smirk on Todd's pale face. "Me and the boys been talking," he said. "We've decided to pick Billy's brain, help him remember what he's destroyed."

Ish had heard the words, heard them just as plain as hearing a church bell, but Todd's mouth still held that grin, his lips never moved. "We want to help him remember before you finish him off."

In the blink of an eye, Joey and Tony were standing beside Todd. One on his left and the other on his right. They too wore the family robes, their hoods almost covering their faces but not enough to hide the grins they wore.

Like a balloon losing air with a slow leak, all the fun Ish was having fizzled out. He'd have to be happy with sloppy-seconds.

■   ■   ■

"The party you have called is not answering. Please try your call again later."

How many times had it rung? Ten, twenty, maybe more? Mitch couldn't recall; he had stopped counting after five. He hit the end button and put the cell phone into his pocket. He couldn't recall how many times the phone had rung because his mind had become sidetracked. Old Jacky-boy was up to his tricks again, trying to make him believe that that's what he needed.

No, he thought, *not tonight.* Tonight he would fight the urge to go to any lengths for a drink. Tonight he would be strong. Mitch watched the flames of the campfire and imagined them burning out all his thoughts of booze.

Was Billy out and about this late or was he fast asleep? *Most likely asleep*, he thought to himself. If that was the case, then he could forget about talking with him; Billy always did sleep like a rock. Nothing could wake him, not even an earthquake.

Mitch closed his eyes, and as he did, his whole body began to relax. It had been a long day, and he walked a nice distance; his body was beginning to feel the effects. He knew it would be easy to fall asleep by the fire, he felt so comfy.

Mitch nodded off.

He dreamed about Vietnam. Something he'd been doing more and more since his divorce. But this time it was more than just a dream; it was as if he was living the nightmare all over again, and time had somehow pulled a rewind.

The smell of death, which was so pungent then, was even worse in his dream world. Explosions from mortar fire, rippled his very core, and bullets tore the air around him, sending him to his hands and knees, crawling through the brush and mud.

"Oh God… oh God, help meeeeeee."

Mitch crawled in the direction from which the cry came. "Please… Please!" It sounded like his partner, and he was obviously in bad shape. "Oh, Godddddddd!" His eyes opened before coming across his bloody mess of a partner, and he was back in the here and now.

He gazed at the campfire's flames; it was almost out.

Was I out that long? The memory of the dream still lingered close and he thought about it, as he threw a couple of logs on the fire. Thinking of the dream only made him feel bad, but thinking about that particular moment in time was all that filled his head. That's where Jack Daniel's always helped out. Drinking himself into a stew would always help him forget about that hell.

He was trying to justify his reasoning for having a drink. Good old Jack was always willing to lend a hand. He could think about drinking all he wanted; it wasn't going to happen; there wasn't a place for miles where he could get his hands on some, but at least thinking about booze took his mind off of his nightmare—a nightmare that never seemed to end.

His thoughts turned to Darla: how it had been she who always seemed to calm the storm in his head. How he could've let her go was beyond his comprehension. It was the biggest mistake of his life. Sure, she was the one who wanted the divorce, but he did nothing to stop it, said nothing that could have changed things. What a fool he had been to let his better-half slip away. Seeing her again at the hospital made him realize how stupid he had been.

For years, he tried forgetting about her, and as he did, his nightmares of the war returned in full force.

Memories of the war, and thoughts of drowning himself in whiskey, were his only thoughts when he first returned home, and since he made the mistake of giving up Darla without a fight, those memories and dreams only grew stronger.

He realized that Darla was his only hope if he wanted to remain sane, and hoped for a way of getting her back. He was afraid that that might not be possible but decided that he would try, if only to keep his mind in check. *But what if she said no?* What if she turned him down, what then? He was too scared to think about that possibility, scared because he knew he just might snap out, and then he would remain trapped in his memories of that hell forever, without a prayer in the world.

She was on duty now; he could call her and try to begin the process of getting his life back together. Mitch pulled out the phone, hesitated with his finger over the buttons, then finally got up the nerve. It would mean major changes in the way he handled his work life and his personal life, but it would be well worth it in the long run.

Darla answered the phone after the second ring.

† † †

Ish was never a complainer. He was an 'ask no questions' follower. He was about to open his mouth when Todd stood up from the desk. Now all three were standing there, the black silk robes twisting in an unfelt breeze. Todd said, "There's some rope under the bed in Mitch's bedroom, Sleaze. Be a good boy and fetch it." He waved him off.

Ish quickly tossed the mop handle onto the small loveseat and moved on about his business like a jester looking to please the king. *Yes'm, Boss*, Ish thought. *No problem, Boss.* He ignored the sign on the bedroom door and stepped into Mitch's domain.

The smell alone was enough to explain the sign. The darkness covered the mess but Ish could see it all. Clothes were hanging everywhere. Food, growing mold, was scattered about, along with tissues, lots and lots of tissues. Mitch either had a really bad cold, or he was cleaning up a whole load of cum, *most likely cum.* Ish chuckled at the thought.

He found the rope where Todd told him to look and hurried back to the living room.

The guys were gone.

Ish headed toward the spare bedroom. With rope in hand, he entered Billy's room and found the guys standing around Billy, watching him as he slept.

Ish gawked, as the three of them raised their hands over Billy's body. He could hear them chanting the same words they always used whenever a sacrifice was about to be offered.

"Day lay, too pa. Day lay, too pa."

He began whispering the words to himself over and over again.

"Day lay, too pa. Day lay, too pa."

They were ancient words. Words that had been spelled out to them while using the Ouija board years before. Words that called for blood. Todd waved him forward and he knew just what to do. While the guys continued to chat, Ish began to work his magic with the rope.

Billy began to moan in his sleep, slowly rocking his head back and forth... back and forth. His moans became more frequent, as the guys chanted even louder.

"Day lay, too pa! Day lay, too pa!"

† † †

Billy's dream, which started out so promising, suddenly took a dark turn. One minute he was about to lay some major pipe, and the next he was lying at the bottom of an old well, looking up at four faces peering down at him.

They were saying something, but he couldn't make out the words. The walls of the well dripped with dew and extended upwards at an unbelievable height, so high in fact, the words they spoke were turned into gibberish by the time they reached his ears.

One of the faces tossed something into the well: something black and slithering, falling toward him. What he thought to be a snake turned out to be a rope. More words jabbered at his ears.

They must want to help me, he thought. Billy reached for the rope and found it dangled only inches from his fingers.

Words still gibbered down to his ears, echoing over and over again as he jumped and grabbed hold. He waited. Expecting to be pulled up, but nothing happened. He could see them staring down at him.

"Hey!" he shouted, "You gonna pull me up or what!"

Unwilling to wait any longer, Billy decided that if he wanted to get out of this hole, he'd have to do some serious climbing. *Pricks,* he thought, as he pulled himself up. With his feet firmly braced against the wall of the well, he pulled himself up inch by inch, his hands and arms aching.

Slowly, he made his way to the top.

It seemed an eternity, the sweat rolling off his forehead and into his eye, stinging it like a bee. He didn't dare try to wipe at it; that would mean falling to the bottom again. He had come too far to start over. He could see the four faces better now, and the words that had been gibberish, came to his ears clearly as well. They were chanting, "Day lay, too pa! Day lay, too pa!"

The closer he got, the more the four faces would back away. Soon they were gone, but he could still hear their chant. "Day lay, too pa! Day lay, too pa!" Billy reached out and grabbed the top of the well and pulled himself up and over the edge. The four faces were now figures draped in black, their backs facing him. They stood around a fire, their arms outstretched over the flames.

Billy knew he was in a dream. He had trained himself to be a lucid dreamer. Now, as he stepped closer to the four figures by the fire, he continually told himself it was only a dream, only a dream...

One of the figures turned to face him, and when it did, memories of the past broke through his wall of amnesia like water bursting through a damn. The next figure turned to face him, then the next, and the next.

More memories crashed through as each face was revealed. It's only a dream... It's only a dream! You can wake up! Wake up and stop the flood! Oddly enough, he didn't want to wake up; he wanted to see the dream through to the bitter end.

All the memories of his life before the accident came roaring in, some good, some bad, but all equally soothing. To know everything, as it filled the nothing, felt refreshing. That is until he looked down at himself and found that he too was wearing a black robe.

As he stared at the faces before him, Billy wondered that if he were to awake, right now, would he still remember, that he remembers. Everything. *Only one way to find out,* he thought. *I'll just wake up. Wake up! Wake up! Wake up!* His dream went black and he opened his eyes.

Billy woke from one dream into what he thought was another.

He found himself bound to the bed with rope, from the neck to his toes. He could sense someone standing over him in the darkness, but he couldn't see who it was; his eyes were still adjusting. His arms, pinned to his sides, he tried to wiggle his way loose. Not in a panic, but calm and deliberate, only to hurt his gut in the process. The rope was too tight; it made him feel like a mummy on display.

"Don't waste your time trying to get loose," said the stranger. "It'll only get tighter."

Was it a stranger? Strangely enough that voice sounded familiar. Yes, he hadn't heard it in a long time, but still, it sounded familiar. It sounded like Ishmael Alastor: a.k.a. Sleaze.

Billy didn't remember the band. He hadn't seen Ish since the accident and hadn't remembered him or the band, until now.

Why would he be doing this, he wondered. Then he remembered the very night of the accident. That was the night he decided to get out of the family practice of witchcraft. The night he cast aside his right to be a warlock, and the night he renounced his pledge to Satan.

He took it all to be a joke, went along with the sacrificial killings of small animals, but when the guys in the band wanted to offer a human baby, that had been the last straw. They wanted to offer it as a thankful offering, one for the band's record deal. He told them he wanted out of the deal as they were riding to get the baby. They knew where they needed to go; only they never made it, because five minutes after saying he wanted out, the accident happened.

Trying to turn his head, he wanted to get a better look at the person standing beside him in the dark. It was useless; he couldn't turn it far enough.

Then he remembered the night he was shot while on stakeout, the killer... Now he understood why the killer's eyes nudged his subconscious. It was Ish; Ish was the Motel-4 Madman.

Billy knew why he was bound to the bed. Knew also that this wasn't a dream; as much as he wanted to believe that it was, this wasn't a dream. *He's here for some unfinished business,* he thought. Knowing full well that it might be a mistake to speak, but hoping he might be able to talk himself out of the mess he was in, he said, "Hey Sleaze. What the hell you doing?"

"You remember me?" said Ish.

Billy thought he sounded surprised; hell, it was a surprise to him as well. "How could I forget one of my best pals?" He hoped he sounded convincing, "We were tight."

"Were is the word," said Ish, his voice sounding edgy. "That was a long time ago, in a different world... Now if you'll excuse me." He left the room, leaving Billy to squirm under the rope, still trying to set himself free. A sharp pain shot through his chest from the struggle. He relaxed and tried to remain calm, but it was getting harder to do by the minute.

A moment later, Ish was back with something in his hands.

Billy strained to see, and could make a guess at what it was; it looked like a mop handle. *What the fuck's he gonna do with that?* He thought. Things were beginning to get out of hand. First, he finds his memory—which you would think was a good thing, but it turns out he's wishing he could forget again. Forget it all for good. His memories put a light on the truth. The truth was something he didn't want to acknowledge; it was just too damn heavy to handle.

Remembering his pact with the devil was the worst memory of all; it momentarily washed out the memories he'd made since the accident, filling his head with the stench of burning ants. That was their first offering to Satan. They managed to catch a large mayonnaise jarful of black carpenter ants, doused them with lighter fluid, and then set them ablaze. Now the memory of that smell stuck to the back of his ever-drying throat.

In the darkness Billy could hear Ish whispering. The words were spoken over and over again, and he understood them all too well. They were words he chanted himself, words that demanded blood.

"Day lay, too pa."

At first it was just one single voice, but as Ish continued to chant, another voice started whispering them too. Two voices chanting? No, couldn't be. There were only two people in the room. *Him and me,* he thought.

The rush of old memories were playing with his head; that's what it had to be, but then the two voices turned into three. Three distinct and different voices, all whispering the same words. "Day lay, too pa..." No, not three, four. Four voices.

Billy tried to look around, hoping to see who was in the room, but there was only one person, Ish. He was standing by the window at the foot of the bed, staring out at the darkening skies.

A quick flash of lightning announced the coming storm. One... two... three, Billy counted in his head. Thunder rumbled as he reached four, making it official; a storm was on the way.

The whispering continued.

Billy tried to ignore it, tried singing out loud just to drown out the droning, but it didn't work. Ish only got louder, but it wasn't only Ish chanting. The other voices were those of Todd Striker, Joey Boil and Tony Sharpton. Hearing their voices brought on even more memories.

This can't be, he thought to himself. They're supposed to be dead, killed in the accident. That's what Mitch told him when he came out of his coma. Memories of the accident played out in his mind. Ish was holding on to the steering wheel like a man on a mission; then the train tracks, the train; the crash, the flash. Billy's mind raced with so many thoughts, it became difficult to remain in the 'here and now.' Panic set in, as he again struggled to get loose from the rope; it tightened even more.

All at once the chanting stopped. Billy kept his gaze fixed on Ish, watching him stare out the window.

Lightning flashed. For a split second, Billy swore he saw four people standing there instead of one. With each flicker of light, he could see four people standing by the window, but when the flash fizzled, there was only Ish.

"What?" Ish shouted.

Todd's face held that same annoying grin. "We've got another job for you, Sleaze. When the storm's at its peak, you know what to do." Ish didn't hesitate to protest, "But... What about him?" He pointed at Billy with rage in his eyes.

Billy tried to stay focused, tried to think of a way out, but it wasn't easy, being forced to listen to Ish as he talked to himself. "Who you talking to, Ish?"

"Never you mind!"

More lightning, faster this time, nature's psychedelic strobe light, and Billy sees four silhouettes; then one, four; then one. Thunder rolled as the rain began to fall. It ticked at the window glass and Billy could picture someone out there, someone with long fingernails tapping. **Tap! Tap! Tap!**

"Don't worry about him," said Tony.

"Yeah," chimed Joey, "we'll look after him while you're gone."

Ish glared at Billy and reluctantly caved, "Fine," he grumbled, "but don't do anything while I'm gone." He turned to the window, looking out at the storm, waiting for his moment of departure.

Billy wrestled under the ropes to no avail. Suddenly a flash of lightning so bright made him stop and stare at Ish. The damn thing must have struck just outside the window, yet Ish never flinched.

Thunder rocked the building, and the mop handle fell to the floor, as moments later, Ish was gone.

Billy never would have believed it if he didn't see it with his own eyes. One minute Ish was standing by the window, and the next he was gone. Puff... like a ghost; he just vanished.

The rain continued its endless tapping at the glass, wearing on Billy's last nerve.

As the lightning flickered, he could see three silhouettes popping in and out, in and out. *Is that Todd, Joey and Tony,* he wondered. No, of course not. It couldn't be, because there's no such thing as ghosts... *Right?*

23

Something wasn't right. Mitch could feel it in his bones. The impression didn't hit him all at once. It was building all night long. First, his call to Darla wasn't nearly as long a conversation as he would have liked; the damn static made it impossible. It was cut short before he had a chance to ask her out for dinner. Then, the storm came.

After hanging up, he felt even more miserable than before. When the storm hit, it rained on his parade. He planned on falling asleep by the fire, knowing full well that sleeping there might bring on aches and pains, but he didn't care, he loved sitting by the fire. He was enjoying himself, thinking about his hopes of winning Darla back, when the storm came out of nowhere, fierce as hell.

It sent him crawling back into the tent.

Mitch couldn't remember the last time he had seen a tempest so ugly. It brought back memories of his childhood, back when he was afraid of lightning; back to a time when he would run to his parents' bedroom, hoping he could sleep between them. His mother would always say yes, while his father would say no. "Be a man!" he would shout. "Get back in your room!" *Be a man?* That son-of-a-bitch wasn't man enough to finish out his life the natural way. During the storm—a storm that seemed to go on forever—he'd been scared. Just like when he was a kid. It seems some things never change. He thought he conquered it. Thought he'd never again be afraid of lightning, because he was a grown man. He found out otherwise. When the rain stopped, he finally fell asleep. Dreams, stacked in his head.

Now, his thoughts were loaded with trepidation.

Mitch tried to convince himself that it was because of the storm, that his dreams meant absolutely nothing, but for the life of him, he couldn't figure out why he felt the way he did. His dreams, after all, were harmless. What's so dreadful about a bunch of kids wailing on a piñata with a stick, or little boys playing stickball in the street? What the hell made him so uneasy over someone beating a dusty old rug with a mop handle? It had to have been leftover jitters from the storm.

Even while packing up in the morning he felt just a tad uneasy. Something was rotten in Denmark.

As he drove toward home, the feeling that started out so small steadily grew at an alarming rate. With each mile clocked off the odometer, it became stronger and stronger. *Something's gone down,* he thought. By the time he rounded the corner of his street, his fears were realized.

Two patrol cars, with lights flashing, were parked out in front of his apartment building. An ambulance was there too, and two men in white jackets were loading someone into the back. Mitch parked his car and ran toward the building, hoping the sick feeling in his stomach was only indigestion. A short, stocky officer was writing something down in a notepad when Mitch tapped him on the shoulder. "Excuse me."

The cop turned to face him; Mitch smiled when he saw his face. It was Bruce "the duke" Horn, a longtime friend on the force. Mitch could always count on him when he needed help on a case.

"Mitch, where the hell you been?" The look on his face was enough to tell Mitch that something was seriously wrong.

"What's happened?"

"Not good, buddy. It's Billy."

Mitch's heart jumped to his throat. He knew something didn't feel right the whole ride home. He should have known Billy was in trouble. "Where is he?" he asked, knowing all the while that Billy was already in the ambulance.

Bruce pointed in that direction and said, "He's in the wagon, man. I'm sorry, Mitch."

Those two words, *"I'm sorry,"* made it final. I'm sorry always meant bad news. *Sorry*, you've been turned down for a loan. *Sorry*, your dog died. *Sorry*, your brother is in the meat wagon. Tears began to well up in his eyes. Mitch tried to hold them back, tried his damnedest, but there wasn't enough will within him.

Damn, he thought to himself, *Damn! Damn! I should have left sooner; I should have known, damn it!* Mitch looked at his friend, not caring if he saw his tears, not caring about anything but finding the son-of-a-bitch that did it. "How?" he asked.

Suddenly the sun broke free of the clouds, casting a beam of light on his friend, as if God himself put a spotlight on him. Officer Horn's voice began to break as he explained, "Some prick tied him up in his bed and beat him to death with a mop handle." Seeing his friend with tears in his eyes made it hard for him to talk about it. "The bastard even left his makeshift weapon behind. He used Billy's blood on the handle, like a fucking fountain pen, and wrote a message on the wall."

A crowd started to gather, everyone trying to see what was happening, but Mitch saw no one else, thought of nothing else but getting up to his apartment.

Without saying another word, he ran up the steps, through the double doors, and up the five flights of steps to his apartment, pushing aside anybody who happened to be in his way. There were still a few cops in his apartment searching for prints, but Mitch paid them no mind. He went directly to the spare bedroom, and found another cop inside taking pictures of the crime scene.

The cot Billy slept on was a bloody mess. Blood seemed to paint the entire room. On the wall, beside the bed, were four words. Each blood-red letter dribbled down the length of the wall, making the words stand out even more.

Don't Fuck With Me!

The words reverberated inside Mitch's brain, as if the wall had shouted them into his ears. The flash from the policeman's camera only intensified the feeling. He wanted to scream in frustration but checked himself. No sense in making a scene. Hell, there was enough of it already, with cops, reporters and nosey bystanders. No sense in having a hysterical brother added to the mix.

He turned away, not wanting to see what he'd already seen, not wanting to believe in the horrible truth, and walked down to his own room.

A few of the officers tried to comfort him as he walked by, but he didn't acknowledge them at all. He just walked into his bedroom, slamming the door behind him. Slumping on the edge of his bed, he began to sob.

†   †   †

Ish was elated. He'd finished off two jobs in one night, yet another first.

The guys wanted him to do his job, so he had. He was proud of himself, filled with joy from his achievement. The job in Portland went off without a hitch, no problems whatsoever. But, it was the job he pulled on Billy that had been a mess. Not that that was a real problem; in fact, he kind of enjoyed it, more so than any other job he ever pulled.

165

Billy screamed like a bitch, but that was only until Ish cracked his skull open like a fresh watermelon. After that, just gurgling sounds, and even that didn't last long.

If any neighbor heard Billy scream, it was a mystery to Ish. He hadn't seen anyone looking out their door when he left. Before leaving though, he had to borrow some of Billy's clothes. He couldn't just walk out in a bloody Zorro suit. When he was ready to go, Ish grabbed a plastic bag, stuffed in his work clothes, then went about cleaning up any trace of being there. Then, last but not least, he took the mop handle, dipped it into Billy's blood and left a message before finally stuffing his black gloves into the plastic bag.

Now, as he lie on his bed freshly showered, he thought how nice it would be when his work was finally complete. Ish knew it would never be complete until Mitchell Blade was dead. He was the only one standing in front of his destiny, and he feverishly plotted ways of finishing him off. Once that was done, he could go on about his business without a care in the world.

When his excitement abated Ish fell into a deep sleep, a peaceful sleep. The kind of sleep he hadn't tasted in a long time. Nearly ten hours had passed before he finally woke up.

The first thing he did when he got out of bed was turn on the television. He flipped through the channels and stopped at *Headline News*. At the top of the hour, the first story was the one he was looking for: microphones from every conceivable radio and television station were jammed in front of Mitch Blade's face. He was standing in front of his apartment building, his eyes red and puffy. Obviously he'd been crying.

That made Ish smile.

He reached for the volume button on the TV and turned it down. He didn't want to disturb Mr. and Mrs. old fart; that meant being as quiet as possible. Otherwise, one or both would end up banging on his bedroom door. They came a knocking plenty of times already; each time being more irritating than the last, and always about the same shit. Turn down the TV! Letting the volume go any louder than thirteen on the dial always made them come hounding him. *Something needs to be done about them,* he thought. Yes, most definitely, and it would be, in due time.

A reporter from ABC asked, "Can you tell us what happened?" The camera panned on to Mitch's face, close enough to see the sweat seeping out of his facial pores.

Nerves got him wheeling. Good, Ish thought.

· "This morning my brother's body was removed from my apartment." He sounded numb. The words that came out of his mouth were just that, words. Numb, without feeling, "Someone's murdered him. The fucking coward tied him up and beat the life out of him with a blunt object."

Oops, too late, Ish thought. The television people must be having a field day. They weren't expecting that. Mitch droned on, "I don't know who is responsible, but I'll find out. I won't rest until I see that—*beeeeep*—scumbag put behind bars."

"Ahh, got that one!" Ish mumbled to himself and laughed.

Another reporter from CBS asked, "Does this have any connection with the Motel-4 Madman?" An NBC guy yelled, "Have you heard that he struck again last night in Portland?"

The first question was like a smack; Mitch's face turned to the right. The second question was a counter punch and Mitch's face turned to the left. For a moment he said nothing; he just stared at the camera as if it were a ghost.

Seconds ticked on. Finally he said, "I don't know. I honestly don't know."

Ish's smile grew even wider.

A moment later, Mitch's face was replaced with Lynne Russell's face, the anchor woman from *Headline News*. Her hair was different; Ish didn't like it. He snapped the TV off, not wanting to hear her little 'let's feel sorry for Mitch Blade' stink.

The thought of that story being shown every hour on the hour made Ish giggle. *Did you see the look on his face?* It was beautiful, just beautiful. Ish planned on watching it every chance he could. Time was on his side. Time was his friend.

■　　■　　■

Mitch was not a happy camper.

Dealing with his brother's death was bad enough, but having his mother find out about it through the news was worrisome. Mitch became concerned about the way she took the news. She never cried, at least not in front of him. He thought he'd at least see tears but there was nothing. It was like his brother was just someone she might say hello to on the streets, someone who meant nothing to her personally.

Mitch felt bad in so many ways.

He felt awful about his brother's passing, felt terrible for being angry with his mother. He felt bad about his failed marriage. The list went on and on. Through it all, he kept his chin up; took the situation thrown at him like a man. His only tears were shed on that first day. He had seen himself on the news, saw how horrible he looked, saw those red puffy eyes. When he saw that, he snapped himself out of his grief like a machine. From then on, he pulled his bootstraps up and marched with the beat of the drum.

He still found it hard to believe, even after three days, but reality slapped him in the face and he turned the other cheek. If Darla hadn't been around he most likely wouldn't have made it. He would have been lost, for good. It was as if he got his strength just by having her close to him.

Now, as he prepared himself for the funeral, he thought that if he had to face this alone, he would have been half tempted to jump in the grave with his brother. Jack was up to his old tricks again, but Mitch still managed a steady hand, still held fast to his sober ways.

Oh, he was tested, tested hard, but he got past them, somehow he managed to get past them all, and he knew he had Darla to thank. He took one last look at himself in the mirror, checking to see if his tie was straight.

It felt odd, sleeping in his old bedroom. The room still remained the same, as if time had stopped, and it made him feel old. He hadn't been back to his apartment since Billy's death, but he knew he wouldn't be able to avoid it much longer.

There came a tap at the bedroom door, and it slowly swung inward. His mother stood in the doorway, dressed in black. She looked at him and smiled. She said, "Darla's downstairs. She just got here."

Mitch straightened his tie once more and said, "I'll be right down, Ma, thanks."

The ride to the church was a composed one. As he drove, Mitch thought about the last time he had seen Billy alive. Billy said he thought he knew the killer, said there was something about his eyes. Had he known him? Was he the one who crushed Billy's skull? And if so, how did he manage to strike twice in one night, in two different cities?

The morning started out so nice weatherwise; the sun had been out, the birds singing, but now clouds were growing, getting bigger and blacker in a hurry. It was as if Mother Nature sensed a funeral and was now preparing herself for it.

The mass and burial were to take place at St. Patrick's Cathedral, where his father had been buried. Mitch had missed that funeral and was glad that he had. He didn't like funerals, not since he was six years old, when his parents dragged him to see his uncle laid out in a casket. He always liked Uncle Norton, but seeing him lying in that damn casket, his face white as a sheet, eyes and lips tight as a zipper, scared the living shit out of a little kid, and Mitch swore he would avoid going to another one if he could.

"Are you all right?" Darla asked. From the back seat his mother said, "Mitch, make the next left." He shook the memories of the past aside and made the left-hand turn. Up ahead, the church emerged.

Its wrought-iron gates were open wide.

Mitch felt a bit uneasy as he drove the car through the gates and followed the path around to the back of the church, where the parking lot was packed to the max. Beyond the parking lot, the tombstones of the dead lay scattered about. Some big, some small, and all reminders of a life lost.

The three of them walked from the car arm in arm, with Mitch's mother in the middle, Darla on her right and Mitch on her left. As they stepped into the church, the sky behind them opened. The first drops of rain began to fall as a teardrop fell from his mother's eye.

† † †

Time was more than a friend to Ish. Time was his everything. He knew where Mitch could be found, and he made it his number-one priority of the day to get there long before he did. He didn't have to wait long at all. Twenty minutes after he found a seat in the back of the church, Mitch came waltzing in with his mother and ex-wife.

Ish watched, as they walked down the aisle to the only remaining seats in the house. Mitch looked in his direction and for a brief moment their eyes meet; Ish's eyes widened with the exchange, feeling the thrill of being at his victim's last hurrah. He brazenly stared into a wounded man's eyes and felt to be the dominant one, the superior one. The fact that he was in the house of God didn't faze him. He had long since stopped believing the stories the preachers tried to jam down his throat; believing instead the lie of the great deceiver: God was jealous of Satan so he threw him out of heaven.

The mass seemed to go on forever, and Ish almost nodded off a few times, but each time, Todd would nudge him awake. "Wake up, Sleaze!" Ish opened his eyes to find the mass over and people filing out of the church, heading to the burial plot.

Nearly three hundred people gathered around the gapping hole in the ground. The mound of dirt on the side of the grave had two shovels sticking out of what was fast becoming a mudslide. As the rain danced off each black umbrella, a weird rhythm of drops began to tap out a beat, a beat to a song.

Ish stood among the other mourners, listening to the tune the rain played out; it was an obvious one. It was Billy's favorite. It was none other than Blue Öyster Cult's "Don't Fear The Reaper."

In his head, Ish sang along. *"LA... la... la... la... la."*

"Ashes to ashes... dust to dust."

Thunder overtook the preacher's words, making them difficult to hear, and the beat of the song began to grow stronger.

"LA... la... la... la... la." Ish started rocking his head from side to side as if he were in a concert. Soon, his whole body was moving to the beat of a song which he only heard.

"LA... la... la... la... la." Todd, Joey and Tony suddenly appeared beside him huddling under a giant red

umbrella. All three were pretending to cry. "Boo hoo," said Todd. "Let's all shed a tear. Boo hoooooo."

Off in the distance, lightning did its dance and thunder boomed even louder.

"Our Father, who art in heaven…" The preacher's voice came out in a whimper against the wind, as many of the mourners struggled to hold their only source of protection from the storm.

The casket was lowered into the soggy earth as the prayer continued, "Hallowed be thy name… "

Ish's head still bobbed with the beat. He smiled at Todd when he gave him a wink; then the three of them were gone.

"… Thy Kingdom come… "

Ish finally noticed the tall black man standing next to him. The man was staring at him hard. He was humongous, at least six foot three. His arms were twice the size of his own. His giant black hands held a small umbrella—one of those cheap things that come with the purchase of an even cheaper piece of luggage. It was comical to see. The man was pretty much soaked to the bone.

"… Thy will be done… "

Ish realized why the man was staring so hard and stopped bobbing his head. He quickly hunched his shoulders instead and began rubbing his arm, as if trying to keep warm.

"Cold out here," he said with a grin. "Wind and rain don't help either."

The black man continued to stare without saying a word. Finally, the guy turned his head and looked in the direction of the preacher before bowing his head in prayer.

"… on earth as it is in heaven… "

When is this going to end? In order to stay in the mood, he decided to immerse himself into the tune the rain still clipped, clapped and tapped out.

"LA... la... la... la... la. Don't fear the reaper. La... la... la... la... la."

"... but deliver us from evil... Amen." Deliver us from evil? Ish thought. He wanted to laugh, but coughed instead. *Hell, I'll deliver your ass, to evil, myself!* He turned to look at the black man, but the man was already gone, pushing his way up front so he could throw a flower on the casket.

He watched as one by one the crowd tossed flowers into the hole, with Mitch being the first. As they all began to disperse, Ish felt like he was watching a scattering of ants moving in every direction. When he was sure things were safe, he stepped up to the grave, pulled out the special flower hidden under his jacket and pitched it in.

"Bye Billy," he said with a smile, "see you in Hell!"

24

Mitch held his mother's arm as they walked back to the car. He tried to hold back his tears as he listened to her sob, "My poor boy... my poor, poor boy."

"It'll be o.k., Mom."

He wasn't sure if he believed that, wasn't sure about much of anything anymore. He kept thinking about what he thought he saw as he stood by the graveside.

As the priest was praying The Lord's Prayer, Mitch had glanced around, seeing who had shown up, and as he did, he noticed a big, red umbrella sticking out like a sore thumb in the midst of all the black ones. Then, in the matter of a blink of the eye—that's what it had been—a blink of an eye. That big, fat, red umbrella disappeared. Poof! Like smoke, it just vanished; nothing but black umbrellas.

"Here Mom, let me get that for you." Darla reached out and opened the car door, looking at Mitch with a look of concern; he was off in his own world.

She helped his mother into the backseat, making sure not to bang her head. Then she took her seat in the front, reached over and unlocked Mitch's door, and waited for him to get in. When she realized he was going to take his time, she closed her door.

Mitch leaned against the hood of the car and lit a cigarette, knowing the two of them would prefer him smoking outside. His thoughts were still on that red umbrella as he sucked on the cancer stick. The rain, still falling, was beginning to taper off. He closed his umbrella and allowed the mist to hit his face. It was cold against his skin.

Am I going nuts? He knew what he saw, yet he wasn't really sure after all.

He took one final drag from the smoke, dropped it on the ground, crushing it with the heel of his shoe. The gravel under his foot crunched, making him momentarily think of what the sound of Billy's head must've sounded like when the killer bashed it in. Mitch reached into his pockets one by one in search of his keys.

The passenger-side window went down and Darla stuck her hand out; the keys dangled from her fingers. "You gave them to me, remember?" He completely forgot. It was something he'd always done when they were married, and he'd done it again without even realizing it.

"Thanks," he said as she dropped them into his waiting hand. "Forgot..." He walked around the front of the car, pulled the door open and flopped into his seat. After closing the door, he sat without saying a word, and stared out the rain-streaked windshield.

Minutes ticked by.

"Are you all right?" Darla asked. The tone of her voice was so soft and sincere, it made him smile. "Yeah, I'll be fine," he said as he started the car and put it into drive. Pulling out of the parking space, he followed the path that wrapped around the west side of the church. On his right was open space with tombstones scattered in places seemingly as far as the eye could see. Rounding the crest of the hill, he could see his brother's newly dug grave. From this height he could see the casket inside with all the flowers on top. Someone was standing by the grave, someone wearing all black.

Mitch slammed on the brakes, put the car in park and immediately jumped out. He could see the guy pulling something out of his jacket, could see him dropping it into the hole. "Hey," Mitch shouted as he ran around the front of the vehicle. "Hey, you!" The man standing by the grave looked in Mitch's direction and waved.

"Hey you! Stay right there!"

Mitch started down the steep hill, his shoes slipping and sliding on the wet brown grass, struggling to keep his balance. He was determined not to fall, willed himself not to fall. He dodged back and forth, from side to side, trying to avoid being tripped up from the gravestones. He stopped long enough to see if the guy was still standing there; the man was already off and running. "Hey!!!!" Mitch shouted.

† † †

Ish ran like a banshee, his legs racing as fast as his heart. He jumped over a grave marker as if he were an elk, laughing as he ran. Running, jumping and dodging, he could hear the guys cheering him on as he ran, "Run Motherfucker run!"

He glanced over his shoulder and saw Mitch trip over a gravestone. As he ran toward the cover of the weeping spruce trees lining the perimeter of the church, Ish laughed. Like curtains on a stage, he parted the branches and stepped under the cover of the trees. Rainwater soaked his clothes, and he laughed again at the thought of Mitch's little spill.

Beer cans were at his feet; some rusted and crushed, others not. Broken condoms and empty cigarette packs outnumbered the leaves on the ground. Someone thought it funny to hang a rubber filled with something nasty from a branch. Two of the bars on the wrought-iron fence were bent apart, as if the Incredible Hulk had pulled them open. Ish slipped through the fence, first the right leg, bend and pull, and then the left. He stood with his back to the fence, staring at the woods in front of him. He wasn't concerned with Mitch, not after the fall he took.

A trail led deep into the darkness of the forest; it was the only choice he had, and he didn't particularly like it. He had parked his pickup truck at a Stop and Shop, a ten-minute walk east of the church. Ish thought he would be able to just slip away without being seen; now his plans of walking back to his truck was a wash. Going through the woods was going to be a major pain-in-the-ass; it meant a detour, turning a ten-minute walk into an hour or more.

Todd's ghost appeared at the edge of the forest, standing at the start of the trail. As if reading Ish's mind, he said, "It won't take that long if you jog, Sleaze."

Tony and Joey appeared at Todd's side and all three of them swung their left arm towards the path and shouted, "Run Motherfucker run!" As if a starting pistol had gone off, Ish broke off into a sprint. If he were to get away, it would take the run of his life.

■　　■　　■

Mitch took a deep breath, preparing himself for the remaining part of the hill. He watched as the man scampered back and forth, jumping over tombstones, looking like the crazy bastard that he was. Mitch's only thought was catching the prick. He braced himself, then took off down the hill.

He was almost to the bottom, about fifty yards to go, when he took his eyes off of what he was doing, wanting to see where the guy was running to, but that was a mistake; his right foot tripped over a small grave marker, and he tumbled and rolled the rest of the way down.

Luckily the gravestones were smaller in this section; otherwise, he could have hurt himself badly. His head did graze one of them, and it left a three-inch gash on his forehead. Blood seeped from the wound. But for the mud packed on it, it could've been bleeding a lot worse.

Mitch pulled himself up off the ground, his clothes soaking wet and caked with mud. His head wound throbbed with the beat of his heart. He tried to run but his left knee nearly gave out, and the pain shot straight to the cut on his head. He steadied himself, his hands on his hips, breathing heavily now; he watched as the man ran under some trees and was gone. Billy's grave yawned wider the closer he came; he hobbled along, like an old man, until he was standing over the hole.

Looking inside, he saw what the stranger had thrown. The bastard left a calling card of sorts. It was lying on top of all the white lilies.

You son of a bitch, Mitch thought. There was no doubt in his mind that that had been Billy's killer. The rose confirmed it. *Who else could it be? But was that the same guy Billy saw on the night he was staking out the Motel-4?* If so, how on earth was he able to kill both Billy and the victim in Portland, the same night, with less than a half-hour between two killings?

He stood there for the longest time just staring at the casket, debating whether he should continue with the chase. He thought about the call he made to the coroner's office in Portland. He'd asked them about the time of the victim's death, and they said the woman had been killed at about 2:30. Billy's last breath came at about 2:48 a.m.

It was impossible; it couldn't be the same man, but something told him otherwise. He felt the same feeling he had when he first became drawn to the case, that feeling of urgency.

He went with that feeling and took off in pursuit of the stranger, in spite of the pain it caused. By the time Mitch reached the tree line and went under the trees, the man he was pursuing was long gone. He had escaped through a hole in the fence. Mitch saw the path, considered giving chase, but decided against it. Darla and his mother would be worrying about him.

Reluctantly, he gave up the hunt and headed back to his car. At least he had something else to go on. Granted, it wasn't a whole hell of a lot, but it was something. He estimated the man to be about five feet, four inches tall, give or take a half inch, one hundred sixty pounds. The man was wearing a wool cap, but Mitch could have sworn he'd seen blond strands of hair hanging out. Mitch knew he'd need more than a vague description of the man; with what he had, he may as well put a third of the men in Seattle on his suspect list.

Finally reaching the car, he pulled the door open, reached inside and popped the trunk. "What's wrong?" Darla asked. "Who was that guy?" Mitch limped to the back of the car and said, "I think that was Billy's killer." He began to rummage through the trunk, pushing things aside—a blanket and some jumping cables—until he found the clean rags he was looking for. He pulled them out of a carryall bag and began to wipe the mud and grass off his clothes.

The passenger-side door slammed and within seconds Darla was standing by his side. His back was facing toward her; he was bent over wiping the mud from his pants leg.

"How do you know it was him?" she asked.

"Well," he said as he straightened himself and turned to face her, "you could say he left a calling card."

"Ouch!"

"What?"

"Your head," she said as she pulled a tissue out of her purse, "it's bleeding." She gently wiped at the gash.

"I'll live."

He could see his mother in the back seat; her head and shoulders were turned to face him. Her face: white and frightened; a tear lingering at the corner of her eye. Darla cleaned the wound as best she could without causing him any pain. "What kind of calling card?" she asked.

He grabbed her hand and held fast. "A rose," he said. "A black rose."

†   †   †

As it turned out, with the help of the guys showing him where to go, it didn't take as long as Ish thought it would. He made a left at the fork in the road, another left through a hidden path, all the while ignoring all the "No Trespassing" signs posted on every other tree.

It took him a total of forty minutes to make the run. The last thirty yards were the toughest, having to push through thick brush, but when he emerged from the woods, he found himself a block away from the Stop and Shop.

Ish brushed himself off, calmly walked the rest of the way, taking in deep breaths, exhaling slowly, and his heart finally began to settle to its normal beat. While he walked, he swung his umbrella in his right hand, the way a Keystone Cop might swing his nightstick. He thought about doing an imitation of Gene Kelly in *Singin' in the Rain* but it had stopped raining.

Damn, he wanted to dance!

He passed a few stores along the way: A comic book shop advertising "Only the best." An ice cream store offering 31 flavors. But the store that really caught his eye was the incense shop, with its huge 12 x 12 front window all painted black and the words "Hal's Incense Shop" sprawled like a signature in its center, under that were the words "Incense, Body Oils and Our Specialty: The Occult."

Should I or shouldn't I, he thought to himself. *Oh what the hell, it should be fun.*

As he opened the door and stepped inside, instead of the usual bell ringing you might normally hear, he set off a motion sensor that when crossed caused a recorded laughter to echo through the entire shop. "Wa... haa... haa... haa... haaaaaaaaaa... ."

Ish browsed the aisles, going down each and every-one. Every aisle lit up with yellow and red overhead lights; each shelf display laid out perfectly for all to see. Spices and herbs, body oils and creams of every flavor; every incense stick imaginable: strawberry, cherry, walnut and chestnut.

He felt like a kid in a candy store.

As he neared the end of the last aisle, he noticed a red neon arrow pointing to stairs that led down to the basement. Ish began his descent, counting all the way: *one, two and three.* The steps curved as he went, *four, five and six.* The lights became dimmer and dimmer; *seven, eight, and nine; ten.* He was in the basement.

The room's ceiling had a majority of red halogen bulbs for lighting, with an occasional dim white one here and there, leaving Ish with the feeling of being submerged in blood.

To his left, bookshelves were stacked with every book you could ever hope to find on the mystical and paranormal. He neared the shelf and began reading some of the titles: *Mysticism*, by Evelyn Underhill; *Revelation: The Birth of a New Age*, by David Spangler; *The Aquarian Conspiracy*, by Marilyn Ferguson. On his right were more shelves with books and games. He noticed the Ouija boards and quickly went over and pulled one off the shelf. *Cool*, he thought to himself.

From behind, a thin voice asked, "Can I help you?"

Ish turned and encountered a tall, bone-skinny white man, who couldn't have been older than twenty. In the murky red lighting, he looked as if he were a puppet on strings.

"Nah," said Ish. "I have what I need."

"I'll take that," said the puppet. His arm swung out, his hand reaching for the game. "The register's over here." His head bobbed to the left as he turned in that direction.

Ish let him have the board game and followed him around to the cash register. Watching the guy from behind, he thought, *Damn, this guy looks like a fucking puppet.* Ish could have sworn he heard the guy's feet clopping on the floor like blocks of wood.

Once behind the counter, Ish handed the man thirty dollars and waited for his change. That's when Todd popped in, standing right beside him. "Gonna make some serious contacts, Sleaze?" His sudden appearance made Ish jump with a start. "Damn! You scared the shit out of me!"

"I'm sorry," said the puppet as he handed Ish the change. "I tend to do that to people."

Ish glanced at Todd and then back to the puppet. "It's o.k. Just don't let it happen again." The sales clerk was about to put the game into a bag, Ish grabbed his arm and said, "That's all right. I don't need a bag." The guy's arm was rail-thin, and touching it felt like touching a wooden stick. It freaked him out.

He grabbed the game off the counter and headed back to the stairs. Todd walked beside him all the way. "You gonna make contact with somebody?" asked Todd as he followed him up the stairs. "Is that it? Huh?"

That's for me to know and you to find out, Ish thought. He'd been looking for a way out of his troubles, wanted to find one ever since he came home, but he wasn't about to let them know about his plans. The moment he saw the board game, his plan suddenly popped into his head: a plan that would show how he was to kill Mitch.

"So what do you say, Sleaze?" Todd followed him every step of the way but Ish never said a word. Returning to the first floor, the lighting momentarily made his eyes hurt. He walked down the center aisle, stomped across the motion sensor and opened the door.

"Wa... haa... haa... haa... haa... haaaaaaaaaa."

Stepping out into the sunshine, the sunlight hurt his eyes even more, bringing watery tears, which he wiped at as he hurried his steps. Todd still lingered beside him, keeping the same pace. "Who you thinking about contacting, Sleaze? We not good enough for you, is that it?"

Ish looked left and right, saw there wasn't any traffic, and bolted across the street towards the Stop and Shop's parking lot. There were only two other vehicles in the lot: a white Chevy Blazer and a silver Mercedes-Benz. The Mercedes was parked way too close to his truck and it pissed him off.

I'll fix your ass, he thought. He pulled his keys out of his pocket, dug them into the side of the car, and with one long swipe, left three stripes as long as the door. He laughed as he pulled his truck's door open and it smacked into the Mercedes. Now there was a dent in the center of the three scratches. "That'll learn ya," said Ish as he climbed into the truck, slamming the door.

Turning the ignition, the truck began its usual cough, and for a moment, Ish thought the damn thing wouldn't start. He jammed his foot on the gas and the piece of junk roared to life. He threw it into reverse, swung out of the parking space and was on the road before the owner of the Mercedes had a chance to see him.

As luck would have it, Todd had decided to leave him alone, at least for now anyway. Forty minutes later Ish was home.

■ ■ ■

What was I thinking? Mitch thought. *Why did I say anything at all?* He wished he could take back telling her, any of it. The look that came over Darla's face when he told her weighed heavy on his mind. Her eyes widened in concern, her mouth hung open in surprise. It was the kind of face that made him feel... what? Mitch wasn't sure; wasn't sure because it made him feel so many different things all at once. It must've been the way he said it; that's it. He did make it a bit dramatic. Thespian enough to cause her obvious worry; after all, a black rose? He could have left that part out. It was bad enough he told her that he thought the guy was Billy's killer.

Mitch pulled her into his arms and kissed her open mouth. She wrapped her arms around his neck, throwing herself against him, closer still, wanting to be held, tightly. She was frightened; he could feel it as he embraced her.

She still loved him. He could feel that too. Her response from his kiss made him feel like a teenager in love; it made him feel young again, alive again.

25

Ish had a scheme. He'd been working on it from the moment he settled into his cousin's old bedroom. Phase one was complete. The elimination of Billy. He was the only person that could finger him as the Motel-4 Madman. Phase two was now in the works, except it was proving to be a bit more difficult task.

Mitch's ex worked the rotating shift at the hospital, making it that much harder to kidnap her. He was never sure what shift she worked; that, plus the fact he had to work the kidnapping into his own schedule. Since moving in with the Browns, Ish found himself a job as a security guard, working the graveyard shift in a Storage Depot. The pay sucked, but the hours worked in well with the lie he told the *old goats*. He told them he had a job as a local radio host on one of the local AM stations; they actually believed it.

They even sat up at night, listening to a Lance Albright, an "Art Bell" imitator, with his ranting and raving about spaceships from other worlds, and every conspiracy theory imaginable.

Once, when Mr. Brown had asked why his voice sounded different on the radio than it did in person, Ish told him it was because his radio voice was a put-on, a show, something everyone could enjoy. He said his normal voice was too soft; he liked to harden it up some when he was on the air.

If there was one thing he liked about the Browns, it had to be their gullibility. They seemed more than willing to believe every word he said.

Maybe the guys had something to do with that, he thought, as he wrote his entry into the hourly check-in log.

5:45 a.m.; all entries secure. He scratched the letters, L.A., and began to circle the initials. Over and over, thinking about the many lies and lives he made for himself.

In another fifteen minutes he would be off duty. If he was lucky, Darla would still be at her job. This cat and mouse game had gone on for over a year and a half now; every time he showed up at the hospital, he either just missed her, or she wasn't on the schedule. It seemed no matter what time he showed up, she was never there. He was beginning to wonder if she even worked there at all.

He had asked about her a few times, each time, making sure never to ask the same person twice. The one thing he didn't want was having 'the hunted' knowing questions were being asked.

He was planning to go to the hospital as soon as he got off work. It wouldn't take long from here; hell, that was one of the reasons he liked this job: fifteen minutes tops and he could be on her like white on rice.

Ish closed the logbook and stared out the office window. The glow of headlights approached the front gate and he looked at his watch: ten minutes till six. *Right on time*, he thought, as he pushed the red button that opened the gate.

A black Dodge pulled up in front of the building and the headlights went out. Behind the wheel was a large, balding white man fumbling through the glove compartment, then grabbing his lunch off the passenger's seat. He opened the car door. It's Ruby Foster, the man otherwise known as the "on-time guy."

Ish watched as Ruby wobbled his way by the front window waving a cheery hello. He smiled and returned the wave, wondering how a man with a five-foot, ten-inch frame could hold three hundred and fifty pounds of unadulterated fat.

The office door swung open and in walked Ruby, his uniform straining to contain the flab underneath; his fat face smiling. "Morning, Lester," he said as he made his way to his locker on the far side of the room.

"Good morning, Ruby," said Ish with a grin, "Damn! You really are the 'on-time guy.'"

Ruby laughed as he fiddled with the lock. "I have to get up pretty early in the morning," he said as he pulled open the locker and dropped his lunch inside.

I'll bet you do, Ish thought.

"When you're as big as me, you tend to get around kind of slow." Ruby slammed the locker shut and without bothering to relock the lock, he turned and hobbled his way over to where Ish was sitting. He was clutching a book in his right hand.

"What's that you're reading?" said Ish.

Ruby placed the book on the desk. It was a Stephen King novel, a good one too: *Misery*.

"Sums up your life, huh Lester?" The fat man smiled.

Ish thought the man's head looked like a football; he wanted to laugh, but instead he said, "You don't know the half of it, Ruby." The fat man laughed even louder as he stood and allowed him to have a seat.

Ish glanced at his watch again: five till six. Smiling, he said, "Time to go... See you later, fat man." He could still hear Ruby laughing even after walking out the door.

■   ■   ■

Darla sat at the reception desk waiting patiently for her shift to end. She'd been rotating shifts since she started working at the hospital and was beginning to grow tired of the whole deal. The woman in Human Resources said it would only be a temporary thing. But it was going on longer than she expected now, and still, she had yet to be assigned a permanent shift. This being her last night on the 10 p.m. to 6 a.m., she was looking forward to having the next three days off.

She glanced at the clock and saw she still had a half hour to go. The night had been a slow one; she spent most of the time daydreaming about Mitch. She started seeing him again, regularly since Billy's funeral. At first she thought it was for Mitch's sake, but as time went on, she realized that she needed him now more than she ever did before. The time that they had spent apart gave her time to think. They were married for seven happy years, because for seven years she wanted what he wanted: a childless marriage.

Things were fine. Fine, that is, until she started talking about having children. That was about the time he started burying himself in his work, filling every minute of every day with anything and everything other than bringing forth offspring. Any mention of the word usually spawned an argument. And yet, being with him again still gave her the same feelings as before, feelings of security in his arms, of passion in his strength.

Her life after the divorce became a mess. She expected a few bumps in the road but never as many as there turned out to be. First, her parents announced their own divorce, making her feel as if it had been her fault, as if her divorce somehow set off a chain reaction, a domino effect, causing her own parents to split apart.

Then, she lost the only job she had since moving to the state of Washington. The bill collectors started calling, threatening to cut off her electric, her gas and her phone. Past-due bills began to pile up. Now that she thought about it, it had been a slow decline in her lifestyle. When they first split up, they sold the house and all that remained inside and split the money evenly, right down to the penny. She found a small apartment, which, in turn, made her feel pretty damn good.

Too bad it didn't last for long. Soon after, her parents split and suddenly someone had thrown a handful of shit at the fan. Splat! Everything became a mess. She nearly lost it all, but God must have been watching over her. She found a job at Northwest Hospital on the same day her landlord handed her an eviction notice. Darla made a deal, promising to get her rent paid up to date within four months. She made good on that promise.

Not long after making the deal with her landlord, she received a phone call from Mitch's mother. She had to admit being surprised to hear from the woman, thinking she wouldn't want anything to do with her since divorcing her son, but his mother had always been nice to her in the past. Darla always liked Beverly, always thought of her as a good person. She had called to tell her about Billy being in the hospital. Darla had promised her she'd make a visit, and that's when she ran into Mitch.

It's funny how everything clicks together, at just the right time and just the right place. When she saw him, he looked a bit ragged, but she still felt feelings for him. Even looking as bad as he had, as if the time they spent apart was meant to happen so they could experience the same feelings for one another once they were brought together again.

She had her doubts if things could be worked out between them, not sure if he felt the same way. The only way to find out was to give him her phone number, even though he could just as easily look it up in the phonebook.

When he finally did call, it was for all the wrong reasons. Reasons she didn't want to hear. Billy had been murdered, pummeled to death with a mop handle. She tried not to think about it, looking instead at the clock on the wall. It showed that she still had fifteen minutes to go.

She couldn't wait to get home, the only thing she wanted to do was to go home and shower and hit the sack.

She wanted to make sure to get enough sleep; after all, they had plans on going out again tonight.

Mitch was the one to suggest they start seeing each other again, and that made her happy. It confirmed the hope that she held in her heart to be true. He felt the same way about her as she for him; she only wished that getting back together with him had been under different circumstances.

It must be true what they say: God works in mysterious ways. Her thoughts were interrupted when the phone she was manning began to clang. Having been awhile since the last time it made a sound, it made her jump. She picked it up on the second ring.

"Northwest Hospital, can I help you?"

She could hear rustling on the other end of the line.

"Northwest Hospital, is anyone there?"

Finally, someone whispered. "Is this Darla?"

Darla's tired face became serious; her eyebrows scrunched up at the same time her forehead muscles crunched down as she strained to hear the person on the phone.

"I'm sorry… Can you speak up? I can't hear you."

Again, a whisper came, only louder this time, "Is this Darla?" *Why on earth is this person whispering,* she wondered. "Yes, this is Darla… Can I help you?"

Click…

The dial tone buzzed her eardrum like a pesky fly. She hung up the phone. *That was weird,* she thought. What was even stranger was the fact that all of a sudden, out of nowhere, the hospital erupted with life. Just a moment ago, before the phone rang, it had been so peaceful, so completely calm, but now there seemed to be people everywhere.

A young woman stood in front of the reception desk, waiting to speak with her. Down the hallway, just finishing up using the courtesy booth, was a man in a security guard uniform. Her eyes were drawn to him like a magnet on a refrigerator door, but she couldn't get a good look at him because his back was facing her and then there were doctors and nurses strolling past the front desk, obstructing her view.

Where did all these people come from? She looked at the clock and saw that it was twenty minutes past the hour. *Ten more minutes*, she thought. *Where the heck's my relief?*

† † †

"Is this Darla?" whispered Ish. He put his left hand over the mouthpiece and glanced over his shoulder. He could see Darla struggling to hear. Up until this point, she hadn't seen him, but it was becoming obvious to him that she might spot him at any second. He looked around, noticing how empty the place was and began to wonder if maybe this initiative of his was a mistake.

"I'm sorry… Can you speak up? I can't hear you," said Darla.

Damn, Ish thought. *I wish there were a lot more people around.* He turned his head and snuggled closer to the phone. "Is this Darla?" he asked.

"Yes, this is Darla. Can I help you?"

Ish placed the phone back on its cradle. He wanted to turn around, wanted to see if she had seen him or not, wanted to more than anything, but something told him not to. He made his way to the exit instead and noticed that people suddenly seemed to be everywhere. Against his better judgment, he looked behind him as the electric doors swooshed open and saw Darla sitting at her desk, looking as confused as a cow going to the slaughterhouse.

She hadn't seen him. Not all of him anyway. He felt her eyes on his back when he walked toward the exit though. Now, as he walked out the door, he could see her glancing around with a look of confusion on her face, wondering to herself where all the people had come from. He wondered himself, as he walked to his truck, but that thought was put to rest after he climbed inside.

Todd appeared in the passenger seat. "Happy Birthday, Sleaze." Ish jumped like always whenever Todd decided to pop in. At least Tony and Joey were civil whenever they showed up, but not Todd. He knew Todd relished the fact that he could scare the piss out of him anytime he damn well pleased. "Must you always do that?" he asked.

That stupid grin was on Todd's face again. "Do what?"

"Scare the shit out of me, that's what!"

"Relax, man. It's your birthday!"

Ish had grabbed the steering wheel when Todd popped in and continued to hold on to it, squeezing it tightly in his hands. Slowly, he began to relax his fingers, wiggling them, until the blood started to circulate again, then he finally let it go.

He completely forgot. He was forty-three today. No wonder all those people suddenly appeared. He had made a wish. He wished for more people around, and sure enough, more people appeared. He made a birthday wish without realizing it.

Ish leaned back in his seat, the springs popping under his bottom as he moved, and forgot about Darla for the moment. His mind raced with more important things—things like time and how fast it goes: how one day you're eighteen without a care in the world, running with a band, being your own man, seeing the world from a whole new perspective. He couldn't believe that twenty-five years had passed. He didn't consider himself old, but he sure felt like it and looked it too.

He stared at himself in the rearview mirror and didn't like what he saw staring back. Wrinkles lined his forehead and eyes; his receding hairline seemed to be receding even further as he gazed at himself. He let his hair grow long in the back, hoping that would make up for what was lost in the front. A big age spot, on his left temple, with another one starting to form on his cheek. *Happy fucking birthday, my ass*, he thought, as he rubbed the larger of the two spots.

Todd said, "That's one good thing about being dead."

Ish turned and looked at him with an expression on his face that said, "How so?" Todd smiled and said, "I don't have to worry about getting old. My face is going to stay just as young as the day I died. You, on the other hand, have to watch yourself fall apart. I mean... look at you!"

Ish looked in the mirror again.

"Some people grow old gracefully, but you're starting to look older than you are. Can you imagine what you'll look like ten, fifteen years from now? Shit, man, you did us a favor when you wrecked that van, and whether you know it or not, you did Billy a big favor too. I mean, he's older looking than us now, but he won't get any older. Not like you, Sleaze. He looks better dead, than you do alive."

Todd laughed and it began to echo within the truck.

Ish rolled the window down, hoping that would somehow relieve his ears of the sound, but it only made it worse. The laughter pounded his ears. He wanted to put his hands to his head, make the laughter stop, but he didn't want Todd to know it was working on his last nerve, didn't want to give him the satisfaction.

With fits of laughter between each word, Todd said, "You... look... like... shit!"

Anger began to bubble up inside. Anger over the fact that he had forgotten his own birthday. *Wasn't that something that happened to old people? What was next— forgetting he left the kitchen stove burning?* Anger bubbled to rage. Rage, over the fact that Todd was right, he did look like shit.

Todd's laughter whipped his rage into hatred. Hatred aimed at life and all that it had to offer.

Again Ish sat up and grabbed the steering wheel, holding on to it like a madman, squeezing it tightly, as if he were strangling someone's neck. With hatred now in full bloom; the veins in his neck bulging, he squeezed and squeezed; he wanted to yell: *Shut up! Just shut the fuck up!* But when he turned to face Todd, he was gone.

Silence fell over him as the laughter came to a halt.

With the quiet came the calm; his heartbeat, which had been thumping in his chest like he'd ran to hell and back, began to settle down as the only sounds he now heard were passing cars, singing birds and a barking dog.

Ish closed his eyes, breathing in deeply, letting it out slowly. He started to feel like his old self again. He could take solace in the fact that, deep down, he knew that Todd secretly wished he had more years than he actually received, and that thought made Ish smile.

Two seconds after opening his eyes and looking in the direction of the hospital's entrance, Darla came waltzing out the door.

This is it, Ish thought, *time to catch me a fox.*

■   ■   ■

Her relief could not have come at a better time.

The woman standing in front of the desk seemed overly anxious, as if under the influence of speed or something. She babbled on and on about wanting to see her father, but Darla barely heard a word; her mind kept trying to comprehend what just happened. *How could people just pop into being? Where did they all come from?* These questions and more filled her head as she glanced back and forth from the clock on the wall to the woman's moving lips.

The whole experience began to make her feel jumpy. She nearly had a heart attack when Mrs. Jasper, her relief, put her hand on her shoulder, causing her to jump two inches off her chair.

"Sorry," said Mrs. Jasper with a smile. "Didn't mean to scare you."

Darla's face became white as a sheet.

"Are you feeling o.k.?"

"Yes... yes, I'm fine." It took her a few moments before she could stand up, her legs felt like rubber.

"Are you sure you're o.k.?" Mrs. Jasper's face looked concerned.

"I'm fine. Really."

Except, that was a lie. She wasn't fine (far from it); she had a gut feeling of impending doom. Darla managed to pull herself together long enough to grab her purse and to get out of her seat, but as she walked around the front of the desk, her legs nearly gave out on her and she had to take a seat next to an old couple. The man, obviously the older of the two, smiled, exposing his brown tobacco-stained teeth.

She closed her eyes, not wanting to look at this strange old man. She could hear him breathing heavily; worse yet, she could smell his rotten breath as it rolled across her nose. The stench was enough to send her to her feet and on her way again. Clutching her purse to her chest, she quickly headed to the exit.

Once outside, she found that the fresh air and sunshine were the cure she needed; both seemed to bring her
back to a state of normality.

She stood there for a moment with her eyes closed;
her face lifted as an offering to the sun, allowing its warmth
to sink deeply into her skin. Darla could smell the many
different types of flowers that were spread out along the
hospital's landscape: roses, lilacs and tulips. She could smell
the freshly cut grass, as well as hear the buzz of a nearby
weed wacker.

She opened her eyes and glanced in the direction of
the buzzing sound, just as the wind swirled her uniform up,
exposing her long, slender legs. The young man cutting the
grass apparently enjoyed the show. He'd been watching her
the moment she stepped out of the building and was struck
by her beauty. The wind only served as an answer to a silent
prayer.

Darla quickly patted her dress down, embarrassed,
but smiling.

The young man wore a khaki uniform, and on his
head he wore headphones to muffle the sound. He waved a
cheery hello; Darla in return waved back, watching as he did
an about-face and continued down the walkway, trimming
the edge. On his back, in red and white, he wore his
company's logo. It read: Levy's Landscaping Service. We
don't just trim the grass, we trim the cost!

She watched awhile longer as the young man continued on his way. As she was about to step off the curb and
onto the crosswalk, a patrol car pulled up, causing her to take
a step back. Behind the wheel was a familiar face. She had
seen it before but couldn't place it, but as the driver's
window buzzed down, and she saw the man smile, she
remembered him instantly.

"Sgt. Horne, good morning... you out and about on
patrol?" She had met him for the first time at Billy's funeral.

She recalled thinking at the time that he seemed to be the type of man who wasn't afraid to show his sensitive side.

"Good morning, Darla." For a second there she thought she saw a twinkle in his eye.

"Looks like it's going to be a real nice one today," said Darla. Before she could say another word, Officer Horne said, "Actually I'm going off duty. Mitch asked me to come pick you up."

That's strange, she thought, *why on earth would Mitch do something like that?* "Are you sure?"

"Yep. He more or less insisted... No, he downright demanded, said it's really important. So, here I am."

"What about my car?"

"Mitch says to just leave it be, says he'll come pick it up later."

This had to be serious. When Mitch got an idea in his head, nine times out of ten it was for a good reason and nothing could stop him from seeing that idea through. If she said no, Officer Horne would continue to insist. It would be better to just get in the car. She could get the whole story from Mitch later. "O.k., if I must."

Officer Horne chuckled and said, "You must. Come on around to the passenger's side. It's open."

She walked around the front of the patrol car, and was about to open the door when she happened to observe a red pickup truck parked in the far corner of the lot. There was no other car in the area, and she could see someone inside. It looked as if the person was banging on the steering wheel in frustration. The window buzzed down.

"Well?" said Officer Horne. "You coming?"

With her attention back on what she was doing, she saw she was still holding on to the door handle. "Oh, sorry about that."

She pulled the door open and slipped inside.

As the patrol car made its way around the parking lot and finally pulled out onto the main road, Darla glanced over her shoulder, and even from this distance, she could see the red truck and its passenger, still furiously beating on the steering wheel.

26

Mitch didn't want to take any chances. The dream he'd had the previous night seemed too damn real. In his dream he was running down a crowded city street, pushing people out of his way, running without a clue as to why or what was so urgent, but he felt as if he needed to reach Darla, reach her before someone or something else did. As he ran, he could see her head in the crowd. He pushed himself to run even harder, run as fast as he could, until he was right behind her. He reached for her shoulder, turning her around to face him. He was shocked to find not her face but a skull.

Maybe it was just jitters, but he wasn't taking any chances. Not this time. The last time he ignored his feelings or dreams, Billy paid for it with his life. When he woke up, the dream, still fresh in his mind, his first instinct told him to call 'The Duke.' He had to play phone tag to hunt him down, but he finally got in touch with him out on patrol.

Mitch tried to explain the reasoning for his demand without sounding unnerved, but it became difficult after Officer Horne started giving him a hard time about it.

He didn't know if it was that time of the month, or if he was just being a pain-in-the-ass, but Mitch didn't have time for games, not when it came to Darla. He finally managed to convince him to pick her up and take her to his mother's house. The Duke said he owed him one, owed him big-time, but Mitch didn't care. Absolutely nothing could have been more important. Sure, he had other important things going on in his life, but she was number one on his list.

There was still one thing Mitch had to face since coming back to his apartment: Reality. He'd been avoiding it ever since his brother's murder. Even though it might cause him pain, he had to go into the spare room. He walked down the hallway towards Billy's old room as if walking his last mile, heading for the electric chair. When he got to the door, he grabbed the doorknob, turned it ever so slowly, and then nudged it open.

The door began to open. Wider... wider... wider, until it thumped against the wall and stopped.

He saw the blood everywhere: on the bed, the walls and the floor and became furious. All this time, and nobody bothered to clean up? He stepped into the room to get a better look; as he did, the room became sparkling clean. There was no blood, no guts, just the smell of fresh paint. His anger began to cool, but the memory of that horrible scene wouldn't let it die entirely. That wouldn't happen until the killer was either caught or killed, one way or the other; and even that might not help.

Mitch began to search everywhere. He went through the closet, the dresser drawers. He didn't know what he was hunting for, but he was hoping, hoping that maybe he would find some kind of evidence the others may have missed, something that could help him find Billy's killer. In the end it turned out to be fruitless; he didn't find anything that would lead him in the right direction, or any direction for that matter.

He spent the rest of the morning going over notes at his desk, something he hadn't done in awhile. The case of the Motel-4 killer was stalled. His brother's killer was out there somewhere. The two cases weighed heavily on his mind; now, here he was, desperately trying to make some kind of sense of it all. He thought by going through his notes, he'd be able to find something he might have missed along the way, something that could shed some light, but it turned out to be wishful thinking.

Old Jack whispered in his ear, asking him to give in. There was just too much pressure. *Wouldn't a drink help the situation?*

Mitch ignored the thought as he thumbed through the pages of his notebook. He stopped when he reached the address section for the Motel-4's. Every location had a checkmark except Portland. That one was circled.

He snatched a pen out of an old coffee mug with the words: Don't mess with the Mitch! Tapping the page with the tip of the pen, *tap... tap,* he made a checkmark next to the Portland address.

He'd never seen a case like this before. Every single murder had taken place under mysterious circumstances: No sign of any break-ins. All the victims were found in locked rooms, with the exception of one. The victim found in Seattle.

Tap... tap... tap.

Murder weapons found, all untraceable steel swords without prints. No sign of any struggle. It's like they were taken in their sleep, never realizing the danger. But, do call girls stay the night? Maybe, if offered the right kind of money. Mitch tapped even faster. *Tap... tap... tap... tap...*

Are all the victims escorts? Were any off the streets? There were so many questions gone unanswered. It felt like he was dealing with a ghost. *Tap... tap... tap... tap... tap...* Every room was unoccupied, rooms where guests never registered at the front desk. And yet, somehow, bodies were found in them. Everything about this case was strange.

What am I dealing with, Mitch wondered. This was definitely one for the books. Every case he ever worked on always had some clue as to who the perpetrator was: some crack, some seam that led him in the right direction, but not this one. *Tap... tap... tap... tap... tap... tap...*

Mitch thought about the case that gave him the most exposure: the one that made him "a star" in the P.I. Business. He remembered the day a respected member of the community came knocking at his door. The man was known for his generosity, always donating either money or other resources for every endeavor the city of Seattle could hope for. He wanted Mitch to find the killer of his little girl. He wanted justice to be served. Mitch wondered why, out of all the private investigators in the city, he would choose him. He even asked the man and was startled by the man's answer.

He could still see the old man's face, with his fluffy gray eyebrows all bunched together, his face totally serious. "I had a dream about you, boy...," he said. "I dreamt I met you on the street and you brought me back to your place. You said you could help me."

When the old man said that, Mitch's jaw dropped because, as the man spoke, Mitch thought he had seen him before, and then, when he said what he said, Mitch remembered his own dream the night before. Sure enough, the man standing at his front door was the same man in his own dream.

Mitch took that case, and when he finally pulled in the killer, he became an overnight sensation. His business of catching the bad guys took off. Gone were the days of petty theft or any other small-time stuff. He became an instant celebrity who worked for celebrities.

But now, since taking on the Motel-4 case, a case he pursued on his own, without payment, it all became meaningless. If he'd done things differently, Billy might still be alive.

Old Jack whispered in his ear again, *"You're not all that, Mitch. Have a drink."* He tapped on the notebook even faster. *Tap... tap... tap... tap... tap... tap... tap.*

Jack is right, he thought, *can't even catch my own brother's killer.* He knew deep down, somehow, someway, the Motel-4 killer was also his brother's killer. Finding the connection was the difficult part, but find it, he must.

†   †   †

Watching her, even from this distance, made Ish's adrenaline flow. He'd been patient, and patience finally paid off. This was the moment of truth. He smiled as Darla's dress fluffed up with a puff of wind. How was he going to pull this off? So far, everything he had done had been off the top of his head, spur of the moment, or an instinct that panned out. Ish decided he would confront her face to face, confident that she would see things his way. He reached into the glove compartment and pulled out the .38 he kept inside a brown lunch bag.

His heartbeat momentarily stopped.

He had taken his eyes off her for only a few seconds, and in that short amount of time it took to pull out the gun, a patrol car had pulled up in front of her.

What the fuck is this, he thought. *Whatever it is, it can't be good.* As far as he was concerned, no good thing ever came from a cop. Maybe the cop knows her, maybe they're just doing the normal morning chitchat; he'll be moving along any second. Ish tried to convince himself, but he found it harder to come up with excuses for believing it, the longer the car sat there.

His mounting frustration started to make itself known; his eyes were squinting and twitching, as if his head might explode. He grabbed the steering wheel, squeezing it tight, and watched as Darla walked around the front of the patrol car.

This is it; she's leaving, right? No! She's... getting... in... the... fucking... CAR! No... No... No! This isn't supposed to happen! His mind reeled with a million thoughts as he watched her look over her shoulder, reaching for the door; she was looking right at him—he could feel her eyes. He started to growl under his breath, "No... No... No!"

His fist went on automatic, banging the wheel, not caring about the pain it caused his hand. The pain only served to make him bang harder. As he watched the patrol car pull off the hospital grounds, he could feel her looking at him, sensed her staring in his direction. So close, yet so far. A little voice in his head told him to follow her and he wanted to, but another voice told him he had some cleaning up to do. He obviously wasn't going to get Mitch Blade through his ex-wife; it was coming down to a one-on-one confrontation. No pussyfooting around anymore; it was painfully clear that the guys were holding out on him; they could have told him he was wasting his time.

Ish stopped banging the moment the car was gone. His hands throbbed with an ache he couldn't feel; his mind raced with questions. *How could I let her slip away? Why didn't I see it coming? Who's going to pay?*

He thought things were going his way, thought he knew what he was doing, but now he wasn't so sure. His plan seemed to be unraveling at the seams. He never bothered to make a backup plan, never even thought it necessary, certain that he couldn't fail. Now, sitting in his truck, stewing in his anger, he tried desperately to come up with an alternative course of action.

Ish began swimming in a mixture of emotions. His anger shifted to sadness. His hands still clung to the steering wheel, but now with his head hung low, his chin touching his torso, his chest heaved up and down with each sob. The tears rolled off his face, into his lap. Then, in an instant, he started laughing. Laughing, because he'd been such a stupid fool, he could almost hear the guys laughing as well. Except they weren't laughing with him, they were laughing at him. Hearing their laughter finally made him stop. He wondered where they were, and wondered why and how his plan could have been so bent out of shape. The more he considered it, the more he realized a change had been coming.

Ever since he bought that board game, that's about the time he felt the change. Sure, the guys still popped in on him, but it became less and less as time went on. Ish figured they trusted him to do what needed to be done; so, he never realized what was happening. The whole thing was like putting a frog into a pot of warm water and gently turning up the heat one degree at a time. The poor frog gets boiled alive without ever knowing it.

But Ish wasn't a frog and he certainly wasn't about to be boiled alive; and his plan, no matter how offbeat it may seem, wasn't going to be wasted. With or without their help, he was going to take care of business. His plan just needed minor adjustments.

He decided he needed to take a nice long drive, needed time to think. The drive would help him sort things out, and when he got home he would finally, actually, use that damn board game. With a smile on his face, he turned the ignition.

·   ·   ·

Mitch reached for the desk drawer and pulled it open. Each file folder was packed with various paperwork concerning the case jammed inside: news clippings or copies of news clippings from all the cities where the murders took place and several from different newspapers that carried the story. He pulled the thickest file out and slapped it on the desk. Flipping the file open, he reached for a cigarette in his breast pocket and lit it up. Smoke curled around his face as he began reading through the clippings for what must have been the millionth time. He had read and reread them so much; he could recite them as if they were verses from the Bible.

Or, at least he thought he could.

While he was crushing his cigarette out in the ash-tray, he came across something in one of the Kansas City newspapers. The manager of the motel had been quoted as saying he couldn't understand how anyone could have entered the room without a key, nor could he explain the phone call that was made inside the room or the victim herself. "It's a mystery to me!"

The manager's words etched themselves into Mitch's mind like the hateful words that had been painted in blood in Billy's bedroom. *It's a mystery to me—Don't fuck with me.* It was the mentioning of the phone call that caught his eye. Mitch didn't know why he never thought of it before, or how he could have missed the information, but it caught his attention now.

What are the odds that the killer used the phone? If he used it once, would he use it twice or maybe even a third time? Mitch smiled to himself. A crack had been found, but he needed to open it wider, had to dig deeper. He could do that by finding out who made that phone call. *That should be easy enough,* he thought. *All I have to do is make a call of my own.*

He reached for the receiver, intent on calling the Mo-tel-4 outside of Kansas City, when it started to ring. Mitch snatched it up and placed it to his ear, "Mitch Blade speaking." He grabbed the pencil, expecting the need to take notes and waited for the other person to say something. So far, he only heard a lot of rustling, as if the person was rubbing the receiver on his or her shirt.

"Hello... This is Mitch Blade. Can I help you?"

His mother's voice grumbled in his ear, "Mitch, it's your mother. Pick up the phone."

She was getting worse; that was painfully obvious. Ever since Billy's passing it had become a slow, steady decline. He tried his best to remain calm, "Mom, it's me, Mitch."

"Oh, I thought that damn machine picked up."

"No Mom, what's up?"

"That nice Officer Horne dropped Darla off." Her voice broke, as a sudden coughing fit came and went. "He asked me to tell you that he's on his way to pick you up."

"Thanks Mom."

"Son... "

"Yes."

"I love you."

"I love you too, Mom. I'll talk to you later." He hung up the phone and glanced at his watch. He had at least a good half-hour before The Duke showed up, plenty of time to do what he had to do. He picked the phone up again and dialed information. A voice came on the line, "What city please."

"Liberty, Missouri."

"What number please?"

"I need the number for the Motel-4."

"One moment... "

A few seconds later, a computer voice gave him the number. Still holding the pencil, he scratched out the number on the back of a Xerox copy of one of the news clippings, and hung up the phone. He picked it up a third time and dialed.

It rang once, twice, three times before a man's voice came on the line and said, "Motel-4, please hold... "

To his surprise, there was no music, only dead air. Mitch looked at his watch the moment he went on hold, and the next time he glanced at it, nearly ten minutes had passed.

"Jeez, ol' man." He grumbled to himself. Finally, the man who answered the phone came back on the line, "I'm sorry for keeping you on hold. How can I help you?"

"I'd like to speak with the manager, please."

"You're in luck. I'm the manager. What can I do for you?"

Mitch could tell by the sound of the man's voice that he was expecting to get an earful of complaints. "My name's Mitch Blade. I'm an investigator working on a murder case that happened at your motel several years back."

Now the man's voice sounded even more irritated, "Listen, I answered all those questions back then. I don't need this shit now. I'm really busy here."

Not wanting to upset the man any further, Mitch tried to be as polite as possible, "I just have one question. It won't take long, I promise."

His politeness paid off. "... All right. What's the question?"

"You were quoted as saying you couldn't explain the phone call that was made in the room where the murder took place. I was just wondering what you meant by that."

The manager's voice suddenly turned serious. "Phones, in rooms that are unoccupied, are usually shut off. It's so employees won't be able to make personal phone calls. Personal phone calls add up to a lot of money. You know what I mean?"

Mitch wanted to laugh, knowing full well how employers could be so cheap at times, but he checked himself and said, "Can you tell me where the phone call was made to?"

The manager coughed and said, "Hold on a sec."

Dead air filled his ear again. Mitch checked his watch and waited for the man to return. *This better not take another*

208

ten minutes, he thought. The Duke would be coming by any minute now.

In the hiss of dead air, a voice whispered his name. *"MMMM*Mitch.*"*

The hair on the back of his neck stood up as goose bumps rippled up and down his spine. Was he hearing things? Or was it just in his head? Mitch rubbed his arm, trying to shake the creeps. *"MMMM*Mitch.*"*

—*CLICK*— "Sorry about that. Yeah, the phone call was placed to an escort service." Mitch's mind was still in Freaksville. He hadn't realized the manager was back on the line. "Hello..." From outside Mitch's apartment window, a police siren gave two quick chirps. "Hello... "

The siren snapped him out of it. "Sorry... What did you say?"

"I said the phone call was placed to an escort service. Heavenly Bodies or some shit like that."

Mitch knew the name all too well. It was Heavenly Escort Service to be exact. One of the many escort services on the list from Kansas City. All the victims (with the exception of one) were escorts. From the street below came two more chirps. "Listen, I have to go. Thanks for your help, I really appreciate it."

"No problem...," said the manager, "... but next time try calling when it's not so busy around here."

"I'll do that," said Mitch, "... thanks again." He hung up the phone. *Try not to call when it's not so busy,* he thought to himself. *How the fuck am I supposed to know if it's busy there? Dickhead!* Again the police siren wailed. Mitch pulled himself out of his chair, went to the window and threw open the screen.

"I'll be down in a second, Duke. Hold your ass!"

The Duke flipped him the bird.

Pushing the screen shut, Mitch paused for a moment. *Who else but the killer could have made that call,* he wondered. *Nobody, absolutely nobody, and if he made one call, then one could lead to another and another; maybe even to someplace other than an escort service.* It didn't matter how the call was made, only the fact that the killer made it.

Mitch pushed away from the window and walked to the kitchen sink. He nudged the faucet handle and let the water flow. The cold liquid felt great as he splashed it on his face. It gave him his second wind, which is sad when you need a second wind at 7:43 in the morning.

He still had a lot of calls to make, still had a lot of work to do, but for now at least, it would have to be put on hold. Mitch thought of the voice he heard in the dead air, remembering it well. It was hard to forget something that sounded like a razorblade slicing paper.

Putting that thought aside, he suddenly became angry at himself. So far, every victim had some kind of ID of an escort service on them when they were found (the senator's daughter being the only exception). He was incensed because he couldn't believe he had never thought to get any information from the escort services, or the motels themselves with regard to outgoing and incoming calls. If he had done that, could a murder or two have been prevented? He had tracked down each victim's place of employment, but he never... *Stop it,* he told himself. There was nothing he could've done to prevent any of the murders. His job was to find the killer; that's all.

He turned the water off and reached for a towel. *Something good is going to come from this,* he thought as he wiped his face. *I just have to keep digging.* Five minutes later, Mitch hopped into the police cruiser, ready to pick up Darla's car at the hospital.

† † †

Ish thought he knew what he was doing, just like he thought he knew what he was doing when he introduced the band members to the practice of witchcraft.

That had blown up in his face too.

It was his little secret: one which he kept to himself since the age of twelve. When he became friends with Billy and the rest of the guys, he felt like they were his family, like he could trust them enough to tell them about his secret, and he did. Everybody thought it was cool; everybody but Billy that is. Ish should have known from the look in Billy's eyes when he mentioned the subject; he should have seen the trouble ahead, but he looked the other way, and now he was paying for that mistake.

Billy had been the weak link in the chain; he was the one that ruined it all.

Ish had the idea that he had paid his dues by putting Billy out of his misery, but that only made matters worse because of his brother Mitch. That son-of-a-bitch wouldn't give up. He felt it in his bones.

The miles clicked on the odometer, but Ish paid them no mind. His thoughts were on ending his pain. He had to stop the bleeding, and the only way he could do that would be to cut Mitch Blade down.

Up ahead, a sign read: Snoqualmie Falls. Ish made the turn and followed the signs until he reached the parking lot. Since it was still early, no one else was around. Ish pulled into a parking space and cut the truck's engine. *What better place is there to think?* He pulled himself out of the truck and followed the trail that led to the falls.

Although Mother Nature was at her finest, the sun shining brightly and the birds singing in the trees, Ish's mood was still sour. He had to find a way to deal with his problems. He kept his eyes on the trail as he walked. Stepping over rocks and tree stumps, avoiding holes. The climb was a grueling one, but one he knew he needed to endure. He walked until he found himself standing on an observation platform at the base of the waterfall.

With the wind blowing in the trees, and the water plunging into the Snoqualmie River, Ish thought of an easy way to end his problem; he could take the dive. Who would know? No one else is around. They'd probably find his body miles down the river, all bloated and decayed, months from now.

"You can't do what you're thinking, Sleaze."

Ish looked to his right and saw Joey leaning against the rail. Joey, the calm one; Joey, the cool one. It never seemed to bother him whenever Joey popped in; in fact, Ish always felt calm around Joey, even when he was still alive.

"You can't jump, man. You have too much work to do. Shit, man, even after Mitch is gone, you'll still have work that needs to be done."

Ish was surprised; he thought once Mitch was dead his days of killing would be done. He thought once he cleaned up his mess, he'd be free, to be. He looked like a little boy standing at a Lost and Found station. He scratched the top of his head and said, "What do you mean I still have work to do? I thought after Mitch, I'd be done... period!"

In an oh so calm, oh so cool voice, Joey said, "No, man. Shit, we got big plans for you, Sleaze. You start out working the Motel-4's; then you take the next step: Motel 6, Super 8. Hell, there's plenty of places you can do your stuff."

Ish's outer appearance was one of irritation, like the whole idea of continuing on after killing Mitch bothered him. But on the inside, where it counts, his heart was overjoyed. When he first began his journey of death, it was tough taking someone out, but he got used to it, got used to it awfully damn fast too.

"So, tell me how to off Mitch."

Joey pushed away from the railing and disappeared. When he reappeared, he was standing in front of his view of the falls. Ish could hardly see him at all. He was standing right there in front of him, but the falling water behind him showed him for what he truly was—a memory from the past.

Joey smiled and said, "You'll have to get that information from a higher source than me, Sleaze… Sorry." With those words spoken, Joey vanished completely.

Ish continued to watch the water as it tumbled over the falls. The wind blew strong enough to blow a mist of crystal cool pellets into the air; the breeze covering his face, bringing a smile to his lips. He thought about what Joey had said, about taking it to a higher source, and realized at that moment that the guys were not leaving him high and dry as he first thought, but instead were doing him a favor.

Everything he had at this point in his life had been provided to him by that higher source and Joey had reminded him of that fact. The guys were more or less his personal cheering section. At the moment though, Mother Nature was his cheering section. The sights, the sounds, all mingled together to fill Ish with a deep sense of satisfaction.

He didn't mess up anything. He was doing what needed to be done, and now he had to get it done. He took one last deep breath, filling his lungs with the fresh nature-kissed air, then did an about-face, and headed back down the path.

It was easier going down, a lot easier. When he made his way up the path, the weight of the world seemed to be on his shoulders, but now that weight had been lifted, and it gave him an extra bounce in his step.

He was wrong in not trusting the guys, wrong in wanting them to leave him alone. Joey had given him the green light on taking the matter to a higher source. The guys must have known all along of his plans. There was no need to try and hide it anymore.

Ish felt like a new man.

As he walked back the way he came, he took in all that nature had to offer, enjoying the outdoor life, the birds singing, the rustling of leaves in the breeze, and insects on the prowl. He spotted a hare running through the brush, but it was gone in a flash, down into its tiny hole. His five senses were powered to the max. His sixth sense told him that Mitch was on the move. He didn't know where, but he knew he was moving; he could feel it.

The walk made him so energized; by the time he got back to his truck he was ready to roll. The drive home shouldn't take long. He started the truck and pulled out of the parking lot and headed for the main road. His thoughts of an easy commute quickly evaporated when he saw the traffic up ahead. Brake lights appeared to go on for miles, and that's what it turned out to be, almost twelve miles to be exact.

Let me guess, he thought. *Someone's been killed and everybody's rubbernecking.* He smiled, pleased that the world had become so morbid. By the time he got to the scene of the accident, the bodies were gone; only the wreckage of a Toyota and a semi were left behind, along with several people still scrambling to remove the mess.

Off to the side, two patrol cars sat with their lights flashing in the morning light. A cop sat behind the wheel of one of them, smoking a cigar, while the other cop stood beside the car chatting with him, his hands waving this way and that as he spoke.

Some asshole late for work, Ish thought. *The stupid prick was probably late for a meeting, or better yet, he was trying to get in early so he could get a quick fuck in with the secretary. Not today, Loser!*

After making his way through the carnage, traffic opened up and Ish pushed the gas pedal to the floor. The truck coughed but quickly got up to speed. Before he knew it, he was doing sixty miles an hour. He hung his left arm out the window, allowing the wind to push his hand back, while it blew his hair everywhere. He didn't care. He felt free on an open road. The traffic around him blew past on his left and right. *Man,* he thought, *I'm doing sixty.* Everybody else had to be doing at least eighty. *You'd think they'd learn something, after seeing that mess back there. Stupid Fucks!*

The rest of the ride home was uneventful, no wrecks, no one stranded on the side of the road, just a nice leisurely drive that settled his mind. Ish felt relaxed: calm, cool and collected. He knew what he had to do; it was plain and simple. He had to get home and make contact. That was his number-one priority. He would find out number two and three and four, once he made contact.

By half-past eleven he pulled his truck into the driveway. The Browns were out and about doing gardening of course; Mr. Brown was busy chopping away at some holly bushes with hedge trimmers around front, while Mrs. Brown helped bag the cuttings into a leaf bag. Ish hoped he wouldn't run into them, but he thought of the bright side. At least they would be outside while he did his thing in his room. The one thing he didn't want was to be disturbed.

Like clockwork, Ish put on his best face with a smile from ear to ear, and hopped out of the truck. Mrs. Brown was the first to speak as she dumped brush into the bag, "Good morning, Mr. Albright."

Ish laughed and said, "Good morning, Mrs. Brown... How many times have I told you to call me Lance?" He kept his smile, but held back another laugh. She looked so comical in the gray dress she wore. It looked as if it had been made in the 1800s. The red apron she wore over it only made it stand out even more.

"I'll call you Lance when you start calling me Dottie." She clapped her hands together, and then pulled off her gardening gloves. Wiping the sweat from her brow with her left hand, she said, "Ain't you getting in kind of late?"

215

Here we go again, Ish thought. *Mrs. Humpback Midget wants to know my business.* He continued smiling, hoping it didn't look as bogus as it felt, and said, "Oh, I had some business to take care of... I'm a busy kind of guy. You should know that by now, Dottie." He was pulling it off; his charm brought an even brighter smile to her lips.

"Indeed you are," she said, "indeed you are."

Mr. Brown suddenly stopped trimming the bushes and began to complain about the chore, "My arms are killing me, Dottie... When can we call it quits?" He stuck the hedge trimmers into the grass at his feet and started rubbing his arms.

The two of them together reminded Ish of that old picture with the farmer and his wife standing in front of the old homestead: the wife with that stupid look on her face, and the farmer holding the pitchfork, or was it the other way around? He couldn't remember.

"How you doing this morning, Lance?" said Mr. Brown. He stopped rubbing his arms and placed his hands on his hips. He truly looked like an old fool.

"Can't complain," said Ish, "besides... who wants to hear it?" He stepped toward the front door and politely said, "I got to get some sleep. I'll talk to you later."

Mr. Brown said, "I'll tell you all about the excitement when you wake up."

Ish stopped in his tracks. Excitement...? He turned, ever so slowly and said, "Excitement? What excitement?"

Mr. Brown saw his chance at escaping the gardening and took it. He hurried over to Ish's side. With a big smile on his face, he said, "There was a P.I. by the name of Blade that stopped by. You just missed him, by about a half hour."

27

What a difference a half hour can make. If traffic hadn't been a mess, he could have run into Mitch, could have walked in on him as he interviewed the Browns. How bizarre would that have been? Ish smiled, showing his pearly whites. He wrapped an arm around Mr. Brown's shoulder and led him toward the front door. "So, tell me all about it."

"Don't you be taking all day, Milton," said Mrs. Brown as she slipped her gardening gloves on. "We still have a lot of work to do out here." Mr. Brown glanced over his shoulder and blew her off with a wave of his hand. "I won't be long," he said, but the expression on his face said otherwise. "You can start without me."

The two men walked into the house, leaving the woman behind to do all the work. Mrs. Brown was not thrilled; being married to Milton for over thirty-five years, she knew all the tricks he used to get out of doing work. She pulled the hedge trimmers out of the ground and picked up where he left off.

Once inside, Ish and Milton each grabbed a cup of hot coffee before settling in the living room. Mr. Brown sat on the left end of the sofa while Ish sat on the right. Behind them, from the open window, a soft breeze filled the room with the scent of recently cut grass. They could hear the sound of the hedge trimmers as Mrs. Brown worked.

Clip... clip... clip... clip... clip...

"So," said Ish, "tell me what happened."

Mr. Brown sat up, grabbed a coaster and put his coffee on the table. With his elbows on his knees, he said, "This guy comes knocking at the door... It must have been... oh, around ten o'clock. The old lady and I were having breakfast, and I'm thinking who's selling what?"

Ish watched as Milton's excitement continued to build. He even started rocking on his toes. Up... Down... Up, down. For a second there, Ish thought the old man had to go the bathroom. "So, I answer the door and there's this big guy standing in the doorway."

Milton, everybody's bigger than you, thought Ish.

Clip... clip... clip... clip... clip.

"And I'm thinking to myself, who the hell is this? Then he flips open his wallet and shows me his ID. Well, I didn't waste any time. No sir, I let him in." Mr. Brown grabbed his cup, blowing away the steam, and took a dainty sip. "Ahhhhh, that's good. So, anyway, he has the two of us sitting on this couch while he's sitting over on the loveseat, and he's asking us questions about a murder that took place in Liberty, Missouri, for God's sake. I'm thinking to myself, what the hell does it have to do with us and I ask him so, and he asked if this was 126 Maple Way, and I say yes... "

His patience (which was never one of Ish's strong suits) was beginning to wear thin. He didn't need all the fucking details. He just wanted the old man to get to the point.

"... So I'm thinking... I've seen this guy on television before, and I'm tempted to ask him for his John Hancock."

"Can we please get to the point, Milt?" said Ish as he finished his coffee and placed the cup on the table without a coaster. Mr. Brown picked it up, grabbed a coaster and sat it back down again. "Don't need to hear any complaints from her," he said as he nodded toward the window.

Clip... clip... clip... clip... clip.

"He said a phone call was placed to this address, then he gave us the number... well, I said that's not our number and he starts asking about the people who lived in the house before we moved in." Milton paused long enough to take another sip of his coffee and then continued, "I tell him only what I could tell him, you know... about them having to put the man's sister in a special hospital; her being nuts and all. Mind if I smoke my pipe?" he asked, then began fishing around in his breast pocket for his tobacco.

Ish was getting sick of looking at the old man's stupid smile, with that stupid gold tooth, that fake-ass gold tooth. "Come on, Milt. You got me on pins and needles here, smoke that shit later."

Mr. Brown put his cup back on the table, taking his sweet time. With his hands cradling his chin, and his elbows back on his knees again, he smiled, even wider this time and Ish wanted to smack him in the face.

"So anyway... he asked if we're living here alone and I say no. I tell him how we're renting a room to an almost famous radio talk-show personality. That's not a slam against you, Lance; it's just that not many people are up between the hours of 1 a.m. and 4, so not many people know who you are."

Suddenly Ish's stomach felt as if he just swallowed a rock. He watched the old man rocking on his toes, smiling that smile with that fucking gold tooth. This could mean nothing but trouble. Panic tugged at the hair on the back of his neck. *Trouble... Trouble... Trouble.* Ish waved his hands and said, "And?"

The old man's mind must have been on his pipe and tobacco. After painful seconds, he said, "Oh... he was pretty much finished by then, he said 'thank you very much' and I showed him the door. Like I said, you just missed him by about a half hour."

■   ■   ■

Mitch's luck could not have been any better. He was expecting Darla's car to give him a hard time starting because that's all she complained about, but it started with no trouble at all. In fact, his luck increased as the day wore on. He got a call on his cell phone from a friend at the phone company. She owed him a favor and he'd called her on it. It's always nice to know someone who works in high places, or at least semi-high places.

Maryann Rawlins was an old flame since before his Army days. Mitch started dating her in his junior year of high school. Everyone told him that she was a floozy but he wouldn't listen. He went out with her for about three months before finding out the stories about her were true. He found out the hard way by walking in on her as she danced on another man's pole. When he heard she was working for the phone company, he remembered the time he covered for her when she needed an alibi. She'd been out drinking with her girlfriends and didn't get home till after midnight, and knowing that her parents liked Mitch, she wanted to use him as an excuse as to why she was out so late. They were already broken up by then, but since she came to his house before going home with her story, he figured he could help her out. If only to show her he held no hard feelings and that she didn't totally fuck up his life.

She never did get in trouble with her parents, and she told him she owed him one.

Mitch asked if she could backtrack phone calls made from each Motel-4. She told him it would take some time since the phone calls were placed so many years ago. That was a week ago today. So, when he got the phone call from Mary, well, his day just kept getting better. She told him things he already expected: a phone call was placed to every escort service, but she also told him something he wasn't expecting. The Motel-4 in Liberty, Missouri, had two outgoing calls from the crime scene. One to an escort service—naturally—but one went to a residence.

She gave him an address and he quickly wrote it down: 126 Maple Way, Duvall, Washington. There was something that made the address familiar, or maybe it was just his imagination running on overtime, but as he drove Darla's car to his mother's house, where she was waiting, he understood why it seemed so familiar in the first place. It was only a mile or so from his mom's home, almost a stone's throw away.

Being so close, Mitch decided to take Darla's car on an unexpected stop. He pulled into the driveway and admired the split-level ranch home with its quaint surroundings. The old couple who lived in the house seemed nice enough. Mitch had apologized for interrupting their breakfast; he smelled the bacon and eggs as soon as the door was opened. The old man said, "Nonsense... don't worry about it. If we can be of any help, then I say come on in."

Mitch couldn't help but notice the man's gold tooth glinting in his mouth; the man kept smiling and shaking his head like some kind of half-wit, making Mitch regret the fact that one day he too would be just as old, if he were so lucky. The old woman's politeness made Mitch a bit edgy too, or maybe it was the fact that he couldn't seem to keep his eyes off the hump on her back, which, he was sure, she noticed. Whatever the reason, both of them irked him to no end, and it seemed the longer he stayed, the more he wanted to bolt.

Now, as he pulled Darla's car into his mother's driveway, he thought of a question he should have asked the old couple: *When did their tenant start renting a room? No big deal,* he thought. *I'll just ask Mr. Albright myself.* Mitch cut the engine and opened the car door. It squealed as it swung open, screaming for oil.

He pulled his nearly six-foot frame out of the cramped space and slammed the door. "Piece of Pinto shit." He mumbled to himself. He couldn't believe that Darla actually liked that car. He remembered her saying, "It's cute." *Cute, my ass!*

Mitch followed the cobblestone walkway and climbed the three steps leading to the front porch. The wood creaked under his foot with each step. Reaching out to ring the bell, the door swung open as Darla greeted him with a warm smile on her face. The beige-colored dress she wore had every imaginable spring flower imprinted on it, and it stopped at her knees. Mitch liked what he saw. "Hey Foxy Lady...," he said with a grin, "... brought your car back."

He reached out and dangled the keys in front of her. When she went to grab them, he pulled back and said, "Where's my kiss?" She threw her arms around him and began kissing his face. First the left side, then the right. Left, right. Left, right. "So what's the emergency?" she asked.

She stopped kissing his face and stared into his eyes.

"Emergency... ?"

He completely forgot to come up with an excuse. He knew she'd be wondering why he had her picked up, planned on coming up with some kind of justification, but with his stop at the Browns, he forgot to come up with one.

"Yes... emergency. Duke told me you said it was urgent that he pick me up."

"First of all, it's 'The Duke,'" said Mitch, trying his best to stall for time, time to come up with a satisfying answer. "And second, I had to see you. Don't you know what today is? It's been a year and a half since we got back together." He hoped like hell he was right; he knew that it was close but wasn't quite sure of the day.

"Actually it's tomorrow, but it's nice to know you're thinking about it." She kissed his face again and again, knowing she had some news for him but wasn't sure if she'd ever find the time to tell him, news that could be taken for good or bad; she wasn't sure how he would take it. It seemed now was as good a time as any, so she said, "I've got something to tell you."

He held her in his arms, enjoying her kisses and her body as she pressed against him. His hands cupped her bottom and he gave it a gentle squeeze. "Is it something I'm going to like?" he asked.

I hope so, she thought as she gave him a quick kiss on the lips. She said, "Maybe..." She let her answer linger in the air and stared into his eyes.

"Well...," said Mitch, "what is it?"

Giving him three quick kisses on the lips, she said, "I'm pregnant."

† † †

Clip... clip... clip... clip... clip.

A lousy half hour, Ish thought. If he'd shown up while Mitch was still here, he could have killed three birds with one stone, could have cleaned up his mess while leaving a mess. He watched Mr. Brown rocking up and down on his toes, and wondered just how much the old man blabbed. "That's it?" he asked.

Mr. Brown grabbed his cup and finished his coffee. When he put it down again, he said, "Pretty much. He asked us some question about you, but we told him if he wanted to know more about you, other than you're renting a room, he'd have to ask you, personally."

Great! Ish thought. He could personally thank Mr. Brown for making his troubles even worse, and he would, soon. He would see to it that everyone saw his thanks, by writing it all over the walls with the old geezer's blood.

"So, what... ? He's coming by here again?" Ish's voice was sharp, too sharp. The look on Mr. Brown's face told him so.

The old man shook his head and said, "Well... he didn't say if he was coming back. I just assumed he would."

Don't you know when you assume something, you end up making an ass out of you, and me, Ish thought. He wanted to say it out loud—hell, he wanted to spell it out on a piece of paper, but he could see the old man was getting nervous and decided against it. Instead, he said, "Maybe I'll save the detective some trouble by going to see him myself, but not now; right now I think I'm going to hit the sack. I'm beat."

He started to pull himself out of his seat, eager to get to his room and make contact, when Mr. Brown put his hand on his shoulder and pushed him down again.

... Clip... clip... clip... clip... clip.

He touched me, Ish thought. *He mother-fucking touched me!* He wanted to grab the old man by the throat, wanted to choke the life out of him, but he kept his composure. "Is there something else?"

The old man's eyes looked like puppy dog eyes as he said, "You're not... sore at us? Are you? The last thing we want is to have a problem with our best tenant."

You mean, your only tenant, he thought. "Sore? Why would I be sore? Wouldn't be the first time I had people hounding me with questions. Guess it won't be the last either." Ish attempted to stand again and made it all the way this time, no touching.

He actually wanted the old man to lay a hand on him again, wanted the chance to grab and snap the geezer's finger. He stretched his arms out and made a lame yawn. "Oh man, I need me some Z's. I'll talk to you later, Milt." Before making it as far as the stairs, Mr. Brown said, "Lance... "

Without turning around, Ish said, "Yes... ?"

"I'll see to it that the Mrs. and I don't disturb your sleep."

"I'd appreciate that," he said, as he began to climb the five steps that led to the bedrooms. He counted them just as he did as a kid; some things never change.

When he got to his room, he closed the door behind him and leaned against it; *alone in my room at last,* he thought. He reached for the doorknob and turned the lock, knowing full well that if he didn't, the odds of having one of the geek-freaks walking in on him would only increase. It was safer this way.

Ish knelt beside the bed as if to pray. Then, he reached under the mattress and pulled out the bag that held the Ouija board. He tore the board out of the bag and stared at the crisp, shrink-wrapped box, and smiled. *Inside this box is the answer to my dilemma,* he thought.

With his index finger, he ran his long fingernail across the cellophane, splitting it open. He reached under and pulled it away from the box. The crinkling noise seemed unusually loud, but he liked the sound, a sound similar to a crackling fire. Still on his knees, he lifted the lid off the box and reverently pulled the game out. He tenderly laid it on the bed and ran his hands over the smooth simulated wood. With his right hand he touched the word NO; his left hand touched YES.

He gazed at the letters in the center of the board. Beginning with the letter A on the left, the letters arched and ended with M on the right; underneath them, another row of letters starting with the letter N and ending with Z. Under those were the numbers in a straight line: one through zero.

They claim it's a game, but it's no game. He knew firsthand. He had seen things, heard things, and it was all real, too fucking real. Ish remembered the first time as if it happened yesterday and began to think about the past. On a rainy night without a gig, everybody in the band decided they wanted some entertainment. They chose the Ouija board. They debated back and forth on whom to communicate with from the dead. They finally decided that they'd call back Billy's father. After all, that son-of-a-bitch committed suicide where they practiced their music. They wanted to know what the hell he was thinking. As if being in a cramped motel wasn't bad enough, the thunder and pounding rain outside made the room seem even smaller. Someone suggested they light candles. Ish wasn't thrilled about it, because he wanted to save them for more important things. To him, they were special candles, used only for ritual purposes, but the guys voted on it and he lost. Four of them surrounded the board, each with their fingers gently touching the pointer. Ish was elected to write down any message from the great beyond. He held his notepad and pen, waiting patiently. Time passed without a word. The thunder outside became intense. Finally, Todd said, "We wish to make contact. Will Mr. Blade, a Mr. Edward Blade please come forth." Minutes passed, minutes spent listening to the storm outside, while waiting for something to happen inside. Everyone's nerves were stretched thin. Ish was glad they didn't call his dad back from the dead. He didn't really remember his dad, only bad things, things he heard from his mother. From what she said about him, he sounded like somebody you wouldn't want to meet in a dark alley. Breaking the silence, Todd said, "Are you here?"

The pointer began to move. At first, the guys started to argue about which one was making it move. Ish didn't know about the others, but he knew he wasn't doing it. Slowly, the pointer made its way to the word YES.

"Wow!" said Joey.

"Shhhh...," said Todd. The dancing candle flames, along with the flashes of lightning, made the hair on the back of Ish's neck stand on edge. A coldness he never felt before filled the room. He could see everybody's breath, including his own. It made him feel as if they were sitting inside an igloo. When Ish mentioned it, it freaked out the others because they hadn't noticed until he mentioned something about it. "Oh man!" said Tony.

"Oh shit!" said Billy. They all felt the cold. They all knew the only possible answer of who made the pointer move. Even Billy, with his ho-hum attitude about the whole process, shivered.

"Will you speak to us?" said Todd. The pointer moved again, only faster this time. It moved away from the word YES and then back again. YES.

"Are you Mr. Edward Blade?" The pointer moved from YES and stopped at NO.

"Who are you?" Moving even faster now, the pointer spelled out a name. Ish wrote down every letter as fast as they came: S-A-M-U-E-L. The pointer stopped. "... Samuel who?" As Ish wrote down the letters, a shiver ran down his spine: A-L-A-S-T-O-R; so cold on a hot, muggy night; in a room without an air conditioner, so cold. Of all the dead fucks out there, his father had to be the one to answer the call. "Who the fuck is Samuel Alastor?" said Tony.

Todd turned to Ish and said, "Ain't that your old man, Sleaze?" The pointer went back to YES, and the others turned their heads and looked at Ish. He thought they were fucking with his head, thought the four of them had the whole thing planned. They swore up and down they weren't doing anything but keeping their fingers on the damn pointer. He still didn't believe them, not until he saw what he perceived to be the ghost of his dead father. He was standing in the far corner of the room, near the bathroom door. Ish pointed in that direction and the guys all looked in amazement. They had seen what he saw, and they too nearly shit a brick.

Ish didn't want to remember any more, didn't want to think about the rest of that night, but he couldn't help it; he remembered how his dad had followed him around, even after they were finished with the game. He asked the guys if they could still see his old man and they said no. His father told him things he didn't understand. Even to this day he couldn't for the life of him remember much of what was said. His mind at the time had been in a million places, trying desperately to shake the fact that his dead father lurked over his shoulder, even when he tried to sleep. The bastard stood by his bed, leering down at him. Before finally falling asleep, his dad said something that later would be confirmed using the board game—Day lay, too pa—the call for blood, human blood. As his memory of that night began to fade, the board game Ish knelt in front of came into focus.

What am I doing, he wondered. He hadn't practiced his belief since the days of the band, and now here he was, about to make contact with the one and only, Satan. He stared at the letters on the board, feeling a bit uneasy. He wondered if believers in God felt the same way after they've gone about doing whatever the hell they pleased, and then go crawling back on their knees the minute a problem comes along. A problem they themselves may have caused.

Could he pull this off, alone? Back then, they never had any luck calling back the people they wanted to talk to. It always ended up being someone different. Every time, no matter how many times, always someone they didn't know, someone who wanted to rant and rave about how unfair life was, about how they shouldn't be dead. That's the last thing he needed, opening up some kind of portal to the other side, a portal of complaints. *Nag, nag, nag...* Then the complaints would become pleas. *Please help me. Please. I shouldn't be dead! Help me! Please!*

He dreaded the thought of using the board game alone, but he decided that he would stay positive; think positive thoughts. He would do this alone, whether he liked it or not.

I can do this... it's a piece of cake. He pulled the bottom half of the box closer and reached inside for the pointer. Opening the plastic pouch, he slipped the pointer out. *No stopping now,* he thought. After all, he knew the guys were with him. Maybe not at this moment, but he knew. He never called on them; they always came to him. They made themselves known to him long ago and gave him his salvation.

With his hands on the pointer ever so lightly, he waited. He kept his eyes closed and his mind on one thing: Contact.

As the fear inside began to subside, his heartbeat slowed; his breathing eased. The sunshine that spilled through the open window became covered with clouds, white puffy clouds, steadily becoming dark ominous clouds. The rustling sound of leaves blew through the window, filling the room with a soft gentle breeze. He could feel the wind blowing through his hair, felt the coolness to his skin. Ish kept his eyes shut, not wanting to break his concentration.

The wind covered his words as he whispered, "Prince of Darkness come to me."

The day suddenly became night as black clouds filled the sky. The wind, blowing through the screen, brought with it voices: thousands of voices, millions of voices, all screaming. From the hallway, Ish could hear the grandfather clock chiming in the noon hour.

"Prince of Darkness... come to me."

He hardly touched the pointer but he could feel something happening, something weird. Electricity prickled at his fingertips. He still couldn't bring himself to open his eyes, not yet anyway, not until he made contact. The cool breeze became even colder, almost winterlike. The screaming voices weren't loud, just under the wind, all screaming his name. *Ishhhhhhhh!*

His eyes still closed, he could see flames flickering, getting brighter as the tingling sensation in his fingers grew. "Prince of Darkness... come to me."

The pointer began to move. He felt it jump off the board, felt it smack against his fingers. He had to open his eyes, had to see what he was feeling. When he opened them, he noticed how dark it had become, and saw a storm about to break. The wind blew stronger still, and the chill in the air brought on goose bumps; goose bumps everywhere.

"Are you here?" said Ish.

He watched with anticipation as the pointer began to slide to the left, could feel the energy running through his fingers. He wasn't touching it, yet it was moving; he knew for a fact that something else made it move, something or someone. The pointer stopped at YES.

Every nerve in his body was electrified; every fiber of his being tingled with a numbing effect. He thought it impossible; thought for sure he'd never actually contact Beelzebub, but the proof of that fact coursed through his veins like dry ice. His voice cracked as he asked, "Are you the Prince of Darkness?"

The pointer moved away from the word YES, then back again. YES.

Lightning flashed and the rain began to fall. Small drops at first, falling from the sky and exploding against the screen. Then, bigger drops still, falling faster, smashing against the screen as the wind howled and hurled the mist into his face while he knelt by the bed.

The voices were louder now. Tormented souls howling with the wind. Ish needed to end this as soon as possible and the only way to do that would be to just come out and ask the question, "How am I to kill Mitch Blade?"

He suddenly realized he asked a question that required more than a yes or no answer and hoped the answer came slowly. He watched as the pointer finally made its move. T-H-E, the pointer stopped. *Yeah,* he thought. It moved again, G-R-E... The pointer circled around and stopped at E again, then moved to N. *The green... what?*

230

Again the pointer moved: D-O-O-R-W-A-Y. It stopped. *Of course,* he thought. *The green doorway!* He didn't know why he never thought of it before; why he had to bother Satan for an answer he could just as easily thought up on his own. He could pop through the green doorway disguised as Zorro and knock Mitch off while he slept. Or better yet, he could catch him awake. That would freak Mitch out.

The pointer started its march again and he wondered why. He hadn't even asked a question. B-E and the pointer stopped. *Be what?* He wondered. Then, as if Lucifer had read his mind, the pointer moved and gave him an answer: Y-O-U-R-S-E-L-F. The pointer stopped.

.   .   .

Mitch thought his day started out great, thought it kept getting better with each passing minute, and it was, too, but all of a sudden he felt scared. "You're pregnant?" he asked.

His biggest fear was about to become a reality. When they were married, he remembered how he avoided the subject of having kids; remembered how just the thought brought on the case of the sweats. His fear of being a lousy father was the main reason the marriage failed the first time around, even though he denied that fact for the longest time.

Darla's eyes widened a little, "You sound disappointed."

He knew he should have kept his mouth shut, knew it would have been better to just grin and bare it, say nothing at all. He should have let her do all the talking, but no, he had to open his trap and stick his foot in it.

"It's not that," said Mitch as his right eyebrow quivered up and down with a nervous twitch. "It's just… "

Darla ran her hands through his hair and said, "It's just what?" Her face looked hopeful and worried at the same time. He couldn't think of a good enough bullshit line, so he decided to go with the truth.

He touched her cheek and said, "The thought of having a baby scares the hell out of me." His eyebrow stopped twitching. *That wasn't so bad,* he thought. He felt relieved, like a weight had been lifted.

Darla smiled, and for a second, the sun shined a little brighter. "What's my baby-kin's so scared of?"

Her fingers felt great in his hair, her smile brightened his soul. He smiled and said, "Of being a lousy father like my old man."

Pulling his head to her chest, she kissed the top of it and said, "You'll be the best dad that ever walked this earth." Mitch wasn't so sure of that, but he wanted to believe it, believe it with his whole heart. He said, "I love you." And gently kissed her on the lips. "Can you give me a ride to my place?"

Darla thought for sure that he would propose marriage, the look on his face made her believe it, but then he went and ruined it by asking if she could give him a ride home. *Oh well,* she thought. *Maybe he's not ready yet.*

The ride back to his apartment was a quiet one. Both of them wondered what the other was thinking; each worried about their future, a future that looked promising on the outside but fragile on the inside. She'd been hurt once before and didn't want it to happen again. She knew the line of work he did: catching the bad guys; she had lived dealing with the lifestyle of a P.I. before. His constant running around the subject of having a family had been the last straw back then, and she began to wish she never said a word about the baby, now.

If Mitch thought he was cramped behind the wheel, the passenger's seat was even worse. He had the seat as far back as it could go, and still he felt like a sardine in a can. He didn't dare say a word; afraid he might say the wrong thing. He could see her lost in her own thoughts, and thought it best to keep it that way. He couldn't think about a baby right now. He had put the hunt for the Motel-4 Madman off long enough. He needed to get home and finish this case. He was so close, he could almost taste victory. He needed to find out more about this guy Lance Albright, needed to meet him face to face.

The closer they got to his apartment, the darker the sky grew. "Looks like rain," he said with a weak smile. He knew he couldn't get into trouble by saying it, knew that those three words, other than I love you, would never and could never start any kind of an argument.

"Sure does," said Darla. She kept her eyes straight ahead, giving Mitch the feeling that maybe she was peeved.

So... he didn't say anything about the baby, so what? He had more important things to worry about. Not that a baby wasn't important—hell, that could be the most important thing, but not right now. Not until he actually held it in his arms. Until then, he would keep his thoughts and energy on finding a killer.

Darla wanted to ask him if he was happy about the baby, wanted to in the worst way, but she didn't want to put any unnecessary pressure on him. He had enough stress with his job. When they were a block away from his apartment, she said, "Will I see you tonight?" She had on her puppy-dog look and it made Mitch smile. "Of course, but do me a favor?" He reached over and stroked her hair. "After you drop me off... go back to my mom's house... o.k.?"

She knew he must have a good reason, knew he must be close to breaking his latest case. If he wanted her at his mother's, then she planned on doing just that. *No reason to rock the boat, right?* "Can I go back to my place and get a few things first?" She turned the corner and was glad to see that no other traffic was behind her. She stopped the car in the middle of the block, right next to Mitch's beat-up Oldsmobile.

"Don't dilly-dally. Get what needs getting and scoot over to my mom's." Mitch gave her a quick kiss and then jumped out of the car. He thumped on the roof twice and said, "Go on, get... I'll call you later." He watched her pull away, watching as she waved her hand out the window; then she rounded the corner and was gone.

The sky grew darker still, and he knew a heavy storm was on the prowl. Mitch grabbed his keys out of his pocket and ran up the front steps of his apartment building. He didn't even bother to try the elevator; instead, he ran up the stairs taking them two at a time. By the time he reached the fifth floor, his head throbbed and his lungs heaved. He knew now that since he was going to be a father, the cigarettes had to go. That, plus the fact that his body more or less demanded it. His youthful days were a thing of the past; he wasn't getting any younger.

The minute he stepped into his apartment, a feeling of doom and gloom dropped on him like a ton of bricks. He learned a long time ago, when he first moved into the place, that the apartment could sometimes give you that impression: Doom and Gloom. It all depended on the weather. If it was a nice bright sunny day, which is how the day started out, then the place could feel so cozy. But, when it got dark or if a storm came along, the place could become pretty damn depressing. Tack on a murder and it became a tomb.

Mitch hit the light switch and waited for some relief. He expected the damn thing to flicker and come on but nothing happened. *Electricity has to be out,* he thought; *must be a big-ass storm if it knocked out the power already.*

The last of the light from the outside finally made its way to his eyes as they adjusted to the darkness in the room.

From the living room, he could hear the cuckoo clock chirping. *Coo-coo, Coo-coo, Coo-coo...* He followed the sound and made his way into the room. *Coo-coo, Coo-coo, Coo-coo...* A cool breeze blew in from the open window, and he could smell rain in the air. *Coo-coo, Coo-coo, Coo-coo...*

Better close the window before it starts to pour, he thought. Mitch went to the window and tried to push it closed. He had to use every ounce of strength; the damn thing liked to stick. He pushed, pushed, and thump! It finally shut.

Coo... coo... Coo... coo... Coo... coo... He'd be damned if he let the coming storm get the best of him; there's no way that was going to happen, not when he felt so close to closing in on the mystery killer.

He began his search for illumination. First, he rummaged through all the desk drawers and came up with nothing. Then, over to the kitchen sink, where he hopelessly searched in vain. First one drawer, then the next, he pulled open the double doors under the sink and found nothing but the water pipes and a can of Ajax.

Mitch could see the light fading, could see the darkness beginning to suck up the room in slow motion. He thought it strange being so dark, when only an hour before, the sun had full reign. After going through the trouble of looking for a flashlight, he finally remembered he kept one hanging on a nail next to the cuckoo clock. He hoped it still worked; he hadn't used it in awhile. He clicked the switch and a beam of bright light swept through the darkness, parting it like the Red Sea. He felt like Luke Skywalker with his light saber, could hear the humming sound of his weapon as he sliced the darkness back and forth across the room.

Funny how the light can make one braver, he thought. Mitch took a seat behind his desk, placed the flashlight on its side atop the ashtray, and proceeded to go through more paperwork, determined to find something else he might have missed. The phone started to ring, jack-hammering his heart with excitement. *Damn,* he thought. He didn't expect that. The room had been so serene, so peaceful and then bam!

It rang again and he picked it up. "Mitch Blade speaking…"

Outside, thunder rumbled, shaking the entire building to its core. "Hello, this is Mitch Blade. Is anyone there?"

Now, it wasn't so tranquil anymore. The wind blew with a vengeance, rattling the windows in the process. Mitch grabbed the flashlight and swung it in the direction of the sound. "Hello… Damn it! Don't play games with me!"

He could hear something on the line, something or someone. The noise tickled the hair in his ear. He wanted to hang up, wanted to stop the 'it' out there on the other end of the line. *That's weird,* he thought. *Why does it feel like it's an 'it'; something not of this world… something dark.*

Why? Because it was something dark, something not of this world, some 'it.' Mitch thought of the Stephen King novel by the same name: *IT.* He was letting the darkness around him get the better of him, letting this clown on the phone rattle his nerves.

"Listen, you son-of-a-bitch. I could have this call traced. I can hear you, you fucking asshole!" He swung the beam of light in the direction of the hallway's entrance. He could have sworn he saw a dark shape standing there, rocking back and forth like an ape, but as soon as the light got there, the thing vanished. *The Thing,* Mitch thought to himself. A movie with the same name brought to the screen by John Carpenter's twisted mind. Mitch was beginning to wonder if maybe he read too many horror books, watched too many scary movies.

With the phone pressed to his ear, the hair inside his ear danced as three different voices came over the line, calling his name. "Mitch... Mitch... Mitch!" Like an echo it was, and then a fourth voice shouted, "Big Bro!"

Big Bro... ? Was that Billy? Billy was the only one who ever called him Big Bro.

A fifth voice said, "Prepare to die!"

"Who is this...?" He shouted. With the fingers of his left hand, he rapped against the top of the desk; he could see the hair on his knuckles standing at attention as the voice on the other end sent shivers down his spine.

"I'm Death, and I'm coming for you." —Click— After a moment of silence came the burp of the dial tone. Just as Mitch hung up the phone, his flashlight went dead.

28

Mr. Brown planned on going back outside to help his wife finish up the yard work, but he never made it. He thought it best to just catch a smoke while the getting was good. He sat at the kitchen table packing his pipe with his favorite menthol blend, looking forward to having a peaceful puff. His better half often complained, making him take it outside. *Why did he think of her as his better half if all she ever did was dish out grief?* She'd give him grief over the most trivial thing. God forbid if he kept the toilet seat up.

He flicked the lighter and touched the flame to the tobacco. The first puff felt great, hitting the back of his throat with a cool mint wave of blessed smoke.

He peeked out the window and could see clouds on the move. After his third puff, his glance became a stare as he watched in amazement at the coming storm. At first, he thought that maybe it had something to do with the tobacco, that perhaps it just made him dizzy, but when the sun happened to get blocked out, the darkness grew like a cancer; he knew tobacco had nothing to do with it. He also knew his smoke break was over, called on account of rain.

As much as he hated the thought, he lethargically pulled himself out of his chair, went to the sink and dumped the still smoldering tobacco down the drain. Grabbing a can of Lysol next to the dish rack, he began spraying around the room using small quick shots, knowing full well she was bound to smell the smoke. Seconds after putting the Lysol back in its proper place under the sink, Mrs. Brown walked into the kitchen through the side porch door. She needed to use both her hands closing it behind her, the wind outside had a mind of its own, pushing the door open, while she struggled to get it closed.

"Looks like rain's coming," she said as she pulled her gardening gloves off. "Coming fast too." Suddenly, she stopped in her tracks, her nose crinkled as she took two quick whiffs. "You've been smoking in here again, Milton. I can smell it."

So sue me, he thought, as he pulled the refrigerator door open. He didn't actually want anything in there, just wanted to make it look as if he did. "You got me again." His face held a stupid grin. "Can't hide nothing from you, can I?"

"How many times do I have to tell you not to smoke in the house?" She went to the sink, pulled the bottom drawer open where she kept her gardening supplies, and tossed the gloves inside. After sliding the drawer shut she said, "You know the smoke irritates my eyes."

"Sorry…," he said, as he closed the refrigerator door. "Won't happen again."

"Well, you just make sure that you don't."

Outside, the wind seemed to be singing… or was it screaming? She started toward the living room as soon as she saw the rain.

"Where are you going?" Milton asked.

"To tell Mr. Albright to close his bedroom window, it's starting to pour."

Milton suddenly felt a twinge of fear. He didn't know why, but the thought of his wife disturbing Mr. Albright sent shivers starting from his feet and rocketing to his head. He reached out and grabbed her arm before she could go any further.

"No! Don't trouble the man, he needs his rest; besides, I think he might already be pissed at us for talking to that detective."

"Nonsense," said Mrs. Brown. She tried to pull her arm out of her husband's grip without success. "Why would he be mad at us for that? What's he got to hide?"

"Just don't bother the man." He let her go, and watched as she walked into the living room. "Now where you going?" She looked at him with a hint of contempt and said, "To close our bedroom window. Is that o.k.?"

Before he could say another word, she was gone. He hoped like hell that she listened to him for once in her life, hoped she wouldn't insist on telling the man to close his window. It sure sounded to him like the man was livid, and if he is, her giving him shit about his freaking window might only make matters worse.

Milton entered the living room, clicked on the television, then flopped onto the couch. The springs creaked under his ass, but he didn't care; he'd paid for the damn thing, he could treat it anyway he pleased. He put his feet up onto the coffee table, knowing he'd hear shit about it, but he figured he was already yelled at once, so what was one more time? One more yap; one more howl. He'd gotten used to her nagging over the years—hell—it was more like becoming immune to it, because it used to bother him to no end. Now, it went in one ear and out the other.

As he considered the news, he began to feel sore from the little work he actually did in the yard. His arms and lower back throbbed. Not a deep thud, just a dull one, but a throb was a throb was a throb. By the time the sports segment came on, he completely forgot about the pulse and fell asleep.

Lightning lit up the sky. Thunder rumbled. Then the electricity went out, sending the sports news and the room into darkness.

† † †

Be yourself! Ish thought. He didn't particularly like the idea, not when he'd previously gotten used to the idea of doing it as Zorro. Every single job he ever did, he did as Zorro, even when he eliminated Billy. Sure, he didn't use his trusty sword, but he was wearing the outfit when he pulled it off, made a bit of a mess, yes, but still. Be yourself? He realized he hadn't lit any candles before getting started. The room was becoming darker with each passing second.

He felt the rain as it blew in through the open window. Could see the mist as it came at his face. In the mist he saw twisted faces, all screaming, rushing at him in 3-D. Then, the mist hit his face and he could feel the pain; the pain of every soul that came.

The pointer started to move again.

He thought he'd have a problem reading the message, but his eyes had quickly grown adjusted to the dreariness that now blanketed the room. I... M... the pointer stopped. *I M,* Ish thought, *what the hell is... I... M... ?* The pointer moved faster still, U... and stopped.

I M... U? I am you? Is that what you're trying to say? I am you? The pointer moved even faster, U, then a pause... R... another pause, and then... I.

I am you; you are I? I am you... you are... I?

He couldn't get the phrase out of his head.

I am you; you are I. I am you; you are I. He understood. He knew because he could feel it, could feel the difference somehow. He felt the pain of the collective, and the pain of the collective made him whole.

I am you; you are I.

He could do anything. The higher source he had sought had found *him* instead; it would make use of him and he would allow it, feeling honored to be considered a worthy vessel.

241

I am you; you are I.

Like a robot, Ish got off his knees, went to the other side of the bed and picked up the phone. There was no ring; he just instinctively knew he needed to pick it up. He listened without saying a word. At first, he heard static, but when he listened closer, he knew that the static was actually the haunting screams of the damned. Listening, he could hear Todd, Joey and Tony all screaming one name: Mitch… Like a domino effect… Mitch… One after the other… Mitch! Then a fourth voice screamed: "Big Bro!"

Was that Billy? Ish wondered. *Billy trying to warn his big brother?* Yes, of course it was, and that's when he knew that Mitch was on the other end of the line.

"Prepare to die," said Ish. He wanted to laugh, was going to laugh, but just then a knock came at his bedroom door. In one ear he could hear the old lady saying something about closing his window, and in the other he could hear Mitch shouting, "Who is this?"

Again the old hag knocked on the door.

"I'm Death," whispered Ish, "and I'm coming for you."

He hung up the phone, and again, the knock came. *This bitch is looking for trouble,* he thought. *If that's what she wants, then that's what she'll get.* Without bothering to give the board game a second look, he calmly walked around the bed, went to the door and opened it with a quick jerk, startling Mrs. Brown as she was about to knock for the fourth time.

"You bellowed?" he asked.

With a flashlight in her hand, Mrs. Brown smiled an awkward smile. "Sorry to trouble you, Mr. Albright. I just wanted you to close your window… it's raining."

You fucking cow, Ish thought to himself, as he opened the door wider. "I'm kind of busy now. Why don't you close it?"

"O.k.," said Mrs. Brown, as she stepped into the room. "It'll just take a second."

"Take your time... no hurry." Ish closed the door behind her, following her every move like a shadow.

"Getting dark all of a sudden. Damn weather can be so strange at times."

"Sure can," said Ish. He watched her close the window, watched her as she turned to face him.

"What's that?" she asked. Pointing the flashlight at the bed. Ish smiled when he saw what she was looking at. The board game's pointer was in the center of the game, standing straight up and spinning.

The old hag is mesmerized, Ish thought. "Oh that..." He snatched the brass clock off the top of the dresser and hid it behind his back. It felt heavy in his hand, like a gold bar. He stepped closer, and before her eyes could meet his, he swung his arm out and smashed the side of her head.

The blow was fierce, her blood splashed across his face before she fell to the floor with a thump. "... That's Death, telling me your time is up."

Ish smiled.

■   ■   ■

The room was completely dark and Mitch jumped in surprise. *Oh shit,* he thought. Not quite in a panic yet, he slapped the flashlight in the palm of his hand and the light came back on, but only half as bright. Since his files were scattered in front of him, he decided to take advantage of the light before it went completely out.

He didn't want to think about the phone call, didn't want to think about it because thinking about it would only make him jumpy, and he was jumpy enough already.

He noticed an odd pattern he hadn't realized before.

The name of every client that called in on the nights of all the murders had been that of a color: Mr. White, Mr. Green, Mr. Black, Mr. Red (spelled Redd), Mr. Gray, Mr. Brown. How he could have missed it before was strange. Mitch found himself thinking about Milton Brown. The odd part about the whole deal was the fact that the client's name at the Liberty, Missouri, murder had been a Mr. Brown, and that second call from the murder scene went to the Browns' address. *No way had that old man with the gold tooth had anything to do with the murder,* Mitch thought.

It had to be a coincidence.

The man was pushing seventy. That would have made him in his early sixties at the time of the murder—not that a man in his sixties couldn't commit murder, but his gut told him the possibility of the old man actually doing it was slim to none.

Maybe that's why he felt so jittery around the old couple—they had something to hide and he could feel it?

Lightning flickered and shadows danced around the room. Had he seen something out of the corner of his eye? Mitch swung the flashlight beam in the direction of the hallway entrance.

The flashlight, now only half as strong, chased away the shadows at a slower pace. This time he did see something, but it vanished before his eyes could focus: a dark shape. Was there someone in the room other than himself? It looked like a man, but he wasn't sure. *It couldn't have been,* he thought. He would have heard someone breaking in.

A creak came from the kitchen sink, then the sound of running water. Mitch shined the flashlight in that direction and saw the water flowing out of the tap. Something walked past the beam of light, moving from left to right. Mitch swung the beam to the right, to the left.

The light became dimmer and he slapped the flashlight again. This time it didn't help. In fact, it seemed to make it worse... *need candles,* he thought. As if thinking about candles could somehow keep him from thinking about what he just saw, or what he thought he saw. Just a shape, like when you turn off the television and the screen goes dark. Only it's not really dark at all, because you might see anyone should they walk past the still glowing green monitor. A shape, a figure, something you can see but can't see at the same time.

Finding he couldn't ignore the running water any longer, he went to the sink and shut it off. The flashlight grew dimmer still, leaving everything it illuminated a brownish-yellow hue.

Mitch's nerves were on edge. Jack Daniel's began its usual insistence on having a shot. He pushed the thought away and began looking for candles. He found them in a cigar box on the bookshelf. The box had been a gift from a client; the finest Cuban cigars smoked a long time ago. Inside, he found a dozen white, twelve-inch dinner candles, some playing cards and a box of wooden matches.

Taking the box over to the desk, he pulled out a candle and stuck it in the pencil holder. After stuffing the holder with a handful of tissues and certain the candle wouldn't fall over, he pulled out a wooden match, struck it and gently touched it to the candle's wick. He could see his hand shaking as he blew the match out.

He didn't like this, something wasn't right. The candle's light barely put a dent in the darkness. Mitch stared at the candle flame and wondered what was wrong. He saw the flame dancing from side to side, up and down, but the flame shined dimly, as if some kind of invisible lampshade covered it. The light just seemed strange.

He decided he'd need to use all of them and proceeded to place each one here and there around the room, until all twelve candles were lit. By the time he lit the last candle, the flashlight died. Now, the only source of light came from the occasional flash of lightning and the twelve dancing flames.

Twelve flames, dancing to their own beat.

It seemed that once all the candles were burning, the light each gave off shined a bright glow, a normal glow, not like it had when only one candle burned. *There's strength in numbers,* Mitch thought.

He wanted to continue working on the case, wanted to find something more, so he decided to call the station where Lance Albright worked. Maybe the man was still there working on his next show. Mitch had to at least give it a try.

He sat behind his desk, ignoring the fact that the water in the sink went on by itself, ignoring the feeling of having someone looking over his shoulders and picked up the phone. It took him a few moments to track down the phone number, but within two minutes he was listening to the phone ring, waiting for someone to pick up.

Finally, after going through the ritual of hearing the station's operator say… "How may I help you please…" and asking for Mr. Albright… "Hold on for a sec, please." He waited a good twenty seconds before a man's voice came on the line.

"This is Lance Albright; how can I help you?"

Mitch sat straight up in his chair, the phone pressed painfully to his ear. "Is this Lance Albright, the radio talk-show host?"

"Yes… Who's this?"

"My name's Mitchell Blade. I'm a private investigator." Mitch could hear a rustling noise over the phone as Mr. Albright leaned back in his chair. "Mitchell Blade? Ain't you the guy who's looking for the Motel-4 Madman?"

"Yes sir, I am. I was wondering… "

"Yeah, I read all about you in the paper. Seen you on television too. How's the case going? Sorry about your brother." His brother's murder had happened over more than a year ago and Mitch was offended by the man's attitude. He sounded as if the two of them had been friends for years, long lost buddies who finally found each other.

"That's what I'm calling you about," said Mitch. He hoped he didn't sound as angry as he thought he did. "I was wondering… "

"Wow, Mitch Blade the P.I. calling me—for help? Who would have thought that?"

If Mitch didn't sound irate before, he certainly sounded irritated now. The man just wouldn't shut up, constantly interrupting every time he wanted to ask him something. "Listen… I was wondering if I could ask you some questions."

Mr. Albright, a bearded balding man, sat back in his chair, twisting his mustache with one hand while holding the receiver with the other. "Questions? What kind of questions?"

Mitch heard a scratching sound, as if a record had come to its end; the needle never returning to the start, or maybe the man was playing with facial hair, but whatever it was, it began to get on his nerves. "Questions concerning the Motel-4 Madman. I was wondering if you could… "

"Oh, I get it. You're a fan of my show. You heard me talk about the case before and you want to know if I can help you with something… Right… ?"

For some reason, Mitch pictured the man on the other end of the line wearing a bow tie. He wished he could reach through the phone and grab him by that bow tie, wanted to pull the man's head through the line and shout in his face: *Shut the fuck up!* Instead, he calmly said, "Right, you're right. I heard you talking about the case and I was thinking, maybe, just maybe, I could possibly get some needed information."

Finally, the man said, "If you think I can help, then go ahead and ask your questions."

"Can you tell me when you started renting a room from the Browns?" There was a moment of silence.

"Browns? Who're the Browns?"

"The people you're renting a room from, at 126 Maple Way."

"Listen buddy, I don't know where you got your information, but obviously somebody's pulling your chain. I never heard of the Browns and I don't live at... "

—CLICK— The phone went dead.

"Hello!" said Mitch. "Hello... Hello!" *Did that son-of-a-bitch hang up on me?* No, the call was cut off in mid-sentence. He never heard of the Browns and he doesn't live there. *Then who's the guy at the Browns' house, claiming to be Lance Albright?*

Just as he was about to hang up the phone, he felt what he thought was a hand touch his shoulder. He looked to his left shoulder and could feel a hand but didn't see one, then a gentle squeeze. Mitch could see the indentation in his shoulder muscles, could feel something as it squeezed, but damn it all, he couldn't see it.

He slowly placed the receiver on its cradle, then quickly tried to grab whatever had touched his shoulder. Whatever it was, it was fast. He could feel it as it pulled away from his hand.

Calm down, he told himself, just nerves, nothing more. Except, Mitch knew that wasn't true; he could feel a presence, sensed he was not alone. No amount of bullshit could change that fact, no matter how much crap he tried to bury it with.

†   †   †

Standing over the old woman's body, still clutching the brass clock in his right hand, Ish stared at his reflection in the mirror across the room. His face speckled with blood, he smiled as the lightning continued to flash. Relaxing his grip on the clock, allowing gravity to take control, it dropped and hit the back of Mrs. Brown's skull with a nauseous thud.

He would do this, he thought. With one exception, he decided he would become invisible. Sure, it had been a long time since he tried it—hell, he was a kid at the time but if he could do it back then, why not now? Besides, he was never told he couldn't.

"Be gone...," he told his likeness in the mirror. "Be gone!"

He never actually saw himself disappear before, and was excited about watching his image in the mirror fade away. When he was a kid, he just made his special birthday wish as he walked down the school hallway, wishing he could become invisible so he could put a hurting on the school bully. Back then, he had his doubts, his unbelief, but he tossed it all aside and went with blind faith; faith in the fact that he was blessed with special birthday wishes every year, wishes that stayed with him throughout the years. After he shoved the kid down the steps, in front of more than a dozen witnesses, he walked away without a word being said. He knew no one saw him. They thought it was an accident.

Ish gazed at his reflection and could see the magic move. Slowly, his blood-splattered face began to fade. He put his hands in front of him so he could watch them disappear, but they were solid, like the rest of him. When he glanced into the mirror again, his reflection was gone. *It's like I'm a fucking vampire,* he thought. He could see his physical self, could see the clothes he wore, but he couldn't see his reflection in the mirror.

It was time to take a walk through the green doorway and pay Mitch a visit.

Ish had a moment of hesitation, a moment where he thought that maybe he would end up in the wrong place; after all, he always ended up in a Motel-4. What if he wound up there? But then he remembered where his information came from. Still, his doubts persisted. If he can see himself, would Mitch see him? *No,* he told himself, *remember: Blind Faith!*

He was told by the powers-that-be to take this walk, and damn it, he was going to do it. He stepped over Mrs. Brown's body and knelt beside the bed, watching as the pointer continued to spin; studying it with such intensity, his eyeballs pulsed. Reaching out his hand, like a child reaching for a hot stove, he put his finger on the tip of the pointer and the spinning stopped. He laid the pointer flat on the board game, then stood up and faced the window.

The rain fell even harder, smashing against the screen, exploding into a mist. Lightning constantly flashed, but thunder seemed rare. Ish stared at the storm and waited, knowing that any moment the time would come, and then... a flash of white light—like a million flashbulbs blazing simultaneously—lit up the room.

Thunder rolled, shaking the house.

Ish closed his eyes and saw the green glob of light. Watched, as that glob of light began to transform; began to morph into the green doorway; an old, thick, moldy green door. In his mind's eye, he pictured himself reaching for the skull doorknob, saw himself walking through the door.

When he opened his eyes, he was surprised to find that he wasn't wearing his Zorro suit. *Maybe that's because I'm invisible,* he thought.

He was certainly in a familiar room. *It's definitely not a Motel-4.* Then he knew without a doubt where he was, and why it seemed so proverbial in the first place. He was in Mitch's apartment.

As he stood in the hallway staring into the living room, he could see Mitch sitting at his desk with a flashlight, going through some paperwork. Ish moved to his right, with the intent of walking into the living room, when the flashlight beam came straight at him. He froze in place and seconds ticked by. Slowly, he began to realize that Mitch couldn't see him. The flashlight beam swung back and forth, up and down; all the while, he stood in the middle of the hallway entrance, waiting for some kind of reaction, but nothing came.

When the beam went back to the paperwork, Ish stepped into the room with mischief on his mind. He moved across the room as if on air—he felt like a ghost. *This is fun,* he thought to himself. *Prowling around, not being seen; man oh man, this is fun.* He was happy in his merriment. He went to the kitchen sink, pushed the faucet handle back. The water started to flow; in seconds, the flashlight beam lit up the sink.

He didn't care; he knew beyond a shadow of a doubt that he couldn't be seen. He walked through the now dimming flashlight beam and began to snoop about the rest of the apartment. His first stop, of course, would have to be the room where Billy took his last breath. He wanted to reminisce, to remember good times. He had loved the feeling of the mop handle in his hand, loved the power he felt as he pulverized Billy's helpless body. He felt that power again as he stepped into Billy's old room.

From there he made his way into the bathroom, where he turned the water on in the sink and the tub, making sure each was plugged up nice and tight. *Let it fill and spill,* he thought. Last, but not least, he waltzed into Mitch's bedroom and was surprised to find the room spotless, and in order, a big difference from the last time he was in there; a big difference indeed.

He went about the business of making it a mess again; enjoying himself, as he tossed clothes from the dresser onto the floor, the bed, and anywhere that looked too damn clean. When he finished, he looked down the hallway and could hear Mitch talking on the phone, could see candlelight flickering up ahead. He knew Mitch's flashlight must've finally died.

At the entrance to the living room, with all the candles lit up, he felt as if he stepped into a church. He suddenly had a fear of being seen, but the fear dissipated when he stepped into the room, walked around, even as Mitch was glancing in his direction.

"Can you tell me when you started renting a room with the Browns?" Mitch asked.

Talking to the real Lance Albright, Ish thought. Knowing something needed to be done, and done now, he walked around the side of the desk, bent down and reached for the phone jack in the wall.

"The people you're renting a room from, at 126 Maple Way."

Ish put a hand over his mouth to stifle a chuckle and with the other yanked the phone line out of the wall.

"Hello…," said Mitch, "hello… hello!"

By now, that gleeful feeling in the pit of Ish's stomach was beginning to settle down. He no longer wanted to laugh. Laughing wasn't good enough. What he wanted more than anything was to instill fear into Mitch's brain.

He stepped around the desk, standing only inches from Mitch's side. Reaching out, touching his shoulder, he gave it a soft squeeze, just the right touch that could scare the shit out of anyone. After Mitch hung up the phone, he suddenly reached over his shoulder.

Ish pulled his hand away just in time. *Oh that was close,* he thought. He was having so much fun! He bent down and whispered into Mitch's ear. "Are you ready?" he asked. He backed away as Mitch stood up from his chair.

"Who's there!" said Mitch, his voice sounded shaken.

. It made Ish smile.

He quickly ran around to the front of the desk. He had to see the look on Mitch's face; it was perfect. It matched the sound of his voice. His teeth were showing through a grin, his eyes squinting, his eyelids constantly blinking; he looked like a man about to have a heart attack.

Ish grabbed the candle that sat in the pencil holder and lifted it, slowly up, and out.

Mitch's eyes widened. He looked like he wanted to say something but the words wouldn't come; they were caught in his throat. He just stood there looking bewildered.

Ish backed away from the desk, giving the candle its floating effect, then stopped at the window. He turned to face the outside world, knowing full well that Mitch would still be able to see the candle floating in midair. He watched and waited.

Lightning flashed, brighter this time, and Ish closed his eyes. The green doorway loomed. He had to go back, go back and get a nice, sharp weapon. He smiled before reaching for the doorknob. "I'll be back," he said, then stepped through the door.

29

Fear gripped Mitch like a vise. He upset himself with the sound of his own scream. As he stood behind his desk, he wondered if he was finally losing it. No, he hadn't imagined hearing a voice. It wasn't a voice inside his head; those words were actually whispered into his ear. *Are you ready?* He even felt a puff of air on his ear when the words were uttered, felt it as sure as if one feels the sun on his face. Warm. *Are you ready?* He thought of the phone call with the Motel-4 manager, remembered being on hold and hearing a voice whisper his name. *That voice—that whisper—sounded like...*

His thoughts were interrupted. His eyes grew large with fright; he couldn't move as every muscle in his body stiffened. He watched, as the first candle he lit slowly began to rise up and out of the pencil holder.

This can't be happening, he thought. It had to be some kind of flashback from the abuse of drugs in his youth. Except this wasn't a hallucination; it was as real as the voice that whispered in his ear.

Mitch stared at the candle as it floated off; he could see the flame bending toward him as it backed away; he couldn't help but think how it looked like an accusatory, pointing finger—a finger pointing at him. With fear still holding him tight, he managed to walk around to the front of the desk, following the candle as it hauntingly drifted toward the window.

Suddenly, the candle began to move to the left; and then, just as fast, it arched toward the right again, stopping only inches from the windowpane.

The candle's flame seemed different somehow; he could see it, but it wasn't so bright. The halo around the burning wick dimmed. Then he saw it! Saw what it must surely be—it. Around the candle, like a halo of its own, was a figure of a man: a transparent man. Mitch stepped closer to the window, reaching out with his hands, wanting to grab whatever—it—that was there.

Lightning flashed like an atomic blast and seconds later that same blood-curdling voice that whispered in his ear said, "I'll be back."

With those words spoken, the candle fell to the floor. Its flame was nearly snuffed as it dropped, but Mitch snatched it in midair; the fire bounced around on the wick like a playful, bubbly infant.

He held it in his hand, wondering if he had imagined the whole thing. Did he actually pull the candle out of the pencil holder, walk to the window and then somehow get stunned back into reality by the flash of lightning? No, what he had seen was real; as crazy as it seemed, it was all too real. Whatever it was, it planned on coming back, and he planned on being ready for it, when it did.

† † †

Ish opened his eyes. Back in the Browns' home, he stood by the window, staring down at the body that lay at his feet. A thick, sticky pool of blood had gathered around the corpse's head. The right-top half of the brass clock was lodged into the back of Mrs. Brown's skull; blood still spurted from the wound like a muddy fountain. He stepped over the body, walked around the bed and opened the bedroom door.

His eyes glowed like a cat as he walked through the darkened house. One, two, three, four... and five... down the stairs he went. He walked past the living room, could see Mr.

Brown lying on the couch with his feet up on the coffee table, fast asleep. He walked by the old man without giving him a second thought and entered the kitchen.

The smell of tobacco and Lysol still lingered in the air, and it nearly made him sneeze. Seconds after starting his search, he opened a drawer and found the weapon he thought would best meet his needs: a boning knife. Its narrow, sharp pointed blade could cut through meat and pull it from the bone. Just the thing he was looking for, nice and neat, strip the meat.

Back in the living room once more, Ish stopped in his tracks as lightning lit up the room. He waited, and seconds later, thunder rocked the house. Loud thunder, a mighty thunder, but the old man still lounged on the couch, oblivious of the sound. The old fart could sleep through Armageddon.

When he was convinced Mr. Brown wasn't going to wake up, he started toward his room, intent on going through the green doorway to finish up his job, but again he stopped. *Should I put this fuck out of his misery,* he thought. He could, and by doing so, he wouldn't have to worry about being found out; the last thing he needed was having Mr. Brown find his dead wife; that would bring the cops and that was definitely a no-no.

Ish turned toward the sleeping Mr. Brown and began to tiptoe, looking more like "The Grinch" sneaking around snatching Christmas decorations, than he did a killer on the prowl. He almost laughed at the thought, knew it must look silly should anyone happen to see, but he didn't care, because he knew no one would.

He stood behind the couch, looking down on the un-suspecting victim-to-be, and observed the man's chest as it heaved up and down at a steady pace. With both hands, he raised the boning knife over his head. Lightning flickered off the tip of the blade, like a distant star twinkling in space.

Rumbling shook the house like an earthquake. The old man's hands, folded, resting on his stomach, and as the thunder rumbled, his left hand reached up and scratched at his nose.

Ish thought the old man was about to wake up, but when his hand returned to his stomach and his chest continued to heave, he knew the old geezer was still fast asleep.

The countdown started in his head.

Five, four, three, two—on one, he thrust the knife down and stopped inches from the old man's chest, as a thought came to mind: *What's a better way to make a mess?*

Ish pulled the knife away and brought it back to his side. Again with the countdown, *five, four, three, two... one!* Like a nail gun blasting a nail from its chamber, Ish jammed the knife into the side of Mr. Brown's neck, twisting and punching through the other side, then ripped the knife out with lightning speed.

In an instant, the old man's eyes bulged open with shock, fear and pain. His mouth, "O" shaped with a scream, but only gurgling... escaped. Clutching at the wounds in his neck, Mr. Brown flung himself off the couch as if on fire. Stumbling over the coffee table, he fell to the ground. Blood spurted in every direction as he managed to get to his feet again and staggered across the living room floor.

On the walls, on the floor and everywhere in be-tween, blood splattered and splashed as if an artist had finally snapped, slapping his paint on everything but the canvas. Ish ogled the whole scene with a giggle in the back of his throat.

Lightning continued to flicker, thunder rumbled.

The show ended when the old man finally collapsed for the last time. When he fell, his body landed between the living room and the kitchen, his legs on the living room rug, his upper-half lying on the kitchen's linoleum base.

Blood poured from the slits in his neck, sloshing out like an over-turned carton of chocolate milk. The white tiles rapidly becoming red as the gore spread across the floor.

Ish began to clap his hands together as he neared the body. "Bravo... loved the show!" He knelt down beside it. Reaching out with his right hand, he dipped his fingers into the blood. Like some kind of sports hero signing autographs, he began to write on the walls. Thank you—Thank you—Thank you! Everywhere around the room, on all the walls: Thank you—Thank you—Thank you! When he finished having his fun, Ish turned, like a robot, and faced the living-room window.

Rain clattered against the glass, the wind howled. A blast of white light from the storm; Ish closed his eyes. The green doorway was there, waiting.

.   .   .

Still holding the candle in his hand, Mitch knew exactly how he could prepare himself. Get the damn gun. His Glock 31 lay in the top dresser drawer in his bedroom. Without hesitation, he sought out his defense. He made it as far as the hallway when he stopped in his tracks. A familiar sound came to his ear. At first it was muffled by the noise of the rain outside, but as he listened closer, it sounded like running water coming from the bathroom.

He made it just in time. The glow of the candle's flame fought a losing battle against the darkness, but it was bright enough to show him the water was just seconds away from spilling out of the sink and tub. If the sink had a decent plug he would have had a mess on his hands.

As fast as he could, with one hand holding the candle, the other turning the knobs, he narrowly avoided a major disaster. The last thing he needed was to have the neighbor below him complain. The man was queer as a three-dollar bill. Mitch had the misfortune of meeting him in the elevator (one of the few times it actually worked) the first week after moving into his apartment. The man made a pass at him and it made him uncomfortable. He made every effort to avoid the guy as much as possible since then. He didn't have anything against gay people, and always thought 'to each his own' but this guy was too gay, flaunting it without regard to anyone else's moral values. That, he didn't like.

Mitch pulled the plugs from the sink and tub and watched as the water slowly receded. Watched as the whirlpools grew and grew, until the sink made its sucking noise and the water went down the drain. Minutes later, the tub followed suit. Satisfied, but confused by the incident, Mitch made his way to his bedroom.

He instantly knew something was amiss when he saw the bedroom door ajar. *What the fuck...* he thought as he pushed it open. He stepped into the room and nearly tripped. Clothes were scattered everywhere and his feet became entangled in a pair of pajamas. He kicked them aside and surveyed the room. The candle's flame might not have been that bright, but it was vivid enough to show him that someone had been in here, and not that long ago. Mitch remembered, in the past, he had lived like a pig, but those days were long gone. He cleaned up his act after Darla came back into his life.

When he saw the drawers of the dresser open, he nearly lost his breath. His first thought, of course, the gun. *Was it still there? Yes!* Apparently whoever or whatever made the mess was not looking for anything in particular. The Glock was still safely hidden in a pencil box under his white socks. He pulled the gun out from its hiding place and held it in his hand. He didn't know if it would be of any use against an enemy he couldn't see, but it still made him feel safe, regardless. He pulled his shirt out of the front of his trousers and tucked the weapon in his waistband. It felt cold against his skin as he covered it over. It reminded him of the chilly bolt of fear that shot through his entire body when those words were whispered in his ear. *Are you ready?*

The events of the day ran through his mind. First, the dream about Darla that started it all. His fierce need to protect her, then finding out about the baby and facing his fear of becoming a father, which turned out to be not so scary when it came to the fear he now fought inside, desperately trying to keep it at bay. Jack Daniel's suggested a drink.

In his mind's eye, Mitch took a swing at the thought and punched it out of his head. The fear of the unknown was bad enough; he didn't need his head fogged up with booze.

Looking out the bedroom window, watching the rain and the lightning, Mitch said a quick prayer. "God, you've got my back; you've always covered me before. Watch over me now, please? In Jesus' name. Amen."

As if his prayers angered the opposition, thunder violently shook the windowpane. Mitch was not about to be intimidated by anything, whether it was the thunder or the invisible man; nothing—absolutely nothing—could shake his resolve. With candle in hand, he made his way back to the living room, constantly looking over his shoulder, expecting something to sneak up behind him, at any second.

That was good; it kept him on his toes. He hadn't experienced anything like it since Vietnam. Back then, it was the fear of getting his head blown off, but this was something all together different; this seemed supernatural, something evil.

Making his way around the desk, he noticed the phone jack laying on the floor. Had he somehow accidentally jerked it out of the wall? He didn't think so. In fact, he knew that was impossible; he was sitting at the desk when the phone went dead; he didn't make any kind of quick movement to cause the wire to pop out of the wall. He plugged it back in and picked up the phone. After hearing the dial tone, he put the candle back into the pencil cup and thought of calling Darla. Then, he decided against it, keeping instead, all five senses alert for one thing: the return of the transparent man.

Mitch dropped the receiver back onto its cradle.

The supplication to his Maker didn't take long to be answered. With his audio senses, now extra sensitive, he could hear the wind and the rain, the continuous clicking of the cuckoo clock's pendulum as it swung back and forth, back and forth, even the slow plunk that came from the kitchen faucet, dripping a drop of water, every two seconds. Plunk... plunk... plunk... His sense of smell was stronger too; the aroma of melted wax, the sooty black smoke that wafts from the wick, even the raisin-bread toast he burned earlier in the day, all floated to his nostrils.

He plopped into the leatherback chair and pushed off. The chair rolled away until it could go no further and hit the wall behind him. *There's no way anything is going to creep up from behind—no way!*

His sense of touch was finely tuned too; the leather cushions under him felt plusher somehow. Even his eyesight seemed clearer, every object in the room more focused. The candle flames, brighter, with undulating heat swirling through the air around them like a pitched stone disturbing the face of a calm lake.

Across the room, under the hum of the refrigerator, a floorboard creaked. Mitch's concentration determined the direction of the sound, and his eyes fixed to the spot in an instant: the window.

He pulled the gun out from under his waistband and laid it on his lap, his finger inches from the trigger.

Lightning glimmered; thunder rolled across the sky.

He thought about the situation he now found himself in. Always the hunter, never the hunted, his feelings swelled like a bag with mixed emotions. At the top of the list: Anger. Anger at himself, for becoming so obsessed with his job, allowing it to send him through hoops, making him drop his guard, and then Billy having to pay for it with his life. The bag filled rapidly: Anxiety, Fear, Worry, Sorrow, Excitement, Determination and Revelation.

He'd always been a skeptic, a doubting Thomas, thinking that every case could be solved, but now he finally realized that not every case could be explained, because there really are things that are unexplainable in this world.

When it all comes down to it, God has the final call. Thumbs up or thumbs down, one way or the other, justice always prevails. Yet, after putting so much time and energy into the case, Mitch found it hard to let it go.

Out of the corner of his eye, a twinkle captured his attention. Without thinking, he quickly dodged to the left, avoiding a deadly blow from a boning knife that appeared out of nowhere. The blade ripped into the leather cushion just missing his ear. Now on full alert, reacting like a ninja, he grabbed the gun and somersaulted off the chair.

On his knees in a flash, arms held straight out, gun in hand, he fired a shot. The discharge echoed around the room as the bullet slammed into the leather chair. Seconds later, the knife pulled out and away from the seat.

With thunder rumbling the whole time, he doubted if anyone heard the shot. *Maybe that was a blessing?* How could he explain taking shots at a homicidal ghost? Who would believe it? He couldn't believe it himself, let alone expect others to.

Like time-lapse photography, he saw the blade thrusting at him in slow motion; then back to real time again, he rolled to his right, narrowly escaping a major wound, as the blade split his shirt at the shoulder. After rolling away from his attacker, Mitch slammed into the desk, hurting his side in the process, nearly knocking out his wind. He didn't have time to hurt; he only had time to recover. With one hand holding his side, the other aiming the gun, he fired a second shot. He didn't know where he was shooting; he just hoped it was in the right direction. The bullet pulverized a few books as it punched into the bookshelf.

Where's the knife, he thought to himself. Mitch lost sight of it when he wheeled out of harm's way. On the floor, on his knees, he scanned the room with eyes like a computer scanning a barcode.

To his left, beyond the desk, on top of the kitchen counter that divided the room, the candle dimmed. Heat fluttered off the flame like sonar, giving him the ability to almost see his attacker. Standing in front of him—there but not there—an outline, a slight shadow, was moving right toward him.

Mitch followed the outline: head, neck and right shoulder. He became so engrossed in trying to see it; he almost forgot what he was dealing with—Death—his own. Right arm, elbow...

Lightning pulsed, thunder growled. The light flickered off the blade, allowing him to see it just in time. Dodging out of the way, but not fast enough, a slit opened on his left cheek, paper-cut thin. Like a tear bubbling up in the eye, the blood oozed from the cut until it finally trickled down the side of his face.

The outline—where's the outline? Fuck the outline! Look for the knife.

Except, he didn't have to look for it, it found him.

To Mitch, it felt like the largest wasp ever created by nature had plunged its stinger into his back and left it there. He reached back and pulled a boning knife out of his left shoulder, gritting his teeth from the pain. He could feel the blood rolling down his back under the shirt.

At first, he thought he needed to find something to stop the bleeding, it felt bad, but when he reached back and pressed his hand against it, he could tell it wouldn't be that much of a problem. Besides, he had other problems right now. His main problem might not have the knife anymore, but it still had the upper hand. By the window, a floorboard creaked.

Outside, a lightning bolt struck a power box several blocks away. The boom from the explosion mixed in well with the thunder. Mitch aimed the gun at the window, ready to blow away death. He always envisioned death wearing a black robe. Like the movies, his vision of the Grim Reaper had no face under the hood, only a bony hand sticking out from the arm of the robe, pointing at its next victim.

Death has no face; Death can't be seen—except to those who are unfortunate enough to see it coming—no one knows when they've used up the last tick of the clock we call the heart.

This was something other than the boogeyman. Death may have a hand in it, pulling the strings like a puppeteer, but it wasn't Death itself. *It couldn't be, could it?*

Something moved. Mitch strained his eyes to see. The aura was there by the window, standing there as if in defiance of his gun, waiting for him to pull the trigger. Before he could lose sight of it again, he aimed the gun and fired. He waited for the sound of shattering glass, expecting the window to explode when the bullet passed through it, because surely he was shooting at a figment of his imagination. But, the bullet simply disappeared, gone... Poof...

† † †

The entertainment Mr. Brown provided was nice, but Ish wanted more, he needed more. Like a crack addict pickpocketing someone's wallet to get another hit, so too was Ish's addiction for blood.

With the dark void behind him, the green doorway ahead, Ish reached out and turned the knob. His first experience of touching that knob shot a host of horrifying feelings deep into his heart, but after turning it time after time, those miserable feelings had lessened, and in its place the feeling of wanting more, of needing more.

Ish opened his eyes and found Mitch sitting in his leather chair. He had pushed it up against the wall, ensuring that nothing could come up from behind. He seemed to be in a state of meditation, and Ish didn't like the look on his face. He looked too optimistic. Ish had to remind himself that he still held all the cards. His only problem, now that Mitch made it impossible for him to sneak up from behind, was making sure Mitch didn't see the knife coming.

Ish started to make his move and the floor under his foot abruptly creaked. He saw Mitch's reaction to the sound and understood why he seemed so confident. *So,* he thought to himself, *he's got a gun.* That alone could be a problem, particularly if he should take a slug. But right now his main problem was looking in his direction. If the hat rack to his right had been placed anywhere else in the room, Mitch most likely would have seen the knife. Ish pressed the knife against the rack, hoping Mitch wouldn't notice, and watched him give the area the once-over.

Look at him, Ish thought, *sitting there, looking so damn cocky, thinking he's safe with that gun on his lap.* He wanted to carve that face, carve that smug look into shreds. Just the thought alone sent a delightful quiver throughout his body, the kind of feeling one gets when taking that first drop on a roller coaster: *Weeeeeeeeeeee!*

With that rush pumping through his blood and that thrill taking him to new heights, Ish moved toward Mitch like a hungry snake slithering to its next meal. Stalking, inching closer and closer, Mitch made it easy as pie as he sat there zoning out, his mind not totally on the here and now. When opportunity knocks, the door must be opened. Ish wanted to take full advantage of the situation. So, holding the knife above his head, fully expecting Mitch not to notice, he began a shortened version of a countdown in his head.

Three... two... one! His target: an eye.

Plunging the knife down with brute force, he missed the intended soft spot and tore into the leather chair instead.

Damn! Damn! Damn!

Mitch's reflexes totally took him by surprise. The fool acted like a fucking ninja in one of those old kung fu movies, rolling off the chair like Bruce Lee on speed. As Ish pulled the knife out of the leather seat, a bullet grazed his knuckles. A slight ache at first, his fingers throbbed with each beat of his heart. Which in turn made them ache even more, until the ache became a full-blown pain.

With the pain came the rage; he wanted to scream. He wanted to shout every explicative in the book. He even knew some in foreign tongues, but he knew that by doing so, he'd give away his position in the room. Instead, Ish funneled that anger into the task at hand, determined not to become frustrated.

Bent on having his way, he turned on Mitch like a crazed pit bull, with rancor swirling inside his head, like a twister cruising down tornado alley. Using all his strength and with an upper-cut motion, he shoved the knife forward, aiming for the center of Mitch's face, hoping to hook him under the chin like a big, fat trout. Except the son-of-a-bitch moved too fast, rolling out of the way with such speed, he barely clipped his shirt. The slight pull on the knife felt like the one that got away.

The whole fishing analogy went out the window when a second shot went off. The bullet zipped between his legs, sending a wave of fast moving air rippling under his balls. Behind him, the bookcase thumped with the impact. Scooting around the desk with amazing speed of his own, Ish crouched behind the kitchen counter, thinking about the next move to make. This whole chess game was becoming more trouble than it was worth. His emotions jumped from being excited one second, to being scared the next. The game was thrilling. The game was hard. But nothing ever comes easy.

Still hunched over, he nudged his way closer, moving like a sumo wrestler.

The game would be played, but by his rules. He would decide the how, where, when. Standing once more, only inches from his target, he would end the game here and now. Ish heaved the knife at Mitch's face, and again, he missed, or at least he thought he did, until the scent of blood came crawling into his nostrils, telling him otherwise.

Unhappy at the difficulty of the game, wanting to put an end to it once and for all, he gave his frustration a foothold in his thinking. Since Mitch had a gun, he'd go back and get a gun of his own. The old geezer had plenty to choose from. He'd go back and grab one. Why screw around with a knife when he could snatch a gun of his own.

His anger, like black smoke, fogged his head. He no longer thought about the game. He just wanted to get this over with right now!

Had he kept his cool, he would have seen his opportunity for what it was, but instead, his mind wandered as he jabbed the knife into Mitch's shoulder and then turned and faced the window. *Have to go back,* he thought to himself, *have to go back. Have to go back.* He waited, watched. Lightning filled the room. *Have to go back, have to go back. Have to go back!* Ish closed his eyes and saw the green doorway pulsating behind his eyelids. *Have to go back! Have to go back! Have to go back!*

Reaching for the knob—*Have to be back!* His hand wrapping around it—*Have to go back!* Squeezing it—*Have to go back!* Turning it—*Have to go back!*

Numb, to the horrifying images that flash through his mind: Heads on spikes. *Go back!* Faces, forever frozen with a scream on their mouths... *Go back!* Fresh blood, dribbling from the stumps of each neck—*Go back!* Opening the door, *Go back!* Stepping through—*Go back!*

Upon opening his eyes, Ish felt the scorching heat of flames, felt the pain as his chest exploded outwards, his insides bursting forth in a miniature mushroom cloud, a cloud of red gore.

A push... shove, or a punch; he fell forward head over heels, tumbling over and over, while all the while, the flames, the insatiable flames, roared. He can hear the screams of other lost souls, screaming an endless scream, but he can't hear his own.

.   .   .

The storm that blackened the day, fierce enough to send the city into darkness with a power outage, winked out with a whimper. The black sky became gray, became white, became blue, as the sun came out once more. The transformation took Mitch by surprise. Staring at the window, still wondering why the glass hadn't shattered, still trying to convince himself that the things he had seen, or hadn't seen, actually happened. All this, plus the sudden change in the weather, made him question reality.

It couldn't have been a dream, unless he had a sleep-walking problem he didn't know about, but he didn't, he knew that for sure. Besides, the bullet holes in the chair and bookcase proved that notion correct. *Right... ?* So, no, it wasn't a dream.

Almost a full minute passed before he finally realized the sun had returned. He went about the room extinguishing all the candles, by first wetting his thumb and forefinger and then pinching each wick out.

By the time he finished, his mind returned to that third bullet. *Where the hell did it go? Did it matter?* After all, the day started out strange—the sun coming out as fast as it had; the bullet zipping into another realm, another dimension, only made it that much stranger.

Maybe the effects of Vietnam decided to pick today to fuck with his head. Maybe he was fighting a gook from the past? *No!* He had to do something, do something before his thoughts totally got lost in that world.

Mitch picked up the phone and dialed the one person who could calm his mind. Two rings and a pickup... Darla's voice—so calm, so peaceful—"Hello..." instantly set him free.

"Hi, Babe... "

30

The sound of her voice may have settled his mind from the stink of the past, but it couldn't cover the stench of the present. It couldn't keep him from wondering if his sanity was still intact.

Trying to understand what had happened only gave him a headache; surely the whole thing must have been brought on by stress. Mitch decided that the best thing he could do would be to play it off like it never happened. If someone asked about the gunshots or bullet holes, he would come up with a reasonable answer if and when the time came. Except, he couldn't play it off like it never happened, not just because of the gunshots or the bullet holes, but the knife too.

The time of questions came sooner than expected; when hours later, he would come upon a scene that set the questions in motion, one after the other.

In an attempt at trying to forget about his escapade with the unseen intruder, Mitch thought he'd be able to do that by paying the Browns another visit. Thinking he would avoid being asked questions by others, he ended up asking himself the first question when he pulled into the Browns' driveway. *What the hell is going on here?*

Two patrol cars with lights flashing and pulsing, police radios chattering, he walked up to the policeman who sat in the first car. The patrolman, who was busy writing his report, didn't see him coming. Mitch read the officer's nametag and said, "Excuse me... Officer Gram. What's happening here?"

The officer glanced up from his paperwork looking a little startled, but smiled anyway, "Got a mess inside, looks like a murder/suicide, but... it's not pretty, mind you, but you might want to see for yourself."

Mitch hurried up the walkway.

The moment he stepped into any crime scene, the first thing he always noticed was the smell of gore (but not this time)—this time, his eyes took notice first. The blood was everywhere; the smell came second. Officer Gram said it wasn't pretty; he wasn't lying, because the scene was downright disgusting. The walls of the living room (a room forever frozen in time with the décor of the '70s) were not only covered with splotches of dried blood, but words as well, two words: Thank you!

Thank you! Thank you! Thank you!

On every wall, in every corner, sprawled out like a child's finger-painting: Thank you! The sight immediately brought back memories of the wall in Billy's room: *Don't fuck with me!*

Thank you? Thank you! What the fuck are you so thankful for? Do you get your jollies watching people die? You sick fuck! Mitch nearly lost his lunch when he found Mr. Brown's body lying across the threshold of the kitchen and living room floor. Blood seeped from the wound on the corpse's neck, pooling around the head, steadily crusting over as it dried, like lava when it's cooled.

"Got another one upstairs..." The sound of the voice, the suddenness of it, made Mitch jump in surprise. He was lost in 'The Zone' and didn't hear the second policeman as he came up from behind.

"Sorry... didn't mean to scare you."

"That's o.k.," said Mitch. He was about to say, *You just spooked me,* but thought better of it, and instead said, "... you just surprised me." The policeman looked familiar; Mitch could have sworn he'd met him somewhere before. "Don't I know you?"

The black man stood a good three inches taller than Mitch, and when he smiled, his pearly whites gleamed. "We met at your brother's funeral. My name's Mason," he said as he pointed to his nametag. "Norman B..." Mitch remembered; some time had passed, but he remembered because in his mind's eye he could see the man standing by the graveside, remembered because it was he who stood closest to the person with that big red umbrella, except, "There was no red umbrella...," Mitch mumbled.

"Huh?"

Mitch saw the confusion in the officer's face and said, "Nothing. It's just... nothing. What's upstairs?"

"Victim #2: female; most likely that geezer's wife." Officer Mason nodded in the direction of Mr. Brown's body.

"Let's show some respect for the dead, shall we."

The smile on Mason's face dropped and he said, "Sorry. Looks like this guy smashed his old lady in the head with a clock, then came downstairs and did himself in with a knife; except, we can't find the weapon. Can you picture that, somebody sticking a knife in their own neck? If you ask me, it's creepy." *I didn't ask,* Mitch thought, *and yes, it is creepy.* "Maybe the knife is under the body."

Raising an eyebrow, Officer Mason said, "Maybe, but doubtful. Look at the way the body's laid out. I would think he'd still be holding it in his hand if he didn't toss it aside."

Mitch had a smile on his face as he watched Officer Mason. This guy he met only once before, yet it felt as if he's known the man his whole life. He watched with a hand held to his mouth, hiding his grin, watching the patrolman, who, with his own hand on his chin, looked like a standing version of *The Thinker*. He felt a connection and remembered the brief conversation they'd shared and an idea came to mind. "Didn't you say you were retiring from the force?"

The officer smiled, pleased that Mitch even remembered meeting him. He had gone to the funeral, not because he knew the victim, but out of respect for a man he admired. "Two more months and I'm done."

Two months, Mitch thought. He could handle two months. Sure, cases were piling up, cases that could've been put to rest, piling up because he was spending most, if not all, of his time hunting down the Motel-4 Madman. They were all cases that put money into his checking account, cases that were no longer doing their job because he wasn't doing his. He was chasing after a killer that seemed to elude him at every turn. One lousy case, a case that never had a client to begin with, a case that brought on a major problem for his business: a problem he needed to fix, if it was to continue to be successful. "Have you ever considered being a P.I.?" he asked. "I could use a man with an eye for details... interested?"

Before Mason could answer yes or no, their conversation was interrupted when the first patrolman strolled through the front door.

"The meat wagon's on the way. So is Forensics." Turning his head, intent on answering Officer Gram's little curt remark about the ambulance, Mitch stopped when he saw the window to his left.

He hadn't noticed it before. With all the blood and the words "Thank you" melting down the walls, but the window was broken. Still in place, but shattered, one touch could send the glass crumbling; a small hole, like a meteor strike on the moon, in the center of the now snowy-white glass, *a stone?* He wondered, *No, not a stone, maybe a bullet hole.*

By now, the two patrolmen were staring at the window as well; neither one of them willing to snap Mitch out of the trance he seemed to have gone into.

A fucking bullet hole, he thought. No one noticed a bullet hole? He turned and asked Mason, "Do you think maybe, just maybe, it wasn't a knife after all?"

Both officers gave each other an embarrassing look, both feeling foolish for not noticing the window. Mitch instantly went into overdrive. "Gram...," he snapped, looking directly at the officer, his eyes serious as a heart attack. "Go around the side of the house and see if you can find a bullet in any of those trees out there."

The officer wasted no time. "Yes sir," he said. Once he was out the door, Mitch turned to Mason. "You guys look like you had it half right. I think we might be able to eliminate suicide." Mitch whipped out his wallet, rifled through it and pulled out a business card, offering it to Mason with a smile. "Just in case you might be interested..."

The patrolman took the card, smiling a bright smile of his own. "I can tell you right now, I'm definitely interested."

"Great...," said Mitch. Before Mason could say another word, he was on the move. There was work to be done, no time for chitchat. As much as Mitch hated the thought of seeing the next victim, he had to do it, had to get it over with, because no matter how many times he had seen Death, it still hurt. But, the more he thought about it, the more that thought seemed untrue. Hurt couldn't begin to explain the effect Death caused. He'd come face to face with it in Nam and was able to walk away, unscathed, but he never forgot his first experience with it.

Even though it pained him, Mitch stepped into the first bedroom to his left. He knew Mrs. Brown's lifeless body waited for him in here; the smell of blood filled his nose.

From the looks of the room, it didn't seem like there was a struggle. Mrs. Brown had obviously been caught off guard. There was no mystery here; the person that did this had to be the guy that was renting the room from the victims, the same person who claimed to be a radio talking head. *Talking head, my ass,* Mitch thought. *The crazy son-of-a-bitch crushed the woman's skull for God's sake. Then what, just for kicks, the bastard decides to embed the thing?*

Mitch could picture the scene in his mind: Mrs. Brown dying, and standing over her is who? *Who are you?* He could see the man's hand opening, could see the brass clock tumbling in dreamlike slow motion—then, Splat! Like a guillotine slamming down, the clock stuck into her skull with a soft crunch.

He shrugged the vision off like a dirty old coat. In all his years as a detective, he had seen lots of things, things that would curl the nerves of the average Joe. It wasn't the first time he'd envisioned such things, and he imagined it wouldn't be the last.

Turning again toward the door, not wanting to disturb any evidence, just wanting to leave death behind, Mitch stopped in mid-turn when he saw the Ouija board on the bed. *That's odd,* he thought. *What's a Ouija board doing here?* Those feelings of dealing with the supernatural came flooding back again. Did the so-called talking head have something to do with Mitch's intruder? Could he have conjured up some kind of entity, some force real enough that could kill?

With a sudden creepy feeling came the rising of the hairs on the nape of his neck. Mitch had to get out of the room, staying any longer was not an option; there was nothing he could do here anyway. Forensic science would have to find the clues, which, in turn, would help identify the culprit. He hoped. Up until now, forensic science hadn't been much help in finding the Motel-4 killer, or his brother's.

As Mitch walked out of the bedroom and started down the hall, the grandfather clock to his right started chiming: Ping... Bong... Ping... Bong. The bells were loud, causing him to flinch—Ping... Ping... Ping... Bong!

He hurried down the short flight of steps with a chill racing up from behind, a chill that longed to penetrate his bones. Alone in the living room once more (Officer Mason had gone out to his car, while Gram searched for a bullet) Mitch stood in silence, staring at Mr. Brown's corpse and then the window, corpse, window. He could feel the chill, feel it as it wrapped its frigid arms around his chest, felt it hugging him, squeezing him.

He shook the chill off his body the way dogs shake water off their backs, then moved in to take a closer look at the window. Taking only five to seven steps, he faltered. It felt as if his foot had struck a piece of furniture. Looking down at the floor, expecting to see his foot resting on a magazine rack or something, he found nothing there.

What the... His foot hovered a good six inches off the floor. Vigorously pressing his leg down, with all his strength, his foot still hung suspended. Then, without expecting it (his mind reeled with the fact that his foot wouldn't budge), his foot slammed on the thick carpet with a thump and began to throb. *What the hell...*

He glanced around, looking to see if anyone else was around to witness the weirdness, but it was just him and his imagination running amuck. Except it wasn't his imagination, his foot really wouldn't move. It felt like he'd been standing on something. *Knock it off,* he told himself. *Just knock it off.*

But he couldn't knock it off; that was the problem. Everything seemed to be bleeding together like a toxic soup. His constant insistence on perfection; his need to leave no stone left unturned; his unwillingness to leave a matter be— would they all lead to his downfall? Is that what this was all about, his downfall? Mitch wondered if maybe he finally snapped the last nerve, the one that kept him grounded to reality.

Staring at the shattered windowpane, observing the intricate web of cracks, Mitch tried to remember what life was like before he took on the task of catching the Motel-4 killer. Simpler came to mind, definitely simpler. It was the only case that ever made him lose sleep, not that his other cases were less important, just never as unnerving. Of course, there was more to it than that, much more. Which other case kept him so preoccupied, or proved to be so compelling? None! Absolutely none! This was the only case that ever gave him grief, and it became personal after Billy died.

Now, he stood on the edge of wonder. The questions kept coming at him like an endless freight train. This *one* tie-in to the Motel-4 Madman had been derailed, leaving the questions jumbled together and scattered about within the wreckage. Answers to some of them may never be known now that the Browns were dead.

Mitch pulled himself away from the window with thoughts of madness on his mind. Every aspect of the case reeked of lunacy. His eyes darted back and forth from the corpse on the floor to the blood-stained words on the walls. *Thank you!*

Stepping closer to get a better look, he can see that whoever did this did it without wearing any kind of gloves to cover his prints. Talk about a cry for help. If the culprit had any priors, there would be a good chance of having the prints on file. The only thing he could do now was hope the bastard had a record. If not, he would be back to square one.

Maybe that's why he had the balls to do what he did; knowing he had no priors, he wouldn't really give a shit now, would he? Mitch had to hope that stupidity played a role, stupidity along with an ounce of luck, his luck and the perpetrator's stupidity.

T. P. Majka

A dull ache began to throb in the back of his head; soon it would find its way to the front. He obviously spent too much time in this house. Mitch hoped coming here would prove to be helpful in getting answers; instead he's left with more questions. As he made his way out the front door, he saw Officer Gram coming up the walk; by the look on his face, it was obvious what the story was.

"No luck on finding any bullet out here," he said with disappointment in his eyes. "I've checked every square inch."

"Every square inch?" said Mitch. Officer Gram was only a year out of the police academy and still green behind the ears.

Looking at Mitch with confusion, trying to be police-like, he said, "Given the position of the window, I estimated the possible trajectory of the bullet and came up with zip!" The fact that he couldn't find the bullet didn't surprise Mitch at all. Not with all the other crap that went along with this case. He imagined there would never be anything that ever surprised him, ever again.

Knowing full well the officer that stood before him was about as street-smart as a newborn sea turtle sprinting to the ocean, Mitch decided he'd give the area the once-over himself. Rather than relying on the officer's judgment, he decided to double-check. Mitch said, "I'll take a look around too."

Officer Gram seemed miffed; he said, "Fine, what-ever," and quickly headed back to his patrol car.

Mitch spent the next half-hour searching every tree, every possible angle, all without results. He even jumped the four-foot white-picket fence at the end of the property line, searching the wooded area for a good two hundred yards before finally giving up the search and going back to his car.

By now, the ambulance had arrived. Two medics were busy loading the body of Mrs. Brown into the back,

278

alongside her husband. Mitch remembered a similar scene upon arriving home from his little getaway.

Billy might still be alive. The thought stung his heart.

He probably should stick around, but he knew Captain Hart, a friend from his Army days, who headed the team, would call him if he found anything. He dealt with the man on numerous occasions and always found him reliable—but just in case, he'd give the man a call anyway. Mitch slid behind the wheel of his car and closed the door. Before starting the engine, he pulled out his cell and placed the call. The woman answered the phone, cheerful as always; Mitch knew his message would get through.

"Hi Amanda, this is Detective Blade. I just wanted to let Captain Hart know I'm working on the Browns' murder case. Two fresh ones are on the way to the morgue now."

Knowing that Amanda was a gabber, always wanting to make small talk at every opportunity, and not really in the mood, he interrupted her before she could say a word, "Tell him I'll see him soon. Thanks... bye," and hit the end button on the phone.

Mitch met the woman at about the time he and Darla had signed the divorce papers. He felt she must have been smitten with him, because at every chance, she constantly asked him out for coffee or dinner. He was flattered that a woman fifteen years younger than he wanted to spend time with him, but he found it hard to believe that she could be interested in him. He was tempted to take her up on her offers. After all, what normal red-blooded male wouldn't? She was pleasant to look at, that was for sure, but he felt it would be wrong to get involved. The one up side to the whole thing was the fact that her showing some interest made him feel good. *Still dashing after all these years,* he thought to himself. *Well, maybe not that dashing.* Mitch smiled at the thought.

Reaching to turn the ignition, someone tapped on the window. The sound, like the chiming of that damn grandfather clock, made him flinch in his seat.

Officer Mason was at the window, smiling. Seeing his teeth so white and shiny made Mitch chuckle under his breath as he rolled the window down, his way of shaking off the jitters.

"What's up?" As soon as he said it, Mitch knew it must have sounded like one of those lame Bud Light commercials. *Wwwwhat's up!*

Mason squatted, like a catcher behind home plate, so he could see eye to eye, his big hands grasping the open window. He swayed from side to side, smiling that big smile and said, "Thought you'd want to know how we found out about this mess."

Mitch scratched at his chin and thought, *Jeez, how could I forget that? Must be getting old!*

Mason's face suddenly became serious, his eyes narrowing. "Weirdest thing... Got a 911 call from somebody named Todd or Tony... something like that... said he was a friend of the Motel-4 killer."

Sitting straight up in his seat, looking like a kid in a candy store, Mitch said, "Yeah... what else?" *Someone who said he's a friend of the killer? This was interesting.*

"He just told the 911 op. where we would find," he made quotation marks with his fingers, "two slow-cooling corpses and hung up."

"Was he on long enough to get a trace?"

Mason burped and put a hand to his mouth. "Sorry... still trying to hold down this morning's breakfast... That's what made the call so damn peculiar. There was no number to trace; it's like the guy was calling from outer space or something. The operator stalled him as long as she could, but like I said, it's like the guy was calling from outer space."

His interest was like a chewing gum bubble expanding, and then Pop! Disappointment stuck to his face. "Damn," Mitch mumbled. He wanted more, hoped for something more, but what he got—what did he get? A supposed friend of the killer called and told them about the bodies. That's it? It had to be some kind of prank, some whack job getting his rocks off. But what they found only proved that somebody out there—maybe even the killer himself—*Stop!* He told himself. None of this was making any sense. "Thanks," said Mitch. After Mason stood up and stepped away from his car, he rolled up the window. With his right hand, he made the 'give me a call' gesture and then turned the ignition over. Throwing it in reverse, he backed the car out of the driveway.

At first, he wasn't sure which way to go. He thought about going home but that only made his stomach feel like it was lined with ebonite. Instead, he decided to go to his mother's house. Maybe Darla would be there—most likely not—but still, she might be. If there was anything that could shake his confusion, seeing his Cinderella again would.

She made him feel the way a man should feel: Strong, Confident. With her having his child, he was proud of the fact that it didn't take any medication to help bring it about—*no Viagra here, thank you very much.* The thought, though amusing, brought images of the words "thank you" finger-painted in blood. It wasn't so amusing anymore.

This was it. There wasn't any point in continuing his obsessive search. He had to put it behind him, no matter how many holes—and there were gapping holes—he had to get past it, had to get on with his life. He had a child on the way, a child that would need all the love he could give. He couldn't do that if he continued on this senseless journey, a journey that was doomed from the start. He had to see to it that his child was cherished; his child would have true love.

Half an hour later, Mitch pulled into his mother's driveway and noticed Darla's car wasn't there. He almost didn't get out of his car. He sat there several minutes debating over the subject with disappointment; he thought for sure she would be here. Then he decided since he was already here, he'd say hello to his mom and maybe even get a sandwich in the process. If he was lucky, Darla might show up while he ate his favorite: peanut butter and jelly on toast.

As it turned out, he didn't stay long. There was only so much crap he could take—his mother, trying to be her usual helpful self, kept insisting he use a friend of hers to help his search for the killer he was chasing. When he asked her how a friend of hers could possibly help, she told him all about her friend's special ability to speak with those who've passed on. A psychic!

Why she would suggest a seer was beyond him. Mitch felt uncomfortable talking to his mother about the case—hell—he felt uncomfortable just thinking about it lately. Her constant jabbering about going to see her friend made him eat his peanut butter and jelly on toast as if it were his last meal, swallowing it down in five bites. He nearly choked on the milk he chased it down with when she told him her name: Evan Buoyant.

31

Months later, when the shock of his encounter with the transparent man finally diminished, and the realization his chasing the Motel-4 killer was going nowhere, Mitch still held on to the hope—no matter how slim—of catching the son-of-a-bitch.

He couldn't believe he was actually considering using his mother's psychic friend for help. It went against everything he believed in, yet he was willing to compromise his beliefs in order to put a killer behind bars. After all, that was the main objective: to get a psycho off the streets.

But there was more to it than that—much more—he just refused to admit it. Ever since he discharged from the Army, from spending a couple of years with the Seattle police department, to venturing off and becoming a private investigator, everything he did, he gave it his all. He never lost at anything and he damned sure wasn't ready to start now.

So, if that meant using a psychic, even though he didn't believe in such things—well then, a psychic it would be.

Now, as he sat outside the chief medical examiner's office, waiting for the chance to discuss the case, he thought of the woman's name: Evan Buoyant.

It had to be a fake; he never heard of the woman before, but his mom said she was well renowned. *Yeah,* he thought, *over in Timbuktu.* Truth be known, some cases had been solved by using a clairvoyant, but Mitch always thought it had more to do with luck than anything else. Maybe he could use some luck, maybe by asking for help, that luck might come his way. It's funny how a person will so easily find a simple solution to every problem, even when that solution could jeopardize your soul.

Mitch sat in a chair that was about as comfortable as sitting in a desk made for a third-grader. Framed in chrome, the cushion under his bottom made him feel like he was sitting on a slab of marble, not a suitable seat for someone with hemorrhoids. He could feel another flare-up starting. *Not now,* he thought as he tightened his cheeks, squeezing and holding them tight, hoping that would quell the beastly turtle from poking its head out. He was spared the misery of waiting any longer, when Hart's office door swung open.

Immediately, Mitch pulled himself out of the uncomfortable seat and felt instant relief. "Hey Bud...," he said with a grin.

Buddy Hart, only days away from his 53rd birthday, looked much older than his years. The bags under his eyes told the story of a man who refused to quit. He was a man who deserved a much-needed vacation from death. "Hey Mitch," he said, his voice sounding hopeless; his smile, weak. He glanced around the room looking a bit confused. "Where's Amanda?"

Mitch tilted his head toward the door. "Smoke break."

Again, Hart gave a weak smile. He stepped aside, his arm swinging out in a mocking gesture, and said, "Come on in..." Mitch walked into the office, eager to hear some good news, but knowing the opposite was more likely.

"Go ahead and take a seat," said Hart.

"I think I'll just stand, but thanks... "

"'Roids acting up again?" he asked. A much warmer smile was on his face as he took a seat behind his desk. He yanked open the drawer to his left and pulled out a pack of Pall Malls.

"Is it that obvious?"

Lighting his cigarette, he said, "Yeah... you got this look on your face that says: stick up my ass." He laughed and coughed a bloom of smoke.

"Hardy har har...," Mitch chuckled. Having known the man for more than sixteen years, he could take the jabbing without getting upset. That was one of the reasons he'd stayed in touch with the man; he knew how to take a joke as well as dish it out. Their friendship had gone through a lot, first his breakup with Darla, and later, Buddy losing his wife after a short battle with throat cancer.

"Amanda told me about you and Darla expecting a baby."

Mitch could tell by the sound of Buddy's voice he was disappointed. He had meant to tell him personally; he just forgot how fast news traveled, especially through the grapevine.

"I would have told you myself...," said Mitch, as he shifted uncomfortably back and forth on his feet. "In fact, I was going to, but I forgot how fast news gets around."

Hart's smile became even warmer. "It's all right; I'm just happy to hear the two of you are back together." He crushed his cigarette out in the ashtray after only two drags and began fumbling around with the paperwork on his desk. When he found what he was searching for, he held the paper out to Mitch. "This is what we've been able to come up with on the Browns' case."

Mitch took the report but did it reluctantly. He didn't want to hear bad news. Without even thinking, he found himself taking a seat in the more suitable chair across from Hart's massive oak desk.

Reading, soaking up the information, the first part sounded encouraging: fingerprints were found on the brass clock that was lodged into Mrs. Brown's skull—oh, even more hopeful news—bloody work gloves were found in a drawer.

Mitch didn't know it yet, but the blood would eventually prove to be that of Billy's.

Had a connection been made? How it fit in with the Motel-4 killer, he had no clue, but he knew, somewhere down the line, the two crossed. Wanting to stay in a good mood, but knowing full well that it couldn't possibly last forever, there was no need to continue reading; besides, Hart obliged him by filling in the details.

"The prints we found do us no good. They're not on file with the Selective Service and the suspect doesn't have a record with the local police." After a slight hesitation and a scratch of his ear, he said, "We also did a nationwide search, but again, no luck." Pushing his 'John Lennon type' reading glasses further up the bridge of his nose, Hart's eyes returned to a state of sadness.

His smile, more a mask than the real thing, unsuccessfully hid the pain he still felt from losing the love of his life. Over five years had passed and still the man mourned for the only person he ever cared about. Maybe things would have been easier had she left him for another man, but death decided otherwise. Death saw to it that Hart's personal life suffered, as if being around the dead—day in and day out—wasn't bad enough.

Mitch wanted to say something to ease the man's pain but couldn't find the words. How do you comfort someone after so much time had passed? How do you even bring the subject up? He wanted to tell him that everything would be all right; that life goes on and so should he. That's what she would have wanted him to do, but there was only one thing that he could think of. He knew he might get himself in hot water but he said it anyway.

"Let's go get a drink."

.   .   .

Five minutes and two city blocks later, the two friends sat in a corner booth inside a quaint, up and coming city favorite hotspot: McShea's Irish Pub. The atmosphere thrived with the steady drove of customers and always-in-a-hurry, lunchtime crowd.

Buddy, always the best friend, even in his own pain, his own private anguish, was constantly looking out for his comrade. "You sure you want to do this?" he asked. "I thought you quit drinking."

Mitch pulled a cigarette from behind his ear and began twirling it between the fingers of his right hand like a miniature baton. "I was going to order coffee, but maybe I should order a shot. That'll help smooth the ache your report caused me... among other things." He flipped the smoke, catching it with his lips, and lit it with a shaky hand. "Besides...," he continued, as gray smoke curled around his face, "... if the shit that happened to me had happened to you, believe me... you'd want a drink too."

Did I just say that out loud? Mitch thought to himself. *I did, didn't I?* The effects from his strange *Twilight Zone* episode still lingered. Thoughts of the knife, the bullet holes, and his attacker: the invisible man—all raced through his head. If he were a betting man, he'd bet his life savings that the knife that was jammed into his shoulder the day he was attacked was also the same knife that killed Mr. Brown.

All these thoughts, and now Buddy would certainly want to know the whole story, and Mitch would be in a world of hurt, because surely Buddy would think him mad if he told the tale.

Of course, without fail, an honest look of concern came across Buddy's face as he leaned forward. "What shit?" he asked. "What happened?"

As luck would have it, the question was left stranded when the waitress, with order pad in hand, strolled up to their table and said, "What can I get ya?" Her lack of an Irish accent was a disappointment, but her red hair and emerald green eyes made her a pleasure to behold. After ordering a pitcher of beer and onion rings, the two men continued their conversation. Buddy joked about the fact that Mitch ordered beer, hoping to break the sudden tension that seemed to surround them. Mitch was in a world of his own, lost in thought.

"So, you going to tell me what happened or do I have to beat it out of you?"

"You wouldn't believe me, even if I believed me!"

Buddy's look of concern became one of confusion. "Slow down, Mitch. You're not making any sense."

As hard as it was for Mitch to understand (because he was still trying to figure things out), he did his best to explain to Buddy what had happened at his apartment. He knew the things he said sounded impossible—hell, it sounded insane: strange voices on the phone, being attacked by an invisible man, and the knife: the very knife that may have been used on Mr. Brown.

"So, you're telling me that you were attacked by something, something you couldn't see, something using a knife; that's what you're telling me?"

Mitch did his best to help Buddy understand, but he could tell that Buddy was having a hard time swallowing the story. The whole thing just sounded too outrageous, something out of a horror flick. By the look on Buddy's face, it was becoming obvious that he didn't believe a word of it. When the onion rings and beer finally were placed in front of them, Mitch wasted no time. Snatching two rings off the plate, he began to chow down.

"So you're telling me you were attacked by a what—a poltergeist?"

Chasing the onion rings with a swig of beer, Mitch dabbed his mouth with a napkin and said, "You don't think I know this sounds crazy? I've been trying to sit on it... you know, forget it. I can't do it anymore; that's why I'm telling you." He looked at his friend with pleading eyes. He needed to be believed. "You're the only person I've told."

Mitch wondered what his friend was thinking. He had said nothing the whole time, just sat there listening, taking it all in. Did he think that what he just heard was true, or even possible? He's a friend, even closer than "The Duke." Didn't he have an obligation to at least give him the benefit of the doubt? That, yes, the whole damn story could be true?

As Buddy leaned back in his seat, Mitch could see the look on his face—a face once immersed in sorrow, now shined with the confidence of a true friend, but still looking like a face that needed convincing.

Mitch's mouth was dry, despite the beer. At least the beer he could handle—he never had a problem with it; his problems came with the hard stuff. At least that's what he liked to tell himself.

Reaching into his jacket, pulling out a brown paper bag from the inside pocket, he placed it on the table. Buddy Hart was a betting man. He'd had his share of lost money on a supposed 'sure thing,' except this had nothing to do with money; this was something between friends. If he were to believe this trip-from-hell story Mitch was throwing at him, he would have to see for himself, and then decide if it was true.

"What's that?" he asked before taking a long draw from his own beer. "Is that my sure thing?" He made quotation marks with his fingers. "Is that something that's going to prove your story? I sure hope so because I'm having a hard time buying all this."

Mitch wasn't sure. He was hoping all the facts would somehow gather as one, hoping he could save his own sanity by telling Buddy, hoping Buddy could put 2 and 2 together, hoping the pressure he felt from all sides wouldn't crush him.

"I trust you might find some needed answers. That's the knife I pulled out of my shoulder. It's got my prints, of course, but I'm betting you'll find another set of prints."

"Another set of prints?" Buddy took the bag and opened it. Inside, there was another plastic bag. He pulled that out and held it up. The knife inside was still stained with blood. "Sure, I'll run it for prints, but I think I'll run a blood trace too."

"I'm betting you'll find two sets of prints as well as two blood types," said Mitch, as he refilled his glass, stopping just short of the rim. When the waitress asked if they needed anything else, Mitch held out the empty pitcher and said, "Fill this up, please... we may need a lot more where that came from."

32

This place is unlike any other place.

Ish quickly realized his blight. The pain he thought he felt when the souls of the damned came crashing through his window screen in the form of mist; that pain could not compare to the pain he felt now. And yet, it didn't faze him. When he first began tumbling head over heels, falling and filled with panic, he screamed for fear of the unknown, not because of the pain.

Control, that's what saved him, control over the panic.

Once that happened, he found that his tumbling head over heels, rolling over and over, finally stopped. He was still falling into a timeless pit, but now he felt as if he were flying, free as a bird.

Flames shot around him, through him, but did not consume him. Oddly enough, they occasionally caused a tickle, making him laugh. The sound reverberated with the crackling of the fire, coming back to him much louder, stronger.

All around him, he can see others thrashing, twitching in agony, screaming for relief. He wonders why he alone has control of his torment.

Below him, so far below him, in the middle of this endless abyss, he saw a mountain, and what looked to be a throne. Closer and closer it came as he floated like a feather, drifting toward what surely must be the underworld's version of Mount St. Helens.

At the top of the mount, a throne made from the bones of the lost and, sitting upon the throne, a beast of unimaginable horror waited.

.   .   .

If Mitch wanted to get Buddy to believe any of what he just told him, he'd have to show him more than just the knife. He'd have to show him the mess that was left behind when he was attacked. He'd left his apartment in such a hurry he didn't bother to clean up; then, after coming upon the crime scene at the Browns and finding that mess, his natural momma's boy tendencies took over; he avoided going back to his own place.

"Tell you what...," said Mitch, as he lit another ciga-rette. "Come back to my apartment; check out the aftermath of my story. I've been staying at my mom's since it happened." He took a long draw on the smoke and held it in. Blowing the smoke out of his nostrils, he said, "Everything's just the way I left it."

Even though he never grew up with the man, having met him late in his military life, Buddy felt as if the man that now sat before him, was a true friend, someone who wouldn't hesitate to drop what he was doing and lend a helping hand. He really had no choice. He knew what he had to do. He looked at his friend and said, "All right. I'll run the test." He slipped the knife back into the brown bag. "I'll come over to your place, check it out. If that's what you want."

He finished off the rest of his beer, slapped the empty mug on the table and said, "Fill 'er up!"

Mitch had to smile; he couldn't help it. Buddy had finally lost that down-in-the-dumps look, and that alone was enough to make him feel great. But having him at least consider the story could be for real, that made him feel reassured. He might not be losing his mind after all. He refilled his friend's beer and then lifted his own. "To friends...," he said.

With a clink of the glass, Buddy said, "To friends."

Once the beer was gone, the two men obviously didn't have plans to return to their respective jobs. Buddy suggested that he would follow Mitch to his apartment, but Mitch insisted that he ride along with him, saying it would be a lot easier since his car was already parked on the street.

Buddy knew better than to argue. When Mitch had an idea in his head, it was best just to let him have his way; otherwise they'd be debating about it all day long.

The ride, surprisingly enough, was a quiet one, which wasn't like Mitch at all. Buddy chose to keep his words few and far between as well. He was still trying to digest the strange events Mitch chose to share with him.

Some of it, he had to admit, sounded off the wall, but knowing the man as well as he did, he was sure that Mitch believed what he said. Believed it enough to tell someone instead of keeping it all locked up inside, afraid people might think he's crazy. And yes, it sounded mad, but (and this thought was even more outrageous) it all sounded real enough.

Hell, Mitch had seen crazy shit in the Army, the real deal. So who was he to say his story wasn't true; it certainly was real enough to Mitch, real enough for him to consider using a psychic.

He knew he might be walking on thin ice by bringing up the subject, so Buddy chose his words, wisely. As he rolled down his window he said, "You know... maybe calling your mom's clairvoyant friend isn't such a bad idea." Buddy grabbed the pack of cigarettes that sat on the dashboard, pulled out a smoke and lit it up. "It sure as shit sounds like a job for one. I mean, damn, it's got all the makings of a supernatural problem, and that's a problem that needs to be solved by someone who deals with that fucking shit."

Up ahead, the traffic light changed from green to red. If it wasn't for the car in front of him, Mitch would have pushed on through, but instead he had to slam on the brakes. Glancing at Buddy with a look of frustration, he snatched the dangling cigarette from his friend's lip, took a drag and said, "As much as I hate to admit it, I think you might be right."

When the light changed, Mitch handed the smoke back and continued the drive. He hated to admit it, but Buddy had a point; if he seriously wanted to catch the Motel-4 killer, he would have to use unconventional means. He had the feeling that once Buddy saw the mess he was going to show him, he'd have no choice but to call the mystic.

Another thing he hated, admitting having the woman's phone number saved on his cell phone.

† † †

The heat here is extreme, but Ish doesn't seem to mind. It's as if it were the norm; it doesn't upset him one bit. While all around him millions of others feel the endless burn, Ish considered it all as just another day at the beach.

Falling, floating, drifting ever so closer to the top of the mount, the heat becomes even more intense. Until now, Ish felt no fear. Soon he would be standing at the foot of the throne, and that thought began to make him feel tremendously vulnerable.

Eye level now with the beast that sits on the throne, Ish feels like an insignificant piece of dust. Its enormous size, along with its hideous form, brought a scream to his throat, lodging there like a piece of fruit and suddenly he couldn't breathe.

Fear has many names, many faces. Fear can freeze you in place, paralyzing your mind, body and soul. Fear covered Ish like a blanket, enveloping him as he finally landed on the mount like a snowflake. Now if he could only melt away... disappear... evaporate... like one. That would be so much better than what he felt was coming.

Pulling himself to his feet, Ish stood before what looked to be a giant wicker chair. Except, this chair was made of human bones: fifty feet in height, a hundred feet wide; the bones—femurs, ribcages, skulls—are stacked and arranged in perfect order.

Sitting, on the throne of bones, a creature with ten heads; in its presence, Ish felt dwarfed by its size. Its hoofed feet alone were as tall as he, with legs that looked as if they belonged to a horse. This was a freak of nature: a body of a man, its shoulders and arms humongous like a bodybuilder's, leading to hands that weren't hands at all—instead, bird claws, with sharp talons for fingers.

The ten heads swayed back and forth on necks as long as a giraffe; the head of a bear, a lion and an eagle; an ape, a man, a cobra, a wolf, a leopard, a hyena and a bull; they all lurched and jerked, screaming with one voice—a voice that sent shivers of dread throughout Ish's soul.

If ever there was a time when he wished he was never born, now was that time. Suddenly nothing else mattered. Standing here, staring at this monstrosity, Ish knew that every corrupt thing he'd ever done would be coming back in a flood of memories, bringing with it all the senses, all the emotions that went along with them. As they came, it caused him to become smaller and smaller, while the beast before him grew larger and larger still.

When it spoke, all ten heads voiced their natural tongues, yet all came together with something unmistakably clear.

"You will be my son!" it screamed. "You will be my Emmanuel!"

Ish continued to grow smaller and smaller, until all around him, the throne, the flames, the heat, the screams, all faded away and darkness cradled his soul.

■   ■   ■

Sharing all this pent-up information with Buddy, information that could make Mitch look bad, he was putting everything on the line by telling someone his—up until now—secret. Now, the cat was out of the bag. Mitch remembered the feeling he had when he first saw Mr. Brown's neck wounds. Visions of the knife, him pulling it out of his shoulder, danced in his head. Instincts told him that the knife he kept in the bag was the murder weapon used on Mr. Brown.

Mitch had a feeling that when all was said and done, when Buddy finished running his tests, they would prove without a doubt that it was, indeed, the murder weapon.

Then what? He wondered. How could he explain having the knife without sounding crazy; because the truth was, it was crazy. Nutty... fruity kind of crazy; the kind of insanity they lock you up and throw away the key for. Buddy may have listened to his story, but that didn't mean he actually believed it. Mitch knew that if he were in Buddy's place, he would be having a hard time accepting it. So yes, Buddy may have been supportive, but Mitch was beginning to think that maybe sharing his secret may not have been such a good idea after all. In all honesty, things didn't look so good.

Now, as the two men stood within his gloomy apartment, examining every detail, Mitch could tell by the look on Buddy's face, that he, too, was just as dumbfounded as he'd been; except, Buddy didn't have the pleasure of wrestling with death.

"You say you fired three shots? Where's the third bullet?"

Mitch pointed at the window and said, "By all rights, that window should be shattered, because that's the direction I was aiming." He stepped closer to the window and ran his hand over the cool glass. "You know, this whole thing sounds nuts, but... you want to hear something even nuttier?"

Buddy walked over to the window, looking a bit pale. "I've got the feeling you're going to tell me anyway."

"I know," said Mitch. "It's crazy... but the window at the Browns' house... the shattered one... the one that looks like it was hit with a fucking bullet. I'm thinking... and believe me it sounds far out but... I'm thinking that's the marking of the third bullet. Don't ask me why, it's just a gut feeling."

Buddy's face suddenly went from wonder to bewilderment. "Do you know what you're saying?" he asked. His tone of voice quickly became businesslike. "You're placing yourself at a crime scene... Think about it. You have a knife that may or may not be the murder weapon and now this... I mean, come on. Who's to say you didn't off the old man and shoot out the window?"

Mitch thought about it for a second; it certainly looked suspicious. If Buddy at any point believed his story, then he was obviously having second thoughts; the look on his face made it clear.

"You don't think I had something to do with that... do you?"

Buddy grinned, then slapped him on the shoulder. "Of course not, but if you ask me... I'd say call that soothsayer... A.S.A.P."

Even though he was having a hard time believing the whole story, he knew Mitch, and if Mitch believed it... well then, he'd do his best to believe in his friend. "Hey... you up for a game of poker this Saturday night?" he asked, hoping to steer the conversation elsewhere. "We haven't played in awhile... what do you say? My place, 8 p.m. sharp... I'll call Duke... "

"*The* Duke," said Mitch.

"I'll call 'The Duke' ... and you can bring..." He pulled his thought up like stopping a running horse; he was about to say... bring Billy, but weakly recovered with, "... bring whoever... 8 o'clock, o.k.?"

Buddy was slick, trying to change the subject, and Mitch understood why; he would probably be doing the same thing right about now: Thank you very much for the show... tip your hat and slowly head for the door. "Saturday night sounds good," he said with a smile. "I'll call Mason... see if he'd be interested."

Mitch watched as Buddy made his way to the door. An uneasy feeling started bubbling below the surface with his every step, uneasy and getting worse by the second. Buddy opened the door and Mitch's nerves began to boil.

"Call me," said Buddy. "Oh, and say hello to Darla for me. Later... "

The door closed and Mitch was alone.

The room began to shrink. Shadows moved closer and closer, smaller and smaller; his state of being had gone from being fine to nervous as hell. Then, in an instant, the door swung open, bringing with it, the room back to its normal size and scaring the living shit out of him when Buddy's head poked inside.

"You drove me here, numbnuts... you have to take me back to my car."

Mitch laughed. Not because he thought anything was funny. No, he laughed to shake off his jitters. "Hey, you want to be there when I talk to that spiritualist?"

Buddy ignored the question, choosing instead to let it hang. Mitch closed the door behind him, and after checking to make sure it was locked, he turned and said, "So... you want to hear what she'll have to say?"

Buddy gave a half-hearted smile and said, "I think I'll pass, but I'm sure you'll fill me in on all the details."

"Oh, no doubt," said Mitch, "no doubt at all."

Mitch didn't mind taking his friend to his car—hell, that was one of the reasons he drove, knowing he'd have to leave the apartment—again. He'd most likely avoid returning. He kept telling himself that if he and Darla were going to get married for a second time, then a home was the first thing they needed. His apartment was becoming a thing of the past anyway. *Why stay somewhere where you don't want to be?*

After dropping Buddy off in front of the parking garage, Mitch felt much better than when they first left. That uneasy feeling was no more.

He planned to meet up with the psychic, hoping she might be able to make sense out of the strange things that appeared to follow him wherever he went. *Would she be of any help?* Doubtful but, then again, stranger things have occurred. *Who was to say? Only the psychic knows...* Mitch laughed at his lame spin of what the shadow knew, then hit the speed-dial on his cell phone.

33

Life and death, shadow and light, black and white...
all is well in heaven and hell.

If Ish could smile, he would do so with delight, for he
would go down in history compared with one of the most
famous mass murderers: Jack the Ripper.

With one exception, whereas Jack the Ripper was in
no way identified or located, Ish would be named as the
Motel-4 Madman, but never found.

The body is one of three: body, mind and soul.

Ish's body was no more, wiped from existence. But
his mind, his soul, has now become the essence to the
scheme of things.

Clothed in darkness, waiting for the light, his soul
knows it'll soon face a struggle. The battle is coming, come
it must. His mind and soul wait. They'll know when the time
is right. Until then, they'll grow in strength as they feast on
the darkness, a meal of misery they so enjoy.

.   .   .

Evan Buoyant was just as Mitch pictured in his
mind's eye: a heavy-set woman, in her mid-fifties, standing
at about five feet, four inches tall, wearing a housedress and
black-rimmed glasses that made her look even older.

When she answered her door, he nearly laughed out
loud. He couldn't believe how close he'd come to reality. He
only missed one thing: the cane she held in her right hand,
presumably to help hall her load around; she must have been
nearly four hundred pounds.

She offered him entrance and a seat as she did often in her line of work. If you can call talking with dead folks work, that is. On the phone, he never mentioned any of the specifics of the case; he merely told her that he was looking for some help and was told she might be able to provide it. The moment Mitch took his seat, she said, "Your brother, Billy, is here... "

He knew this was coming, but he didn't think it would come so soon. He thought there would be some small talk first, maybe get to know her before getting down to business. "You don't waste any time, do you?"

The woman smiled; a creepy smile; the kind of smile that could just as well have come manufactured, like one of those clear plastic masks, with rosy cheeks and all. "I don't believe in small talk," she said. "You don't need to know me, and vice versa."

Mitch felt—no—he *knew* the freak was reading his mind.

"Oh... and for the record... I'm not a freak."

He sat straight up in his chair, looking more than a bit shaken. "O.k.," he said. "Now you're freaking me out. What am I dealing with here? I thought you were connected to the dead."

"I connect with the living as well as the dead," she said matter-of-factly. "I have many abilities, abilities that you could not comprehend."

"Listen, Mrs. Buoyant is it?"

"... Ms."

"... whatever..." Mitch was becoming agitated. He had a hard time making the decision to see this woman and now he was having second thoughts about the whole thing. "I came here hoping to get some answers to... "

She stopped him in mid-sentence. "Your brother Billy has given me all the answers that you need. Since you first called, he's been with me... telling me things... showing me things."

Mitch's eyebrows wrinkled up, skepticism clearly showed on his face. He knew there were people out there waiting to pounce. How was he supposed to know if what she was saying was true; for all he knew, she could've done her homework, could have come up with some kind of information she could use as truth, play it off as truth, a false truth.

"Showing you what kind of things?" he asked, the tone in his voice confirmed his suspicions.

She sat across from him at the dining room table; her glasses perched on the tip of her nose. His question suddenly seemed to transform her into a zombie. Her eyes glazed over. Her mouth dropped open.

"Are you all right?" he asked. There was something about her eyes, something that wasn't right, something totally out of place. Mitch stared at those eyes with the glazed-over look and watched as those eyes changed color. A moment ago they were a sparkling green, now they'd become a chocolate brown.

Her voice, when she spoke, sent a chill through his veins. "Mitch... I know who you're looking for..." It wasn't her voice at all, but it sounded all too familiar. He knew it was impossible, knew that what he was hearing had to be a dream, but he also knew that anything was possible; after all the shit he'd gone through, it could just be possible that he was hearing his brother's voice.

"... he's crossed-over, but he's coming back... "

Mitch thought of the morning when Billy had called him, waking him out of a sound sleep and hung over. The morning Billy was doing surveillance in front of the Motel-4. He remembered how excited he had sounded, and that excitement echoed now as his voice spilled out of her mouth. "... Mitch... he's coming back!!!"

† † †

Within the deep, dark matter of space, within the very fabric of the cosmos, there is a place where time and space meet to set destiny in motion.

Ish (or what used to be Ish) wrestled with, and for, control of an unborn soul. It rolled with the flow, reeled about in ease, because it knows its purpose. Knows that all that there is, and all that will be, is its for the taking. To do with as it pleased.

The innocent and trustworthy are the most vulnerable, even more so when they have yet to enter the world.

Even now they dance. One with the knowledge of what is to be; the other prancing about in what it perceives as play. But, like a black hole twirling in distant space, with its force sucking in every ounce of light, the unborn soul does not stand a chance.

Then, when the time is right, when the full moon rises at midnight, all play is stopped—Slam, Bam, like two magnets colliding together, the soul it sought was captured.

Suddenly... things are different somehow. The change is slight but noticeable, warm and wet. It may take some time to get used to this new home. Listening, straining to hear, a sound vibrated all around, throbbing through and through. It penetrated its whole being.

It's the muffled voice of the mother-to-be. "Oh honey... come feel... the baby's kicking."

. . .

Mitch wouldn't have believed it if he hadn't experienced it firsthand. If someone had told him the story he was telling the fellows, he'd say the whole thing was hogwash, but, true to form, Buddy was more than willing to listen to what he had to say. Mason, on the other hand, was just being polite, smiling and nodding in agreement, while The Duke laughed it off.

"I'm serious...," said Mitch, as he tossed his cards on the table. "... Give me two."

The Duke tossed two cards on the table and said, "So this psychic lady says his name is Ishmael Alastor?" He glanced at Mason and asked, "How many?" Mason quickly tossed three cards on the table.

"It was Billy's voice coming out of her mouth...," said Mitch. He didn't say anything about the whole eye-color changing thing either. He was having a hard time trying to concentrate on the poker game and telling the story of his talk with the clairvoyant at the same time. "... He told me where to look to make the connection... where the evidence is buried."

The Duke looked at Buddy and said, "Your call... "

Buddy glanced at his cards and again for a second time, then tossed them on the table and said, "I'm out."

Mitch stared at the hand he was dealt: a jack of hearts, seven of spades, four of clubs and a pair of threes, a diamond and a spade. Not a promising hand. He thought about the hand he'd been dealt in life.

In the telling of his story, he neglected to mention about Billy's warning of the killer's crossing over and coming back, mainly because he wasn't quite sure of what that meant, but also because he wanted them to believe him. "I don't have shit," he said as he dropped his cards on the table. "I'm out too."

"You'll have to let me know when she's going to take you to the evidence," said Buddy. "I'd like to be there."

"First thing Monday morning," said Mitch.

"I can't believe you guys actually believe all that mumbo-jumbo," said The Duke, as he tossed more chips on the table, raising the pot. When Mason raised it five more, The Duke wasted no time at all slapping his chips on the table, raising it ten more. Finally, Mason folded.

After another lousy hand, another bite at his wallet, Mitch was ready to call it a night. He was past his usual limit anyway. Besides, Lady Luck seemed to be leaving him hanging high and dry anyway. He knew that at least one of his friends might give him a hard time about leaving—that one person being 'The Duke.' But, he had a woman-with-child at home and knew that was always good for an easy out.

Just then, The Duke stood up while slapping his belly. "Gots to take a leak," he said with a grin. Mitch took this as a cue and stood up as well. "I'm out of here, fellows. Darla's waiting on me."

The Duke pulled out his air-whip, and made the gesture of snapping his wrist, ending it with a slightly slurred crack. "Whipped...," he howled, as he made his way to the bathroom.

"That's right... and proud of it."

Using his first two fingers of his right hand, Mitch pointed at his eyes, then pointed back at Buddy and Mason. "I'll be seeing you guys later."

As he walked out the door, he could hear The Duke, shouting from the bathroom, "Hey! Don't be a stranger!"

Mitch knew Darla would be waiting up. Even though the house he was going home to belonged to his mother (he left his apartment for good), it still felt nice knowing Darla was there. He'd talked his sweetheart into moving in with him about three weeks after that early May morning, when The Duke so graciously agreed to pick her up at the hospital. He never said a word about the dream he'd had that sparked the action. The two of them now spent most of their time looking after his mom, who had grown frail so fast after his brother's death.

He was planning to let Darla in on his secret search for a house; a place they could call their own. He found a promising piece of property and was sure that she would love it as much as he did. But, if not, then he'd keep looking until he found one they both loved.

† † †

While Mitch drove home, fantasizing about his future dream house with the white-picket fence, the forces of Evil were busy doing their own thing.

Todd, Joey and Tony were given a second task: a task so much better than the first. They had proved themselves worthy by helping Ish in his first life; now they would show their appreciativeness by completing the ultimate task of helping the soon-to-be child of Darla and Mitch: a boy for sure, a boy who was destined to become the Man of Perdition.

For now, they watch and wait, content just to linger close to their Master.

Before them, Darla was sitting up in bed, waiting for her husband-to-be (for a second time) reading the latest Danielle Steel novel. With her back propped up with three fluffy pillows, she placed the book on her swollen belly, stretched her arms and yawned.

The baby inside her appeared to reject the idea of reading Steel by rumbling around, kicking and punching as if to say: Get that sappy crap off me!

The three of them can sense their Master's agitation and suddenly they've become riled as well. They begin to run around in circles, faster and faster, whirling around and screaming an ungodly sound, until a slight breeze can be felt, a cold, spine-tingling breeze.

Darla put the book aside and pulled the covers up to her chin. She wondered if perhaps she was coming down with something. The last thing she needed was getting sick just before having her baby. Her very first baby; a child she planned on spoiling. Making sure she, or he, had everything she herself did not. Giving all that was possible to make the child happy, something she missed out on way back when.

The child settled down once more, and all is calm. So too, the three mad screaming fools. They now stand at the end of the bed like pillars, wondering what kind of mischief could possibly be had.

Dreams are their outlet. Dreams, which happened to be in motion right now; one after the other, they smile. They know just what to do.

"I've got an idea," said Todd. "Let's go mess with the grandmother-to-be."

.   .   .

At half-past eleven, Mitch walked through the front door. Inside, the house was dark and quiet. A night-light lit the way to the foot of the stairs. Without bothering to flip the light switch (he knew the house like the back of his hand), he climbed the steps. Four stairs from the top, he could see that his mother's bedroom door stood ajar. Within the room, another night-light cast a shadow on her bed; under it, a pair of slippers and some dust balls.

Three steps from the top, a distorted shadow flashed in front of the night-light. *Was she out of bed?* Two stairs and another shadow; finally at the top, still a third shadow flickered by. *What the hell is she doing in there?*

At the end of the hallway, the door to the master bedroom was closed. He could see light under the doorjamb and knew Darla was waiting for him. He had to look in on his mother first. After that, a hot shower would top off his day.

Pushing the door to his mother's room, it squealed on its hinge as it slowly opened. The sound raked at his nerves and he suddenly became spooked by the memory of walking into Billy's room long after his murder—the blood splattered everywhere; the words "Don't fuck with me" on the wall— all flashed through his head like a bolt of lightning. A trickle of sweat began to slide down the side of his face.

Stepping into the room, he could see his mother lying on her side in the bed; her form under the covers and in shadows. Moving closer to the bed, wanting to see if she was asleep or faking it, he had convinced himself that she had somehow jumped into bed just before he entered the room; even though it had been a mere second or two after seeing the moving shadows.

Leaning over his mother, inches away from her head, he could hear her usual soft, almost whisperlike snore. Had she been lying there awake, trying her best to fake it, she would have been snoring louder than the norm, a dead giveaway.

Satisfied she was asleep, he began to pull the blanket over her shoulder. He stopped when he thought he saw something. Glancing to his right, his own reflection stared back at him from the mirror.

The shadow on the wall behind him, from the reflection in the mirror, showed four shadows; all leaning over, pulling the blanket—his own, and three others, all lined up like dominoes.

Chills crawled over his body as each nerve, one after the other… popped.

Mitch peeked at the wall behind him and found only one shadow. Then, glancing into the mirror again, he saw only one shadow. *That's because there was only one to begin with*, he told himself. But he knew full well, that that thought, at least for a split-second, may not have been true.

Finally, finishing what he started, Mitch pulled the blanket over her shoulder and tucked it around her neck. With one last look at the mirror, just to make sure, he backed out of the room, pulling the door closed behind him.

Once in the hallway, he stood there debating whether to go directly to the master bedroom, or to take that hot shower he so desperately needed, especially after getting spooked like he did. He decided to stick with his original plan.

The feeling of being watched began the moment he stepped into the shower. He tried to play it off as just built-up stress, hoping that the hot water would wash it away, but the feeling persisted even as he toweled himself off. With a towel around his waist and one on his head, Mitch left the bathroom in a hurry.

His paranoia level set on high, he glanced over his shoulder every three or four steps, anxious to get some distance from those perceived prying eyes. After one more look behind, he stepped into the master bedroom, finding Darla right where he expected, lying in bed with a book in hand.

"Hi baby," she said with a smile. "Win any money?"

Again, as always, her voice eased his racing heart. That feeling of being watched, those unseen eyes, was crushed by the sound of her sweet, soft voice. Mitch smiled a weak smile, and she knew without a doubt that it wasn't a lucky night. "How much did you lose?"

He let the question hang for a moment, choosing instead to put on some clothes. Slipping into his checkered pajamas, feeling relaxed despite what he felt in the shower, he climbed into bed and snuggled up to Darla. "You know I don't like to lose more than fifty...," he said, as he leaned over and kissed her temple. "Besides, I wanted to get home. I had a feeling you'd be waiting up."

Leaning his back into the comfort of the pillows, he knew sleep would not come easy tonight, and not just because of the feeling of those leering eyes. He couldn't shake it. He thought curling up close to the love of his life would somehow make it better, but it didn't. This feeling, this weird idea hadn't always been on his mind. It started right about the time her belly began to grow.

He glanced in her direction and watched as she engrossed herself in her book. It seemed the bigger her stomach grew, the more that feeling grew as well, and now, lying next to her when she was so close to giving birth, the thought suddenly repulsed him. It was unexplainable.

He pulled away gently, ashamed of how he felt. He hoped she kept her nose in the book so she wouldn't see his sudden uncalled for feeling. He should be happy but that objective seemed far away. *Jack's busy tonight,* he thought, *more than usual.* He imagined what life would be like when the child came, and that thought made him feel threatened. He knew why, and the reason was a stupid one: added responsibility.

Mitch slipped out of bed and opened the dresser drawer. He found his sleep mask, knowing full well he was wearing it so he couldn't see Darla's belly and not for sleep. He glanced at the digital clock and watched 11:59 change to 12:00.

"Oh honey, come feel... the baby's kicking."

Mitch started having second thoughts about leaving the poker game. If he'd stayed out late enough, he might have missed this opportunity. Just seeing the ultrasound irked him; he was afraid of what touching her belly, while the child kicked, would do to him. And of course, he was afraid he'd experience something that most fathers-to-be do not: that being the feeling of wanting to hurl.

Just the thought of feeling the baby's head or foot or arm or whatever other part it was, stretching through her flesh, sent shudders through his nerves.

He managed to put a smile on his face as he placed his hand on her belly, expecting to receive a horrifying shock, an attack of the heaves, but surprisingly, it never came. His nerves steadied. Maybe it was just the thought of the added responsibilities, or it could just as well have been the fact that he couldn't see the future, and not knowing what was coming next made him feel as if his whole life was about to spin out of control. Whatever the reason, that feeling of wrecked nerves would probably be something he could expect to experience for the next eighteen years, at least.

After getting the o.k. to turn off the lights, Mitch hit the switch, slipped his mask over his eyes and settled into the pillows. The two of them lay in the dark; Darla's head nestled against his shoulder, she thinking how grand it will be when the baby arrived, and him thinking that maybe things were going too easy.

His mind returned to his job (always working, this boy). Having the name of the man you're looking for given to you by a medium was bad enough, but knowing he'd met the killer before, that chewed at his mind. He remembered how he felt when he met him for the first time in that hospital room back in Pittsburgh more than twenty years before. The jackass who was driving the van on the night Billy lost his memory wasn't more than three rooms down from where Billy had been laid up.

He remembered how he couldn't wait to get out of that room. They'd had a staring contest of sorts, staring to the point where it seemed as if the kid's pupils had snaked out of his head and touched his own eyes three feet away. It was a freaky feeling Mitch would never forget, that feeling of almost having your core stolen.

Despite his thinking otherwise, sleep did manage to wrap its arms around him, pulling him gently into la-la land. His dreams, though fuzzy as they were, would prove to work their way into his reality. His fears, as well, would make themselves known in due time.

In his dream he was running. He didn't know if he was doing the chasing, or the running away. It didn't matter. In the morning he would awake thinking he'd had another dreamless night.

34

Holidays tend to have a way of sneaking up on us all. With his investigation of the Motel-4 murders completely on his mind, October 31st came and went without being missed. Thanksgiving went by just as fast. No big bash this year, just a nice night out, having dinner with the woman he loved.

They seemed to flash by with the blink of an eye.

Evidence was mounting against one: Ishmael Alastor. DNA taken from his mother (who was unaware, because she was in left field, without a glove at the time) matched up with DNA they got from hairs found in a hat. A black Zorro hat was buried right where the psychic said it would be, along with a loaded .22, some black gloves and a black mask. That practically sealed the deal, since evidence of the two sets of prints were found on the knife that killed Mr. Brown, one set being Mitch's and the other set matching those found on the gun and the brass clock that killed Mrs. Brown.

Everything pointed to the friend of his late brother with enough evidence to throw the book at him, that being the gas chamber, of course. Now that he had a name, he was more determined than ever to find justice for Billy.

Since Christmas was his favorite holiday, he found enough time to buy gifts for his wife and his due-any-day baby. Their second wedding wasn't elaborate, just a few close friends as witnesses, along with a justice of the peace. It was quaint. There would be no honeymoon, at least not until after the baby was born. But that was o.k. .... when the time was right; till then, the absence of said honeymoon makes the thought of eventually having one grow fonder.

On December 25th, at 3:12 in the morning, Darla woke Mitch out of a sound sleep.

"Honey... wake up... I think my water just broke."

†   †   †

The moment of truth finally arrived. The waiting was worth the trouble. Not only was there about to be two proud parents, but there would also be one happy little hell-raiser.

Like a mob wanting to rush the doors of a shopping mall during a Christmas sales event, the baby pushed and prodded, pulled and pounded, desperately wanting out from its confines.

People around the world were about to celebrate the birth of the Savior, even though half the population cared more about receiving presents from Santa Claus, than they did about the gift God had to offer.

The world had its chance. Everyone has heard the good news, what they do with that news has been entirely in their own hands. Take it to heart or toss it to the curb. Unfortunately, the good news has become old hat: seen it, heard it, did it, time to move on already, because many have chosen to cast it aside, which is why this pivotal moment in time was made possible.

The continual pushing and punching, pounding and banging, bring forth the birth pangs. The liquid world that once held the child has been shattered; now, it's only a matter of time before feeling the light at the end of the tunnel.

.   .   .

She didn't have to say it twice. Mitch jumped out of the bed as if he'd been practicing for this moment for months. Sleep still clung to his shoulders like a jilted lover trying to pull him back to bed, but he shrugged it off similar to the way an experienced drunk might shake off a hangover. He pulled his khaki pants over his pajama bottoms and slipped his feet into a pair of sneakers, anxious to get on the road. Luckily, they already had a bag packed for just such an emergency.

Darla was across the room, pulling her parka over her nightgown. Garfield's printed image played peekaboo as her coat flapped open and closed, open and closed. She was doing her best to remain calm; it hurt like hell but she didn't want Mitch to see. That might freak him out and that's not what she needed right now; instead, she did her best to keep him calm by constantly telling him everything was going to be all right.

"What about your mother?" she asked. Mitch wrestled with his jacket, trying to pull it on. "She'll be fine," he said, sounding flustered. "I'll call Buddy when we're on the road, ask him to come over; keep an eye on her." He finally managed to pull it on, his mind racing with a million thoughts. He looked at her, eyes wide with excitement. "Are you o.k.?"

"I'm fine," she said. "Everything's fine."

Snatching the overnight bag off the floor, Mitch wrapped his arm around Darla's. "Let's get the heck out of here," he said with an awkward smile.

She knew he was nervous. Patting his hand, she said, "Let's...." They left the house quiet as mice so as to not wake his mother. Mitch made the call to Buddy before pulling out of the driveway; he wanted to make sure he kept his mind on his driving once he started out. With that done, they drove off at a slightly higher rate of speed considering the circumstances, but not fast enough to get pulled over by the cops, mainly because of the time of day. Not many cars are out at 3:30 in the morning.

† † †

By 3:45, Buddy arrived at the house as instructed, found the spare key hidden under the ceramic frog by the back door and let himself in. The moment he stepped through the door, a feeling of uneasiness settled around him, making him extremely uncomfortable. That was odd too, because he'd been in the house a number of times and never had a problem before. He decided to ignore the feeling, considering the time of day as being the reason for it, and made himself at home in the kitchen.

After turning on the lights, he put water and coffee into the coffee machine and waited for Mr. Coffee to do its thing. Taking a seat at the table, he grabbed the remote and switched on the 13-inch color TV atop the kitchen cupboard. Since it only provided local channels, there wasn't much on but color bars. Channels 3 and 6 were off the air; channel 10 was just now playing the National Anthem while the Stars & Stripes swayed in the wind under a cloudless blue sky.

Flipping through the rest of the channels, he found nothing but snow and hiss. He hit the off button, the set winked out with a loud thump. When the smell of the brewing coffee reached his nose, he instantly wanted to light up a smoke. Buddy was in a sound sleep when Mitch had called and wasn't upset to help him out; he did, after all, offer to help should it ever be needed, anytime, all the time. That's what friends do.

Mitch sat at this very table with him after his wife's death, mostly listening. He'd been there for him then; he would damn sure be here for him now. Fifteen minutes of waiting and the coffee was ready. Mugs lined the wall to his left on hooks, everything from plain black to others with various silly sayings like: World's #1 Dick or I need my Java. He chose the Felix the Cat mug and poured the brew just shy of the rim.

As far as Buddy was concerned, anyone who put milk and sugar in their coffee was a pussy.

Bringing the cup to his lips, he gently blew on the black liquid before taking a gulp. The warm caffeine hit his stomach and he instantly felt the lingering sleepiness fall away. He was about to pull out a cigarette when a sound caught his ear and he stopped. It was a soft murmuring sound, and at first he thought he might be allowing his overactive imagination to run wild, but when it came again after his third gulp, he put the cup down.

From where he stood, he could see the dining room and beyond that, the living room. All was dark except for a night-light. He could also see the silhouette of the Christmas tree standing by the front window.

The sound seemed to be coming from that direction.

His brain told him to check it out, but his legs lagged behind a full minute before they finally moved. Entering the dining room, a cherry wood table and eight straight-back chairs were on his right; a glass cabinet that held the special dinner plates and cups was on his left. The light that spilled in from the kitchen seemed to fade the further he went. What little light that glowed from the night-light made it feel like it was so far away and it was only a few feet from the stairs that led up to the second floor.

Halfway between the dining room and the living room, the hardwood floor creaked, but it wasn't his foot that caused it. The sound came from the right. He glanced in that direction, and suddenly heard the Christmas tree bristle as something brushed against it.

He knew Mitch didn't have any animals, so whatever it was, it shouldn't be here. Buddy started to wish he'd stayed in the kitchen; that weird feeling he'd had when he first entered the house was back with a vengeance.

A murmuring sound again, except it sounded more like blubbering now, coming from his left, and up the stairs. He moved in that direction, banging his shin against the La-Z-Boy and cursed under his breath. Following the noise, he tried not to think about what may or may not be lurking near the tree. He convinced himself that it was a Christmas ornament falling off a branch. And yet, in the back of his mind, he knew that the creaking noise he'd heard wasn't an ornament falling, because the creak came before the tree was disturbed.

Buddy glanced over his shoulder as he began to climb the stairs, expecting something or someone to come charging. Nothing came of course, but the night-light began to flicker off and on, off and on.

The sound was louder now, and it was more than just blubbering. He wasn't sure what it was, but it sent a chill through his veins. At the top of the stairs, the first room on the right, Mitch had said that was his mother's room and that's where the strange noise had led him.

Buddy wished he still had the coffee with him; he could use another gulp right about now. His mouth was dry. From behind the door, he could hear mumbling and blubbering. He was about to reach for the doorknob when he stopped.

The knob was already turning.

With a quick click, the door opened a small crack, then came to a halt. The only thing he could see for sure was that there was another night-light in that room as well, and it was flickering on and off, on and off. He looked over his shoulder, glancing down the stairs, expecting to see that night-light flickering too, but it wasn't; it was out all together.

Pushing the door open wider, he reached in and flipped on the wall switch. The lamp next to the bed lit up, showing him what the ruckus was all about and he immediately regretted having followed the sound to begin with. Mitch's mother was in the bed, her back up against the headrest; her hair all wired, looking as if she'd stuck her foot in a bucket of water and her finger in a light socket. Her face was as white as a sheet as she clutched a pillow to her chest.

Mitch told him about her deteriorating health since Billy died, but she looked a lot worse than he let on. She obviously had some kind of bad dream, but, if he didn't know any better, he'd swear she looked as if it were time to consider putting her in a home. Buddy took a seat beside her on the bed and rubbed her clenched fist. "It's o.k., Beverly... just a bad dream."

She clutched the pillow even harder, staring at him but not seeing him. She had stopped mumbling the moment the light went on; now her lips quivered as she stared through him. She seemed to want to say something but couldn't get the words out. He wondered if maybe she were still asleep, still in her own private nightmare, but then her eyes widened as if lifting from a fog and she realized who he was. "Buddy... what are you doing here?"

He didn't hear her; his mind had suddenly turned to other things. Things like that doorknob turning, the door creeping open. Sure, it might have been dark, but his eyes were adjusted just fine, and he knew what he saw. *If she didn't turn it, then who did?*

"Buddy... ?"

"Huh... ? Oh yeah, Mitch asked me to keep an eye on you."

She glanced around the room, her pale face turning pink with what looked to be embarrassment. Her lips stopped quivering but her eyes now darted back and forth with concern. She looked at him with eyes bouncing around in her head. "What happened... ?"

"Everything's fine. Darla's about to have the baby."

The word 'baby' seemed to turn her concern into fear as she grabbed the pillow even tighter and her lips started to quiver again. The sound which brought him up here began to escape from the depths of her being and out of her mouth.

"It's o.k.," said Buddy as he touched her hand for a second time. "It was just a bad dream." She stopped her whimpering and looked at his hand. She looked at his face, then his hand again. "They told me he's going to kill me first," she said.

"Who are they?"

Her voice dropped to a whisper, "Manny, Moe and Jack... The Three Stooges... I don't know who they were..." Buddy leaned in so he could hear her better when suddenly she shouted, "... he's going to kill me first!"

He jumped back with a start, his heart nearly coming to a complete stop, but it did tick on, racing a mile a minute now. The residue from his next question seemed to stick to the back of his mouth, as his throat dried up when the words passed his lips, "Who is *he*?"

"The Baby... the Baby... !"

† † †

While words of prophecy were being spoken, another mother sat in her padded cell, her back to the north wall, her feet fixed in a yoga position; she gently banged the back of her head against the cushioned cinder block, mumbling under her breath.

Sondra Alastor, known as Sandy to the doctors and nurses in the south wing of Overlake Hospital, was placed into isolation for the third time since being admitted.

She tried to hurt someone other than herself this time.

The doctors believe her mental condition could be hereditary. The people that put her in the State's control believe her mental well-being was lost when her son ran away from home. In actuality, it was a combination of the two that brought her here.

At 4:25 in the morning, she sat in her cell, repeating the same words over and over again. Sometimes she whispered, sometimes she screamed, as she struggled back and forth in a straightjacket. The only source of light came from the four-inch squared window on the door of her cell. It shined like a beam, into the darkness, cutting a path to her face; a face that seemed distorted as she wrestled with her restraints.

Suddenly her struggling came to a stop. Her face with closed sunken eyes, her nose flaring, her lips curled back, exposing clenched teeth, she looked to be trying to absorb the light as if the sun would tan her pale skin. Except it's not the sun, only a fluorescent bulb out in the corridor.

A growl began to bubble in her throat.

Louder and louder still, until it sounded almost like a wild beast. "KKKKill... the... child!"

† † †

As the first snowflakes began to fall from the morning sky, a baby boy was born. Time of birth: 8:06 a.m. The child weighed in at six pounds, six ounces. There were no complications; everything went about as smooth as usual, except for the fact that Mitch decided not to be in the room when it happened.

They made it to the hospital with plenty of time to spare. They even talked about experiencing it together, but when the time came, he froze. Darla had wanted him to be there, needed him to be there, but she didn't push the issue. She thought it made no sense to cause a commotion; she knew he had a lot on his mind, and if he said he needed to stay away, well then she could understand, but that didn't mean he wasn't out of the doghouse, not by a long shot. She didn't have time to get angry; she had more pressing matters to deal with. They rolled her through the double doors of the delivery room, and as the doors rocked back and forth until they closed, she could see the look on his face. He was scared.

No sooner were the doors closed when Mitch headed for the exit. Not that he was running out on her or anything like that, he just needed a cigarette; his nerves were on edge. He fought the urge on the ride over and saw his shot at fulfilling it now; besides, he planned on quitting anyway, so this was most likely his last, depending on how long it took to have a baby.

A baby? Him? He felt proud and frightened at the same time. What if he didn't measure up or, worse yet, what if the pressures of parenthood sent him over the edge? The last thing he wanted was to end up like his old man. He remembered the letter his mother sent, explaining what had happened; remembered it, as if it were yesterday.

He was halfway through his second smoke when the snow started to fall.

Merry Christmas, he thought, *snow and all.*

He stuck his tongue out and caught a half-inch flake. It melted on contact, cooling his apprehension. Maybe fatherhood—the ups and downs of it all—would be good for him. He crushed the remaining butt between his fingers, allowing the head to fall to the ground, then tossed it in the trash. Wiping his hand on his jacket, he turned to go back inside and the doors swished open, making him feel as if he were in a *Star Trek* episode. He stepped through and headed for the elevators.

By the time he got back to the waiting room, a nurse was waiting for him with a sour look on her face. His leaving obviously was an inconvenience to her; he hoped his smile would ease her mood.

"Mr. Blade?" she said. Her voice didn't match her look, he was expecting a harsh, nasally sound; instead it was quite soft, too soft for the flare in her eyes. Mitch read her nametag, Maria Wise, and wanted to ask if she were any relation to the Wise potato chip family but thought better of it. So, instead he said, "In the flesh... "

He knew it sounded corny, and regretted it the second he said it. She gave him a frown and said, "Everything is fine... your wife is in her room, and the baby is in the process of being cleaned up." She started to walk off, antsy to do other things and peeved for being delayed.

"Excuse me... nurse?" He and Darla had waited in an office for nearly three hours before she'd been taken into the delivery room; either the nurse didn't know that or she was just being a bitch about telling him where his wife could have gone after giving birth.

Nurse Wise turned in his direction with a half-hearted smile. "Yes?"

"What room?"

"608." She turned and pranced off with a cocky swagger.

Mitch wanted to throw a few nasty words to match her attitude but chose to be civil. "Thanks...," he said as he watched her turn the corner. He couldn't believe it. He was officially a Dad. A full-fledged, 100% POP. The waiting was over and it didn't take long at all. It was amazing knowing his life had just been changed forever, and all the fears, the worry, he had up until this point were just precursors of things to come, but it didn't matter now; he realized, even if it was just a small fraction, how God must have felt when He created it all.

He knew why the nurse didn't specify whether it was a girl or a boy; he could see Darla asking her not to mention it, wanting to be the first to tell him. He also knew he had to stop at the gift shop and pick up some flowers, but doubted whether they'd help get him out of trouble.

He could have been there for her, could have held her hand for comfort, but something just overwhelmed him at the time, and it wasn't just a cigarette jones. He thought for sure he would throw up, and he didn't want to look like he couldn't handle it. He'd seen far bloodier things on the job, but still, he didn't want to take any chances.

He was glad she didn't plead her case.

Mitch bought the only thing available, one half-dozen red roses bunched in with baby's breath, and hoped they could put a dent in her armor.

Any thoughts of his being in hot water evaporated the minute he entered her room. The smile on her face was enough to convince him that all was well between them. Physically she looked drained, but her pearly whites made up for the rest. "Hi baby...," she said as she reached for his hand.

An odd numbness crawled up his arm as he took it, and gradually, that smile that told him all was well didn't appear to mean that anymore. It took on a whole new scary dimension. Her teeth were saying one thing, while her eyes were saying something entirely different. It said: I love you... I'll kill you!

"She didn't tell you... did she?" said Darla.

Mitch thought that once the baby was born things would get back to normal, but the look on her face, plus the vibe he seemed to be getting, told him that it might be longer than he anticipated.

It was as if her seeing the baby, holding the baby first and knowing that she had brought a beautiful child into the world, a world the child needed to be protected from, had flipped her primordial switch.

"Did she...?"

"Did she what?" said Mitch.

"Did she tell you the sex of the baby?"

Mitch scratched the top of his head with his left hand, still holding the flowers and told her that her secret was safe. That peculiar sensation seemed to ebb some as he took a seat in the chair beside the bed.

They decided that they didn't want to know the sex of the child, wanted to find out together, but it didn't turn out that way. Since Mitch chose not to be in the room, he'd missed out on that plan. That gave her an advantage somehow, an edge up. He'd missed out on the chance of having that first-time bonding experience with her; sure, he'd get his chance to bond, but even so, she was definitely ahead in the game.

"Well?" said Darla.

"Well what?"

"Don't you want to know?"

That was a dumb question, he thought, *of course I want to know.* Mitch put the roses into a vase half filled with water and said, "Yeah... don't leave me hanging. Of course I want to know." He hoped he sounded convincing enough. He had a twinkling of an idea that it was a boy but didn't want to let on.

Her face seemed to sparkle like an angel at the prospect of revealing her secret. Even though she'd been upset with him for leaving her when she needed him the most, in her heart she had forgiven him, especially after she thought about the frightened look on his face. "Thanks for the flowers, they're lovely...," she said, purposely delaying. She may have forgiven him, but that didn't mean she couldn't have any fun with him.

"Oh, come on...," said Mitch.

Her eyes, her beautiful blue eyes, appeared to twinkle for an instant, as if catching the light of some unknown star.

She knew that he was hoping for a boy, praying for a boy, and she wanted to hear him say it. "Guess…"

Mitch had a hunch this was some sort of setup. If he said a boy, she might get peeved and then the scale would tip in her favor even more than before. But then, it might tip in his favor if he's right because she might see it as him being there for her in some way. He thought his best bet would be to go with what worked: Go with your gut. He knew when to trust the right judgment. He kissed her hand and said, "A girl?"

Her face beamed even brighter, her smile again showing those pearly whites.

He might have achieved victory here. His guess just might get him off the hook for good. Sure, he secretly wanted a boy, but if it turned out otherwise, he could live with that.

"Yes!" said Darla with a devilish grin.

"Yes?" said Mitch, his heart beginning to sink.

Again her pearly whites flashed, "No… I'm just playing… it's a boy!"

His heart seemed to do a reverse, as it felt like it was starting to grow in his ribcage, realizing that his suspicions were true; he could see himself playing catch in the backyard with his son. "A boy?" he asked.

"Yes!"

They hugged. A warm hug, a loving hug, and then in an instant, and only an instant—like a jolt from a 9-volt battery after sticking your tongue on the coils—that primal force coursed between the two. His natural proud heart overwhelmed by the power of bringing forth an heir and her natural protective nature melting together as one; it was official, they were a family. Now it was only a matter of time before seeing the fruits of her labor and of his loins. As if stepping onto the set of a soap opera, Nurse Wise walked into the room holding the baby, wrapped in a white cotton blanket.

The child murmured in her arms. With their embrace now broken, Mitch turned and smiled a proud smile. The nurse no longer harbored an attitude, her face strictly business now. She appeared to be enjoying herself; her eyes laughing at an inside joke. Something deep down told him that normal just went out the window.

In the blink of an eye, Mitch saw the baby lunge at the nurse's throat. Fangs sprung from its mouth and began shredding open the soft flesh. The baby looked in his direction, a jugular vein dangling from its blood-covered mouth. Then just as fast, the child was back in her arms as if nothing unusual just went down.

Gone, he thought, *out the window.*

Mitch glanced at Darla and held her gaze. That feeling was back. That "I love you... I'll kill you" feeling covered him like a fisherman's net.

He looked at the nurse again, struggling to free himself from this imaginative web of confusion. She was smiling; not only her lips, her eyes too, they were smiling and dancing. Without a word being said, and what seemed like time slowing to a crawl, she began to reach her arms out, extending them... ever so—God-forsaken—slowly.

The child now wiggling around in her outstretched hands. "Merry Christmas and Happy Father's Day," she said with a smirk.

The baby was covered from head to toe, but now he could see it had a full head of hair; an unnatural amount of hair, and it was ghost white. Its arms, now flailing, were white too; its face all wrinkled like a morgue sheet.

What are the odds, he thought to himself as he took the child in his arms, *my son, the albino.* His heart froze as he held the baby close.

There went all thoughts of having a game of catch, melting away like an ice cube in the hot sun. He felt happy and sad, proud and ashamed, scared and alone, lost and confused. He felt that nature had played a joke; one that would always keep her in stitches. He felt anger; he felt remorse, regret; all these things and more, slowly twisting his guts inside.

Mitch looked at the child, now asleep in his arms, quiet as a mouse. A tinge of joy, and still more pain; he had gotten what he'd asked for... a baby boy... that's all that mattered. He tried to convince himself that everything would turn out just fine, but the shock of finding out your son is not what you call normal—that stung his heart.

A tear slipped from his left eye, rolling along the side of his face and finally falling from his chin. His heart felt heavy as he watched the sleeping child, with its eyes closed, looking so peaceful.

Forget about what could have been, he told himself; *think about what could be.* His tear landed on the baby's face and trickled down its small nose until it curved to the left and pooled into the corner of its eye.

The child began to vibrate like some kind of play toy in his hands, its tiny arms waving a cheery hello.

In his mind's eye, Mitch could see the psychic's face, could hear Billy's voice and the warning that spilled out of her mouth. He tried not to think about it, tried instead to put it out of his mind altogether by being thankful for this new challenge in his life—and it would be a challenge.

Then, the eyes of the baby were open, staring up at him. For how long, he didn't know. Looking at his son, he wrestled with the urge to scuttle but found he couldn't move. Those crimson eyes of the newborn were pulling him in, like quicksand.